G⊕NE H⊕NTING IN DEADWOOD

"Laugh and shiver your way through this chill ride that deserves its own theme park!"
~**Patricia McLinn**, USA Today Bestselling Author

"GONE HAUNTING IN DEADWOOD has it all—snappy dialogue, nail-biting paranormal mystery, and of course that special Ann Charles brand of humor that keeps us all coming back for more!"
~**Joleen James**, Award-winning Author of the Hometown Alaska Men and Wilding Point Romance Series

"Ann Charles effortlessly weaves together snappy dialogue, action-packed scenes, and complex plots with incredible attention to detail into one amazing story!"
~**Diane Garland**, Continuity Specialist at Your Worldkeeper

"Don't get too comfortable in your favorite reading chair. GONE HAUNTING IN DEADWOOD will have you on the edge of your seat from page 1!"
~**Paul Franklin**, Software QA Engineer

"GONE HAUNTING IN DEADWOOD is full of suspense and humor that will make you laugh out loud. Charles brilliantly creates an exciting adventure that doesn't stop until you close the book and say, 'Wow! What a ride!' "
~**Karen Runge**, Reporter for The Parkston Advance

For more on Ann and her books, check out her website, as well as the reader reviews for her books on Amazon, Barnes & Noble, and Goodreads.

Dear Reader,

When I was younger, I spent my days exploring the Black Hills on a dirt bike or with my stepdad in our version of the Picklemobile. I came across many falling-down remains of small mining settlements that were once loud and rowdy but now abandoned, silenced by time. I tiptoed through the decaying structures, walked what remained of outer walls and fence lines, and searched the weeds for evidence of those who had inhabited the area. Sometimes I would just sit under the shade of a pine tree and daydream, looking out over what was left of the civilization that had occupied the land many moons ago.

Slagton is an amalgamation of several such ghost towns built on veins of silver, tin, or gold ore. When I created it, I wanted to tell you about a different kind of ghost town—one that was still alive under the surface. The sort of ghost town I'd sometimes imagined while sitting under a pine tree, back before I had any clue that my spelunking and exploring were going to be written about in books starring a wild-haired woman with a wicked windmill swing and balls of steel, not to mention her shotgun-toting bodyguard and his nephew, a snarly detective.

This ninth book in the still-growing Deadwood Mystery Series takes the focus off Deadwood and Lead for a short time, drawing us deeper into the hills to uncover what time has hidden away from the world … or tried to bury until Violet and her big nose came along.

This book was a fun challenge for me, pushing me to stretch my writing muscles, making me trust the storyteller in my head more than ever, giving me room to explore Black Hills memories I'd stored up from long, long ago (yes, I'm that old).

I hope that you enjoy reading about Violet's "long way from ordinary" life as much as I did writing it. I'll end with a nugget of advice from Old Man Harvey:

"Just 'cause trouble comes visitin', doesn't mean ya have to offer it a place to sit down and take off its boots."

Ann Charles

www.anncharles.com

GONE HAUNTING IN DEADWOOD

ANN CHARLES

Illustrated by C.S. Kunkle

To Shelly
The nicest sister ever!
(shhh ... don't tell Laura)

Cover Art by C.S. Kunkle
Cover Design by B Biddles
Editing by Eilis Flynn
Formatting by B Biddles

Library of Congress: 2018904065
E-book ISBN-13: 978-1-940364-54-4
Print ISBN-13: 978-1-940364-55-1

Acknowledgments

Every book I write involves many people helping me behind the scenes. Many, many thanks to:

My husband for your love, patience, and appreciation of good tequila. You help me plot, edit, format, corral the kids, eat healthy, and so much more every damned day.

My kids, Beaker and Chicken Noodle, for making me smile with your daily observations of the world around us.

My First Draft team: Margo Taylor, Mary Ida Kunkle, Kristy McCaffrey, Jacquie Rogers, Marcia Britton, Paul Franklin, Diane Garland, Vicki Huskey, Lucinda Nelson, Marguerite Phipps, Stephanie Kunkle, and Wendy Gildersleeve. You deal with me leaving you hanging often and only threaten to tan my hide every few chapters.

My critique partners, Jacquie Rogers and Kristy McCaffrey, for putting up with my sorry ass.

My editor, Eilis Flynn, for tolerating me giving you my manuscripts in chunks.

My WorldKeeper, Diane Garland, for helping me keep story details straight and nitpicking the hell out of me on the page.

My Beta Team for helping me keep secrets and doing a bang-up job finding those final sneaky errors hiding in the manuscript.

My brother, C.S. Kunkle, for illustrating what is lurking in my imagination and kicking ass on cover art.

My graphic artist/cover designer, Mr. Biddles, for your patience while I peek over your shoulder.

My readers for your cheers and shared laughs both online and in person. Without you there to swear to the authorities that the voices in my head are a good thing, I'd be writing from a padded cell.

Author Patricia McLinn for your awesome cover quotes!

And as always, Clint (my brother), for exploring ghost towns in the Black Hills with me long ago on those warm summer days.

Also by Ann Charles

Deadwood Mystery Series

Nearly Departed in Deadwood (Book 1)
Optical Delusions in Deadwood (Book 2)
Dead Case in Deadwood (Book 3)
Better Off Dead in Deadwood (Book 4)
An Ex to Grind in Deadwood (Book 5)
Meanwhile, Back in Deadwood (Book 6)
A Wild Fright in Deadwood (Book 7)
Rattling the Heat in Deadwood (Book 8)
Gone Haunting in Deadwood (Book 9)
Deadwood Shorts: Seeing Trouble (Book 1.5)
Deadwood Shorts: Boot Points (Book 4.5)
Deadwood Shorts: Cold Flame (Book 6.5)
Deadwood Shorts: Tequila & Time (Book 8.5)

Jackrabbit Junction Mystery Series

Dance of the Winnebagos (Book 1)
Jackrabbit Junction Jitters (Book 2)
The Great Jackalope Stampede (Book 3)
The Rowdy Coyote Rumble (Book 4)
Jackrabbit Junction Short: The Wild Turkey Tango (Book 4.5)

Dig Site Mystery Series

Look What the Wind Blew In (Book 1)
Make No Bones About It (Book 2)

Goldwash Mystery Series (a future series)

The Old Man's Back in Town (Short Story)

Kindle Worlds Short Story (Amazon only)

Feral-LY Funny Freakshow

Cast

KEY: Character (Book # in which they appear)—Description**

Violet Lynn Parker (1–9)—Heroine of the series, real estate agent

Willis "Old Man" Harvey (1–9)—Violet's sidekick and so-called bodyguard

Dane "Doc" Nyce (1–9)—Violet's boyfriend, medium

Detective "Coop" Cooper (1–9)—Deadwood and Lead's detective

Zoe Parker (1–9)—Violet's aunt and mentor in life

Layne Parker (1–9)—Violet's nine-year-old son

Adelynn Parker (1–9)—Violet's nine-year-old daughter

Natalie Beals (1–9)—Violet's best friend since childhood

Jerry Russo (4,5,6,7,8,9)—Violet's boss, owner of Calamity Jane Realty

Mona Hollister (1–9)—Violet's coworker and mentor in realty

Ray Underhill (1–9)—Violet's coworker and nemesis at work

Benjamin Underhill (1–9)—Violet's coworker

Jane Grimes (1–9)—Violet's previous boss

Cornelius Curion (3–9)—Violet's client; so-called ghost-whisperer

Reid Martin (2–9)—Captain of the fire dept., Aunt Zoe's ex-lover

Jeff Wymonds (1–9)—Violet's client; dad of Addy's best friend

Prudence (2–9)—Ghost who resides at the Carhart/Britton house

Zelda Britton (2,4–9)—Owner of the Carhart house in Lead

Tiffany Sugarbell (1–9)—Rival Realtor; Doc's ex-girlfriend

Susan Parker (1–9)—Violet's evil sister; aka "the Bitch from Hell"

Quint Parker (1–3,7–9)—Violet's brother; Layne's hero

Freesia Tender (5–9)—Owner of the Galena House

Stone Hawke (5–9)—Coop's ex-partner; detective called in to solve cases

Rex Conner (3–9)—Biological father of Violet's children

Rosy (6–9)—Camerawoman from TV series called "Paranormal Realty"

Eddie Mudder (3,6–9)—Owner of Mudder Bros Funeral Parlor

Dominick Masterson (4,7–9)—Previous client of Violet's old boss, Jane.

Mr. Black (2–4,6,8,9)—Mysterious, pale-faced Timekeeper

Ms. Wolff (5,8,9)—Previous resident of Apt. 4 in the Galena House

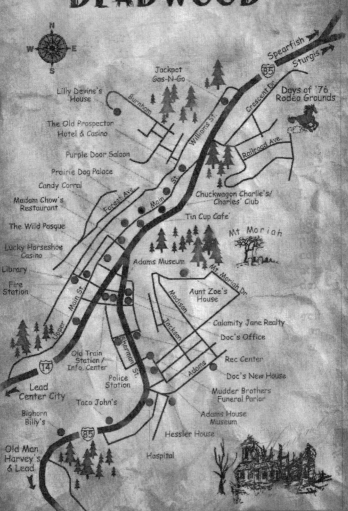

Chapter One

Friday, December 14th
Slagton, South Dakota (in the boonies south of Deadwood)

If Hell had a butt crack, the town of Slagton would be located one freckle north of the sphincter.

"Not that Slagton can really be called a 'town' anymore," I said aloud, grimacing out the pickup's passenger-side window at the rusted SLAGTON sign peppered with bullet holes and buckshot. "All that's left here are the decaying shadows of lives built on silver ore."

"Quit yer bellyachin', Sparky." My shotgun-toting, self-appointed bodyguard, Ol' Man Harvey, reached across the front seat and poked me in the ribs. "We'll be in and out quicker than a greenhorn at a whorehouse."

"You two screwups aren't going inside with me," Detective Cooper said from the back seat. "Especially not Parker. She's not even supposed to be here."

For once, I agreed with the steely-eyed, often-obstinate detective. Normally, he and I made a habit of ramming our horns together, especially after I solved one of his cases for him, which tended to spur plenty of bristling on his part. But today neither of us wanted *me* to be joining Cooper and his uncle on this snowy joyride back to Slagton—

for good reason, too.

Decades ago, the EPA had shut down the mine operating outside the town, listing contaminated water among the company's many crimes against nature. The federal government strongly encouraged the locals to pack up and hit the road, offering financial help to relocate. Most of the folks took the deal, but not all. A few stubborn diehards lingered, peeking out from behind closed curtains with loaded shotguns whenever strangers came calling. Strangers like a hard-headed detective, a cantankerous old man, and a hungover blonde who should have stopped celebrating her best friend's birthday after the fourth shot of tequila last night.

"Whether you like it or not, Coop," said Harvey as he glanced at his nephew in the rearview mirror, "we need Sparky's help with this mess ya done got us into, and I ain't talkin' about her house-sellin' talents."

Cooper cursed under his breath. "First of all, this isn't a mess. It's a minor situation that needs clarification in order to determine if it's even a legitimate problem. Second, I didn't get you two into anything. You stuck your big nose in my business and now you have it in your whiskey- and women-addled brain that the three of us are some kind of damned team."

"My noggin' ain't spoiled with whiskey." Harvey shot me a wink. "I prefer my grandpappy's homemade hooch with my women."

I cringed. "I know too much about your female preferences." No amount of plugging my ears over the months I'd known Harvey had saved me from the intimate details of his love life, which he shared on a daily basis.

"Finally," Cooper continued through gritted teeth, "nothing is going to happen today. I'll go inside *alone*, interrogate my informant, and then leave. There will be absolutely no sniffing around or gunplay done by either of you while I'm inside."

"I don't have any guns," I said, wishing I were home in my aunt Zoe's kitchen nursing one of her hangover concoctions. Better yet, I could be stuffing my cheeks with the molasses cookies she'd been making this morning when I'd left for work instead of visiting a creepy ghost town with Detective Pissypants.

"I brought two guns," Harvey told me, frowning at the dilapidated shack up ahead on the left. Smoke seeped from the side of the crumbling chimney. Snow lined the barbed wire fence surrounding the yard and coated the caved-in porch roof. "Better to be safe than sorry back in these here parts of the hills."

"I don't want to see a single footprint in the snow outside of this pickup from either of you. Understand?"

I rolled my eyes. "Yes, *Coop*." I purposely shortened his name, poking the bear.

"That's 'Detective Cooper' to you, Parker, and you know it."

Harvey snickered. "Why'd ya drag us along if all we're gonna do is sit and count snowflakes?" He slowed as the snow started to fall harder, covering the windshield almost as fast as the wipers could clear it.

"I didn't drag you along, Uncle Willis. I asked to borrow your damned pickup. That's it. You're the one who showed up at the station with Parker here and refused to remove your stubborn ass even after I threatened to fill it full of lead."

"You should have known your uncle would call your bluff. He always kicks your ass at poker." I glanced over my shoulder at the detective. His blond hair was slicked back this morning. His jaw was rigid, matching his cheekbones. Not even the furry collar on his black police bomber jacket could soften up his chiseled features.

"Shut up, Parker." Cooper glared at me. The black eye I'd given him a week ago had finally faded to a dull yellow-green with a few spots of purple.

"Ya shouldn't come out here alone," Harvey told him. "None of us should. Things are gettin' too hairy. Bessie and Violet will go to the well with ya if shit hits the fan."

Bessie was Harvey's favorite shotgun. She rarely left his side, day or night. "You're putting me on the same level as Bessie now?" I smiled at the old buzzard with his freshly trimmed beard. "Dang, Harvey, that makes me feel all warm and fuzzy inside."

Harvey grinned back, flashing me his two gold teeth.

Truth be told, I'd lay my money on Bessie. I was still pretty new at this Executioner gig I'd been born to play. My résumé as a killer was splattered with blood—my own—and had several pages of screwups and near misses listed under Past Experience.

"I've been a cop for close to two decades." Cooper leaned forward, his head butting into Harvey and my greeting card moment. "I believe I can handle a visit to a backwoods shithole without needing a babysitter."

Harvey's focus returned forward. "You underestimate Slagton, boy. The whangdoodles back here aren't yer normal sort of agitators."

I slunk down in my seat as we passed another rundown shack, this one with oil drums lining the porch. Last time I was here with Harvey, there'd been shotguns holding down those drums, the barrels aimed at the road. The shredded curtains in the window twitched as our tires rolled through the slushy snow now coating the gravel road. For a moment, I thought I saw a ghost of a face behind the window, but a blink later it was gone.

According to local lore, something still lingered in Slagton besides the contaminated water. Whatever haunted the streets of this ghost town had supposedly added an extra dose of insanity to the people who'd chosen to stay behind. I had no desire to see these "whangdoodles" up close and personal to decide for myself if the rumors about them were true. The bloodthirsty mutants in *The Hills Have Eyes* had nothing on the Slagton residents. At least that was the story my best friend liked to tell after a hearty dose of liquor at the Purple Door Saloon.

Natalie and I hadn't touched on the topic of Slagton last night while celebrating her birthday—at least I didn't think so. Truth be told, I couldn't remember much of what happened after our fourth tequila shot. I glanced over my shoulder at Cooper, recalling one particular blurry moment amidst the drinking that involved him, the birthday girl, and a steaming-hot kiss that had left Natalie reeling for several beats. The question was, did Natalie remember that kiss this morning? Or had last night's tequila overdose completely fogged that memory?

Cooper grunted, sitting back again. "I'm not wet behind the ears, Uncle Willis." I glanced over my shoulder. Cooper had his Colt .45 out. He checked the cylinder before stuffing the gun back into his shoulder holster. "I've seen and talked to more people back here in Slagton than you have."

He looked up, catching me in the middle of a scowl. I couldn't help it. Cooper and his guns always gave me heartburn. As often as my curly blond hair and I irritated the detective, I figured I'd end up facing off with the wrong end of his pistol one of these days.

His gaze moved beyond me. "That's the place up ahead on the right," he said to his uncle.

The house sat off the road in the shadows of several pine trees.

"I'm not talking about the regular folks," Harvey said, hitting the brakes and pulling into the front yard. He let the engine idle, turning in his seat. "I'm talking about the sort that require a visit from Sparky here and her war hammer."

Cooper aimed a frown at me.

"What did I do?" I held up my hands in surrender.

"You let this old man drag you along."

"Wrong again, Detective. He pulled the wool over my eyes, too. You'll have to snarl and bark at someone else for now."

Harvey had called me at Calamity Jane Realty and told me that he wanted to drive out and look at a place with Cooper. I'd assumed he meant a new home for his nephew now that the sale on the detective's house was wrapped up. A trip to Slagton was what I got for assuming around Harvey.

"The day is young," Cooper said. "It's pretty much a given that you'll do something to piss me off before the sun goes down."

I stuck my tongue out at him.

"Real mature, Parker." He opened the back door. "Neither of you two leave this cab, got it?"

Harvey grunted.

I scoffed.

"Do. You. Understand?" He bit out each word.

"Yes, Detective Cooper." I gave my best robot impression.

"Sheesh, boy. Yer a real buzzkill, you know it?"

The slam of the pickup door was Cooper's answer.

We watched Cooper through the windshield. He strode through the snow toward the drooping front gate that looked like it was one swing from breaking free of its hinges and dying a slow, rusty death in the weeds below. Pausing at the gate, he turned his head slightly as if listening.

"Did he hear something?" I whispered to Harvey.

"Between the pickup engine and the muffle of the fallin' snow, I doubt it."

Cooper pushed open the gate. It quivered as it swung, but didn't keel over. He hesitated at the base of the porch steps, testing each stair before putting his weight on it. The porch sagged, the right end dipping a couple of feet lower than the left. Cooper leaned toward the higher end, standing to the right of the door.

I couldn't see through the falling snow if he knocked or not, but I'd reached a count of eleven when the door opened inward.

Darkness greeted the detective.

"Do you see anyone?" I asked Harvey.

"Nope. The butler must be a ghost."

If that were true, Cooper would've reeled back. He hadn't learned to control his reaction around the ectoplasmic crowd yet since he'd only recently been "blasted open" by a pair of ghosts during a séance that had taken a turn for the worse. Since that night, his world had been turned upside down and shaken to hell. The ability to see ghosts only added to his crabbiness most days and gave him another reason to growl at me, thanks to my "oops!" part in his eye-opening ordeal.

After one last glance in our direction, Cooper stepped inside the rundown shack and closed the door behind him. Several clumps of snow fell from the drooping porch roof in his wake.

The waiting began.

I chewed on my knuckles. My gut grew heavier by the minute, feeling like I'd swallowed the lump of coal I was probably going to get from Santa this year after all of my grand fuckups.

Harvey and I sat in silence, both of us watching out the windshield, waiting to see if Cooper would crash out the front door and sprint back to the pickup. At least that's what I was half-expecting, eerie as the house looked.

"Have ya ever heard of a woman undertaker in the Old West?" Harvey asked.

I did a double take, ending with a scowl as I stared at his profile. "No. Why on earth would you ask about an undertaker right now?" I didn't need any help thinking about death while parked in Slagton.

He shrugged. "Fer some reason, I keep thinkin' about a woman gravedigger from way back when. It's the kookiest thing. I can even picture her in my mind standin' in the middle of the street in Deadwood."

"Well, stop thinking about her until we're clear of this place," I snapped.

"Breathe easy, Sparky. We'll be back in Deadwood in two shakes." Harvey shut off the pickup. Apparently, his fight-or-flight meter was pointing in the opposite direction of mine.

"What are you doing?" I shot him a worried glance, not wanting to take my eyes off the shack for long.

"Savin' gas."

"Don't you think we need to keep the engine running in case Cooper is chased out by a one-eyed mutant working a shotgun?"

His bushy brows drew together. "Girl, why is yer neck bristlin' so much?"

"Something doesn't feel right here."

"We're in Slagton. Not Disneyland. Things haven't felt right here since the Feds shut 'er down."

"Yeah, but this is different. I'm telling you, there is som—" I gaped at Harvey's backside as he shoved open his door and stepped out of the pickup. "What are you doing? We're not supposed to leave the cab."

"Try explainin' that to my prostate."

"Oh, sweet Lord! Your prostate is going to get me shot one of these days." It had landed me in jail already due in large part to the prickly detective now dinking around inside of the shack.

"Don't be pourin' short sweetenin' into long," he said. "Sit tight. I'll be quick as a jigger-wiffer."

Having no idea what a jigger-wiffer or short sweetening was, I huffed. "Pee right there next to your door. I promise not to look."

"I'm not going to show my doodads to the world right here."

"Why not? You flash them at the ladies down at the senior center every weekend."

"That ain't one hundred percent gospel. Besides, I got me one of those shy bladders. Like a turtle, it doesn't like to stick its head out of the shell too quick and when it does, it takes its time tellin' a tale."

I held out my hand to make him stop. "That's too much information for a Friday morning."

"Then ya shoulda let me take care of my business without badgerin' me."

"Fine, go already. But leave me the keys in case Cooper comes running."

He tossed the keys on his seat and shut the door. Instead of going through the rickety gate like his nephew, Harvey detoured around the right side of the house and meandered on back toward what looked like an ancient, two-story woodshed. Several of the windows in the upper floor were broken. The gray weathered wood reminded me of an old, tired lumberjack whose shoulders were weary from lugging an ax around for centuries.

"Just pee already," I muttered.

Harvey disappeared around the side of the woodshed, leaving me alone.

Alone in Slagton.

My stomach knotted.

I locked the pickup doors and huddled inside my quilted down coat. The seconds ticked by, turning into minutes. Outside, nothing moved besides the falling snow. My gaze darted back and forth between the front door of the ramshackle house and the old woodshed, willing Harvey and his nephew to get their butts back to the pickup pronto.

At the five-minute mark, I sat up and scowled at the woodshed. How long did it take the ol' buzzard to drain the lizard, dammit?

More seconds ticked by. Still there was no sign of life from either man. My patience was growing tired of pacing.

I wiped away the steam my breath left on the side window with my coat sleeve and peered through the smeared glass. If Harvey didn't return soon, I was going to honk the horn, even if it brought the town nutters out in full force.

Something moved on the other side of the woodshed back near the pine trees. Something dark and lower to the ground.

"What's that?" I pressed my nose against the glass.

It sort of looked like a large cat—mountain lion size. But its fur was dark, more black than tan. Its body was longer, too, sleeker even, reminding me of a Doberman pinscher mixed with a panther. The head was thick, like a mini-lion with a full mane encircling it. Was this one of those weird dog hybrid breeds I'd heard about from my daughter, the wanna-be vet?

I wiped off the window again and tried to see the creature clearly through the heavy snowflakes. It moved like a predator, slinking low as it crept along the tree line toward the woodshed, hunting.

My heart quickened.

Crap. Had Harvey slipped and fallen in the snow? Was that dog-thing stalking him? Pickings in the forest food chain were slim this time of year. A human would make a tasty meal.

I felt under the seat for Bessie. My fingers touched her cold barrels. I pulled her out, careful not to blast myself to smithereens in the process.

When I looked back at the woodshed, the creature was no longer in sight. I opened the door, listening for a growl or a bark.

My ears were muffled thanks to the falling snow, but my fingers tingled. Something wasn't right. I could feel it deep inside. Anxiety played me like a harp, plucking my nerves one by one.

I glanced at the shack, willing Cooper to step outside.

The porch remained empty.

"Bloody hell!" I stuffed the pickup keys into my pocket. Cooper was going to be doubly pissed now. Careful of Bessie's trigger, I crawled out of the pickup, easing the door closed. Maybe Harvey and I would return before Cooper noticed we'd disobeyed his order and went on a walkabout. Although there'd be no hiding our footprints in the snow.

The snow sloshed and crunched under my suede boots. Silly me, since while choosing my outfit today, I'd gone for fashionista, not frontier woman. I should have known better considering that I lived in the hills, where winter snowstorms were as legendary as Wild Bill.

I followed in Harvey's footsteps, hugging the fence line. The snow fell with purpose now, covering much of the ugliness surrounding the old shack and matching woodshed. It made for a peaceful scene, looking like one of those bucolic scenes Thomas Kinkade sold by the thousands.

I followed Harvey's trail around the side of the shed. I thought about shouting his name, and then remembered Cooper's order to stay in the pickup and kept my lips pinched.

Harvey's tracks led into the open door on the backside of the woodshed.

So did the predator's.

I bent down to take a closer look at the creature's tracks. I'd expected paw prints, the sort I used to make on steamed covered windows on the school bus alongside the hearts and various boys' names over the years. These weren't paw prints, though. I reached down and held my hand over one, fingers spread. There were three, forward-facing "toes" as long as my middle finger, if not longer. A fourth toe of about the same length pointed to the side, reminding me of a dewclaw.

Standing upright, I frowned toward the tree line, searching the shadows underneath for movement.

What kind of animal had finger-like toes on its feet? The prints reminded me more of a bird, but what I'd seen through the window was no bird. Could they be long claws rather than toes?

Something clunked inside the woodshed.

I turned back to the doorway, trying to listen over the commotion of my pounding heart.

All was silent.

I lifted Bessie's double barrels, keeping my finger off the trigger, but nearby just in case. After one last glance to my right and left, I eased into the woodshed.

It took a moment for my eyes to adjust to the darkness.

A board creaked overhead.

Something rustled to my left.

There was a soft clink in front of me.

"Harvey?" I squinted into the shadows. "Are you in here?"

Something huffed behind me.

I whirled around, Bessie leading the way.

A hand grabbed the barrels and yanked her out of my grip. "Dammit, Parker! Did I not tell you to stay in the pickup?"

The sight of Cooper made me breathe a sigh of relief in spite of his glare.

"Your uncle had to see about a mule."

"A man."

"What?"

"He had to see a *man* about a mule."

"Whatever. Are you going to stand there and correct my English all day, Detective Wordsmith, or help me find your dang uncle?"

"I wasn't correcting your English, Parker, only the idiom you were using incorrectly." When I held my fist up in front of his face, he almost cracked a smile. "Why do we need to find him if he's just taking a piss?"

"Because he's been gone too long."

"His prostate slows him down some."

"Dammit, Cooper. I know all about your uncle's stupid prostate. I'm telling you, something is wrong. He's taking too long and I saw something prowling around this woodshed."

"What do you mean, *something?*"

I pointed out the doorway. "Look at those tracks. Whatever made those is hunting your uncle."

He stepped over to the door. "Those look like turkey tracks."

"Then that's one big-ass turkey with long, fat toes."

This time he smiled wide. "Reminds me of you."

I narrowed my eyes. "Are you looking for another black eye? Because the last one I gave you has almost faded and I'd hate to have the boys down at the Deadwood dog pound be left with nothing to yip and bark about over their daily doughnuts."

"Touch me, Parker, and I'll handcuff you again."

"Handcuff me and I'll—"

Something growled off to our left from inside the shed.

The hairs on the back of my neck stood up on their tiptoes.

Cooper raised the shotgun, pointing it in the direction of whatever was hiding back in the shadows.

"That is no turkey," I whispered.

He grabbed me by the wrist and pulled me behind him.

I tugged free. "I can handle myself, remember."

"Fine, get yourself killed, but first make sure you write a note in blood to your boyfriend that I tried to save you."

Doc Nyce and I had exchanged a note written in blood before. Once was enough for me. "Shut up and give me back that gun." I reached for Bessie.

He shoved my hand away and moved deeper into the shadows.

I followed behind him, practically stepping on his heels. "Fine, then hand over your pistol."

"No fucking way in hell."

"Dammit, Cooper."

"Go outside and wait for me."

"If it's one of the *others*, neither gun will protect you."

Cooper and I had faced off with *other* supernatural creatures before that only grew more ferocious when filled with hot lead. Apparently, the detective hadn't learned his lesson.

"You're overreacting. It's probably just a mountain lion."

"That is no mountain lion." I could feel that truth in my bones. "It's more like a cat and turkey mixed. A cat-urkey."

"A cat-urkey?" He snickered. "Are you still drunk from last night?"

"I'm not drunk. I know what I saw." I looked around for a makeshift weapon, picking up a weathered two-by-four. The pointy end of two rusty nails stuck out from the wood, one bent, one straight. I hefted the board, practicing my swing.

When I looked up, Cooper was frowning at me. "Seriously, Parker?"

"Whether you like it or not, hot shot, you need me."

" 'Hot shot'?"

"You know. You like to fill things with hot shots of lead."

"Jesus, Parker. I need you like I need a—"

From the darkness came a shed-rattling roar. Something dark and lithe flew between Cooper and me so fast that all I saw was a blur of black before the creature disappeared into the shadows at the opposite end of the shed.

The shotgun boomed next to me.

"What the fuck was that?" Cooper shouted.

My ears rang from the shotgun blast. "I don't know, but it's not a freaking three-toed turkey."

"Then what's with the damned feathers floating in here?"

He was right. Small black feathers, like goose down, drifted to the ground between us. I bent to pick one up and noticed a long gash in Cooper's pant leg. "You tore your pants."

"I did?" He looked down.

"Yeah, right here," I pointed at his knee. The material looked wet. I touched it, frowning at the red on my fingers when I pulled them back. "Cooper, you're bleeding."

"Get back up here." He hooked me under the armpit and hauled me upright. "That thing must have sliced me with its claws as it passed." He squinted into the shadows. "How did it move so fast?"

"Is the cut deep?"

He put weight on his leg, grimacing. "It's just a flesh wound."

Cooper was covered in scars. I had a feeling his definition of flesh wound and mine were quite different. I stepped between him and whatever the hell was in here with us, blocking him from another attack.

"You should go outside," I said, raising the two-by-four.

"You're in my way, Parker."

"Cooper, this thing isn't a normal animal. I'm telling you that what I saw sneaking around the woodshed was unnatural. Your informant has a pet he forgot to tell you about."

"My informant didn't tell me anything."

"Why not? Did you piss him off, too?"

"The house was empty. He's missing."

"Missing?" I took a step forward. "Or dead?"

"I don't know."

Something blocked the light in the doorway.

We both turned, Cooper with the shotgun raised, me with the board cocked to swing.

"What in tarnation are you two doin' in here?"

I frowned at Harvey. "What are you doing *out there*?"

"I was waitin' fer ya in the pickup and then I heard Bessie's sweet music."

She had more of an eardrum-exploding bellow. "Your nephew got trigger happy."

"Yer bleedin', Coop," Harvey said. "Did ya shoot yerself again?"

"Again?" I asked.

"That's none of your business," Cooper told me.

The creature growled.

"Shit." I gripped the board, my right elbow out, ready to hit a home run.

"What was that?" Harvey whispered.

"Something that doesn't belong here," I said loud and clear. "Neither do you two right now."

"Give me Bessie," Harvey told Cooper, who complied without argument and then pulled out his handgun.

Focusing on the growls, I inched further into the shadows.

"Parker, get back here."

I sniffed, picking up a cloying, mildew odor. The hair on my arms lifted, my warning system lighting me up. The urge to bludgeon and destroy drove me deeper into the darkness.

"Where are you?" I said aloud. There was no use trying to hide. It had a better vantage point. I needed to rely on my instincts. "Come out and play."

"Jesus, Parker. You think it speaks English?"

"*Scharrrrrrfrichterrrrr,*" said a scratchy voice from the shadows.

The creature knew my name—the killing one, anyway. I could hear it breathing through its teeth. I tightened my grip on the board.

"Don't kill it." Cooper came up behind me. "I need to know where my informant is."

"I'll try not to." I stalked closer.

My eyes weren't of much use, so I zeroed in on the creature's sounds. The quick huffs of breath. The scratch of claws on wood. The rumble of its low growl.

"What are you?" I asked.

Garbled sounds were its reply.

"That sounds like turkey talk," Harvey said.

"I told you, Parker."

"Shut up, Cooper." I was thinking more of a crow than a turkey, or maybe a raven.

"What did it say?" Harvey asked, cocking his shotgun.

"I don't know. My ears are still ringing from Cooper firing your damned gun."

I heard the start of its roar deep in its chest. Reaching behind me, I shoved Cooper toward the opposite wall.

The scratch of its claws on wood as it sprang from the shadows gave me the cue I needed to anticipate its course. I kicked out, connecting with its flank and sending it sprawling sideways into a chunk of log. It scrambled upright onto its four legs, hissing at me, its long fangs bared.

It looked more like a big cat than turkey, but the snout was longer, wider than normal, filled with a shitload of teeth. Tufts of fur and black feathers rounded its mane and sprouted from its elbows. Armed with finger-like toes ending in wicked talons, this beast could take down a human with a single swipe.

The creature lunged.

I swung the board, nails facing out, landing a hit to the side of its skull. The blow was so solid it jarred my teeth.

A screech of pain filled the woodshed, followed by a crackling boom. I stepped back, shielding my face.

When I lowered my arm, fine gray powder covered my coat. I touched my hair, coming away with more powder, and sniffed my hands. The smell of rotten eggs made me recoil.

That wasn't powder. It was ash.

Harvey coughed. "Holy hell's bells!" He brushed ash off his chest and shook out his beard. "The darn thing done exploded."

"Goddammit, Parker!" Cooper glared at me. Ash coated him from head to toe. He must have been at ground zero. "I told you not to kill it."

I winced, letting the board clatter onto the floor. "Oops."

Chapter Two

In spite of the modern conveniences of the day, I had no frickin' cell phone signal all of the way back to Deadwood. Harvey blamed the whangdoodles back in Slagton, claiming they had some sort of radar that short-circuited cell signals in order to help keep their secrets safe from the government.

Unfortunately, Harvey's phone was sitting on the counter at Doc's house where he'd left it in his haste to pick up Cooper and me this morning, so I couldn't see if he had enough signal to reach the outside world. Cooper scoffed at my useless phone and declared it a piece of junk that sent random incoherent messages. After I called him a few not-so-nice, yet very coherent names, he refused to let me use his phone. On top of it all, he then proceeded to blame me for the missing state of his informant.

My request for Harvey to pull over and kick his nephew out at the top of Strawberry Hill went unheeded.

Due to my lack of signal situation, I wasn't able to warn Doc that I was about to tornado into his office, which I did with Cooper spinning in right behind me while Harvey parked the pickup.

"Doc?" I called as I stomped off the snow from my wet suede boots on his back doormat inside the dimly lit hallway.

Cooper bumped me from behind. "Don't stop in the doorway."

"Wait your stinking turn, pushypants."

And *stinking* we still were from that gray ash on our clothes and in our hair. We'd used snow to wash off what we could, but it would take a long, hot shower to scrub off the rest of the exploded remains. I shuddered at what might be soaking into my pores.

"That's 'Detective Pushypants' to you, Parker." He nudged me again, closing the door behind him.

"I don't want to get snow all over Doc's wood floor." I elbowed Cooper into the door while tugging off one arm of my coat. "I thought you needed to rush back to all of that paperwork you keep crying about."

He shrugged off his coat, glaring at me. "Not until I shower, thanks to you and your latest fuckup."

"Newsflash—there's no shower here." I pulled my other arm free of the smelly garment. "And it wasn't a fuckup."

"It definitely wasn't part of the plan." He stomped his boots on the mat. "I need to talk to your boyfriend before I go to his place and hit the shower, so move aside."

Cooper was living temporarily at Doc's house when he managed to escape his job long enough to sleep. Harvey was bunking there, too, along with his yellow lab, Red. It was a regular stag house, only my stag was hanging out in my bed more often than not lately, letting the other two enjoy his home without him.

"I need to talk to Doc, too," I said. "So get in line, because I was here first."

"Christ, Parker, we're not in third grade. There is no damned li—"

The overhead light came on, silencing us in the midst of our fifth tiff of the day. We were off to a dandy start.

The sound of a particular someone clearing his throat made Cooper and me turn.

Doc stood on the threshold of his office's back room, his arms crossed, his brow furrowed. His dark eyes widened as he inspected us from head to toe. Then he sniffed, cringing. "What happened to you two?"

Cooper pointed his thumb my way. "Your damned girlfriend took a whack at a hybrid turkey back in Slagton with a two-by-four and the thing exploded in my face."

"Holy horny toads, Cooper! For the umpteenth time, it was not a stupid turkey. I saw it. If that was a bird, then I'm an alligator. And for the record it exploded on all of us, you just happened to be front and center in the blast zone."

Doc cocked his head to the side, his gaze settling on me. "Was it Puff the Magic Dragon?"

Cooper and I exchanged frowns.

"Doc thinks he's a comedian," I said. When Cooper continued to frown at me, I explained, "Get it? You said a bird and I said a reptile, so Doc mixed the two and came up with a flying dragon." Still nothing from the stone-faced detective. "Listen, if you're not going to share our sense of humor, then you could at least pretend to laugh so that hanging out with you isn't on a par with hugging a crotchety porcupine."

"I get it, Parker," he bit out. "I'm just trying to figure out why you feel the need to kill instead of maim. Just once, can you *not* kill something?"

I raised one eyebrow. "You're still alive, aren't you?"

"She has you there, Coop," Doc said with a chuckle. "And she has maimed you multiple times."

"You're a regular Rodney Dangerfield today," Cooper grumbled.

"I get no respect." Doc even sounded like Dangerfield when he used the comedian's favorite catchphrase. He crooked his index finger toward me. "Come here, Killer."

I hung my smelly coat and purse on the hooks he had recently installed on the back wall and joined him, peeking around his shoulder into his back room. A row of computers lined the floor, a maze of cords snaking everywhere. "What's going on?" Then I noticed the one-horned Viking helmet next to one of the monitors. "Is Cornelius moving in?"

Cornelius Curion had a penchant for ghosts. His need to communicate with the dead was spurred by an ancestral line containing ghost whisperers and seers, along with plenty of old money to finance his love of all things wispy. From his stovepipe hat, dark round glasses, and gangly limbs, to the haunted hotel on Deadwood's Main Street that he'd recently purchased, eccentricity fit him like a floating white sheet. In spite of Cornelius's kookiness, he'd grown on Doc and me, securing a place not only in our lives but now apparently in Doc's office, too.

"He's experiencing technical difficulties." Doc cupped my chin, turning my face one way and then the other. "It's a little early in the day for an execution, isn't it?"

"It was an accident," I explained, noticing the smudge on Doc's hand when he let go of my chin. I thought I'd gotten the worst of it off before we'd climbed into Harvey's pickup. I was going to need a wire brush to clean off all the ashes. Cooper might need two showers as covered as he was.

"Tripping is an accident," the detective said, hanging his coat next to mine. "You belted that thing square in the face with a two-by-four full of nails."

I rolled my eyes at his fussing. "It was sort of an accident mixed with instinct."

"Are you okay, *cara mia?*" Doc's eyes zeroed in on my mouth.

"I am now, *mon amour.*"

He sucked a breath through his teeth. "That's French, Tish." His hand slid around the back of my neck, pulling me toward him. "What flavor of lip gloss are you wearing this morning?"

Doc must be desperate if he was willing to kiss me while I was covered with the charred remains. "You'll have to see for yourself."

Cooper's hand shoved between us.

I contemplated biting it.

"Enough lovey-dovey shit. We have a problem here. A big one, thanks to Parker and her need to kill without prejudice."

Doc released me. "Coop, you have a true gift when it comes to ruining a moment."

"You're sleeping in her bed." Cooper lowered his hand. "Take your moment then. Here and now we need to sort out this mess before it turns into an all-out shitstorm."

I pshawed his squawking about the sky falling. "This is a mere squall." I led the way out to the front office, hopping onto the edge of Doc's desk.

Cooper followed, stalking to the front door and flipping the Open sign to Closed. He shut the blinds covering the door and then moved to the front windows, frowning in the direction of the Deadwood police station.

After giving me a questioning glance, Doc lowered into his chair behind the desk. "What's really going on here, Coop? You're off your game."

"And don't blame it on me." I beat him to the punch.

Cooper plowed his fingers through his hair, stirring up a small puff of dust. "Today's visit was not on the radar. None of this Slagton shit has been."

"Detective Hawke doesn't know about this?" I asked, my upper lip wrinkling at the mention of Cooper's official partner in crime solving.

Detective Stone Hawke made me mad enough to eat fire ants. The pea brain had a fascination with proving I was a witch. Not the sexy sort, with a cute black mini-skirt and tight corset, but rather the green kind with hairy moles and thick yellow fingernails. He had made it his current life goal to pin all of the wrongful deaths that were filling the police's unsolved cases drawer on me. I was one final straw from shoving his head down a toilet and flushing repeatedly.

"Not at the moment," Cooper said. "But if my informant is missing, I need to report it."

"What makes you think he's missing and not out having a picnic in the woods?" I asked.

"His lack of appearance today."

Doc steepled his fingers. "Was there any evidence of foul play?"

"Besides the cat-urkey?" I joked, receiving a squint from Cooper for my efforts to lighten the mood. "Get it, *fowl* play? Wait, better yet, we could call it a sabertooth turkey. What do you think of that name?"

Doc laughed out loud. "Sabertooth turkey?"

A hint of a smile crossed Cooper's lips. "Keep it up, Parker, and I'm going to shoot you." He turned to Doc. "There was no evidence indicating a problem, but he should've been there."

"You see any footprints in the snow around the house?" I asked.

Cooper shook his head. "Only ours."

I crossed my arms. "Just because you're a cop doesn't mean you have to say anything to your buddies in blue about this."

"Not yet, anyway," Doc added. "Not until we're sure the informant is actually missing."

"Maybe he went out hunting," I threw out.

"Why would he set up a meeting with me and then go hunting?"

"He's old and forgetful." When Cooper gave me an exasperated look, I added, "What? Not all of us are half robot, Cooper, with computers for memories."

He started pacing. "I don't think he went hunting. There was a Remington 12-gauge shotgun and a Ruger 10/22 rifle hung over the fireplace. Both were well-used but clean and ready to fire."

"What else did you notice in the house?" Doc pressed.

"There were dirty dishes in the sink."

I snorted. That could be almost any house, especially one with two children, a pet chicken, and a cat. "Like stinky dirty with mold growing on them?"

"No mold. The food remnants were relatively fresh."

So, he'd been there recently. "Did you check the fridge?"

"He didn't have a refrigerator."

No refrigerator? That reminded me of a house in Lead where my predecessor in the Executioner business, Prudence, still resided in her now-translucent form. Prudence's house had a fridge, but never any ice cubes. "How's he keep his beer cold?"

"Apparently cold beer isn't high on his must-have list," Doc said. "A hunter without a freezer for his game meat is a bit odd, though."

"There was a rusty deep freeze in the dining room."

The guy must like to keep his frozen goods close at hand. "Were there any human heads in it?"

That earned me a smirk. "He's an informant, Parker. Not a serial killer."

I shrugged. "You never know. Maybe he needed to take on a second job to make ends meet."

The back door creaked and then slammed shut. We all paused, waiting as boots clomped on the doormat. Harvey joined us a few floor creaks later, his thumbs wrapped around his suspenders.

"What took you so long?" I was the first to speak.

"I was doing a little spyin' fer ya."

"Spying?" My heart skipped a couple of beats. "Spying on whom?"

"That hornswoggler who's out for yer blood."

"You'll have to be more specific than that," Cooper said. "Violet's list of enemies doubles by the day."

I wrinkled my nose at the detective.

"Yer boss and Tiffany Sugarbell. Apparently, there was a parkin' lot meetin' that you weren't invited to."

My shoulders cinched up tight around my neck. "Crud," I muttered. I was hoping that possibility would fall flat on its face.

"What's going on with Tiffany?" Cooper asked.

"My rat-bastard coworker is trying to get Tiffany hired."

"At Calamity Jane Realty?" At my nod, Cooper cringed. "I'd better make sure we're all stocked up on crime scene tape at the station."

"Ray has this big idea that if he gets Tiffany in there, I'll get fired."

If assholes could pay for fake tans and talk real estate, then Ray Underhill is what they'd look like. The jerk had been trying to get me canned since the first day I started at Calamity Jane Realty. We tended to rub each other wrong daily, periodically producing enough friction to light one of us on fire. Unfortunately, he'd never exploded in my face, unlike whatever it was I'd killed earlier in Slagton. However, there were times I'd like to aim a two-by-four at his huge arrogant head.

"Yer boss may be thick-skulled on some of the finer things about women," Harvey said. "But that boy is hot to trot and already a-saddled."

I wasn't even going to try to decipher that. "Meaning what?"

"Two fine-lookin' heifers in the pasture are better than one." Harvey did a little giddy-up jig. "I need to go tap the ol' maple tree and let the sap drip." Without another word, he headed back down the hall, shutting the bathroom door behind him.

I looked over at Cooper. "What exactly is the law defining wrongful death versus accidental death?"

Doc crossed his arms. "Hiring Tiffany would be a mistake after all Jerry's done to build your sales. Those billboard ads aren't cheap."

My face warmed at the reminder of the two billboards starring me caked in makeup posed in asinine positions now gracing both east- and west-bound lanes of Interstate 90.

"True," I said, "but Tiffany has hot sex written all over her." With her long red hair, Barbie-like waistline, and rock star boobs, she had male clients panting after her on sight alone.

"You think you don't?" Doc asked.

"I've told you before, you're biased."

"More like smitten," he said, openly admiring my curves.

"Want some advice, Parker?"

"Advice? From you?" At Cooper's nod, I braced myself. "Sure."

"I've watched Tiffany and you go head to head multiple times."

My cheeks darkened. Unfortunately, that was true. Tiffany was really good at humiliating me in front of Cooper.

"You let her bully you."

"She intimidates me."

"Do I intimidate you?"

Was this some kind of police interrogation trap?

"Do I?" he pressed.

"Sometimes."

"How do you handle me?"

"I hit back."

"Exactly. Maybe you should pretend you're dealing with me. Better yet, pretend she's Detective Hawke. You've been holding your own with him since the first time he clicked his pen at you."

"I don't know if I—"

"Quit being such a namby-pamby. Now, if you're done crying about Nyce's ex, let's get back to the problem at hand—my missing informant."

"I have a thought on that," Doc said.

"I'm not a namby-pamby," I said to Cooper.

"Then quit playing victim around Tiffany." He turned to Doc. "What's your thought?"

"You hold off on reporting anything until tomorrow."

"What's tomorrow?" I asked.

"Another trip to Slagton to pay a visit to Coop's informant, only this time I'm coming along."

"You think you'll be able to detect a ghost?" I asked.

Doc looked at Cooper. "Did you see any ghosts back there?"

Cooper shook his head.

"Then probably not. However, some do tend to hide, and in that case I might sniff one out."

Doc had been dealing with ghosts since childhood. When he wasn't in his office playing financial planner, he was finessing his skills as a mental medium. Over the years, he'd gone back and forth between fine-tuning his ghost interaction skills and trying to bury them in a dark corner of his mind so he could enjoy a normal life. Since coming to Deadwood, he'd given up on normality, especially after meeting me and finding out my purpose in this world—executing troublemakers who don't belong on this plane of existence.

At least that was what Aunt Zoe told me I was supposed to be doing. Lately, I'd been more focused on keeping out of jail and not dying a painful death since my enemies often came equipped with big muscles and sharp claws. Reading the family history book about Executioners in my ancestral line could help me stay alive, but the nightmares spurred from what I read in those pages messed with my head too much. Doc now kept the book and helped prepare me as much as possible for what lay in wait for me.

"If it's not about seeing a ghost," I said to him, "then why do you want to go along?"

"Because I have a theory."

The wrinkles lining his forehead inspired a few of my own. "You think somebody is up to something fishy?"

"I think somebody is dangling bait."

Bait? I'd used bait myself when hunting trouble in the past. "What are they trying to catch, a monster?"

"More like an Executioner."

No sooner had Doc spoken his sobering theory, my cell phone rang playing the Harlem Globetrotters theme song. That was my boss on the line, Jerry Russo, the ex-professional basketball player turned realty guru.

I gulped, another round of doomsday bells clanging in my head.

When I answered, Jerry told me to meet him in an hour at Bighorn Billy's Diner for an emergency huddle with the rest of the Calamity Jane crew. I sent a prayer to the real estate gods that Tiffany wouldn't be joining us today and hopped off Doc's desk. Before my meeting, I needed a good scrubbing to wash off the remains of my last kill.

Doc walked me to the back door. I passed Harvey in the hall. Apparently his tree was done dripping sap.

"I'll see you tonight," I told him.

It was his turn to cook supper for whoever joined us at Aunt Zoe's place, where my kids and I were living for the time being. On the way out to Slagton, Harvey had mentioned something about *carnitas* and his momma's blue-ribbon coleslaw, and I was holding him to it.

Doc kissed me at the door. "Raspberry," he whispered, taking a second taste before helping me with my stinky coat.

"I'll see you tonight?" I asked, shouldering my purse.

He was still staring at my lips. "Definitely."

"And tomorrow morning for breakfast?"

His gaze met mine, heat spreading through me. "That depends."

"On what?"

"If you're going to use me for a foot warmer again all night long."

"How about I use you for a hand warmer instead?"

"Deal."

I zipped home, stuffed my coat, boots, and clothes in a garbage bag until I decided if I should keep or toss them, and took a shower. Both kids were at school and Aunt Zoe's pickup was missing, so I had no distractions and set to work removing the dead creatures' ashes from all of my nooks and crannies.

When I arrived at Bighorn Billy's Diner, Tiffany's Jeep wasn't in the parking lot. I breathed a sigh of relief, but didn't fully lower my shields. It would be typical of Jerry to surprise us with Tiffany breaking through a *GO TEAM!* paper banner midway through the meal.

Inside the diner, Jerry waved at me from the large back corner booth already occupied with two of my three coworkers. He stood to let me slide inside. When standing next to Jerry with his fair-haired Thor build, I often felt like a hobbit minus the hairy feet. At least I had the curly hair for the role.

"You're late," Ray said as I slid into the booth.

I ignored him.

"Settle down, Sunshine," Mona told the buffoon. "It's only been a couple of minutes."

Mona Hollister had been on my side from the get-go at Calamity Jane's. While she had a good decade and a half worth of birthdays more than me, she would still give Grace Kelly a run for her money in both fashion and class. I aspired to be like Mona when I grew up and got my shit together, only with crazy blond hair instead of her stylish auburn tresses.

"Sorry," I said to Jerry. "I needed to stop off at home. I stepped in a slush puddle this morning and soaked my boots." More like stepped in a steaming pile of trouble.

"No problem. We're still waiting on Ben. How did the house showing go with the detective?"

After Harvey had called me this morning, I'd told Jerry what I thought was happening—Harvey, Cooper, and I were going out to see some houses. In reality, we'd seen a rundown shack. Unfortunately, something was home besides the owner.

"He's interested in going back." No lie there. Tomorrow morning I'd be in Slagton again, only this time I was dressing for it. Suede boots didn't grow on trees, especially anywhere near my bank account.

"What house did you show him?" Ray asked with narrowed eyes.

Before I had to come up with an answer, Ben Underhill showed up full of warm smiles for one and all. He took the other end of the wraparound bench and filled us in on what he'd learned yesterday at a seminar down in Rapid City on new rules for selling historical buildings. Ben might be Ray's nephew and share several of his uncle's physical features, including dark hair and good teeth, but he was from the non-reptilian side of the family.

By the time coffee was delivered all around and lunch orders taken, my worries about Tiffany showing up to join us had eased.

Jerry started the meeting with a request for status updates. In his typical style, Ray gloated about all of his big-ticket clients. Mona itemized her impressive pipeline, while Ben listed statistics along with his potentials. I wrapped it up with my usual stumbling and stuttering. Public speaking was not one of my finer skills. I was much better getting my meaning across with a two-by-four.

Our meal arrived and we settled into eating and sharing property rumors and home staging ideas. My food went down easily in spite of the sneers Ray periodically shot my way. I thought about asking Jerry why he was talking to Tiffany in the parking lot earlier, but I didn't want to give myself heartburn, so I held off for the time being.

I was finishing the last of my salad when Jerry glanced at his watch for the third time in the last few minutes.

Was he anxious to get back to work, or was he waiting for someone to join us? Someone with red hair, perky everything, and an ultra-competitive personality who was out to steal my job?

Jerry looked toward the door a few seconds later, his smile widening. "Here she is."

"She who?" Ben asked, shooting me a wrinkled brow.

"My special guest." Jerry stood, holding out his hand. "Thanks for coming. Everyone, you remember Rosy, of course, from the *Paranormal Realty* crew."

Sweet manna from heaven! My smile matched Rosy's. Boy oh boy, was I happy to see her pink cheeks and friendly eyes instead of Doc's ex.

"Did you drive the moving truck through this snow?" I asked.

Rosy had recently purchased Cooper's place from me. I'd grown fond of the reality TV show's camerawoman, especially after she filmed me with an eerie clown-loving ghost and then did me the favor of deleting the footage to save me from the hell that would have followed had it gone live.

"No. I hired a company to deliver most of my furniture. The truck should be here on Sunday." Rosy shucked her winter coat and slid into the booth seat next to Ben. "I just brought my camera equipment and some clothes and booked a room at The Old Prospector Hotel."

She leaned on the table. Lugging a camera around for a living had beefed up her arms and shoulders. From the first time we'd met, something about her reminded me of those "We Can Do It!" posters from World War II starring Rosie the Riveter. She had the name for it and all.

"You're staying at Cornelius's hotel?" I asked. "But it's under construction."

"I know, but he gave me one hell of a discount that covers the cost of earplugs, and it's only for a couple of nights. I'm in one of the farthest rooms from the action. Since I'm usually up at dawn, I'm good with it."

But was she good with all of the ghosts Cornelius had lured there over the last few months via what Doc referred to as his Pied Piper abilities?

Jerry cleared his throat. "I invited Rosy to join us today because I've hired her to help prepare for the release of the *Paranormal Realty* episode starring Calamity Jane Realty in January."

I fidgeted with my spoon. I'd sort of wished all of the filming we'd done last fall for that reality television show would disappear into thin air like some of the *others* I'd killed around that time.

"Prepare how?" Mona's tone was wary and for good reason, too. Jerry's marketing ideas often made at least one of us grind our molars down to nubs.

"She's going to hang around and do some filming for our website blog."

"We have a website blog?" I asked. I hadn't noticed a blog tab the last time I'd visited the site.

"Not yet, but we will come January." His grin was as wide as his huge shoes. "We're going to have a collection of ongoing vlogs there. My goal is to have several ready to post for each of you by the time the show goes live."

"Vlogs?" Ray asked through a brittle smile.

"A video blog," Rosy answered. "Jerry wants me to spend time with you guys, creating both a video biography and several short pieces of video fun stuff for your future fans."

Jerry's head bobbled with excitement. "Each of you will have your own page on the website with a collection of vlogs."

"Each?" Mona's smile was tight. "Don't you mean just Ben and Violet, since they were the only two on film?"

"Oh no, Red. You don't get out of it this time. Each of us, including myself, will have videos. We're the number two realty office in the region, and I aim to have us in the top spot by spring."

The waitress brought a cup and the coffee carafe, pouring some at Rosy's nod.

"What sort of stuff will you be recording?" Ray's tanned brow wrinkled at the edges where his latest injection of muscle relaxer hadn't reached.

"Don't worry," Jerry said. "It will be partially scripted, at least at first."

"Who's writing the script?" Mona asked, her pinched lips giving away her feelings on the whole plan.

"Rosy is."

I nailed the camerawoman with a raised brow. She winked back. "I help a lot with the script for the show. I actually started out writing scripts before being seduced into stepping behind the camera."

"So this is your big news?" I asked, wanting to make sure he wasn't going to pull a mid-court Hail Mary shot and have Tiffany show up in a cheerleader outfit.

Jerry nodded. "I'm excited to get Rosy busy with her camera. We have a lot to do before the website goes live, and lucky for us Rosy is hanging around here for the next month while she settles into her new digs up in Lead."

He ordered dessert to celebrate and more coffee. For the next half hour, we brainstormed concepts for our individual vlogs. I tried to pretend I wasn't worried about what Rosy might see on camera when filming me after our last experience, but the reassuring grins she aimed my way in between bites of her apple pie à la mode said I was doing a bad job of hiding my fears.

As we all stood to leave, she touched my arm and nudged her head toward the hallway leading to the restrooms. I followed her into the ladies' room.

After checking underneath the stalls, she leaned back against the door and stared at me while chewing on her lower lip.

"Is everything okay with Cooper's place?" I asked, wondering what had spurred this impromptu bathroom rendezvous.

"Yeah. I need to talk to you about something else."

"What?"

"Cornelius Curion."

Cornelius? He seemed to be on the minds of multiple people this morning. "What about him?"

"He called me a couple of days ago."

"To invite you to stay at his hotel?"

She shook her head. "He wants me to join you two on a hunting expedition."

I was going hunting? That wasn't going to work for me since I didn't own a single piece of camouflage or bright orange clothing.

"Did Cornelius say where we were going?" I asked. Or what we were hunting?

"Sort of."

"What do you mean?"

"Well, in addition to my camera gear, he told me to bring a rope ladder." She crossed her strong arms. "Then he mentioned something about a 'Hellhole.' "

Chapter Three

As afternoons went, mine sucked big boughs of holly.

It turned out that while Tiffany Sugarbell hadn't yet been hired as a new employee of Calamity Jane Realty, she had officially stolen one of my clients.

Jeff Wymonds had signed a contract for me to sell his house last summer. It was a modest one-story rambler in Central City that had cleaned up pretty well with a lot of sweat and elbow grease, some of which had been mine, but our first open house had started with a bang. And by bang, I meant *BOOM!!!* Good-bye, garage roof. Even though Jeff's insurance company had fixed the roof, I hadn't been able to hook any potential buyers since hanging my sign in his front yard. Between the lack of bites and Tiffany's multiple seduction attempts to lure him away, Jeff had succumbed to the red-haired siren.

He called me shortly after I'd returned from lunch with the news that he'd taken the client-stealing, two-bit whore up on selling his place. At least I think that's what he said, although my brain may have thrown in a contemptuous adjective or ten.

Jeff's call had sent my afternoon into a tailspin. After he'd apologized all over the place, he'd asked if Addy could spend the night with his daughter this evening, promising he was staying home alone to hang out with the girls and string some popcorn for fun while watching *The Grinch* on television. In spite of my teeth still gnashing about his using his penis meter to choose his Realtor, I agreed. Maybe his leaving me was for the best, since I'd refused to let him plow my fertile fields and plant his seed within a hundred-mile radius of my uterus.

Ray's gloating grin when he heard the news about Jeff Wymonds accelerated my downward spiral. I had no proof, but I was ninety-nine percent sure he had been working on the sly with Tiffany to screw me over on the Wymonds deal. Or screw Jeff via Tiffany. Either way, it appeared Jeff and I both got screwed.

Jerry's disappointed frown when he returned from an afternoon appointment and heard that I'd lost a possible sale to Tiffany made me feel like gum on the sole of one of Ray's fancy Tony Lama cowboy boots. I'd spent the rest of the afternoon fuming in silence. Ray and Tiffany were tag-teaming up on me. What would they pull next? Woo Cooper away from me?

My pipeline was sounding hollow from a lack of sellers. I did have several interested buyers thanks to Jerry's billboard ads, but since they came in based off a giant photoshopped picture of me sporting a pen between my super-sized red lips, I wasn't expecting any long-term commitments, especially if Tiffany played the temptress card again.

I needed more properties to list.

And more buyers with bulging wallets.

And more time focused on selling real estate instead of killing sabertooth turkeys. I snorted at that. I was partial to that silly name even if Cooper wasn't.

Finally, five o'clock came and I was able to scurry home and hide in Aunt Zoe's cozy yellow kitchen while hugging her Betty Boop cookie jar. I'd scarfed down three cookies before she found me grumbling to myself at the kitchen table.

"What's going on at work?" Aunt Zoe asked, heading straight to the sink to wash her hands. Her long silver-streaked hair fell in soft waves over her shoulders.

"How do you know something is up at work?"

"Baby doll, you've attached yourself to the cookie jar." She searched my face while drying her hands. "That usually means something isn't going well at work. If you were snuggling with a tequila bottle, I'd be worried you hit another snag with the cops or worse."

"The tequila is next. I needed to lay a foundation of sugar and flour first."

She tossed the towel on the counter. "Spill it, Violet Lynn."

I pointed a cookie at her. "You're all snazzed up. Got a hot date?"

Smoothing her sparkly tunic over her black velvet bohemian skirt, she avoided my gaze. "Tonight is the Deadwood Chamber of Commerce holiday party."

I grabbed another cookie. "You didn't fully answer my question."

Crossing the room, she snatched the cookie from my hand. "That's enough cookies. You'll spoil the dinner Willis is planning for tonight."

Whenever anyone called Ol' Man Harvey by his first name, it took my brain a moment to put the two together.

I reached for another cookie, but she took the jar away from me.

"I'm going to the party with Reid," she admitted, taking a cookie for herself.

My mouth fell open. "Reid Martin?"

"Yes. Close your mouth. You still have cookies in there."

I obeyed, finishing my bite and swallowing before saying, "Reid, as in the captain of Deadwood's Fire Department?"

"Yes, that Reid."

"The same man you threaten to fill full of bullet holes every time he crosses your threshold?"

"Not every time, and I shoot pellets, not bullets."

I waved off her correction. "Nine times out of ten, then."

Her dark blue eyes narrowed.

"I don't understand," I said.

"There's nothing to understand. I asked Reid to join me in case Dominick Masterson shows up."

Ahhh, the Earth's magnetic poles were realigning and all was well again in the land of Deadwood.

Dominick had recently taken a strong liking to Aunt Zoe. Normally, that wouldn't be such a bad thing considering how charismatic and heart-palpably handsome he was. However, Dominick was the devil's first cousin in Aunt Zoe's eyes. He had the ability to charm the pants right off her, literally, and could wipe out all of her resistance in one smoldering glance. Lucky for me, Dominick was not human, and I'd been born with a natural resistance to his kind and their tricks due to my Executioner genes.

"So, you're taking Reid as a bodyguard?" I asked.

"Exactly."

"Is tonight going to end up like that old bodyguard movie with Kevin Costner and Whitney Houston?"

"You mean *The Bodyguard*, and no. Reid understands the rules and has agreed to keep his hands to himself all evening."

I grinned. "Yeah, but can you keep your hands to yourself?"

"Of course."

"Liar."

Her chin jutted. "I've answered your questions, now you answer mine. What's going on at work?"

I spilled the beans about Tiffany stealing Jeff from me.

Aunt Zoe's mouth thinned. "That explains why Jeff was acting so antsy earlier when he came by to get Addy for the night. He must have been worried you'd told me about his switching agents."

"Probably." I sighed, sitting back. "I understand his wanting to mix things up and try a different agent. I just wish he'd picked someone other than Doc's ex."

The doorbell rang.

"That's probably Reid," she said, kneading her hands together.

"I'll get it," my son, Layne, called out. He tromped down the stairs.

Aunt Zoe shot a worried glance toward the dining room. "Don't let Tiffany get to you, kiddo." She checked her reflection in the side of the chrome toaster. Unfortunately, it was smeared with my kids' fingerprints. "You'll have to keep a brave face and pretend losing Jeff was not a big deal or she'll figure out a way to keep throwing salt in your wounds."

The sound of Layne's voice coming closer made us both turn. My son bounced into the kitchen, followed by Cooper, whose arms were laden with grocery bags.

"Why look, Aunt Zoe," I said as Cooper set the bags down on the table. "The Grinch came down off his mountain to have a Christmas feast with us poor little Who-folk."

That earned me a squint. "Funny, Parker. You have crumbs on your face."

Of course he'd notice that. I brushed off my cheek. "I'm saving them for later. What's with the groceries?"

"Uncle Willis called the station and left me a list of things to pick up for tonight."

"You're making supper?" If we weren't having Harvey's *carnitas*, I was going to need more cookies.

"No, he is. It's my turn to pay for it."

I tugged open one of the bags. "What all did you buy?"

He pulled the bag out of my hand. "That's police business."

Aunt Zoe chuckled. "Better be careful, Coop. She's pissed off and hungry. She's liable to bite first and apologize later."

The doorbell rang again. Layne headed to get the door with Aunt Zoe on his heels.

Cooper unloaded the bags, placing a six-pack of beer, two packages of taco shells—corn and flour—peppers, limes, a head of cabbage, shredded cheese, and several different brands of salsa on the counter next to the stove. I joined him, inspecting his take.

"There's no meat," I said.

"Uncle Willis slow-cooked the pork at Nyce's house."

I licked my chops. "Did you hear anything from Slagton?"

"No." He handed me the empty bags. "Who is coming tonight?"

I stuffed the bags in the pantry. "Your uncle, Doc, and you for sure." When his mouth drooped a little at the corners, I added, "But I invited Natalie, too. She was down in Rapid this afternoon and said she'd try to make it back."

His frown deepened. "Did she happen to mention anything about what happened last night?"

"You mean about your bending her over backward and kissing her senseless at the Purple Door Saloon?"

"Shhhh." He shot a look toward the dining room.

"Don't shush me, Cooper. If you didn't want the world to know, you shouldn't have put on that public display of affection for one and all at the bar."

"It's not that I'm trying to keep it a secret, but I'd rather you didn't broadcast it to the whole damned town." He popped open a beer. "And I didn't bend her over backward."

"Practically."

He pointed his beer bottle at me. "Not practically. You were drunk and not supposed to be watching. You're remembering it wrong."

I crossed my arms. "Whatever. Natalie didn't say a word about the kiss, but that doesn't mean anything because our conversation was short and I didn't ask about it."

He took a swig from the bottle. "Did she mention anything at all about last night?"

"She said her head hurt like she'd been run over by Santa's sleigh, and she spent half of the night doing the tango with the toilet."

"When I helped her up to her apartment, I told her to eat something before going to bed. She said she wasn't hungry and promptly passed out on the couch."

"Did you remove any restrictive clothing from her body, Detective? You know, to help her sleep better?" I winked at him.

His gaze narrowed. "What do you think I am, Parker? Some kind of sexual deviant?"

"I think you're frustrating most days. Sometimes downright annoying."

"Good. Then I'm doing my job."

"How come I don't remember you taking her up to her apartment?"

"Because you were snoring in the back seat by that point."

I was just glad to make it through the night without tossing my cookies since Doc was there beside me in bed. There was nothing like a drunk, puking girlfriend to make a man want to run for the hills.

Aunt Zoe joined us in the kitchen again with Reid in tow.

I whistled, eyeing him up and down. "Wow, Reid. You look hot enough to catch fire." His deep red shirt made his blue-blue eyes stand out. His salt-and-pepper hair was combed back, his mustache trimmed. His black corduroy pants and cowboy boots added a final suave look.

"Thanks, Sparky. You have crumbs on your cheek."

I brushed off my other cheek.

"She's saving them for later," Cooper told him, leaning against the counter. "Why are you so dressed up, Martin?"

"I'm taking Zo to the Deadwood Chamber holiday party."

Cooper's brows climbed upward. "No shit." He looked over at Aunt Zoe, who was slipping on a pair of elegant glass earrings of her own making. "Did you lose a bet, Zoe?"

She chuckled, reaching for the long wool coat that Reid held out for her. "Something like that."

"Shut up, Coop," Reid said, helping Aunt Zoe with her sleeves. "At least I have a date tonight. You're stuck here with your uncle." He smiled at me. "No offense, Sparky."

"None taken. I thought we'd play a game of pin the tail on the donkey after you two left, but Cooper would probably get tired of being poked with tacks all night long and shoot me."

"Zoe," Cooper said, "how about I take you to the party and leave these two knuckleheads here."

She patted him on the shoulder. "Thanks for the offer, but Natalie just pulled up outside. A little birdy told me you have something to talk about with her."

Cooper's steely eyes nailed me to the floor. "Jesus, Parker. Did you take out a fucking ad in the *Black Hills Trailblazer*?"

I raised my hands in surrender. "I was drunk last night. I can't be held responsible for my loose lips."

"What's the deal with Natalie and Coop?" Reid asked.

Cooper cursed under his breath and went over to the refrigerator, stuffing the rest of the beers he'd bought inside.

"It's police business," Aunt Zoe said, grabbing Reid by the arm. "We'll be home around eleven," she told me.

"You sure?" I wiggled my eyebrows in the fire captain's direction.

Reid grinned, wiggling his back.

"Positive," she said, elbowing him as she headed for the door.

He grunted, and then waved at me before following Aunt Zoe.

After they were gone, I turned back to Cooper. "What are you going to do about Natalie?"

He squeezed the bridge of his nose. "I don't know yet."

"But last night you said something about—"

The sound of footfalls in the dining room made me pause.

Natalie joined us in the kitchen, faltering when she saw Cooper standing there. She recovered quickly, but her smile was banana-wide, looking almost manic. "What's going on?"

"Nothing," I said too quickly.

Her gaze narrowed.

Cooper shot me an exasperated glare, and then he turned back to Natalie. "How are you feeling after last night, Beals?"

His question weighed heavy in the air, layered with all sorts of hidden undercurrents and sexual tension.

Her cheeks darkened as she held his gaze, but then she glanced down at her pink fleece shirt and pretended to wipe something off it. "A little hung over, but otherwise same ol', same ol'."

"Do you remember anything that happened?" I fished.

She took her sweet-ass time answering—at least it felt that way for me. It must have been an eternity for Cooper. "Well," she said, moving over to the refrigerator, hiding her face in it. "I remember a lot of tequila talk." She pulled out Aunt Zoe's pitcher of lemonade. "Oh, and you sucking at pool."

"I didn't suck." At least I thought I'd done decently. Or maybe I was thinking of another tequila pool party we'd had.

She set the lemonade on the counter next to Cooper, bumping him aside so she could reach the glasses. "What do you remember besides me out-drinking you?"

"I held my own just fine, thank you very much." I crossed my arms. "Didn't I, Cooper?"

He smirked. "You were equally shitfaced when I showed up."

It was shortly after his arrival last night at the bar that he'd kissed Natalie, although there'd been some words first, but I couldn't remember them.

"Yeah, but Vi passed out first, so I won."

"You remember me carrying you up to your apartment?" he asked.

She poured the lemonade, her forehead creased. "You didn't carry me. I walked on my own two feet."

"You call that walking?"

"I call it staggering."

"More like leaning heavily."

She set the lemonade pitcher on the counter and hit him head-on with a stare. "What's your point, Detective?"

His eyes searched hers.

I waited with my breath held to see if he'd bring up the kiss.

"Did you sleep okay?" he asked, chickening out.

She looked away first, carrying the pitcher back to the refrigerator. "I don't remember that either."

Either? I caught the hurried frown she shot him before opening the fridge door. She was hiding something, and I'd bet my purple boots it had to do with Cooper's lips and her reaction to his kiss.

Rather than push her further in front of Cooper and add to the tension swirling around us, I decided to change the subject.

"Did you hear any ghosts last night?" I asked.

Natalie lived in the Galena House, my only remaining listed property besides Harvey's ranch out in the boonies where dead body parts kept showing up. The Galena House was an old multi-story, Italianate-style boarding house that had been built in the late 1800s by

Big Jake Tender, a freed slave known for his large stature, impressive abilities, and legendary feats. Over the decades, the house had passed down from one generation to the next. It now belonged to Jake's great-great ... and maybe one more great in there ... niece, Freesia. While Freesia appreciated the bones of the building and all of the hard work her family had put into it for generations, she was a young, single woman trying to make ends meet. The Galena House needed repairs beyond her abilities and cash flow. Enter Natalie, a handywoman extraordinaire, who was helping Freesia fix up the house to sell so that Freesia could be free to roam and find her own place in history.

"No ghosts," Natalie answered. "Ever since you guys played musical chairs with the attic ghosts, I haven't heard a peep."

Last week, Doc, Cooper, Cornelius, and I had held a séance in the attic of the Galena House. Our purpose had been to find a killer from the past. As it turned out, the answer had been in the mirror all along.

Anyway, before we'd had the séance, Natalie had been hearing noises in the middle of the night. Sounds like footfalls on the stairs and golden oldie country tunes coming from an unplugged antique radio in the attic. Doc had guessed the noisemaker to be Big Jake Tender in his ghostly form, whom Doc had run into at a séance in one of the downstairs apartments months prior. Apparently, Big Jake's love for Ms. Wolff, who'd lived in the house during his lifetime, had been undying—at least his ghost thought so and kept playing the golden oldies to remember her. I'd used that same antique radio as a channeling device for the séance. Maybe that séance had sent Jake on his way to whatever came next.

"Although," Natalie continued, pulling me out of the past. "After all of the tequila I had last night, I probably wouldn't have heard a marching band playing on the floor above me. When I crashed onto my couch, it was a head-on collision that knocked me out cold until I relocated to the bathroom to begin my worshipping of the porcelain goddess." She sat down at the table, raising her drink toward Cooper. "Thanks for the blanket and pillow."

He nodded once.

"I wonder if Big Jake is gone for good now," I said.

"Gone to where, though?" Natalie asked, taking a sip of lemonade. "All this talk about multiple planes and physical mediums has me scratching my head a lot lately."

"Physical medium" was one of the labels Cornelius and Doc had given me, due to my ability to find frightening creatures on other planes of existence and somehow drag them back to this one. That was only one of my many new talents I'd discovered that left me staring at the woman in the mirror and wondering who in the hell she really was.

"Scratching your what?" Harvey asked, joining us in the kitchen.

I did a double take. "Where did you come from?" I hadn't heard the front door open or close.

"My momma's womb." He jabbed his thumb over his shoulder. "Yer stallion is here, too."

I glanced over Harvey's shoulder. "Is he wearing his invisibility cape?"

"He was hoofin' it upstairs to change."

Doc had brought a few sets of clothes over this last week, stowing them in my closet. If he was going to keep spending the night, which was an integral part of my diabolical plan to make him my sex slave for life, we were going to have to make some space in my dresser drawers.

Harvey hustled over to the counter, inspecting Cooper's groceries. "Ya forgot the cheese for the kids, boy."

"It's in the refrigerator."

Harvey handed Cooper the head of cabbage. "Get to choppin'."

Layne burst into the kitchen, spreading several sheets of paper on the table in front of me. "What do you think, Mom?"

I picked up one of the sheets. He'd drawn a medieval-looking sword with a long blade dripping blood. I complimented him on the detailed work on the handle.

"That's not a handle, Mom. It's called a hilt."

Lately, Layne had been spending his recess in the library reading instead of going outside to get some fresh air. My son took after his father with his big science brain. If it weren't horse anatomy 101 Layne was reading about in some huge tome, then it was other complex subjects such as the Maya or Deadwood's ghost-filled past. The kid devoured books like he was a Himalayan monk locked up in a mountain temple. It appeared that his latest fascination was medieval weapons.

Layne picked up another drawing and held it in front of my face, talking excitedly about pommels, grips, scabbards, and more, making my head spin. While Layne pointed out the details of his weapon collection, Natalie kept sneaking peeks at Cooper, who was too busy helping his uncle make supper to notice. Every time she'd find me catching her in the act, she'd glance down, pretending to focus on her glass of lemonade.

Doc interrupted the scene, striding into the kitchen and stealing my attention with his faded jeans and black Henley.

"Hubba hubba," I whispered.

He stopped to drop a hello-kiss on my mouth. "Molasses cookies?" he asked, his voice low and husky.

"Let me guess, I have more crumbs on my face?" I wiped off both cheeks this time and my nose, too.

His eyes crinkled in the corners. "Your kiss was extra sweet. I'm going to need more later."

"I left a few in the jar."

"I wasn't talking about cookies." Doc left me and my heart smoldering and walked over to the cupboard, pulling down plates. "Layne," he said, holding out the plates, "you want to help me set the table?"

"I can help you," I offered, starting to rise.

Doc shook his head. "It's not your turn, remember?"

"Yeah, Mom," Layne said, pushing me back into my seat. He dropped his artwork on the table. "Tonight is guys' night. You just sit there and look pretty for us boys."

Chuckling, Doc handed Layne the plates. "Nice touch, kid."

I picked up a couple more of his drawings. Damn, Layne had even noted details on lengths and widths on several of the weapon diagrams. "Hey, Layne, did you copy these from one of the books at the library?"

"No." He set a plate in front of me. "I saw them in that old book about women gladiators that I found in your room."

More like sneaked from my room. I'd been doing a rotten job of reading the family history book about previous Executioners in our family line. Having the flu hadn't helped my ability to focus. One night when I was passed out during my flu coma, he'd come into my room to check on me and found the book on my bed. Unable to resist, my curious child had "borrowed" the book without telling me, hiding it under his bed so I wouldn't know he was reading it.

Doc paused in the midst of setting out silverware. "You drew them from memory?" He kept the book at his place now, so Layne wouldn't have been able to copy them.

Layne nodded. "They were cool weapons."

"Let me take a look at those." Doc joined me, leaning over my shoulder as he stared down at Layne's penciled sketches. "Damn, he did an amazing job with the details," he said under his breath, pointing at one that looked a lot like the very ax a juggernaut-sized troublemaker had used to try to slice me in half during one of our séances at the Galena House.

Natalie leaned over my other shoulder, frowning down at one of the war hammers he'd drawn that resembled the one I had hidden in my closet at this very moment. "What's this for?" she asked, pointing at the long spike sticking out the opposite side of the hammer.

"Piercing armor," Layne explained. He lined up the silverware on the napkins. "In medieval times, a warrior had to break through the heavy plates used to protect the enemy's chest and back during battle."

"Yikes," Natalie said, handing it to Cooper, who'd come closer to take a look.

He stared at the war hammer for a few seconds, his forehead wrinkles deepening. When he looked up at me, his scowl was back in full force.

What? I mouthed.

He snorted in reply and returned to helping his uncle.

Ten minutes later, the table was set and the food was almost ready to eat when my daughter's chicken, Elvis, came strutting in from the dining room.

I growled. "What is she doing out of her cage?"

Layne shrugged. "Addy couldn't find her before she left with Kelly."

I reached for the damned bird, but she dodged my hand. "Do me a favor, Layne, and go put Elvis in her cage for the night."

He scooped up the chicken and headed down into the basement, where Addy had made a two-story henhouse for the bird.

As soon as he was out of earshot, Cooper said, "Where is that war hammer, Parker?"

"Somewhere safe, why?"

"Don't you think it's quite a coincidence that your son drew a picture of it?"

"That's not my war hammer he drew."

"What makes you so certain?" Natalie asked.

"Because I know my weapon. It's similar, but mine has the horns curling around the headpiece. The horns on the one he drew pointed straight out, more like spikes."

"You need to take care and not let your son find that weapon," Cooper warned. "It's listed as stolen evidence at the police station and should it turn up in one of your offspring's hands, Detective Hawke would be all over your ass again."

"Detective Hawke can kiss my—"

The thudding of shoes on the basement steps made us both turn.

Layne rushed through the door, his eyes wide. "Mom, guess what?"

"Elvis laid a golden egg?" Harvey teased.

"Funny, Harvey, but no."

I shrugged. "I have no idea what has you so breathless all of a sudden, Layne." He'd probably discovered a new species of insect inside Elvis's cage.

"You remember that spooky clock Addy found in a box next to the stairs?"

"You mean the box that had my name on it?" The box containing a Black Forest cuckoo clock with a carving of a pointy-eared beast with a long snout that I suspected was some sort of Hellhound–werewolf mix? The one I'd stuck down in the basement in spite of Aunt Zoe's protest so that I didn't have to listen to its incessant ticking with ever-growing anxiety.

"Yeah, that one."

Of course I knew that clock. I'd recently learned that it had been a gift from the other albino-looking juggernaut, Mr. Black, who was supposedly a sentinel acting as my ally. He had come clean about his anonymous gift via a note after my last visit to Ms. Wolff's apartment in the Galena House. Mr. Black was also a Timekeeper and had the job of training me in that same role, which I now shared with him.

"What about it?" Doc asked.

Layne pulled out his chair and dropped into it. "Well, I was putting Elvis in her cage and I noticed that the clock isn't ticking anymore."

It wasn't? When had it stopped? I hadn't heard any cuckooing, but then again I'd been gone all day.

In the grand scheme of timekeeping I knew very little at the moment. However, one bit of information I'd gleaned was that when the clock cuckooed or chimed, it meant that whatever being was tethered to that clock was either entering or leaving this plane of existence. In short, it meant a change was occurring. Whether or not the clock's arms started or stopped moving indicated whether the "traveler" was among us.

Mr. Black had written in the note that he had given me the Hellhound clock as a means of protection. The traveler it monitored purportedly had one goal while on this plane—to hunt me. The idea was to eliminate me from the game of life for good, along with my kids, Aunt Zoe, and anyone else who carried the Executioner gene and could potentially slay those bent on wreaking havoc.

"Did you hear any cuckooing today?" Doc asked. He knew as much as I did about timekeeping and the telltale clocks that came with the job.

"No," Layne answered.

I breathed a sigh of relief. While Layne hadn't gone through the step-by-step process required to become a Timekeeper, his picture had played a role in turning me into one. Doc and I had both wondered if that minor connection had somehow pulled him into the loop. His not hearing any cuckooing or chiming answered that question, since only Timekeepers could hear those sounds. Then again, Layne had been at school for much of the day. He might have been gone when the clock was cuckooing.

Cooper joined us at the table, setting a big bowl of coleslaw in the center. "You mean the clock's arms aren't moving, right?" The detective also knew the rules of the clock game.

"Yes. It's broke, I think."

"You didn't move the clock arms, right?" Manually moving the arms was a big no-no in the Timekeeping world, screwing up gates between realms.

"No, Mother. You've made it clear that we are not to move or touch anything on the clock."

"Good."

Doc and I shared a frown.

Maybe it was time to contact Mr. Black for another lesson on the clocks. Somehow I needed to figure out which traveler that clock was monitoring and how much time I had before the predator returned to continue the hunt.

Chapter Four

"Have you ever wondered why there weren't any women undertakers in the Old West?" I asked Doc, who was staring out the kitchen window into the darkness beyond. The only light in the room came from the string of Christmas lights Aunt Zoe had taped around the window. Shades of blue, green, yellow, and red added a colorful glow to his olive complexion.

"There were female undertakers." He took a hit from his bottle of beer. "And you're avoiding my question."

"I'm not avoiding."

It was more about not wanting to explore the rocky territory where my answer might take us. Not tonight, anyway. Big snowflakes were falling outside and lights were twinkling on the Christmas tree in the living room. Couldn't we take a break from the insanity that was now my life and enjoy an evening of snuggling under a blanket on the couch and watch a holiday movie? A normal date night that ended with us wrapped in my bed, naked, exploring skin, pretending we were going to live long enough to grow old and wrinkly together.

"Definitely avoiding," he said, glancing at me. "Same as earlier when everyone was still here."

"It wasn't a good time, especially with Cooper listening."

Shortly after Doc had asked me his question earlier, Cooper's phone rang. Work wasn't ready to let him go for the night. When Natalie made a biting remark about Cooper living for his job, the detective nailed her with a scowl and explained that he was on call this weekend. She glared back, not backing down, leaving me to suspect the burn of rejection still stung after a steamy night years ago when he'd chosen his job over her.

An hour later, after Natalie and Harvey had left, I went upstairs to find Layne already in bed reading a book about the history of medieval weapons and their uses. Sheesh, obsess much? I asked him about his newfound interest in weapons, trying to see if he'd figured out my Executioner secret somehow. Without removing his nose from the pages, he answered that he thought they were cool. After a peck on his forehead and a reminder to brush and floss, I'd gone to my bedroom to change into pajamas and a robe.

I'd returned to the kitchen to find Doc staring out the kitchen window. Grabbing a beer, I'd leaned on the counter beside him. That was when he'd once again asked the question I still wasn't ready to answer.

"How come I've never heard of any female undertakers in the Old West before now?" I asked.

"If memory serves me right, you're not into reading about history, including your own." He shifted, resting his hip against the counter, facing me. "Deadwood had a female undertaker early on, but there isn't a lot written about her in the books in the library."

I needed to tell Harvey about her. Maybe he'd seen something on a television show or in a magazine about her and that's why she was bumping around in his thoughts. "You'd think a woman undertaker would be something worth talking about in the newspapers and history books." I wondered if Eddie Mudder, the owner of the Mudder Brothers Funeral Parlor, knew anything about her.

Doc drained his beer and set the empty bottle on the counter. Moving closer, he lifted me onto the counter and settled himself between my knees, and rested his palms on my fleece-covered thighs. He smelled delicious—sugary sweet along with his usual woodsy scented cologne.

"Did you get into the molasses cookies without me?" I asked.

His lips curved. "I left you plenty. Answer my question, Killer."

I sighed, leaning my head against the cabinet. Doc had his teeth sunk into this. There'd be no changing the subject short of tearing off my pajamas and resorting to a naked diversion, and even then he'd come back around to his question once we finished taking care of business. I might as well open the can of worms and let my worries wriggle around between us.

"I don't know when I'm going to start hunting the *lidérc*, but it has to be soon," I told him.

The smoky Hungarian devil had slipped through my fingers last month when I'd tried to kill it. Now its previous owner wanted his pet back and had shared information in exchange for my Executioner services. In spite of my being a killer, not a *catcher*, Dominick Masterson was certain I was the woman for the job.

I wasn't so sure about that, but I had little doubt that he'd follow through on his threat if I failed to deliver on the deal we'd made. The slick charmer had set his sights on Aunt Zoe, and if I didn't bring his pet back to him, he planned to wrap her around his finger until he grew bored of toying with her. Since Dominick had already lived many human lifetimes, Aunt Zoe's remaining years would be a blink for him. Neither she nor I wanted to see her end up in his bed.

"I want to go with you on all hunts." Doc's tone left no room for argument.

I shook my head, bucking his tone. "Aunt Zoe thinks the hunt is going to be even more dangerous now that the *lidérc* knows it can't trick me with its usual mind games."

"I'll be extra careful and take precautions."

Care and caution might not be enough. "Doc, I don't want anything to happen to—"

"You agreed to let me try to protect you, remember?"

Of course I remembered. It was part of the outcome of one of our louder arguments where I'd said a lot of stupid shit that I still regretted voicing aloud. I'd learned a few things that night after our fight, including who killed my old boss and how powerful Dominick Masterson was.

I took one of Doc's hands in mine, threading our fingers together. "That was before I knew what I really was." Finding out I was born to kill had been an eye-opener, a fact about myself that I still didn't want to face most days. Especially when I tucked my children in at night.

"You need an extra set of eyes and ears even more now." Doc wasn't giving up easily, not that I expected him to. Like me, he was stubborn when he'd set his mind to a task.

"It's a bad idea, Doc. I'm still learning how to hunt and kill. What if I screw up and the *lidérc* latches onto you?"

Hungarian devils were parasitic, feeding off humans until the host was sucked dry. If anything happened to Doc because I messed up during the hunt, I would spend the rest of my days in gut-aching hell.

He tugged on one of my loose curls. "Violet, nobody learns anything important without getting it wrong at first."

"Doc …"

"If the *lidérc* attaches to me, you'll figure out how to remove it."

He sounded far more confident in my abilities than I felt. "I don't even know where to begin looking for it."

"I do."

I blinked. "What? How?"

"I have my ways." He lifted our entwined fingers and kissed my hand. "You need me, Boots."

More than oxygen some days.

Seeing an avenue of escape from the topic at hand, I batted my eyelashes at him. "Need you? I don't know. You're getting sort of old and worn out. You are *almost* forty."

"Old and worn out, huh?" He tugged me closer, pressing into my inner thighs. My pulse ratcheted as he untied my robe and slid his hands along my ribcage.

"It's only a matter of time," I teased.

"Until what?" His hands cupped and rubbed, his thumbs circling closer and closer.

"You tire of me," I said, sharing one of my fears with him.

His catty ex had made a habit of warning me time and again that Doc would grow bored of curvy blondes, the same as he had of sexy redheads. As much as I tried to shield myself from her sharp claws, my skin was only so thick, especially around my heart.

His thumbs stilled. His brow tightened. "Are you serious?"

"Maybe."

His eyes narrowed.

"Sort of, yes."

He lowered his hands to my hips. "Has Tiffany been hissing in your ear again?"

"No, not recently anyway. But let's be serious for a moment about my whole situation."

"Okay," he said cautiously and waited for me to continue.

I licked my suddenly dry lips. "I live a very messy life."

"I like your messy life."

"You had a nice, quiet life before I came along."

"Quiet? I've been dealing with ghosts since childhood, remember?"

"Besides the ghosts, you like to be in control of your days. Your car has no stains on the seats, the chrome fixtures in your house have no fingerprints, you hit the gym regularly, and you own a growing financial planning business."

"That sounds really boring when you put it that way," he said.

"Not boring, try nice and stable. I, on the other hand, have been surrounded by drama daily since I had those two kids. Hell, even before they entered this world, I had a knack for stirring up trouble. Ask Natalie."

His jaw tensed. "I don't like the direction this is going."

I didn't either, but we needed to take this trip sooner or later if we were going to keep playing "house" together.

"Sooner or later …" I paused. "You're going to experience burnout when it comes to me and then what?"

"Are you trying to push me away, Violet? Is this what you meant when you told me about sabotaging your previous relationships?"

"No. This is different."

"How? Because you seem determined to find reasons for us to fail."

More like afraid. Life had a history of smacking me with a flyswatter when things appeared too good to be true, like the man before me. "Doc, I love you."

One dark eyebrow lifted. "Do I hear a *but* in there?"

"*But* I come with all sorts of baggage."

"I've told you already that I adore your kids. Try again."

"I'm not talking about Addy and Layne."

"I don't mind Elvis, even when she leaves eggs in my shoes."

"I'm not talking about that damned chicken, either." I licked my lips, and lowered my focus to his Adam's apple. "I screwed up back in Slagton today and killed that creature before I'd even realized what I was doing."

"Better it than you."

"One of these times somebody is going to get hurt. I know you're the king of the mountain when it comes to dealing with ghosts and other mental medium mindboggling stuff, but today …" I looked up.

"Today, I got a taste of what I'm going to be dealing with until my life as an Executioner comes to an end—one way or another."

When he didn't say anything, I added, "They murdered Prudence's husband along with her son."

"I know."

"She was an accomplished killer. Earlier, in that woodshed, I was swinging at that creature like a bumbling rookie."

"You are learning to rely on your instincts."

"I lucked out."

"You underestimate yourself, Violet."

"Cooper got hurt because I didn't react fast enough the first time it rushed us."

"It's a minor cut."

I sighed. "Doc …"

He put his finger over my lips, silencing me. "If you're worried about not being good enough at your job, then do something about it."

I pulled his finger away, but didn't let go of his hand. "Like what? Ask Santa to bring me a superhero cape for Christmas?"

"Read your family history book or ask Prudence to share some lessons she learned before they caught and killed her."

"I can't show up on Prudence's doorstep without a tooth."

The last time I was up at the Carhart-Britton house in Lead where Prudence held court, I'd promised to bring her a trophy tooth the next time I visited her in exchange for her not extracting any of Detective Hawke's teeth. The dead Executioner's fetish for teeth gave me another reason to keep Doc and my friends at arm's length. How long would it be until I lost touch with reality and began collecting macabre souvenirs from my kills?

He captured my other hand and squeezed it. "At the least, let me show you a few self-defense moves and teach you how to fight."

My chin jutted. "I know how to fight." If fighting dirty counted, which it did in my rulebook.

He smirked. "Your windmill swing is a classic, but you need to have an arsenal of moves at your disposal."

I looked over at the Christmas lights lining the window. I wanted my old simple life back, dammit. Only I wanted Doc in it, too.

"You need to stop hiding away in your castle, Killer, stepping outside of its walls only to play defense. If there is going to be some sort of war, like the other Timekeepers told you, then you need to prepare for battle."

My gaze snapped back to his. "I'm not hiding in my castle."

"What do you call putting that clock in the basement where you can't keep an eye on it? Mr. Black gave it to you as a means of protection. You're supposed to keep it where you can watch it and use it to track your enemies' travels between planes."

I covered my ears. "I can't stand the tick, tick, tick."

His dark eyes filled with a compassion that made my throat tight. He pulled my hands down. "Violet," he started in a husky voice.

"It's a constant reminder of what I am now. What I don't want to be." I swallowed the lump in my throat. "I don't even like to squish spiders, Doc."

He cupped my face. "You're an amazing woman."

"But …"

"There is no *but* this time. Before you came along, my life was empty. I kept it neat and tidy because I had nothing else to do."

"You had the ghosts."

"I was alone."

"There were women." One redhead in particular who was currently trying to steal my job.

"Not many and none like you. I don't want to go back to that stale and lonely life. You've filled my world with color."

"You mean chaos."

"I mean excitement." His gaze lowered to my mouth. "And passion." He ran his finger down my cheek. "Sweetheart, you have people surrounding you who want to help you win this war. Let me help you hunt the *lidérc.*"

I snorted. "As if you'd take no for an answer."

He threaded his fingers into my curls, his intent clear in his smoldering eyes. "Do you have any idea how nuts I am about you?"

My heart sighed and fanned itself. "Nuts enough to hunt a Hungarian devil that could strap itself to you while it slowly sucks the life from your body and soul?"

"When you say it like that, it sounds so sexy," he whispered. "Kiss me, Boots."

He didn't have to tell me twice. I closed the distance between us, taking my time kissing him, enjoying the taste of beer on his lips. When

I stroked my tongue along his, he groaned and dropped his hands to my hips, pulling me against him. I wrapped my legs around his and let him take over the kiss, sliding my hands under his shirt. His skin was hot. His mouth was hotter. I fired up in a flash, burning for a lot more.

When his lips moved to my ear, I gulped. He wasn't playing fair. "Okay. Okay." I gave in. "You can teach me some moves."

He pressed against me, his body ready to relocate the show upstairs behind a locked door. "Do you mean in the bedroom or the ring?"

"Both."

His chuckle was short-lived, thanks to Aunt Zoe stomping into the kitchen. She threw her shawl on the table. "That bastard needs to learn a lesson!"

Before I could get a word out, she tugged off her necklace, breaking the chain and sending glass beads scattering across the table. Curse words flew as she pulled off her earrings and threw them on the floor, crushing the glass and metal under her boot heel.

I unwrapped my legs from around Doc. "What bastard?" I asked her backside as she marched to the fridge and yanked open the door.

"What happened?" Doc helped me to the floor, settling me in front of him to shield the evidence of our foreplay.

She grabbed a half-full bottle of wine and shut the door. "Dominick was at the party." Tugging out the cork, she chugged several gulps.

Uh-oh! "He didn't try anything on you, did he?"

She lowered the bottle. "He followed me into the women's restroom to give me this." She drew a piece of paper from the inside of her shirt and held it toward me.

"What is it?" A love note? I took it from her.

"Read it."

I opened the note and read aloud, " 'Your time is running out, *Scharfrichter.*' " I crumpled the note in my hand. "Blimey, he's relentless."

"That's not all," Aunt Zoe said, taking another swallow of wine.

"What else did he say?"

"It's not what he did or didn't say." She gulped more wine.

"Aunt Zoe, stop drinking and explain, damn it."

The bottle lowered again. She wiped her lips with the back of her hand. "I didn't give him a chance to say anything else. I ran out of the bathroom before he could get into my head, but the son of a bitch followed me out. In front of a crowd of Deadwood's business leaders, he drew me to him with his damned mind game." She scrubbed her hand down her face. "He got in my head so fast, Violet. My charms were worthless, not even a hint of protection against him. What a fool I must have looked, mooning over him like that."

Having seen Aunt Zoe moon over Dominick in the past, my face heated for her. "Did you kiss him?"

She grimaced. "I tried to."

"What do you mean, *tried?*" Doc asked.

"Reid stepped in before I could actually plant my lips on Dominick's. He pushed me aside and punched the bastard square in the face." She planted her fist in her open palm. "Bam."

I covered my chest with my hand. "Oh, no!" Dominick could break through brick walls with his bare hands. "What did he do to Reid?"

"He didn't *do* anything. There were too many people watching." She crossed her arms, frowning out the window in the back door. "He just rubbed his jaw and smiled at one and all. You know Dominick, all handsome charm and slick charisma."

That was the shine on her from Dominick's magic still talking. I didn't find him charming at all, only tricky and dangerous.

"But on his way out the door," Aunt Zoe continued, "he walked by Reid and warned that his time was coming."

"What's that supposed to mean?" I winced on Reid's behalf.

Aunt Zoe's face creased. "I'm afraid to find out."

* * *

Saturday, December 15th

The bright light of dawn found me alone in my bed with Bogart the vegetarian cat lounging between my ankles. My daughter's shy cat rarely made an appearance outside of Addy's room, so I wasn't sure how I warranted Bogart's companionship this morning or her purring. Maybe she sensed something about me that I needed to heed, like impending death in a derelict mining town full of shotgun-toting whangdoodles.

Sheesh! Enough with the negativity.

I sat up, leaning forward to pet her, and froze.

I wasn't the reason she was purring.

Under Bogart's front paw lay a mouse. It blinked and wiggled its whiskers as the cat licked its ears, cleaning the mouse like it was one of her own freaking kittens.

I screeched.

Bogart shot off the bed and out the door in a blur.

The mouse rolled onto its feet and took a run straight at me. I squealed and threw up the blanket, sending the mouse airborne. It cartwheeled across the room, squeaking as it twirled, and landed on my dressing chair. For a second the two of us stared at each other in silence, breath held, and then it made a mad dash into my closet.

"You've got to be kidding me!" I scrambled off the bed and shut the closet door, jamming dirty socks in the space between the door and the floor.

I leaned against the door, breathing a sigh of relief. I had the beast contained for the moment. I looked around my bedroom for something to use as a mousetrap. Dang Doc for sleeping at home last night. I could use a big hunka-hunka man to ... Elvis! Of course! I'd watched Addy's chicken chase mice around the backyard several times this fall, pecking at their hindquarters as she raced after them.

After a dash to the basement to collect a mouse-hunting chicken, I shut Elvis in my closet with a grimace of what carnage I might find when she finished the job. Thankfully, my purple boots were downstairs by the front door, safe from the bloodshed. Elvis squawked from the other side of the door. Then something thumped against the wall.

Grumbling about my daughter and her damned weird pets, I escaped to the shower, putting the cat, mouse, and chicken from my mind as I washed my skin twice. Lord only knew where else that mouse had crawled while in my bed.

As I shampooed my hair, my thoughts returned to last night.

Doc had ended up taking Reid to the hospital emergency room to have his swollen hand X-rayed. Initially, when Reid joined us in the kitchen shortly after Aunt Zoe's tale of the evening's events, he balked at having his hand examined by a doctor. His stubbornness made Aunt Zoe drink, stomp, and cuss more. When she threatened to grab her shotgun and give Reid another reason to go to the ER, he'd wisely caved. Since she was too tipsy by that time to go with him, Doc volunteered.

Around midnight, I received a text from Doc saying Reid had no broken bones, only a lot of swelling. Instead of returning to Aunt Zoe's, he decided to go home and research late into the night to prep for our pending Slagton visit. When I joked about not making it through the night without him next to me, he sent me a heart picture and told me to come see him at work around lunchtime. His request for me to wear the red lace bra and panties that he loved earned him a heart picture in return.

Before crawling under my covers, I'd gone down to let Aunt Zoe know about Reid's hand. She was out in her glass workshop toiling away, the effects from the wine gone judging by her steady hands. The swear words were still flying, though. When I asked how long she planned to stay out there, she said, "When I can think about tonight without wanting to scream the house down."

My thoughts snapped back to the present as I rinsed the shampoo from my hair and shut off the shower. When I returned to my bedroom, all was quiet on the battlefield. I peeked in my closet and found Elvis nesting on a pair of my knockoff sheepskin boots. The mouse was nowhere to be found. For the time being, I was happy to be ignorant of its whereabouts.

I left the closet door open a crack and headed to the kitchen, which was empty. A fresh pot of coffee steamed on the counter. Movement outside the kitchen window drew my gaze. I watched Layne lift a lopsided ball of snow. He set it on two bigger snowballs, giving his snowman a head. The sound of Aunt Zoe cheering made me look down. She sat on the back porch steps, a steaming mug in her hand, her long silver-streaked hair draped over her shoulders. I soaked in the scene, my heart warming at the matching grins on both of their faces.

I poured myself a cup of coffee, planning to head out to join them.

The doorbell rang.

Setting my coffee on the counter, I padded to the front door. I peeked out through the curtains, making sure it wasn't Dominick Masterson here to terrorize my aunt some more. Instead, Cornelius stood on the porch in his long black overcoat and stovepipe hat.

I opened the door. "Cornelius, what are you doing here so early?"

The man usually didn't like to be awakened until after eight-thirty-seven. My awareness of that fact, sad as it was, showed how long I'd been involuntarily acting as Cornelius' assistant.

"Hello, Violet. I've come to take you fishing."

Fishing? Knowing Cornelius, I doubted he was talking about using fishing rods and worms.

I peered around him. "How did you get here?" Currently, he didn't have a car and relied on various Deadwood taxis to get around town, but there was no taxi to be seen out at the curb.

"My mode of transportation is not relevant to this conversation." He reached out and touched my robe's lapel. "Where on earth did you find a trench coat made of pink terrycloth?"

"It's a robe, Cornelius, not a coat."

"Why are you wearing a robe at this time of day?"

For Pete's sake, it wasn't even eight yet. "That's not relevant to this conversation," I threw back at him. Cold air swirled around my bare ankles, making me shiver. "Come inside." I held the door wide for him to join me, closing it quickly behind us. "What do you mean, you're here to take me fishing?"

"We need bait." He took off his round sunglasses and looked down his long nose at me. His cornflower blue eyes seemed extra bright for so early in the day, his smile lifting both corners of his mouth for once.

"Who are you and what have you done with the real Cornelius?"

"Violet, quit being silly. Now," he pulled off his gloves and stuck them in his pockets. "Do you have any monkey skulls? A howler monkey would be preferable, but I suppose we could make do with a common marmoset."

"Sorry, no monkey skulls here," I said with a straight face. "But my son reconstructed a horse skull last summer and we've found all but three of its teeth."

"A horse, huh? That might ..." He stopped at the sound of clucking behind him, turning around.

Elvis stood at the top of the stairs, looking down at us with her head cocked sideways.

"Did you get that damned mouse?" I asked her.

In answer, she cocked her head to the other side and clucked.

"What did she say?" Cornelius asked me.

"I don't know. I don't speak chicken."

Elvis clucked again, and then she leaned her head down. When she lifted it back up, the mouse dangled by its tail from her beak.

I watched with a gaping jaw as Elvis fly-hopped down the stairs holding onto that damned mouse the whole time. It squeaked as she hit the bottom step.

I opened the front door for her. "Take it outside, Elvis."

To my surprise, the bird strutted over the threshold and onto the porch. She flew down the steps, holding on tight to the mouse's tail.

"Well, butter my butt and call me a biscuit," I said, speaking in Harvey-ese. I laughed. "Can you believe that crazy chicken?"

Cornelius joined me in the doorway. "How long have you known that bird?"

"My daughter chicken-napped her last July."

Elvis strutted along the sidewalk, veering around the side of the house and out of view. Maybe I should have been more specific on where to drop the mouse.

I closed the door. "Now, where were we? Oh, yeah, drinking coffee." I headed for the kitchen.

Cornelius followed.

"Why do you need monkey skulls?" I took a sip of coffee.

He walked over to the refrigerator and opened the door. "For good luck. Skulls ward off evil influence. I prefer smaller monkey skulls because they fit in my coat pocket."

"Ew! Remind me never to borrow your coat."

He bent lower, searching the fridge. "Where do you keep your ginger?"

"On Gilligan's Island with Mary Ann and the sexy Professor."

I'd grown up with a big crush on Russell Johnson and his broad shoulders and windblown hair. Maybe he was the reason I had a hard time resisting smart men, a weakness that had landed me neck-deep in trouble in the past. By *trouble,* I meant pregnant with twins from an egocentric scientist who wanted nothing to do with his offspring. Although I'd scored with Doc, who I had little doubt could give my ex a run for his money in the big-brains department.

"I was more fond of Mrs. Howell and her pristine white gloves." Cornelius shut the refrigerator. "I've been reading an old German spell book that I picked up years ago in a pawn shop outside of Cologne. It was written by a male witch."

"You mean a warlock?" Or were males called a wizards?

"A witch is a witch regardless of his or her gender."

"Witches can be men or women, got it."

I took another drink of coffee, thinking about Detective Hawke accusing me of being a witch. Cooper had warned me repeatedly to watch my Ps and Qs around Hawke when it came to playing along with the dipshit's witchy idea. So far I'd failed on keeping my big mouth shut—cackling at him like the Wicked Witch of the West and casting phony penis-shrinking spells I made up on the fly. If only I could hire a monkey to fit with fake wings …

"… and found a love spell you can use on the Tall Medium," Cornelius said.

Say what now?

The "Tall Medium" was what Cornelius called Doc rather than the three-letter nickname everyone else on the planet used. There were so many questions that popped in my head from the last bit of Cornelius's sentence that it took me several seconds to sort through them.

I took a gulp of coffee this time. "A love spell, you say?"

He walked over to the table and pulled the lid off Aunt Zoe's Betty Boop cookie jar. "If you put a turtledove's tongue in your mouth and coerce the Tall Medium to kiss you, he will fall deeply in love with you and never be able to love any other."

Tempting as it was to make Doc my love slave for life, I wasn't thrilled about sticking a dead bird's tongue in my mouth. "Why are you reading a German spell book?"

"I would think it's obvious."

Sure it was—to the mentally deranged. I chugged the last half of my coffee, beer-bong style. "How long have you known how to speak German?"

"I can't speak German. It's too guttural and full of hard sounds. I prefer Spanish."

"I thought you said you don't speak Spanish." Ironically, Natalie and I had been speaking pig Latin at the time he told us that.

"I don't." He plucked out a molasses cookie and inspected it. "However, I prefer the sound of it over German."

"If you don't know German, how are you reading the spell book?"

"Via a translator, of course."

"So you have some sort of German-talking cricket in your pocket?"

He took a bite of the cookie and groaned loud enough to make me jump. "What is this morsel of ecstasy?"

"Uh, that's a molasses cookie."

"I've had molasses cookies before. They are dry and crunchy. This is soft and melts in my mouth."

"Maybe you're confusing molasses with gingerbread."

He shoved the rest of the cookie in his mouth, moaning as he chewed. "Are you aware," he said before he swallowed and grabbed another from the jar. "In the late Middle Ages Europeans used ginger to stimulate arousal in men and women?"

Was that why he was looking for ginger in the fridge? "So I need to pick up some turtledove tongue and ginger root at the grocery store in order to woo my Tall Medium?"

"Feathers from a rooster's tail pressed into his palm works, too," he spoke through a mouthful of cookie.

And miss out on sticking the dead bird's tongue in my mouth? No thanks. Tail feathers made for boring foreplay.

I set my empty coffee mug in the sink, looking out at Layne who had made a second snowman, this one smaller than the first. As I watched, he adjusted their stick arms, lining them up so they were holding hands. Wasn't that sweet? I smiled, my son's tender nature making my eyes misty. The first girl who broke his heart would die a thousand painful deaths via the pointy end of my war hammer.

Another round of groans and moans played out behind me.

"Cornelius," I said as I watched Aunt Zoe jam a row of different-colored glass buttons on the smaller snowman's middle section. "Does this German spell book have anything to do with you wanting to take me fishing this morning?"

"Yes," he mumbled.

Layne noticed me in the window and waved. His smile filled his cheeks, pink from the cold.

"What are we trying to catch?" I waved back, blowing Layne a kiss.

I had a feeling Cornelius wanted bait for that spooky Hellhole he'd found under Calamity Jane Realty.

"Wilda Hessler's clown."

My heart screeched to a stop.

I rather preferred the Hellhole.

Chapter Five

A half hour later, my Honda SUV crunched along the snow-covered streets. My white-knuckled grip on the steering wheel had nothing to do with the icy roads, though.

In the midst of sharing molasses cookies for breakfast with Cornelius, I'd received a call from Cooper ordering me to meet him four hours earlier than we'd discussed last night. My neck was still bristling from our short but loud conversation over the phone. For one thing, I did not have a big fat nose. For another, I didn't appreciate the high and mighty detective demanding I drag my sad sack to Doc's office in forty-five minutes and then threatening me with an "or else!" When I told Cooper where to shove his "or else," he told me to quit being such a pansy and proceeded to blame today's return trip to Slagton on *me*.

Of all the nerve! That bullheaded man and I were going to come to an understanding one of these days that would probably end with one of us sporting a broken nose—again. Maybe I could train Elvis to drag Cooper out by the tail next time he was over for supper.

Or just peck him on the ankle under the table.

"You're being excessively challenging this morning, Violet," Cornelius said from the passenger seat.

I guffawed. Hell, I was just getting revved up. He should have seen me battling the killer mouse earlier. "You ain't seen nothing yet," I said through clenched teeth.

I predicted an all-out brawl with Cooper before the sun set, envisioning climbing on his back, monkey style, and beating him over the head with a banana. While I suspected the stubborn oaf was suffering from tension overload that was partly due to sexual frustration thanks to my best friend's long legs and full lips, he didn't need to use me as his punching bag.

"You could use an internal cleansing to calm your nerves and open your mind," Cornelius said. He was still trying to convince me to help him fish for a dead girl's clown doll, or rather the ghost version of it.

"Are we talking about my black aura again or my clogged chakras?"

"The last time I flew back from Nevada," he said, "I read an article in a renowned parapsychology magazine about how hydrotherapy for the colon can widen a channeler's receptors, allowing spiritual energy to flow with more ease."

There was no way I was sticking a hose anywhere near my nether regions anytime soon. Although I wouldn't mind taking a fire hose to Cooper's keister one of these days. "Cornelius, an enema isn't going to cure what ails me."

However, a lobotomy might do the trick.

"Oh, it's not an enema. Those procedures clear only the lower end of your—"

"Gahhh!" I shouted, turning into the parking lot behind the office building. "This subject is officially off limits for us from here on out until the end of eternity." I made a karate chop in the air several times for emphasis.

"See." He poked my karate arm. "Look at that tension. Your sphincter must be coiled up tighter than a—"

I reached over and covered his mouth. "I mean it, Cornelius. One more word and I'm going to stab you with a trident."

His black eyebrows rose. "You have a trident?" he mumbled through my hand.

Placing both hands back on the steering wheel, I shot him a scowl. "Not yet, but my son wrote it on his Christmas wish list so I've been searching online for one. He wants the real deal, though, not a plastic one." Layne's list this year had made me laugh when I'd first read it the other night. A laugh that bordered on hysteria, which made Doc look up from the dining room table where he'd been working on his laptop. When I'd shown him the list, he'd reached for his beer and muttered, "Like mother, like son."

"I may have a trident source for you," Cornelius said.

"Why does that not surprise me?"

"But you'll have to help me lure a clown ghost."

"You play dirty."

"You would too if the little terror had carved a fiendish message into your skin."

A month ago, Wilda Hessler's ghost had possessed Cornelius for a couple of weeks, making his world a living hell. During her stay inside of his head, she'd manipulated him into carving words into his arm, leaving scars that would spur paranormal groupie chatter for years to come.

I parked in my usual spot and killed the engine. "Explain to me how a ghostly clown doll can be possessed by an evil presence. And don't try to use that *Chucky* movie as an example, because that shit is fiction and he isn't a ghost. He's plastic and yarn, or whatever they use for his doll hair."

Cornelius stroked his goatee. "I fail to see why you are having trouble comprehending the situation at hand. This is basic paranormal studies. The changeling is possessing Wilda's ghost."

"And by 'changeling,' you mean ..."

"Wilda Hessler's twin. Did your Tall Medium neglect to inform you of his discovery?"

"Oh, he told me about the clown in the old picture of the Hessler family." We'd been up at the family grave markers in Lead at the time.

"But did he explain what he has since learned about that clown?"

"He said there was a notice in the paper about the Hessler twins' births saying both babies were healthy, but that one child seemed to have suffered distress in the womb."

"The twin was disfigured," Cornelius stated.

How could he know that based on an old newspaper photo of a kid in a clown costume? "Did Doc find another picture?"

"No, I saw the twin."

"Recently?"

"Wilda was in my head for weeks. I saw things during that time. Things I didn't understand. Now that I'm free of her and I've learned of the existence of her twin, those visions make sense."

"What visions?"

"I thought I was seeing a distorted version of Wilda. She would appear with gnarled limbs and a contorted face, lurching more than walking, sometimes with a clown mask, other times not." He frowned out the windshield. "That wasn't Wilda I was seeing. It was her disfigured twin."

I covered my chest with my hand. "That poor child."

"Apparently," Cornelius continued. "The Hessler family didn't like having their jewelry empire tarnished by a disfigured child. My belief is they dressed the daughter in clown attire when in public to hide her in plain sight. At some point early on in Wilda's young life, the 'clown' twin disappeared entirely, never to be seen again."

My heart hurt for Wilda's twin. Her family hadn't even given her the honor of an official gravestone, hiding her existence well after death. A small rectangle of concrete mostly covered by weeds and dirt was it for the child.

A disfigured child? I returned to what Cornelius had called the twin a moment ago—a *changeling*. "I thought a changeling was a nefarious child that was secretly exchanged during infancy by evil fairies." An idea the old movie *The Changeling* had played upon with chilling effects.

"There are various definitions of a changeling depending on the culture and paranormal subgroup in which one participates. Would you like me to list them all?"

I narrowed my eyes in response.

"Violet, it appears the tightening in your sphincter has spread to your eyes."

I pinched his arm, making him squawk while he laughed.

"And your fingers, too." He chuckled still as he rubbed his arm.

"So, you think Wilda the ghost is actually being manipulated by yet another ghost?"

"Another entity," he clarified.

"Whatever. She's the puppet and the changeling is pulling the strings?"

"That is mostly correct."

The twin was reaping revenge. "But if it's inside of Wilda's ghost, how is the changeling inside the clown doll Wilda carries, too?"

"The entity is using the doll as a vehicle for its non-physical form. A separate apparition, if you will, created via telekinesis from Wilda and visible to you and me through telepathy."

I let that gobbledy-gook speak bounce around in my brain for a few heartbeats. "I'm sorry, but that's too nuts to believe." I reached for the door handle. I didn't have time for this right now. I had a ghost town to visit.

"It's a solid theory."

"Seems more gelatinous to me, and I reject it."

Cornelius frowned at me over his round sunglasses. "You can't reject my theory, especially when it's still in the formation process."

"I just did."

"You can dispute it and provide another theory, but you don't have the power to reject."

"Oh, yeah?" I smiled across at him. "Watch this." I traced an "R" on my open palm with my finger and then slammed my other fist into it, as if I had a stamp in my hand.

"What's that mean?" he asked.

"It's the letter 'R.' It stands for 'Rejected.' "

I climbed out of the Honda, scanning the parking lot for my coworkers' rigs. Mona and Ben were at the office, but there was no sign of Jerry's Hummer or Ray's SUV. That explained why Mona had answered when I called in earlier about taking the day off to run some errands. I didn't mention that my errands involved another venture into a creepy mining ghost town, and Mona didn't prod for details.

The Picklemobile, Doc's winter set of wheels, was parked a couple of spots down. I wondered how late he stayed up last night reading my family history book, and if Cooper had been as bossy with Doc when setting up our morning meeting as he'd been with me. Probably not, since Cooper liked Doc more. Hell, I had a feeling Cooper liked just about everyone in town more than me, especially when he was looking in the mirror at his crooked nose.

Cornelius joined me at the bumper of my Honda. "I reject your rejection." He walked beside me toward Doc's back door. "And I trump it with a prediction."

"You can't trump a rejection. You can try to fight it, but there's a lot of bureaucratic red tape to cut through and darn it, we're all out of scissors." I stepped over a mound of dirty slush. "What prediction?"

"You'll change your mind."

"Why would I change my mind?" I paused outside the door, kicking the snow off my boots.

Cornelius did the same before following me inside. "Because the Tall Medium wants to go fishing, too."

"He does?" Why hadn't Doc mentioned anything about it last night? As soon as the door was closed, I said, "How in the world did you convince Doc that trying to lure this ghost clown out of hiding is a good idea?"

We wiped off our boots on the bristly mat.

"I had him listen to my EVP recordings from the séance we had in the Hesslers' root cellar."

I paused, frowning up at Cornelius. "What did you pick up?"

"It took some cleanup work with all of that other noise, but I was able to single out some voices, including the changeling's."

Goosebumps peppered my arms. "You're kidding."

"There are two things I never joke about, Violet: malevolent spirits and toy poodles."

I blinked away all poodle questions. "What did the changeling say?"

"You mean, what did *you* say?"

"Huh?"

"It spoke through you."

I shook my head, words log-jamming in my throat. I'd acted as a microphone for the dead once before for Harvey's grandpappy, but he was a harmless old romantic who liked to mix his homemade hooch with blondes. This was different. This was a creepy clown doll, or rather an evil twin pretending to be a clown. Either way, I didn't like the idea of being its speaker.

A sound at the other end of the hallway made us both turn. Doc stood, his hands stuffed in the front pockets of his jeans, leaning against the wall. His cheeks and chin were dark with beard stubble, adding a shade of ruggedness to his face. Cooper must have rushed him this morning, too. How long had Doc been standing there?

"Cornelius thinks Wilda's twin used you to channel more than her mother," Doc said, answering my unspoken question. "He suspects your services were used to bring over a parasitical entity that has attached itself to Mrs. Hessler's ghost."

Shit. I was starting to see why Doc had waited to talk to me about this. Snaring Wilda and her entourage would be tricky with more risks than Doc or I had anticipated, and I already had plenty of other problems stacked high in my head like a leaning tower of unread books.

"You mean like the *lidérc*?" I asked Doc.

Cornelius looked back and forth between us. "What *lidérc*?"

"Sort of, but the *lidérc* feeds off the living. This is more of a ghoul that feeds off spiritual energy."

"A ghost leech?"

He shrugged. His shoulders looked broader in the green flannel shirt he wore over his black thermal undershirt. "If you will."

"And in your EVP recordings …" I turned back to Cornelius. "You could hear this ghoul speak?"

"Technically, we can only hear you speak."

"You know what I'm asking."

"I believe we can hear the changeling and the ghoul speaking, but the latter is not comprehensible."

"Is it a foreign language?"

"Maybe," Doc answered. "There were noises that weren't normal human sounds mixed in with your voice."

I grimaced. "Mrs. Hessler stood right next to me." I held my hand a couple of inches from my cheek. "She was this close, Doc."

"I know."

I closed the distance between us with Cornelius on my heels until he reached the door to Doc's back room where his equipment now resided. At that point, he veered off course and left Doc and me alone.

Crossing my arms, I frowned up at Doc. "You also know that I've had nightmares with her whispering terrifying threats in my ear, touching my face with her icy dead fingers, and turning my skin into a charred black shell that cracked and oozed with pus."

Doc reached out and ran his thumb down my cheek. "They were only nightmares."

"For now, maybe, but what about when I run into Mrs. Hessler and her soul-sucking ghoul next time? We don't know what that thing is capable of doing to the living—to me."

"We need to send it back where it came from before it wreaks havoc on some innocent bystander."

"True, but *we* don't know how to do that, do we?"

His mouth set. "*We* have some theories on the subject."

"Theories? Now you sound like Cornelius. Just a warning, I'm in theory rejection mode today." I ran my knuckles along the scratchy stubble on his jaw. "This five-o'clock shadow look is really sexy. It makes me want to play pirate with you. I think Aunt Zoe has a headscarf with skulls on it in the attic along with a fake cutlass and scabbard. What time did you go to sleep last night?"

"Around two, matey." His gaze dipped down my front side. "The way those jeans hug your hips makes me want to wrap your legs around me while I squeeze your sweet pirate booty. If I don the skulls headscarf, will you wear one of those corsets over a white frilly shirt that laces up the front? I've always wanted to see what happens when I slowly loosen those strings."

"Aye, Captain."

His focus slid northward. "We'll need some rum to wet our pipes."

"Oh, I'll wet yer pipe, swashbuckler." I wrapped my arms around his neck and went up on my toes to whisper in his ear. "And I know just the trick to hoist your Jolly Roger."

His hands slid down my sides, his mouth lowering. "Yo ho ho," he whispered over my lips.

The backdoor creaked open, letting in a blast of freezing air.

"Jesus, you two!" Cooper slammed the door. "It's too early for that shit."

"Go away, Coop. I'm busy." Doc teased me with soft kisses.

Cooper stomped his feet on the mat. "Save it for tonight. We need to hit the road. They're calling for another storm later this afternoon."

With a growl of frustration, Doc pulled away. "I'm thinking mutiny is in order," he said to me. "What say you, lass?"

"I'll poke him with a cutlass all the way down the plank."

"Parker, get in the pickup," he ordered, grabbing the doorknob. "Let's get this surefire catastro-fuck underway."

Doc grabbed his thick winter coat from his desk chair along with his gloves and stocking hat. "Ready?" he asked me, pulling on his coat. At my nod, he ushered me down the hall.

"Cornelius," he called out. "Lock up on your way out."

As we passed the back room, Cornelius waved absently from where he sat on the floor next to one of his monitors.

Outside, Harvey's pickup waited for us with chains on the tires and Harvey in the back seat.

"You want the front?" Doc asked me.

Next to Cooper's canines? No, thanks. "I'll keep Harvey company."

Doc held the door for me before climbing in front with Cooper. "Let's roll, Coop," he said, aiming the heating vents toward the back.

"Hey, ol' buzzard," I greeted Harvey, clicking on my seatbelt as Cooper shifted into gear.

"How's yer tobacco taste today, Sparky?"

I had a feeling that was some sort of greeting, so I answered, "Bitter with too much sour law dog sprinkled in the mix."

"Save it, Parker," Cooper said, his focus on the slushy parking lot. "I left my pity party hat and balloons at home."

"What has your stinger sticking out already?" Harvey asked.

"Your nephew blames me for his informant going missing." I glared at Cooper's profile.

"That's not true," Cooper said. "I'm blaming you for me having to return to Slagton again today. Had you not gotten out of the pickup yesterday, as I requested—"

"You mean *ordered*," I interrupted.

"As I requested," he repeated in a louder voice, "I would've had time to scout around the place and possibly find clues to my informant's whereabouts."

"Any news on that situation?" Doc asked.

"Not one damned bit." Cooper turned onto US Highway 385, heading out of town. "I've reached out to the other contacts I have in Slagton, and none of them have seen or heard from him. The son of a bitch seems to have disappeared into thin air."

I tried to ignore the heavy feeling in my gut about his missing informant and today's task, but I couldn't shake the anchor of unease sloshing around in it.

"What's the plan for today?" I asked Cooper. Maybe if I had an idea of what I was riding into, I'd be able to get a grip on my anxiety.

"Are you going to bite my head off if I answer you?"

"Probably, but tell me anyway."

"Did you bring your war hammer?" Harvey asked under his breath.

"She better not have." Cooper must have his bionic ears turned on.

I shook my head. "Your nephew told me I'm not allowed to kill anything today."

Harvey snorted. "You can't tame a natural-born killer, boy."

"For starters, we're going back to the house." Cooper moved to the side of the road to allow a snowplow to pass and lead the way. "I want to check for any clues I might have missed yesterday thanks to you two yahoos."

"You're the silly yahoo," I muttered.

"What's that, Parker?" His steely eyes glared in the rearview mirror.

"Just drive the damned truck."

"And after that?" Doc asked.

Cooper shrugged, pulling back onto the cleared road. "We'll see where the wind takes us."

Settling into the back seat, I stared out the window at the snow-covered landscape as we climbed Strawberry Hill and made our way south, deeper into the Black Hills. In the front seat, Doc and Cooper talked about truck engines for several miles and then various kinds of firearms, with Harvey joining in when they somehow wandered into a discussion about cannons.

I zoned in and out, thinking about what I needed to accomplish yet before Christmas when it came to my kids' gifts from Santa. Addy's wish list was full of pet accessories, including several items for pets she didn't have, which made me wary of what she was up to. Why on earth would she want a fish tank with a castle, a warming light for reptiles, and an igloo-style doghouse? As far as I knew, we had a cat, gerbil, and chicken.

Layne's list was all about the family business. He'd included a chainmail armor shirt, the trident I'd told Cornelius about, throwing stars, and a morion helmet, which Doc told me was used in the 16th and 17th centuries. Other than battle equipment, Layne listed books that fueled his recent obsession with weapons and medieval warriors, along with several thick tomes about the ancient Maya, including one about how to read their glyphs. I swear the boy took after his uncle Quint more every year.

Before I realized it, we were passing the battered Slagton town sign.

I did a double take at what looked like fresh paint on the metal. "Hey! I didn't notice that skull and crossbones spray painted on the Slagton sign yesterday."

"That's because it wasn't there." Cooper slowed the pickup as he rolled into the congregation of shacks and rusty old buildings that remained along the old town's main drag.

"Well," I huffed. "That's just freaking great, isn't it?"

"Relax, Parker. It's probably just some kids out on their snowmobiles screwing around."

"Right," I said, looking through the back window at the other side of the sign. "Kids."

I didn't believe that for one minute. That emblem was a bona fide warning. There was something back here. A killer, and it wasn't me.

At least I didn't think so.

Then again, yesterday I'd killed something unnatural in that woodshed. Now the town's sign had a death emblem on it.

Maybe I was the killer.

I settled back into my seat, worrying out the window as we cruised by a ramshackle house and teetering shed covered in snow. Smoke puffed from the dilapidated chimney that looked on the verge of tumbling over any minute.

Dark clouds blocked out the cold winter sun. We crunched along in silence, the easy-going conversation squelched in the ominous atmosphere. I searched the shadows under the tree line, watching for signs of something strange hiding in the pine trees.

Cooper eased off the gas as we neared the informant's shack. The house looked the same as yesterday—ready to keel over. There was no smoke from the chimney, no fresh tire tracks in the drive, no signs of human traffic. My breath steamed the glass. I wiped my window and peered into the trees behind the woodshed, looking for another one of those weird black creatures. Clumps of snow fell from the lower branches of one of the pine trees. Breath held, I watched for a sign of movement. It must have been a breeze, or the snow melting enough for gravity to win.

Pulling into the drive, Cooper stopped and shut off the pickup.

He pointed out the windshield at the front of the house. "What do you make of that?" he asked us.

Harvey and I leaned into the middle, peering out between Doc and Cooper's shoulders at something hanging from the porch rafters.

"What is that?" I asked, trying to make sense of what I was seeing. "Is that a fur coat?" A raggedy, torn-up one, if so.

Harvey grunted. "Looks like a headless carcass in the process of having its blood drained."

I recoiled at the dark smears on the gray hide and the pool of something shiny on the porch boards under it.

"What kind of carcass, though?" Cooper asked.

"It's too bulky to be a deer," Doc said, pulling on his stocking hat. "Reminds me more of a bighorn sheep, but its legs aren't right."

"It's been gutted," Harvey said.

I made a face. "How can you tell?"

"There's a pile of intestines on the porch steps."

I looked at the steps and gagged, sitting back.

Doc pushed open his door, climbing out into the snow.

"Where are you going?" I asked, rolling down my window.

He slipped on his gloves. "To see what's waiting for us inside of the house. You can wait here if you'd rather, Killer." He winked at me and then moved to the front of the rig.

Cooper joined Doc outside, checking his handgun before trudging through the snow toward the front gate.

I looked at Harvey. "I have to go in there, don't I?"

He shrugged. "It's up to you, but those boys will be in a hell of a fix if something comes at them that bullets won't stop."

"Damn it." I sighed. "I should have ignored Cooper and brought my war hammer."

"We goin' in then, Sparky?"

"I don't have a choice, but you do."

"If you go, I go, bein's I'm yer bodyguard and all."

"Did you bring Bessie?"

He guffawed in answer.

"Does Cooper know?"

"It's none of his goldurn business."

"Good. Grab her and let's go."

I tried to walk in Doc's and Cooper's steps to keep from adding to the amount of foot traffic in the snow, since Cooper might need to check tracks later. Harvey trudged along behind me, not caring where he stepped.

I caught up with the guys at the base of the porch steps. I avoided looking at the pile of guts, staring out toward the woodshed instead.

"Them there innards ain't normal," Harvey said when he reached my side.

"How can you tell?" I asked, still looking the other way.

"Well, fer one thing, they're blue."

"What?"

I looked down. Sure enough, they didn't look like normal innards. Not that I was an innards expert.

Doc stepped through the snow and weeds over to where the carcass dangled. "I still don't know what this thing was." He scanned the yard. "If we could find the head, that would help."

"I'll take a look inside while you three wait out here." Cooper skirted the mess on the stairs and paused at the door. He stepped to the side, bracing his back against the wall next to the door, and held his Colt .45 chest level. "Uncle Willis, get Parker out of the line of fire."

Harvey nudged me through the snow to the corner of the porch where a rusted oil drum sat in the yard and pulled me down behind it. At the other end of the porch, Doc leaned against the trunk of a tree, shielded from view.

I heard the sound of knocking, and then Cooper shouted, "Police! Anyone inside?"

We all waited.

A branch cracked in a stand of trees across the street. More snow tumbled to the ground.

The sound of hinges creaking made me peek above the oil drum. Cooper looked around the doorjamb and then disappeared into the darkness beyond.

I started to stand, but Harvey yanked me back down. "Hold yer horses, girl. Wait 'til he gives the all-clear."

My thigh muscles started to burn as we waited. I looked over at Doc, who was focused on something down the road. I followed his line of sight, frowning when I locked onto the crumbling two-story building that had been a store at one time according to Harvey. Now, it had a mix of broken and boarded-up windows with bullet holes peppering its walls.

"Nyce," Cooper called from the doorway. "You need to see this."

I stood, stretching the kink in my lower back. "What is it?"

Cooper looked at me for several seconds. No snarls, no glares, no scowls. He just stared.

" 'Fess up, boy," Harvey said from behind me.

"I think it's a message."

"From whom?" Doc asked, moving to the first of the porch steps. He waited for me to reach his side. "Want me to boost you over the mess, Killer?" At my nod, he grabbed me around the waist and lifted me up onto the porch, making sure I had my footing before he let me go. "You need a hand, Willis?"

"Teach yer grandmother to suck eggs."

"I think that means, 'No thanks,' " I told Doc, who was looking down the road toward the old store again. "What is it? Do you see something?"

His forehead furrowed. "When I was waiting by the tree, I thought I saw something race along the covered boardwalk in front of it, but then it was gone."

I stared at the building, trying to remember the exact wording of the message spray painted on one of the walls. I'd noticed it that day several weeks ago when Harvey and I had traveled here to pick up a message for Cooper. If memory served me right, it said: *Trespassers will be gutted and hung!*

Whoever wrote the message must have stolen it from a greeting card company's "Wish You Weren't Here" product line.

Wait a second! My gaze moved to the carcass hanging from a porch beam. ... *Gutted and hung.*

Holy shit! Was this creature some kind of trespasser? Had a local done this, sending a message to the *others* out there roaming the hills? Maybe it was a warning for that curly-horned thing whose image the missing informant had caught on film and passed on to Cooper. Or were those words on the old store building not meant to *threaten* humans, but rather alert them of the dangers hidden back here in Slagton?

"Violet?" Doc asked, tugging on my hand.

I blinked, hitting the brakes on my runaway train of thoughts. "What?"

"You ready to go inside?"

I looked at the doorway. It was empty. Cooper had disappeared inside the house again.

"Sure," I told Doc and led the way.

The rancid smell inside the room made my eyes water. It took a couple of seconds for my pupils to adjust to the dark room. When they did, I gasped and took a step back, colliding with Doc's chest.

He grabbed me by the shoulders, steadying me. "What the hell is that, Coop?"

"I was hoping you could tell me since you're the one studying Parker's freaky family history."

"Ho! What the …?" Harvey said from the threshold. "Now that there is far from normal." He shuffled up next to me, nudging me with the stock of his shotgun. "Looks like we got us some wasps in the outhouse again, Sparky."

Chapter Six

And I thought waking up with a mouse on my bed was hair-raising. "Trespasser," I read aloud the words scrawled in blue-tinted blood on the wall above the creature's severed head, which sat lopsided on the deep freezer in the dining room. It appeared that somebody had gotten a little too rambunctious with a handsaw. Shit criminy, these Slagton folks were tight as banjo strings when it came to infringing on their property.

"Well, at least we know where the head is." I turned to Cooper. "Looks like you won't need your crime-sniffing, canine partner to find this body part for you, Detective."

Over the past few months, Harvey's dog, Ol' Red, had discovered several body parts before the cops could at Harvey's ranch—a fact with which I liked to poke Cooper every now and then.

His steely eyes narrowed. "I'm laughing on the inside, Parker."

Doc approached the head. His breath steamed in the air as he touched one of the curled horns. "It's similar to a bighorn sheep, but the head is too round. The snout is more elongated than what's typical of the *ovis* species, more like something from the crocodile family with its V shape." He bent down, leaning closer. "Willis, hand me your screwdriver."

Harvey tugged a screwdriver from his leg pocket. "Always like to be ready for a screw," he told me with a grin.

I rolled my eyes. "You tell me that every time you pull it out."

"Better than waitin' 'til after I shove 'er in, eh, Doc?" He snickered.

"No comment." Doc took the screwdriver and lifted one side of the creature's mouth.

I yanked on Harvey's beard. "Don't make me hurt you, old man."

"Willis," Doc said, "you wouldn't happen to have a pair of pliers on you, by chance?"

"Sure as a goose goes barefoot." Harvey dug in his other leg pocket and handed Doc one of those folded multi-tools.

"You're a regular tool chest today," I told the old buzzard.

"Aren't ya glad ya brought me along?"

"That's still up for debate," Cooper answered.

I watched Doc inspect the creature's face. The nostrils were large and round, protruding up from the snout. It must have been able to pick up scents from a great distance. Its two black eyes were wide open but murky in death. They faced forward above the snout. "It's a predator," I said. "Forward-facing eyes allow for binocular or stereoscopic vision. They need the depth perception to track and pursue their prey."

When Doc hit me with a raised eyebrow, I explained, "Layne likes to watch National Geographic documentaries."

Harvey harrumphed. "This varmint is an all-new breed of hunter."

"Or an old breed that's returned to this neck of the woods," Cooper said, walking over to the mantel. "Shit."

"Did you see the long arms and hair-raisin' claws danglin' from the front end of it?" Harvey asked nobody in particular. "You'd think somethin' with horns like this would have cloven hooves, not fingers and toes. I tell ya, one swing from this sucker and yer head would go flyin' a helluva ways from home."

It must have stood upright. I stared at those horns, remembering a photo I'd seen recently. "It's the creature from the picture in that manila envelope." The envelope Harvey and I had driven to Slagton to pick up for Cooper a week and a half ago. "Isn't it?"

Harvey scratched under his beard. "That photo was purty fuzzy, but the horns look 'bout right."

I glanced Cooper's way to get his two cents, but he was gone. I saw a glimpse of his black coat through the grimy front window.

Doc used the screwdriver to prop open the jaws. Apparently rigor mortis hadn't set in yet. Then again, maybe this thing didn't experience the chemical changes in the muscles that caused post-mortem stiffening.

"If you're right about this being a hunter," Doc said, squeezing the pliers on the multi-tool a few times while he stared at me, "then who's killing the hunters?"

I knew what he was thinking. I was a hunter, too.

Cooper strode into the house, snaring our attention. His cheeks were pink, either from the cold outside or whatever had his forehead puckered up. "The rifle is missing."

"What rifle?" Harvey asked.

Cooper jabbed his thumb at the mantel. "There was a Ruger 10/22 rifle above that Remington 12-gauge yesterday. Now the Ruger is gone."

Sure enough, only one gun sat in the wall rack.

Cooper joined Doc over by the head, pulling out a small flashlight. He shined the light around the backside of it. "See that hole?" he said to Doc, pointing at something with the light. "It looks like an exit wound."

"Where's the entrance wound?" Doc asked.

Cooper moved the flashlight around, his forehead wrinkling. "I don't see one."

"Wait," Doc said. "Let me see your light." He took the flashlight and peered into the mouth. "Check out the back right side. A bullet would explain why some of the teeth are broken."

I joined them, peering into the propped jaws at a small hole behind some broken molar-like teeth. I covered my nose. Even in the cold I could smell the rank odor of death. Then again, maybe this thing reeked while alive, too.

"Its mouth must have been open when the shot was fired," Doc said, his words painting a scene in my head of holding a rifle steady in the face of all of those pointy teeth coming at me.

Cooper stepped back, his gaze darting around the room. "I'll need to find the bullet and take it to ballistics to see if the Ruger was used to kill it."

"You could take the head to Eddie Mudder on the sly," I halfway joked. I wondered what the local mortician-slash-pathologist would say if Cooper plopped this thing on the autopsy table. Eddie had seen his fair share of kookie shit lately, but this one might take the cake.

Cooper turned on me. "This whole Slagton situation keeps getting more and more fucked up, Parker. Now I have a missing informant and rifle."

"And a dead hunter," his uncle added.

"This is not my doing, Cooper, so you can quit glaring at me."

Harvey prodded the side of the severed head with his gun barrels. "Ya think this thing was one of the good guys or another troublemaker?"

"That probably depends on who's asking." Doc handed the tools back to Harvey.

Cooper was still staring at me. However, instead of pissed-off wrinkles lining his face, he had a perplexed crook to his mouth, as if I had a pair of curling sheep horns sprouting out of my head.

"What?" I crossed my arms. "Whatever you're thinking, I'm innocent. I had nothing to do with it."

"Didn't Dominick Masterson say there were hunters coming for you?"

"Yeah, but why would they be here in Slagton? I'm easy enough to find in Deadwood." Too easy, actually, which gave me night sweats when I thought about it in the dark hours.

"I don't know, but my gut tells me this is the tip of the iceberg."

Cooper's gut wasn't alone in that line of thinking.

"So, what now?" I asked. "Are we going to scour this place for more clues or go door-to-door with questions and cross our fingers we don't get shot, hanged, and gutted, too?"

"You two troublemakers aren't doing anything besides waiting in the pickup." Cooper ushered Harvey and me toward the door. "Nyce and I are going to head out back and check the woodshed, looking for any new tracks."

I didn't like him dragging Doc with him on rounds when there were non-local predators roaming about in the shadows. "Don't you think I should go with you after what happened yesterday?"

"You killed it, Parker. I doubt the damned thing will rise up from the ashes like a phoenix. If it does return in spirit form, I'll be able to see it now thanks to the ghost vision you cursed me with, won't I?"

Son of a peach! The stubborn detective would blame me if he cut himself shaving these days. He seemed to be stuck in the anger stage of grief since losing his ghost blinders. If he didn't snap out of it, I was going to drag him by the ear to the next stage whether he liked it or not. "Try to be positive, Cooper. Think of it as me giving you the gift of sight."

"There was no giving. You hit me with it like a Mack truck."

Now who was being the pansy? "Move over, princess and the pea, we have us a new drama queen in the ranks." I held up my fist in front of his face. "What I should have done was shove it up your nose."

He pointed out the door. "Go get in the goddamned pickup and don't either of you step one toe outside, got it?"

"What if I have to milk my snake?" Harvey asked.

"Don't start, Uncle Willis."

"Violet, wait," Doc said, stopping me on the porch. He held his closed hand out toward me. "Take this."

"What is it?" I held out my gloved palm and he dropped a long brownish-yellow tooth in it. "A tooth?" At his nod, I grinned. "Shucks, Doc. Are you asking me to go steady?"

"Why are you giving her that?" Cooper asked.

With a wink, Doc closed my fingers around it. "It's a canine tooth for Prudence."

"Oh!" This would give the old girl a surprise.

"Prudence told Violet that she needed to bring her a tooth the next time she came over," Doc explained. "Or Violet would have to forfeit one of her own."

"Right," Cooper said. "I'd forgotten about that. Will that be good enough?" he asked me.

"We'll see."

"Take your tooth and my uncle and get your asses in the pickup." When I grumbled in response, he said, "I've told you before, I do not fornicate with monkeys. Now go!"

Like good little kids, Harvey and I skirted the mess on the porch steps and made our way toward where the pickup was parked in front of the place. Cooper waited until we were shut inside the cab to lead Doc around the side of the house and across the snowy yard to the rickety woodshed near the tree line.

"Where did Doc get a gun?" I hadn't noticed it on him earlier when I was patting him up and down in his office.

"Coop brought an extra."

"Dang it. Your nephew never shares his toys with me." I shivered in the cold cab. Slouching in the back seat on the driver's side, I looked out my window toward the center of Slagton. The clouds were growing darker, heavy with snow. *Ominous* was a good word to describe them, especially with that derelict two-story building in the foreground. As I stared down the street, the sky started to spit snowflakes.

Aunt Zoe's living room beckoned. Flames crackling in the fireplace, lights glowing on the Christmas tree, a rugged Tall Medium sexing up me and my cockles under a blanket on the couch while buttered rum warmed my …

A large, black creature slunk across the road by the old store.

I sat up straight, pressing my nose to the cold window. "Harvey! Do you see that?"

"See what?"

I pointed out my window. "One of those big cat-bird things. It's about forty yards down the road in front of the store."

He leaned closer. "You mean the one standin' in the middle of the road? Or the other doozy on the boardwalk in front of the ol' building?"

"Shit!" Now there were two. Even from this distance I knew they were the same breed as the creature I'd killed in the woodshed yesterday. There was no mistaking that body shape and the way they skulked while walking.

Harvey scratched his beard. "They look like some sorta mutant griffin. Ya know, one of those mythological critters with a body like a lion that has wings, talons, and a beak? Only these suckers don't have wings or a beak."

"Right." A mutant griffin. I liked that. "They have lots of pointy teeth instead."

As we watched, the beast in the road stopped and turned in our direction. Its snout lifted in the air as though it was looking at the falling snowflakes.

Or sniffing the air.

Its body stiffened, head lowering.

"Oh, crap," I said. "It's picked up our scent."

"Not ours, girlie. We're cooped up in this cab safe as a banker's wallet. I'm thinkin' it's sniffin' out Coop and yer stallion."

The other one turned toward the informant's house, its head lowering. A deep, growling sound filled my ears. "Do you hear that?"

How was I hearing it from this distance was a better question. Maybe the growling was extra loud.

"I don't hear anything but yer breathin', bucket mouth."

I frowned at him. "You can't hear them growling?"

"No." He pointed out my window. "But I got a good hunch 'bout their intentions."

I turned back and gasped.

Both were stalking in our direction. As I watched, they split up, one on each side of the road, using the pine trees lining the ditches as cover. All that stood between them and the informant's woodshed off to our right was the pickup.

Make that the pickup, Harvey, and me.

Harvey grunted. "Those sons-a-bitches are gonna launch a surprise attack on the boys."

Oh, lordy, I had to do something. Those things moved too fast for Cooper's guns. I reached for the door handle.

Harvey grabbed my wrist. "What're ya doin'?"

"We have to alert Doc and Cooper somehow."

He flashed his two gold teeth at me, holding up Bessie. "This'll perk up their ears. Grab the crowbar under yer seat and let's go."

We climbed out, armed but probably not prepared for what was coming at us. Leaving the safety of the pickup, we stopped in the middle of the road and faced our foes like gunfighters of the Old West.

The two creatures slowed at the sight of us, sniffing the air again. I could still hear their growling.

"Ready?" Harvey asked.

"For what?"

He pointed his shotgun in their general direction. "Cover yer ears, Sparky. Bessie has a loud bark."

I raised my hands right before he pulled the trigger.

An explosion boomed from her double barrels.

Down the street, both beasts stopped. Their stances were rigid, ready to spring into action.

Heat filled my arms and legs, making me itch to fight or take flight. I took a calming breath. On the inhale, a multitude of scents slammed into me—the pine trees, Harvey's cologne, my hair gel, wood smoke, and the pickup's air freshener, to name a few. But underneath it all, I noticed the same sour odor that I smelled yesterday in the woodshed. As I exhaled, the growling deepened, growing more guttural and menacing.

"Why aren't they leaving?" I asked.

"Maybe they're waitin' to see what we do next."

I knew what we had to do next—or rather, what I had to do now. It was time to take off my gloves and get my hands dirty. Literally.

Stuffing my gloves into my pockets, I gripped the cold, steel bar.

In a blink, everything around me slowed, like someone had downshifted reality. Sounds became muffled, except for the rapid beat of my heart. The snowflakes drifted down so slowly that they almost seemed to hover in midair. I looked over at Harvey. He was cocking his shotgun in slow motion, his gaze locked on the two predators. A slurred shout behind me made me turn. Doc and Cooper were rounding the woodshed, running our way at a snail's pace. Snow sprayed up around their boots, floating behind them.

What in the hell was going on?

Goosebumps lifted on my arms, spurred by the adrenaline rushing through my body. I could hear the whooshing roar of my blood and feel energy sparking in my muscles, making me twitch.

I turned back to the two predators, my vision tunneling and gaining focus. With their necks bristling, they reminded me even more of lions with full manes. Black feathers stuck out here and there, fluffing up their size even more. Their thick heads were lowered for battle; their sharp teeth were bared. Drool hung from the bigger one's massive lower jaw. The smaller one had a streak of white up the middle of its black snout that split into a Y above its yellow eyes and continued through its mane, reminding me of the Bride of Frankenstein.

I didn't remember yesterday's woodshed visitor being as big as these two, but then again I had caught only glimpses of it before I made it explode.

Frankenstein's Bride turned its head toward Cooper and Doc. I saw it crouch, preparing to pounce.

It was time to fight.

I took off like a shot, running full-bore toward the two predators with the crowbar in hand. Shouts rang out from behind me, but the predators' huffs and growls soon blocked them out.

I raced down the street, breaking all of my previous sprint records for the ice cream truck. Both predators came at me at once, two against one. I lowered my head and plowed forward into battle.

Gunfire echoed loud and long behind me.

I saw the bullet fly past me and slam into the bigger mutant griffin on my right, knocking it sideways.

Crowbar raised, I charged in, dodging Frankenstein's Bride's biting jaws as I slammed the bar into its ribs. It screeched and tumbled into the ditch.

I heard the other predator grunt behind me. I whirled in time to see it push off the ground a good fifteen feet away, going airborne with its lips pulled back, massive jaws extended. Its front arms reached toward me, parachute-like flaps of skin attached from its elbows to hips giving the impression of wings.

I swung the crowbar, throwing my body weight behind it as I'd learned in softball. The curved end of the crowbar connected with the side of the griffin's head. *Whack*! I'd rung its bell like a Buddhist monk.

Its drool plastered my face while shattered pieces of teeth peppered my coat. The bar vibrated hard in my cold hands, stinging like hot pins. I almost dropped it as the beast slid on its side across the snow-covered road.

Wiping my face on my coat sleeve, I tightened my hold on the crowbar and prepared for round 2. Frankenstein's Bride was working its way around my back, trying a sneak attack. I turned so I could see both predators out of the corners of my eyes.

The drooler scrambled to its feet. Something black and viscous dripped from its now-crooked jaw. It shook its head, its yellow eyes rolling around in their sockets for a second before locking onto me.

Another gunshot rang out. The griffin stepped to the side, dodging the bullet with ease this time.

"Well, fuck-a-doodle-doo," I said. "You're smarter than you look."

"*Scharrrrrfrichterrrrr*," Frankenstein's Bride hissed, lowering its head. Its yellow eyes watched me with an intensity that made me grip the crowbar even harder.

"Why are you here?" I asked. "Are you bounty hunters?" I doubted they spoke English as a second language, but it was all I knew.

"*Scharrrrrfrichterrrrr*," the Bride repeated in that hissing voice.

Apparently that was the only word it knew.

"You could stand to take a few English lessons from a parrot."

Frankenstein's Bride made several gobbled guttural sounds and took a step back toward the trees. The same sort of vocalizations I'd heard from the one yesterday in the woodshed. The drooler nodded its head once and then lunged at me again with its jaws wide and aiming for my throat.

Instantly, I gauged the trajectory and velocity of its jump. I ducked, spinning on my heel while the griffin vaulted over me. I popped up as it touched earth and swung the crowbar in a downward arc, landing a solid blow to its back. Something cracked like a dry tree limb and the beast dropped flat on its belly. It tried to stand and walk, but its hind end dragged.

"Where do you think you're going?" I asked, stalking after it.

The griffin stumbled, falling onto its side where it hissed at me with blackened teeth. The dark gelatinous goo must be its blood.

"That's no way to talk to a lady." I flipped the crowbar around and jammed the pry bar through its head. "Give Hades my love."

Its body convulsed, its legs twitching. I shielded my face before it exploded in a puff of gray ash.

Expecting Frankenstein's Bride to attack next, I raised the crowbar again, blinking through the ash from the dead griffin falling along with the snowflakes. But the other was gone. I glanced toward the trees. Where did it go? And when had time shifted back to normal speed?

"Violet!" Doc slid to a stop beside me, grabbing my arm. "What in the hell were you thinking?"

My mouth opened, but I didn't really have an answer other than, "I had to kill it before it got to you or Harvey." Behind Doc, Cooper ran toward us. "Or Deadwood's most lovable detective."

"Christ, woman!" Doc's chest rose and fell as he caught his breath. "I almost died from a damned heart attack watching you charge hell with a bucket of ice water."

I smiled. "You're starting to sound like Harvey."

Doc rattled off a string of curses that made my jaw drop. He rarely swore in front of me with such zeal.

"Wow. Cooper is rubbing off on you, too. Be careful. The way that man foams at the mouth most days, he probably has rabies."

"I heard that," Cooper said, catching up to us. His breath steamed like a locomotive.

"Jeez! Do you have a bionic implant crammed in your ear?"

"Dammit, Parker!" He didn't even pause for a breath before jumping right into chewing me a new asshole. "You need to wait for backup next time."

Movement over his shoulder caught my eye. I watched Harvey crawl into the driver's seat of the pickup and close the door. Good, that should keep him safe while I hunted for the Bride of Frankenstein.

"I had backup." I focused on Cooper. "Your uncle caught the big griffin in the side, giving me a chance to take them on one at a time."

"Griffin?" Doc asked.

"Harvey said they look like mutant griffins," I explained.

"That wasn't Uncle Willis's bullet." Cooper raised his handgun. "It was mine. Neither he nor Nyce were willing to risk taking a shot with you in the picture."

But Cooper was, of course. "Good shootin', Tex." I tipped an imaginary hat at him. "Did you see where the other one went?"

"It ran into those trees," Doc said.

I started after it, but Doc caught my arm. "What are you doing?"

Pounding on my chest, I spoke in a caveman voice, "Me Executioner. Me kill bad beast."

Doc guffawed, frowning over my head at Cooper. "She's going to be the death of me."

"I warned you months ago about dating girls with crazy curls."

"Leave my curls out of this or I'll bust your kneecaps." I tugged free of Doc's grip. "Now if you gentlemen will excuse me, I have a three-toed menace to ship back to Hades before it tears someone's throat out with all of those pointy teeth."

"Hold up, Killer." Doc grabbed me by the coat lapels and yanked me toward him. His lips were cold, but his kiss branded me. It was over before I had a chance to respond, and then he let me go. "I'm coming with you. Lead the way."

Cooper followed us, staying about twenty feet off to our side as we crashed through pine tree limbs drooping low with snow. He had his handgun out and ready for a rootin' tootin' shootin' good time.

The griffin's long-toed tracks zigzagged through the pine trees, weaving a drunken path. Five minutes into the trees, Doc snagged the back of my coat.

"Violet, wait." He studied the forest floor, frowning to the left and then right.

"What is it?" Cooper asked.

"There are tracks all over the place here," he told us. Doc was right. The tracks doubled back, fanning out in multiple directions. "We've lost its trail."

I looked toward the north, sniffing. My gut told me it had gone that way, but the scent of pine trees was all I smelled in the air. With a nod, I told Doc, "You're right. I should have gone after it as soon as I finished off the other one. The fun is over for today, boys."

"Fun. Right." Doc scoffed. "We're heading back," he called to Cooper.

The detective nodded, scanning the trees.

I looked down at my red pea coat as I stepped over a half-buried log. Darn it, this was one of my favorite coats. I'd just sewed on several new buttons. Stupid pet chicken and her button fetish. How hard would it be to get dead predator ash out of the wool blend? Maybe I should …

I didn't hear the tree branch crack until it was too late.

A black blur bulleted out of the trees in front of us. I started to raise the crowbar when Doc shoved me hard.

"Doc!" I cried as I stumbled sideways.

Frankenstein's Bride rammed into his chest. Doc flew backward through the air, landing on his back inches from a large rock. His face creased in pain as he stared up at the sky, gasping for air.

I raced to his side, putting my body between him and the griffin.

The beast bared its teeth, pawing the ground with me locked in its sights. I braced myself for impact, trying to read its intentions from its body movements like I had earlier with the other one.

"Get the hell out of the way!" Cooper shouted from behind me.

I knew without looking that the detective had his Colt .45 trained on the creature, but I also knew that bullets wouldn't stop it.

"Cooper, help Doc," I ordered, running straight at the sharp-toothed bastard, my crowbar cocked and ready to swing.

It roared and came for me, springing into the air. At the last second, I veered to the side, dodging its long claws, and took off running away from Doc and Cooper, racing deeper into the trees.

The griffin crashed along behind me, gaining on me when I tripped over a branch hidden under the snow and stumbled for a few seconds before finding my balance again. As soon as I heard its ragged huffs right behind me, I dropped to my knees and skidded to a stop. It tried to hit the brakes, too, but momentum carried it past me, sending it tumbling through the snow.

Before the beast could get its footing, I hopped to my feet and charged. It tried to dodge as I swung, but it was too slow. I slammed the hooked end of the crowbar into its head, knocking it into a tree trunk. The predator slumped to the ground, a crumpled wreck of black fur and feathers.

I marched over to it, my body pulsing with adrenaline. "And that's what it feels like to be hit by a girl."

Its upper lip curled. A rusty growl rumbled in between rapid pants.

"Who sent you here?" I asked.

It stared at me with its yellow eyes for a moment, and then looked down at the crowbar.

"*Scharrrrfrichterrrr*," it said in that hair-raising hissy voice again.

"What?"

The creature extended its long claws and slashed its own throat right before my eyes. Thick, black fluid oozed from the wound.

"Damn it!"

Cooper was going to be pissed at me. For once I'd maimed instead of killed. "It's not my fault," I told the yellow-eyed beast.

It lay there blinking up at me, its lips pulled back in a toothy grin.

Several minutes later, I was still brushing off the griffin's ash when I caught up with Doc and Cooper. They were making their way back to the road. As usual, Cooper's gun was out and ready. Next to him, Doc held onto his left side as he struggled through the snow, his face tight with pain.

I jogged to Doc. "Are you okay?" I wasn't sure if I should try to help him or if my touch would only make things worse.

He nodded. "Had the wind knocked out of me. You?"

"A couple of scratches from my own clumsiness."

We walked in silence for a moment. The pine trees whispered and hummed in the growing wind.

"I killed it."

"We heard." Cooper sounded tense. "Heaven forbid you actually detain something for further investigation."

"I tried interrogating it." Well, sort of. "It wasn't interested in chatting."

"You're three for three on fuckups, Parker, and I still have no informant or clues to his whereabouts."

"At least you're consistent," Doc said, chuckling, and then

grimaced at the effort.

"You're going to the hospital," I told him, in case he thought he'd pull a Cooper and self-administer first aid at home.

"I'm fine."

"You look *fine* with your pasty face and sweaty brow."

"It's just bruised ribs." Cooper took Doc's side. "He'll be back swinging in the ring in a week or two. That is, if you can refrain from using your deadly windmill move on him and inflicting more damage."

I ignored the unprofessional assessment of Dr. Cooper, Proctologist Gigantic-us. "Bruised or broken?" I asked Doc.

"Bruised. I know what broken ribs feel like and this isn't it."

When had his ribs been broken? And how? Was it when he got that long scar on his knee? Or the one above his eyebrow? I wanted to touch him somewhere, but was afraid I'd jar him so I kept my hands to myself. "Is your head okay?"

"I'm fine." He grinned at me. "Although my ticker nearly popped at the sight of my girlfriend taking on two huge ... what did Willis call them?"

"Mutant griffins."

"Two huge mutant griffins on her own."

Everything had happened so fast, including Frankenstein's Bride slamming into Doc. "I'm sorry you got hurt."

I hadn't seen the griffin coming for me through the trees, damn it. I'd been too busy thinking about my stupid coat. My lack of focus could have gotten Doc killed. The memory of how close he'd come to hitting that rock made my hands clammy.

"Violet, I stepped in front of it of my own free will."

"Yeah, but—"

"And I'm the one who said we'd lost its tracks. Stop taking the blame for my mistakes."

Head lowered, I walked alongside him in silence.

I'd raced into battle without thinking it through. In hindsight, that was stupid on my part. I had two kids relying on me. If I were going to live to see them through their next birthday, I needed to learn how to control that adrenaline-fueled impulse.

What would Aunt Zoe say about my poor judgment today? I cringed at the disappointment I'd see in her eyes.

I fingered the canine tooth Doc had pulled from the severed head back in the informant's house. I knew what Prudence would say if she'd seen me rush in swinging. She'd drone on and on about my sloppy style, ending with how I was an embarrassment to the Executioner name. I sighed. Why did my predecessor have to take after the ghost of Christmas future—all doom and gloom while pointing out my shortfalls?

Harvey was waiting for us at the road, his pickup idling. I helped Doc into the back seat behind Harvey.

"What happened to Doc?" he asked as Cooper climbed in the front passenger seat, leaving me to join Doc in the back after stuffing the crowbar under the seat.

"He fell for a nutty broad with a bunch of wild hairs."

I tried to flick Cooper's ear, but he dodged my fingers while smacking my hand away.

"He took a hit for me," I told Harvey.

As the pickup started to roll, a tremor rippled through me, leaving my freezing cold hands trembling. I clutched them together, hunching my shoulders. My muscles felt drained and limp, my lower back stiff.

Doc tapped my arm, beckoning me to slide to the center of the bench seat.

"I don't want to hurt you."

"I'm bruised, Killer. Not broken. Besides, you're on my good side."

"You say that now," I joked, "but wait until we get you naked." He was going to have some colorful bruising for a week or two.

Cooper groaned. "Jesus, Parker. Can we not talk about your sex life right now?"

"Mind your own business, detective." I scooted to the center, securing my lap belt before carefully leaning against Doc. He wrapped his arm around me and stroked my shoulder.

"Well, Sparky?" Harvey glanced at me in the rearview mirror.

"Well what?"

"Did you kill both of them humdingers?"

Cooper scoffed, shaking his head.

"Yeah," I said, frowning out the front windshield.

"You moved like greased lightnin', girl." Harvey looked at Cooper. "Did you see her fly down the road?"

"You mean did I see her race headlong into a dangerous encounter with deadly predators without the appropriate backup?"

Harvey blew a raspberry. "You saw those things move, Cooper. They were fast, but she was faster." Harvey sounded like a proud coach. "How do you move that fast, anyway? I'd break a hip at that speed."

I shook my head. "I wasn't fast. Everything else slowed down."

"What do you mean?" Doc asked, grunting when Harvey hit a pothole.

"One minute, I was standing next to Harvey and everything moved along at the same speed as always. Then it was like time downshifted, but I didn't."

I went on to explain how even the snowflakes seemed to slow down, and how my vision telescoped on the two predators. When I finished, we were past the Slagton town sign and Harvey's ranch, nearly to the main road.

"That's nuts." Cooper crossed his arms, firm in his evaluation. "First ghosts, then some bizarre creatures from some other realm or plane or whatever, and now Parker has the ability to slow down time. I can't wait to see what's next on this freak show merry-go-round."

"I didn't say I can slow time. I said it seemed to slow in my head."

"Where'd ya learn to swing a crowbar like that?" Harvey asked.

"I played softball in high school. Earned a scholarship to college, thanks to my mad batting skills." Not that I'd followed through on that scholarship for long, dropping out of college after a couple of semesters to figure out what I wanted out of life before heading back years later. A lot of good all that pondering did me.

"Sparky looked like Babe Ruth out there," he told his nephew.

"I wouldn't go that far." Cooper glanced at me. "You got lucky, Parker. Had you slipped on the snow, they would've ripped out your throat, and there's nothing Nyce and I could've done to stop them. You were too far away. That's a rookie mistake in my line of work."

As much as I didn't want to admit it, Cooper was right. Luck had been on my side. Prudence would have used skill. She wouldn't have needed luck. I'd taken one hell of a chance with my life—a reckless risk I couldn't afford again, especially now that catching the *lidérc* was on my to-do list. I had no doubt Doc would throw himself in the line of fire again if I failed to focus on the game, and with the *lidérc* that would result in way more pain than a couple of bruised ribs.

Doc squeezed my hand, drawing my gaze. His dark eyes held mine.

Lifting his hand, I kissed his knuckles, and then rubbed my cheek over them.

He pulled me closer, his lips warm on my forehead. As we bounced along the dirt road, he leaned his head against the headrest and closed his eyes. His chest rose and fell steadily, but his muscles stayed tense.

After we hit pavement, the storm let loose and dumped snow on us. It slowed our progress, but Harvey knew how to handle his pickup and made it down Strawberry Hill with minor slipping and sliding.

Doc remained steadfast about not going to the ER, telling Harvey to keep driving as we rolled past the hospital. I agreed to stop pestering him about getting an X-ray when he promised to stay with me for the night so I could keep an eye on him.

The house was quiet when Harvey dropped us off. Doc made it inside with only a few winces. I settled him on the couch and brought some ibuprofen and a bag of ice.

"What else do you need?" I asked.

"You here next to me."

I smiled. "I have to shower first. Do you want me to get you something to eat?"

"No. I'll be fine."

"If you need any—"

"Violet, go take a shower."

I did as told, scrubbing my hair twice with shampoo.

A half hour later, I came downstairs and found Doc in the kitchen, leaning against the counter drinking a glass of lemonade. "You're supposed to be resting."

He gave me a look that silenced me on the subject of his physical health. "Did Addy and Layne even cross your mind when you raced into battle?"

I grimaced at the guilt his question kindled in my chest. I joined him at the counter. "No."

"I wonder if that's some sort of innate self-preservation in Executioners."

"What do you mean?"

"You go into fight mode and nothing else matters."

"Something else mattered."

"What?"

"You."

"Violet, you don't need to try to win me. I'm already in your bed."

"I'm serious. When I saw that creature lock onto you, I knew I had to stop it."

"I was supposed to be protecting you, not the other way around."

"You did protect me. Your bruised ribs are evidence of that."

He grabbed my hand and tugged. "Come here."

"Are you sure? I don't want to—"

"Now, Boots."

I moved into his arms, careful of his left side. He smelled sweet and safe, like molasses cookies and home. I wanted to crawl under his shirt and hide there until all of this weird Slagton crap subsided. "Let me know if I'm hurting you."

"Quit coddling me, woman." He frowned at me. "You scared me today. If I'm going to continue hunting with you, I need better gear."

"You think Cooper would lend you one of his Kevlar vests?"

"I was thinking more along the lines of a suit of armor."

I laughed, resting my forehead against his shoulder. "What do you think is going on back in Slagton?"

"I don't know, but I think it extends beyond the town limits."

"What do you mean?"

"Don't forget about Harvey's ranch."

I looked up at him. "What about it?"

"All of the odd crimes and bodies turning up there."

"Oh, yeah. Those."

"I have a theory," he said.

"What is this? National Theory Day?"

"Maybe." He pulled on one of my curls. "You know how Harvey's ranch butts up against the mining company's land outside of Slagton?" He shifted slightly, grimacing. "It's essentially the last stage stop before entering the old mining town."

"Last stage stop? Did you read that somewhere in the history books?"

"No. It's my own observation. Think of it as a way station, if you will."

"A way station for whom? Or what?"

"Others leaving and entering Slagton, like the bone cruncher."

"Do we know the bone cruncher actually came from Slagton?"

"Not definitely, but Cooper told me a story about something

digging up the graves back there and—"

"Eating the bones," I finished. "I heard about that, too."

"Don't forget about those masks Harvey found in the floor of his toolshed. During our séance, Harvey's grandfather said they were used by the *others* to disguise themselves."

I leaned back with raised brows. "What are you saying, Doc?"

"What if these creatures that we're running into back in Slagton aren't hunters, necessarily? I mean they're predators, but maybe they've been there for a while now, only whatever or whoever was keeping them tucked away is no longer around."

"Do you think Cooper's informant has something to do with them being loose?"

"I don't know, but I'm afraid it's going to take an experienced hunter to round them back up." He lifted my chin, his gaze traveling over my face before stopping at my eyes. "Someone who moves as fast as they do and isn't afraid to charge headlong into battle."

Chapter Seven

"There's nothing wrong with pumping my kid for a little information on an ex-client," I told Aunt Zoe later that evening.

She stood next to me at the kitchen sink, drying the supper dishes I was washing. "Jeff Wymonds is more than an ex-client, Violet Lynn."

I didn't like what she was insinuating. Thankfully, Doc had gone upstairs to take a shower, leaving the two of us alone with Natalie, who'd made baked chicken tenders to dip in her mom's infamous peanut curry sauce. Add the salad Aunt Zoe had tossed together and my belly was as happy as a puppy with two tails.

I stopped washing a plate and frowned at her. "Really? What do you know that I don't? Besides that one time Jeff used his tongue to play bumper cars with my uvula, which I remind you was only because he'd been lured in by the smell of beef jerky on my breath, he and I have maintained a client–agent relationship."

"He's the father of your daughter's best friend."

"True, but—"

"And you've eaten meals with him on several occasions."

"Not like on-a-date kind of meals, though."

"And," Natalie jumped into the conversation, "you've seen his bare ass flossed with a red G-string in the midst of football-themed kitchen counter sex." When I glared over at the table where she sat drinking hot buttered rum, she raised her glass to me and then grabbed another piece of chocolate-covered toffee from the serving plate in front of her. "Just keeping it real, babe."

"Don't make me come over there and give you a wet noogie."

"All I'm saying," Aunt Zoe continued, "is if you want to know what's going on in Jeff Wymond's life, then you should put aside your pride and pay him a visit."

"I don't want to know what's going on in his life, only what Tiffany has done to his house to prep it for sale. For business purposes." I finished washing the plate and rinsed it before handing it to her. "There's a big difference between the two, trust me. Knowing Jeff, if I try to talk business with him, he'll tell me all about his love life in explicit detail and make it even harder to look him in the eyes."

Natalie let out a snort of laughter. "If you're making it *harder* for Jeff, I doubt he'll care much about looking you in the eyes when you're taking care of his business."

Aunt Zoe and I both turned to stare at Natalie.

She wiggled her eyebrows at me in Groucho Marx fashion. All she was missing was the cigar. "If you know what I mean, jellybean." She finished her drink, setting the glass down on the table. *Thunk.*

I looked down at her glass. "How many hot buttered rums have you had so far tonight?"

She held up one finger. "And this was my third."

I exchanged frowns with my aunt. Her counting was off.

"What's going on, Nat?" I asked, rinsing the last of the silverware. I grabbed a clean towel from the drawer and dried my hands, joining her at the table. "Are the ghosts getting to you in the Galena House?"

She scratched at something on the table. "Yeah. It's the ghosts," she said in a flat tone.

Before I could shift into psychiatrist mode, the front door opened.

"Hello?" Cooper called from the other room. "Nyce asked me to bring him his laptop and a couple of books from his place."

Aunt Zoe walked over to the archway leading into the dining room. "You can set them on the dining room table, Coop, and then take your coat off and come join us. I made some homemade toffee."

"I can't stay long," he said, striding into the kitchen. He came to an abrupt stop at the sight of Natalie sitting at the table.

She seemed intensely focused on her fingernails all of a sudden.

It took Cooper a couple of beats to snap out of his trance. He dragged his gaze to Aunt Zoe. "I'm on call, but I'd love some of your toffee."

I was of the opinion that Cooper could use a lot of sweetening up, so the more sugar we could cram down his throat the better.

"Give me your coat," Aunt Zoe said, holding out her hand. "Certainly Deadwood can go a little while without a detective on a snowy Saturday night."

"I suppose." He unzipped his coat and handed it to her.

After she left the room to hang it up, Cooper grabbed a piece of chocolate-covered toffee from the plate and leaned against the counter. He snuck a glance at Natalie before focusing on me. "Have you killed anything since I saw you last, rookie?"

I stuck my tongue out at him.

"Are we in kindergarten, Parker?"

"You're just mad because your bullets didn't do anything."

"Did you get hit in the head this afternoon?" He took a bite of the candy. "My bullet slowed the bigger bastard down so you didn't have to take on two at a time."

After supper, when the kids had disappeared to watch a Christmas show, I'd told Aunt Zoe and Natalie about the problem we ran into back in Slagton. Doc filled in the holes in my story, including the bits and pieces I couldn't remember because of being in the thick of battle. He continued to insist the bruised ribs were his own fault when I tried to take the blame again. As far as I was concerned, though, he wouldn't have been in the woods with me if I hadn't been so gung-ho to follow the other mutant griffin into the trees.

When I asked Aunt Zoe if she'd heard of such creatures as the black predators or the gutted, decapitated hunter, she reminded me that if I'd read my family history book, I wouldn't need to be asking her that question. Stalemated again.

"Why is Coop calling you a rookie?" Natalie asked, fidgeting with her empty glass.

"He thinks I acted recklessly today."

"What would you have had her do?" She looked at him, only to drop her gaze to his chest almost immediately.

What was going on with her tonight? First she'd downed three hot buttered rums like they were tequila shots, and now she was acting like a virgin in a strip club.

"She should've waited until Nyce and I were there to help her."

"What if you hadn't been there at all?"

"That point is moot because we were there."

"But what if, Coop?" She knocked the glass back and forth on the table with her fingers, like it was a hockey puck. "What should Vi do if she ends up in a situation like that and has nobody there to help her?"

"It depends on the situation and the weapons at her disposal."

"What's your point, Nat?" I asked.

"Instead of criticizing you, maybe Coop needs to train you on how to handle situations like what you experienced today." She stared at him, a challenge in her eyes. "Put his money where his mouth is."

His gaze narrowed at her dare.

"And in exchange," she continued, turning to me. "You could school Coop on how to deal with his ability to see ghosts."

"What do I know about dealing with ghosts? That's Doc's territory."

"Not entirely," Doc said, joining us in a pair of faded jeans and a blue and black plaid flannel shirt. His wet hair was finger combed. Stubble still darkened his jaw. His bruised ribs were obvious in his stiff posture and by his wince when he settled into the chair next to me.

"Okay, it's your and Cornelius's territory then," I said.

He pointed at the plate of toffee pieces in the middle of the table. "Will you hand me one of those, please?"

I reached across and grabbed two, setting them on a small plate in front of him. "You could use some extra sugar tonight." Not that he needed any sweetening up, unlike Cooper.

"I could use extra sugar most nights." His flirty grin made me blush since Natalie and Cooper were watching us. He lifted a piece of candy, his face sobering. "Have you forgotten that you're a physical medium when you're not swinging your weapons around playing Executioner?"

"I try to forget about talking to ghosts as often as possible."

"You're cute when you're in denial." He took a bite of toffee, swallowing before continuing. "My experiences and interactions with ghosts are different from yours. You've been able to converse with them upon occasion, whereas I'm forced to experience their past from first-person point of view."

Lucky for me, my interactions with ghosts were rare. I had enough headaches with my Executioner playdates.

"Coop follows more along your footsteps when it comes to interacting with entities," Doc added. "Only he doesn't have to go under in a séance to see them."

"See," Natalie said, standing and stretching. "Coop could teach you how to follow whatever police procedures he uses during altercations to stay alive, and you could teach him how to keep from getting his tighty-whities in a wad when he sees a ghost."

"I don't wear tighty-whities," he growled.

She swung her gaze his way, her eyes glancing down over him. "I remember, Coop. It was merely a turn of phrase."

His cheeks darkened, but he kept a poker face. "Parker doesn't want to learn from me."

"He's right. Have you seen how many scars he has? I'm not sure I like his methods for avoiding bodily harm."

Not to mention that Cooper often reminded me of Yosemite Sam, Bugs Bunny's fiery archenemy, minus the red mustache. Both men had hair-trigger tempers, a fondness for weapons, and a cannon barrel full of unchecked aggression. One wrong step during the detective's daily lesson and he'd probably blast a hole in me.

I crossed my arms, leaning my elbows on the table. "Cooper will lock me in the hoosegow for days if he has to spend that much time with me, and I have Christmas shopping to do."

Doc chuckled and then grunted in pain, holding his left side. "In spite of both of your reservations, I think Natalie's onto something here. The two of you could learn quite a bit from each other. That's if you can handle being in the same room for more than ten minutes."

"I can handle it," I said, looking over at Cooper's stony expression. "But the detective tends to get hurt around me. I'd hate to accidentally add another notch to his crooked nose."

Cooper scowled at me. "I've watched Parker in action multiple times now. I don't think she's trainable."

"What?" I scoffed.

"I'm serious," he said. "You're a loose cannon. You have no code of conduct, and regulations make your wild hair stand on end."

"You had to get that jab about my hair in there, didn't you?" I turned to Doc. "See, he's impossible."

Doc's eyes crinkled in the corners. "You do tend to have a problem with rules."

"Rules are for fools," Natalie repeated a mantra we had in school.

I raised my glass of hot buttered rum to her. "You're singing to the choir, rock star."

Cooper pointed at Natalie. "You're in the same boat, Beals."

"Of course she is." I defended my best friend with gusto. "Her cousins are the notorious Morgan sisters, remember? Bucking the law is in Natalie's DNA, just as slaying freaky nasties is in mine."

"Maybe Coop could teach both Natalie and you some tricks of his trade," Doc suggested. "He could help you both be more aware of unseen dangers."

Natalie walked over to the counter, swaying a little along the way. "Nah. Coop doesn't like to play with local girls, does he, Vi?"

I played dumb. "I don't know what you're talking about."

She giggled as she poured more rum into her glass. "Yes, you do. I bared my soul on my birthday, remember? I told you all of the juicy details even though you pretended we weren't talking about Coop."

Dear Lord. Somebody stuff a grapefruit in her pie hole.

I looked over to find Cooper's squint drilling into me with a soul-sizzling intensity. It didn't take any sort of detective training for me to see how he felt about my knowing the details of his makeout session with Natalie behind the Purple Door Saloon.

Shaking my head at him, I mimed tipping the bottle and glugging. "We just played a few rounds of pool."

"And I kicked your ass." Natalie raised the glass of rum minus the hot butter and took a sip.

"How are you getting home tonight?" Cooper asked her.

She shrugged. "What's it to you?"

"You're not driving, especially in this snow."

Her chin jutted. "I can walk. It's not that far."

"You'll wander into a snow drift and freeze to death. I'll take you home."

"Or I can call your buddy down at the station. Detective Hawke is still sleeping downstairs in Ms. Wolff's old apartment, guarding all of those clocks, right?"

Detective Hawke had become obsessed with counting clocks in the murdered woman's apartment after several had gone missing. While he'd initially come to Deadwood to act as Cooper's temporary partner and help solve some of the cases stacking up on Cooper's desk, his inability to find solid answers was making his grip on sanity slip and slide right into Nutter Alley. That was Harvey's latest assessment, anyway.

"Hawke's down in Rapid for a week on a mandatory stress leave."

"No way." I gaped. "How did you manage that?"

"I didn't. You did."

"What? I didn't do anything."

"Right, you only pretended to be a witch who could talk to ghosts in front of him, and then you put a hex on him and planted a trigger word in his head that makes him bark like a mad dog."

Hawke had made the mistake during our first meeting of talking down to me like my brains were made of cotton candy. His second mistake had been poking fun at my hair. After that, it had been one rowdy and raucous Pecos promenade after another for us. How could I resist stirring the pot when he came up with such outrageous accusations every other time we met? A mother of twins only had so much patience to spare.

"To be fair," I said, "I didn't plant the trigger word. Prudence did."

"But you were the one who suckered him into going to the Carhart house to act as Prudence's karaoke machine," Cooper pointed out.

"True, but I had no idea that exposing him to her mental manipulations would cause his mind to short-circuit."

"That's because you've never had her inside your head."

Cooper and Doc had both battled Prudence, at least mentally, and lost. Apparently, Executioners could retain some of their abilities even after death. A fact I hoped not to find out for myself anytime soon.

"I don't know if Prudence can go into Violet's head," Doc said.

My fingers were crossed she couldn't. It was bad enough facing off with her puppets every time she wanted to tell me how shitty I was at my job.

"Anyway," Cooper continued. "Yesterday afternoon, the chief informed me that Detective Hawke had been told to take the week off and get his shit together."

A week without the asshole threatening me at every turn? What would I do with all of my unspent stress? Oh, yeah. Worry about what was going on back in Slagton.

"I don't need a ride from you, Coop," Natalie said. "I'll call a taxi."

He pointed out the kitchen window. "The roads are covered in several inches already. There aren't any taxis out tonight. Either I drive you home when you're ready, or you stay put for tonight."

Natalie scowled at me over the rim of her glass. "Coop's bossy."

"That's news to you?" I scoffed. "You can sleep on the couch if you want."

"I think I'll take you up on that offer and save Coop a trip through the snow."

I had a feeling her reason for rejecting his ride home had more to do with whatever had her drinking more than usual, but I kept my mouth shut.

Aunt Zoe cruised back into the room, wearing her fleece pajamas under her robe. "You want some coffee, Coop? I just made it." When he hesitated, she added, "It goes great with the toffee."

"Sure. Where's Martin tonight?"

She frowned, moving to the coffee maker. "How should I know? Where's your uncle?"

"There's some Christmas shindig at the senior center that he didn't want to miss." Cooper grimaced. "He was wearing a Santa costume with a sprig of mistletoe taped to his belt buckle when he stopped by the police station earlier to bring me a sandwich for supper. Said something about trying to get kissed under the mistletoe before the night was through."

"Oh, Willis," Aunt Zoe said, chuckling.

I grinned at Harvey's ingenuity when it came to getting tail. "I'm surprised they're having the party with it snowing like it is." Hunkering down until it cleared seemed safer to me.

Cooper shrugged, taking the cup of coffee Aunt Zoe handed him. "They're old-timers. Snow doesn't scare them. Besides, one of our off-duty officers is in charge of transportation for the party. He has a custom-built snow crawler with a cab that fits six. I've seen him go up Mill Street in Lead when it's iced over with hardly a slip."

"I'll have to check it out one of these days," Doc said. "Might be fun to build one of those for myself."

Addy came into the kitchen with Elvis the mouse-catcher tucked under her arm. Her straight blond hair was pulled back in a ponytail, her cheeks rosy from sitting in her beanbag next to the fireplace. Her glasses looked crooked on her face. I'd have to have Doc take a look at them again and see if he could straighten them out.

"Hey, Coop." She filched a piece of candy from the plate on the table. "Are you spending the night again? You can stay in my room if you want. It doesn't stink like perfume that much anymore." She hit him with a double-dimple smile.

Cooper had spent over a week with us, day and night, earlier this month thanks to Detective Hawke's determination to pin the murder of Ms. Wolff on me. Luckily, I was able to dodge that bullet, but at a steep cost. Plus, I had to put up with Cooper in my business 24/7. While we managed to find some common ground in our mutual appreciation for middle-of-the-night westerns, I danced a jig of joy when he packed his duffel bag and traded places with Doc.

"Thanks, Addy, but not tonight," Cooper said, smiling down at her. "I'm on call, so I'll crash on the couch in the chief's office at work."

"Hey, kid, I'll take you up on that offer," Natalie said. "But only if you stay in there and keep me company."

"Yes! It'll be a slumber party!" Addy turned to me, bouncing up and down. "Can Elvis stay in there with us, too?"

"No!" Natalie and I nixed the idea in unison.

The bouncing stopped. "Fine! What did you do with my Christmas list, Mom?"

I smacked her hand away when she reached for more candy. "That's enough candy for tonight, child. I mailed your list to Santa, why?"

"Dang it. I wanted to add something else."

"What?" My tone was wary. I couldn't help it. If she asked for a rabbit cage or a pot-bellied pigpen, I was going to have to put my foot down.

"A gun."

"No," Cooper said, beating me to it.

I crossed my arms. "Absolutely not, Adelynn Renee."

"Do you mean a toy gun?" Natalie asked. "Like a Nerf gun?"

"Why do you want a gun, Addy?" Doc asked.

She shifted Elvis to her other arm. "To protect Mom," she answered Doc, her expression earnest.

Aunt Zoe lowered her coffee cup, her brow furrowed as she looked from Addy to me. "Protect her from what, kiddo?"

"The hungry wolf-monster."

Wolf? Had she been watching one of those horror movies that played on the Red Riding Hood fairy tale? Or was it a werewolf movie? Surely Jeff didn't let Kelly and her have free rein with the television last night. He said he was going to be there with them all evening. Maybe he fell asleep early ...

"What hungry wolf-monster?" Doc pressed.

She hugged Elvis close, her worried gaze meeting mine over the chicken. "The one that keeps trying to eat her in my dreams."

* * *

Sunday, December 16th

Nothing tried to eat me in my dreams, but I did wake up the next morning to find two pairs of eyes watching me.

"What are you two doing?" I asked Addy and Layne, who stood beside my bed staring down at me.

"You had a slumber party, too," Addy whispered.

I blinked, sitting upright. "A slumber party?" I whispered back.

Layne pointed behind me. "Why is *he* sleeping in *your* bed?"

Oh, crud.

I looked over at the man lying next to me with his eyes closed. What was Doc doing still asleep? He usually woke before the sun. Then again, he'd had a rough time trying to relax last night with his bruised ribs. Finally, he'd drifted off in the early morning hours after I convinced him to take a dose of over-the-counter sleeping medicine. It was the same stuff Aunt Zoe had bought me earlier this fall when I was having trouble with nightmares every time I closed my eyes.

Shooing the kids out of my room, I grabbed my robe and slippers and followed them into the hall. After one last peek on Doc, I quietly pulled the door closed and led Addy and Layne down to the kitchen where Natalie and Aunt Zoe sat at the table sipping coffee.

"Both of you sit," I ordered the kids, earning raised brows from Aunt Zoe. I poured myself some caffeinated brain juice and joined them. "There is something you two kids need to understand about Doc sleeping in my bed."

"Are we really doing this now?" Natalie interrupted.

"Why not?" Was there something I needed to know?

"Well, it's just that we're close to Christmas and everyone seems so happy." She glanced pointedly toward Layne.

I looked at my son, whose arms were crossed. His eyes narrowed as he waited for me to continue.

"I thought you'd decided to hold off until after Santa's visit," Natalie added.

A few days ago, she and I had weighed when the best time might be for me to tell the kids the truth about Doc sleeping in my bed. Up until now, they hadn't noticed where he crashed because he was always up before them to go to the gym. After considering the pros and cons, I'd decided to wait until after Christmas so that Doc's first holiday with us wasn't filled with angry glares and snippy attitudes.

Addy leaned her elbows on the table, lowering her voice like we were speaking in secrets. "What do we need to understand?"

"Doc got hurt yesterday," I said.

"We know." Layne shifted in his chair, sitting up straighter. "He hurt his ribs. He told us."

"Did he tell you how?" I asked.

"He said it was an accident." Addy pushed her glasses higher on her nose. "But he told me not to worry about him, that he'd be as good as new in a couple of days."

In other words, he'd skirted the truth without openly lying. "He will be okay," I assured her. "However, last night was a tough time for him. He was hurting pretty bad because it was a fresh injury. You know, like that first night after you broke your arm."

"Right." She turned to Natalie. "I cried off and on all night. Mom let me sleep with her and stroked my hair while I was awake."

"You're lucky to have such a good mom," Natalie said.

I winked at my daughter. "Who loves you, baby?"

"You do, Momma." She winked back.

"Did Doc cry during the night?" Layne broke up our mini love fest. "Is that why you let him sleep in your bed?"

"He didn't cry, but he moaned and groaned a lot until I gave him some medicine to help him rest. After he took the pills, I was still worried about him. You see, sometimes the wrong medicine can make a person feel even worse."

"So, you wanted to watch over him all night?" Addy asked. "That's why you had him sleep in your bed?"

"Yes." There was no lie there.

Layne tipped his head to the side, watching me like I was in a little room down at the cop shop under bright lights. "Are you going to let him sleep in your bed again tonight?"

"Yes."

Resting her chin on her palm, Addy's eyebrows pinched together. "Should we be worried about Doc?"

"Nah, kid." Natalie ruffled Addy's hair. "Doc's a big strong man. Your mom is fretting over him because that's what moms do, right?"

My daughter nodded, patting my hand like she felt sorry for me for being so motherly.

Layne, though, still had his interrogation face in place. "Where's Doc's mom? Why doesn't he ask his own mom to take care of him?"

"Doc's mom is no longer alive, Layne. He doesn't have anyone to look after him."

"What about his dad?" Layne pressed.

"His dad is gone, too."

"Ohhh." Addy's eyes grew watery. "You mean Doc is all alone?"

"No." Aunt Zoe squeezed Addy's shoulder. "He has us now, doesn't he?"

I smiled at my aunt, my adoration for her overflowing my heart.

Addy jumped up from her chair. "We should make Doc breakfast in bed, Mom. You know, like you do for us when we're sick."

I almost pooh-poohed her idea, not wanting to wake Doc, but the excitement in her eyes swayed me. "Sure, we can do that. What should we make him?"

"He likes French toast." Addy ran over to the pantry and grabbed one of Aunt Zoe's aprons.

I turned to Layne. He'd been hanging around Cooper too much, practicing his smaller version of the detective's stony expression. "What are you thinking, kid?"

"How old was Doc when his mom and dad died?"

"Younger than you."

He mulled that over. "Did he grow up in an orphanage?"

"No, his grandfather raised him."

"His grandpa?" At my nod, his forehead puckered between his light brown eyebrows. "Is his grandpa still alive?"

"No. He died when Doc was in high school, I think."

"Does he have any brothers or sisters?" Addy asked while Aunt Zoe helped to tie the apron on her.

"Nope."

She covered her heart with both hands. "Oh, my molies. That is so sad. We need to get Doc something extra special for Christmas, like a puppy."

"No puppy, Adelynn. Try again."

She twirled in circles in the apron, smiling as it puffed out around her. "How about a rooster then? A rooster would fit right in at Doc's house with all of those boys, don't you think?"

"Absolutely not."

"I know!" Natalie raised her hand, waiting for all of us to look at her. "We could dress your mom up really nice and send her out on a date with Doc."

I nodded, liking the sound of that.

"Nahhh," Addy said, skipping over to the refrigerator. "Doc has seen Mom with no makeup and her hair all messy. We can't fool him about her anymore."

Hey! I scoffed under my breath, patting my tousled curls. What did that mean? I wasn't that hideous in the morning ... was I?

"We could get him some goldfish and let him keep them here in my room." Addy added under her breath, "In my new fish tank."

"No fish, Adelynn. You have enough critters running around here."

"Nice try, kid." Aunt Zoe chuckled, joining Addy at the counter where she was attempting to crack an egg in a bowl. "How about I help you with this?"

"Sure! Doc likes cinnamon in the mix, too. I helped him make French toast for Kelly and me last time she spent the night."

"I know what we could get him," Layne said.

"You do?" I waited, my breath held. Was Layne going to give an inch or two on accepting another man in the house for the long term?

He nodded. "But it's a Christmas secret."

"Okay, my lips are sealed."

"It's a secret from you, too, Mom."

"What about me?" Natalie asked. "You can whisper it to me."

Layne guffawed. "No way am I telling you, Nat. You tell Mom everything."

I grinned at my best friend. "He has you there." Although there was something going on in that gorgeous head that she wasn't telling me, something that I was going to drill out of her as soon as we had some time alone.

A half hour later, Natalie left to slip and slide her way back to the

Galena House. I headed upstairs with Doc's breakfast on a tray. Both kids tiptoed in after me. Addy carried syrup and a napkin, and Layne balanced a cup of coffee and a glass of water. Loaded down with a tray of food—a plate with several slices of French toast, a small dish with bacon, and a bowl of grapes and orange slices—I paused outside my bedroom door.

"What's wrong?" Addy whispered.

"The door is open." Hadn't I closed it? Maybe it was sucked open when the furnace kicked on. Old houses were tricky that way.

"Isn't that a good thing?" Layne said with a layer of sarcasm from the back of our food train.

Before I could answer, a clucking chicken threaded between our legs and strutted into my bedroom as if it were her own boudoir. Elvis headed for the chair by the window, flutter-jumping up onto it, joining Addy's cat, who sat on top of a pile of clean clothes. Bogart the cat paused in the midst of cleaning her back leg in a rather risqué pose, eyeing us for a second before returning to her task.

"Addy," I murmured, nudging my head toward the cat as I rounded the end of the bed with the tray of food. "Get them out of here."

My daughter ignored me, her eyes wide as she stared at the bed. "What's that?" She pointed the bottle of syrup toward it.

"Shhh." I looked over. What was the problem? Doc hadn't moved since we'd left earlier. His chest rose and fell in a slow, even rhythm. His face appeared relaxed, pain-free.

On my side of the bed, a small lump moved south under the covers, heading toward Doc's feet.

I gasped.

That damned cat had struck again.

Scowling, I watched as the lump skirted his right foot. Hold up. That thing looked too big to be a mouse.

Oh, my God! What was under there?

Frozen in horror, I watched as the lump made a sharp left, traveling north between Doc's ankles.

Shit! Shit! Shit!

I looked around for someplace to set the tray where the cat and chicken wouldn't be able to scarf the food Addy had worked so hard to make.

"Mom!" Layne whispered, grimacing as the lump made it to Doc's knees. "Do something before it reaches his private parts."

Doc stirred, his legs moving under the blankets.

The three of us watched with bated breath, none of us moving a muscle as Doc shifted. I winced in anticipation of his shout of surprise that undoubtedly would be followed by a bellow of pain when he tried to sit up too fast.

The lump was only inches from his knee when Doc stilled again.

"I have an idea." Addy put the syrup on the floor. She stepped around me, hovering at Doc's side. "I'll pull back the covers and get it out." She grabbed the edge of the comforter.

"Wait!" I stopped her before she could flip back the blanket.

Doc was wearing only his boxer briefs under the covers. I doubted he'd appreciate being gawked at by the three of us in the morning light.

"I'll do it." I reached across Doc to set the tray on my side of the bed.

Elvis chose that moment to take flight from the chair, landing in a puff of feathers on the end of the bed at Doc's feet.

Still bent over Doc, I glared over my shoulder at Addy. "Get. That. Chicken."

Layne inhaled quickly. "Mom, it's moving again."

I looked between my arms at the bed. The lump was slowly moving toward Doc's thighs.

"Uh-oh," I whispered, letting the tray bounce onto the bed so I could stand upright again.

Elvis squawked loud in my ear.

Doc's eyes opened. He looked from me to Addy to Layne to the chicken, which had paused mid-hunt with one leg in the air. "What's going on?"

"Don't move," I said. "There's a big mouse between your legs."

His brows furrowed. "That's not a mouse, Violet."

Elvis took a step closer to the lump, which was now a few inches from Doc's nether regions.

I hushed him with my finger to my lips. "I'm gonna reach under—"

The dang chicken went into ninja mode between Doc's legs.

Wings flapped!

Feathers flew!

Elvis screeched and squawked!

I jerked back and stepped down on Addy's bare foot. She cried out and shoved me back onto the bed. I fell toward Doc, who caught me before I came down on his ribs. Grunting in pain, he tried to kick the bird off from under the covers, but Elvis rode the waves, bent on her task.

Doc's knee bumped the serving tray, flipping the tray and dishes upside down on the comforter.

A loud squeak came from under the covers. I looked down as Elvis hopped between Doc's knees, pecking in mad-chicken mode at the lump running in circles under the covers.

"Christ!" Doc growled, trying to push me upright as the lump headed further north to burrow for safety. I tried to get my footing only to have Addy bump me forward onto Doc again as she scrambled up onto the edge of the bed.

"Don't worry, Doc," she yelled. "I got her!" Addy tried to grab Elvis, but the bird slipped free, squawking and pecking him on the knee.

"Ouch!" he shouted, shoving me lower where I had a close-up view of the lump being chased by a very determined chicken.

"I'll get it!" Layne set the coffee down on the floor and dove onto the end of the bed, playing whack-a-mole with the lump under the covers.

"No! Layne, stop!" I shouted, but Layne didn't hear me in the commotion. Pushing off Doc's hipbone, I shoved my hand under the covers. "I'll get it!"

Layne kept smacking at the lump while Addy struggled to hold onto the flapping chicken. A feather floated up my nose as I reached south between Doc's legs, making me sneeze.

"Everybody freeze!" Doc bellowed.

All three of us stopped and looked at Doc, who'd managed to push himself into a sitting position.

"Addy," he said in a calm voice. "Put the chicken down on the floor." When she obeyed, he turned to Layne. "Please get off my shins." Layne rolled through the mess of French toast and bacon onto my side of the bed and beyond, taking some grapes and orange slices with him.

"Violet," Doc frowned down at me. "Remove your hand from under the covers and step away from the bed."

I scrambled to my feet, almost knocking the glass of water over onto the carpet.

While the three of us watched, Doc reached under the covers and pulled out a large, tan-colored rodent.

"Duke!" Addy cried out. She grabbed her pet gerbil from Doc and held him to her chest, petting him between the ears. "How did you get out of your cage, you poor baby?"

I crossed my arms, glaring at where Bogart the cat had been sitting moments ago but was now suspiciously absent. "I think I know who sprung your gerbil out of jail. Did you lock the cage?"

"No. I never do."

"Why not, Adelynn?"

"Because Duke's too short to get out, and I have trouble opening it on my own, remember?"

I sighed. "Take Duke back to your room." I pointed at Elvis, who was trying to open my closet door. "Layne, return Elvis to the basement for now."

After apologizing to Doc and telling him they hoped he was feeling better, both kids left the bedroom along with the troublemaking pets. I closed the door behind them, locking it for good measure, and leaned against it.

Doc picked up a piece of bacon from my comforter and took a bite. "You guys brought me breakfast in bed."

"And then some." I scrubbed my hands down my face, wondering if he'd want to pack his clothes and head home for the next couple of weeks where he wouldn't risk further injury upon waking up each morning.

He grabbed a piece of French toast from my pillow. "So, the kids saw me in your bed." He brushed a feather off the piece of bread and took a bite. "Mmmm, cinnamon." He nodded in appreciation. "Nice touch."

"Addy made it." Well, Addy and Aunt Zoe, but right now I figured my daughter could use some bonus points for the mess her chicken, cat, and gerbil had made of his morning.

"She's a good egg." He took another bite. "Will you hand me the syrup?"

I crossed the room, grabbing the bottle from where Addy had left it on the floor. "I told them you slept in my bed because you were in pain and needed my help, just like when they're sick and hurting."

He took the syrup and popped open the lid. "Is that why I was getting breakfast in bed?"

"Something like that." I watched as he poured a few dollops of syrup on the French toast and then took a bite. "How are you feeling this morning?"

He swallowed. "Like I was run over by a chicken chasing a gerbil and then bounced on by two kids and a wild woman."

Groaning at the catastrophe, I sat down on the edge of the bed next to him, my hand finding the comforter's edge. "I guess it could've been worse."

His dark eyebrows lifted. "Really? How?"

"Elvis could've attacked something else hiding under the covers."

He looked downward. "You mean like what you just found?"

I smiled at him from under my lashes. "Why whatever do you mean, Mr. Nyce?" I spoke in a sweet, southern voice.

"Lady, you have one hell of a wake-up call at this joint." He drizzled more syrup on the piece of French toast and held it out to me.

"Welcome to my crazy life." I took a bite, licking my lips. "Mmmm, she really did do a good job with just the right amount of cinnamon."

He stared at my mouth, his body stiff all around. "Boots, either you need to stop what you're doing or finish what you've started."

"Your ribs are bruised," I reminded us both, pulling my hand out from under the covers.

He closed his eyes and groaned. "Now my ribs aren't the only place that aches, vixen."

"Yeah, but it's a good ache."

"No. No it's not."

"Lie back and let me look at your ribs."

"I'd rather lie back and have you finish what you started."

My smile teased. "Ribs first, big guy."

I propped the pillows behind his head and helped him lean back into them. When I pulled the comforter down, I sucked air between my teeth at the sight of the mottled colors on his left side. "My, what pretty bruises you have, Doc."

"Thanks. I was trying to outdo Coop's from when that bone-eater used him for a trampoline back in Harvey's graveyard."

"Well, I didn't get a look at his after that first night, but you certainly would look good next to my purple boots." I frowned down at the evidence of yesterday's screwup. "I should have been more careful, Doc."

He cussed, holding out his hand. "Help me out of bed." With a few winces, he made it to his feet with little actual assistance from me.

"You want me to help you get dressed?"

"No, Nurse Violet. I got this. I appreciate your offer, but a guy doesn't want to look like a complete wimp in front of his girl, especially after almost having his nuts and bolts pecked off by a chicken."

I frowned. "You probably want to wake up in the safety of your own bed tomorrow."

He squinted down at me. "Are you kicking me out of your bed?"

"No, just offering you an escape option."

"It's going to take more than sharing a bed with a rodent to scare me off, woman."

I closed the distance between us and slid my hands around his waist, slipping my thumbs inside the elastic band of his boxer briefs. "Good, because I have big plans."

"For your bed?"

"For you."

His smile creased his eyes. "Do tell, please."

"Well, for starters, I'm—"

Someone pounded on the door.

"Mom!" Layne shouted. "You need to come downstairs quick!"

"Why?" I stepped back from Doc. "What's Elvis chasing now?"

"It's not Elvis. It's Aunt Zoe."

I grabbed Doc's jeans off the chair where Bogart had been cleaning herself and tossed them to him. "What about Aunt Zoe?"

The boom of a shotgun blast rumbled through the house.

Chapter Eight

"Please tell me you didn't shoot Reid," I said, racing into the kitchen. Aunt Zoe wasn't there. Neither was Reid, thank the Maker. Layne and Doc joined me several hand-wringing seconds later.

I grabbed my son by the shoulders, searching his wide eyes. "Layne, what was Aunt Zoe doing before you came upstairs?"

"Ummm, well, she was rinsing out her coffee cup in the sink. Then she made a weird screeching noise that sounded like somebody pinched her. When I looked at her, she was staring out the window. She said a couple of swear words—sort of like you do, Mom, only she wasn't as loud. Then she grabbed her shotgun off the top of the fridge and told me to go get you and Doc."

Doc walked to the sink and peered out the window. "There are footprints in the snow." Before I had a chance to fully register his words, he stepped out the back door, closing it behind him.

Layne and I looked at each other with matching lined brows.

"Where's he going?" Layne asked.

I wasn't going to wait around for Doc to return and tell me. I grabbed my cell phone from the kitchen counter. "Layne, go upstairs and make sure Addy is okay, and then stay up there until I call and give you the all clear." I handed him Aunt Zoe's cordless phone.

"Where are you going?"

Grabbing Aunt Zoe's work coat hanging inside the laundry room, I slipped my arms into the sleeves. "To help Doc find Aunt Zoe." I snatched a set of house keys from the rack next to the fridge. "Lock the door behind me."

"But … but … I don't want you to go out there."

I kneeled in front of him. "I'll be okay. Doc will protect me."

His cheeks darkened. "But I'm supposed to protect you."

Now was not the time to get into this. I kissed him on the cheek. "I know you are. Right now I need you to protect your sister for me while I help Doc find Aunt Zoe."

Layne shot another frown toward the back door, and then he nodded. "Okay, but you better call me as soon as you find her."

"I promise." I walked out into the freezing morning air, waiting until Layne had flicked the deadbolt before joining Doc, who was standing at the bottom of the porch steps. He'd slipped his boots on at some point between my bedroom and the kitchen. Smart guy. I only had my slippers, which wouldn't do much good if we had to trek up to Mount Moriah cemetery.

"Where do you think she went?" I asked him.

"Her workshop." He pointed out the footprints leading to the door. "The question is, who's in there with her?"

"What makes you think someone else is in there?"

"There are tracks coming from the side gate."

I tried to see the tracks, but the sun was reflecting off the snow, blinding me. Were they Reid's? Or maybe Dominick's?

"I don't see any blood in the snow," I said, unsure if that was a good thing or not.

"Me neither."

The door to the workshop opened and Aunt Zoe leaned out, waving for us to come inside. She turned back, leaving the door ajar.

"Something isn't quite right here," Doc said, not moving.

I agreed. Her wave had seemed stiff.

"We might as well find out what's going on in there." I tried to see inside the window, but the snow's reflection lit the glass. "Whoever is with her knows we're here."

"Do me a favor, Killer." Doc took my hand. His fingers were cold. "Let me lead this time."

"Be my guest." I followed him through the snow across the backyard, retracing Aunt Zoe's tracks. Once inside, I stomped the snow off my slippers and closed the door behind me.

I looked around her workshop. Her glass cutting tools, paddles, and blocks were hanging on the pegboard, the old radio she kept high on the shelf was playing the Allman Brothers Band's "Midnight Rider," the scent of cinnamon from her plug-in air freshener spiced up the air. Everything seemed normal, so why were my hands and fingers tingling? Maybe it was nerves, but something didn't feel quite right in my bones.

I walked over to Aunt Zoe, who sat tall and stiff at her worktable. Her shotgun lay on the table in front of her.

"We heard a gunshot."

She grimaced. "I slipped on the porch step and accidentally pulled the trigger before I caught myself."

"Why did you have your gun?" Doc asked.

"I saw someone."

"Who?" I pressed. "If Masterson is bugging you again, I'm going to find that slick bastard and—" And what? That guy could bust through brick walls. Short of pulling out his nose hairs one by one, I wasn't sure what I could do to hurt him.

"It wasn't Dominick." Aunt Zoe pointed her thumb behind her.

Mr. Black stepped out from the back room.

I squawked, taking a card from Elvis's deck. Stumbling backward, I collided with Doc. He steadied me, holding onto my shoulders even after I had my footing.

The dang juggernaut always brought out the chicken in me upon first sight. It wasn't so much his extra-tall stature that made my knees wobble after the initial shock wore off. It was the similarity to another of his kind whom I'd battled twice and barely scraped by with my life both times.

Mr. Black's thick tufts of white hair contrasted sharply with his black coat, which hid his tall lanky frame. His high cheekbones looked more prominent today, his eyes sunken—not as bulbous. But his skin was still as pale as Layne's snowman outside in the yard. Had his kind evolved to blend in with the snow? A northern European chameleon?

"You have been busy, *Scharfrichter*," he said in clear English, no Slavic accent that I'd heard from others of his sort. I wondered how long he'd practiced to get rid of that telltale sign of his origins. The last time I'd heard his deep voice was over the phone almost a week ago when he'd told me we needed to talk soon about my Timekeeper duties.

"He knows about Slagton," Aunt Zoe said. "About your kills."

Already? Jeez Louise. I hadn't even had time to clean the deads' ashes out of my pea coat yet. "How?"

"When *ein Scharfrichter* performs an execution in the middle of the street in the daylight, it is sure to cause a ripple."

Who was watching? The ghost town had been a … well, a ghost town. Or had it? There were several ramshackle buildings hiding back in the trees near the informant's place. Did Mr. Black know about the blue-blooded carcass hanging on the front porch, too? Did he have any answers on the whereabouts of Cooper's informant?

"I couldn't help it. They attacked in the daylight." I crossed my arms, my hackles rising. "Is that why you're here? To tell me I'm screwing up? That I shouldn't kill while the sun is up?" I should give him Cooper's phone number. The two of them could form a peanut gallery and holler insults at me, like those cranky old men on *The Muppet Show*.

Mr. Black spread his hands wide. "Who am I to tell *ein Scharfrichter* when or how to slay? I mention this only because you have undoubtedly captured the attention of an enemy who will not be pleased to lose two allies."

I cringed. "Actually, I've killed three—another one attacked me in the woodshed the day before yesterday."

"Three?" His pale lips curved upward. "There will be retaliation for this loss. A battle will ensue."

Great. Splendid. Shit. He didn't need to look so happy about it. I shuddered mentally at his ghoulish grin. He reminded me even more of the other juggernaut who'd tried to kill me in my nightmares too many times to count.

"Retaliation by whom?" Doc asked, still holding onto me.

"Their master. These are not simple creatures. They are bred and trained to obey the commands of the leader of the hunt."

"The leader of the hunt," Doc repeated under his breath, as if contemplating each word.

"Where is their master?" Aunt Zoe asked.

Mr. Black held up one long finger. He crossed to the door, peered outside through the glass for a moment, and then left the workshop.

Doc walked over to the window, squinting in the brightness. "The hunter," he said more to himself than Aunt Zoe and me, rubbing his stubble-covered jaw. "How do I know that …?"

Shoot! I'd forgotten to call Layne. I pulled out my cell phone and dialed the house phone.

Layne answered on the first ring.

"It's me," I said. "Aunt Zoe fired her gun by accident. You and your sister can go downstairs, but stay inside the house for now."

"Where are you?" he asked.

"Out in Aunt Zoe's workshop. I'll be in soon." I had to go to work this morning. While there wasn't a big rush to be at Calamity Jane's since it was a snowy Sunday and I had no appointments, I'd agreed to go in and hold down the fort while Jerry and my co-workers were out of the office. Although Mona had mentioned being in and out throughout the day, so I'd probably see her at some point.

"What aren't you telling me, Mom?" Sheesh. Layne was beginning to sound like Doc.

"That you need to brush and floss your teeth."

At Layne's groan, I hung up and tucked my phone inside my pajamas.

Doc turned from the window. "Zoe, isn't there an old story about a hunter and its hounds?"

Before she had a chance to respond, Mr. Black returned with a mid-sized wooden crate. He closed the door behind him and placed the crate on the counter in front of Aunt Zoe, standing across the worktable from her.

Shazbot. Not another wooden crate. I joined him at the worktable, waiting to see what was inside this version of Pandora's box.

My hands and fingers tingled again, as they had when I'd first entered the workshop, yet the sensation was more of a pleasant tickle than something to set my teeth on edge. I sniffed, waiting for the usual punch of nausea that came with being in close proximity of the *others*. I smelled something akin to licorice—not uncomfortable, merely a subtle yet distinct scent. Where I was unable to get close to Dominick Masterson without upchucking my cookies, Mr. Black caused only a minor reaction. Why the difference? Did it have to do with a level of danger? I was going to need to keep testing to find out.

"Have I passed?" Mr. Black asked, one white eyebrow lifting.

There was no use playing games with him. "For now." I pointed at the box. "Please tell me this is a big chocolate Santa Claus for my stocking."

"There is only coal for *der Scharfrichter*."

Aunt Zoe chuckled.

I did a double take. "How do you know about receiving coal in Christmas stockings?"

He shrugged. "One does not exist among humans as long as I have and not understand the rituals associated with various calendar dates."

Doc rounded the table as Mr. Black lifted the lid off the crate, standing across from us next to Aunt Zoe's chair. "A weapon or a clock?" he asked the juggernaut.

"Both, if used correctly." Casting a sideways glance at Doc, Mr. Black set the lid down on the table. "*Der Scharfrichter* has chosen you to mate with, yes?"

My face warmed at the juggernaut's words. When he phrased it in that way, I felt like a horny monkey being observed by a group of grad students with clipboards.

Doc shot me a grin. "That's one way of putting it." His focus dipped to the black velvet material filling the crate.

"An interesting choice," Mr. Black said.

He made it sound like I'd had an option when it came to falling for Doc. As if my heart hadn't leapt into his arms after that first kiss and begged to be carried off into the sunset.

"Why's that?" Doc asked, his brow tightening.

Wait! Did Mr. Black know about Doc's ability to trade places with the dead? That he could sniff out ghosts? If so, how had he found out?

"You see what most cannot," Mr. Black said matter-of-factly while reaching into the box. "*Ein Orakel* is a rare gem coveted by many who crave power."

Orakel? Was that the same thing as an "oracle" in English? Like the high priests and priestesses in the ancient times sought out by leaders for advice and prophecy? Or more like the mediums in movies, who could bend spoons and read minds?

"Selecting *ein Orakel* to guide her through the other realms was wise beyond her experience."

Wise? I looked Doc up and down. Dark hair, sexy eyes, thermal hooded shirt, faded jeans, and boots. Even fresh out of bed he looked like the cover model for a magazine about rugged woodsmen, whereas my morning guise leaned more toward the loony old hag who lived under a dead tree and had pieces of forest flotsam stuck in her hair.

Mr. Black had it wrong. There hadn't been much wisdom involved on my part when it came to Doc, let alone any conscious "selecting" going on in my head.

The juggernaut drew back the black fabric. "But *seeing* is not your only gift, is it?"

Doc glanced at me, his expression guarded.

I looked back and forth between Mr. Black and the man with whom I shared a bed. What did Mr. Black mean? Did Doc have some other ability that I didn't know about yet?

"What have you heard?" Doc asked Mr. Black.

"Nothing yet, but time will shed light on even the deepest shadows. It always does."

"What makes you think Doc has other gifts?" Aunt Zoe asked, rising from her chair. She leaned her shotgun against the side of the table.

"I do not think, I know," Mr. Black said, still eyeing Doc. "He was near *der Scharfrichter* when she executed the other Timekeeper. I could feel him."

What? Doc wasn't in Ms. Wolff's apartment that night, only Cooper and me.

Then again, when I'd initially "woken" during the séance, before I'd tiptoed down the attic stairs, only Cornelius had been in the room with me. Both Doc and Cooper were absent. I'd run into Cooper a short time later in Ms. Wolff's apartment because he'd been following me in real time. Doc, on the other hand, was nowhere to be found. Yet he'd been able to pull Cooper out of the time loop I'd been caught in until Ms. Wolff's death.

"His kind are rare," Mr. Black's voice pulled me back to the present. "And they are quite ancient. A primeval lineage left over from a rather dark period of time when tyrants reigned with unchecked violence."

"How do you know his 'kind' by sight alone?" Aunt Zoe asked, staring at Doc as if he'd just stepped off the stagecoach in a remote desert town.

"They have evolved to blend in seamlessly with humans, but I interacted with one many years ago. Different beings, such as this one," he indicated toward Doc, "have distinct, telltale characteristics. Sight is not the only means of identification. Some features cannot be muted, not even after generations of crossbreeding with humans." Mr. Black blinked, his pupils morphing into black snake-like slits. He leaned over the table toward Doc. The juggernaut's nose protruded as he sniffed several times, growing snout-like for a moment before sinking back into his face. "They have a unique scent when their mate is near, especially when they perceive the presence of a threat. It is one of their few weaknesses, but this is obvious only to those who have familiarity with their kind."

I thought back to the night in the basement of the old Opera House when Dominick had sliced my palm and smelled my blood, and the day Prudence had sniffed my neck. Both had been able to detect by the scent of my skin that I was an Executioner before I even knew what I was. What other signs defined a species besides smell and looks? Was this something Mr. Black could teach me?

"Besides Doc's ability to see what others cannot," Aunt Zoe said. "Why is Violet choosing him as her partner an interesting choice?"

"This mating is a rare combination that gives *der Scharfrichter* an advantage over her enemies. They will expect her strength and fortitude in battle, but the vision of *ein Orakel* allows her to have advanced information in order to prepare for what is to come."

But at what cost? I frowned across the table at Doc, who was looking beyond Mr. Black toward the window, his body rigid. His life was even more at risk because of me than I'd thought, damn it. The doom and gloom surrounding me just kept billowing bigger and bigger. What was next? A plague of flesh-eating locusts? An army of Tiffany clones? My evil sister Susan moving in with me?

Without further comment, Mr. Black lifted a clock from the box. It was another Black Forest masterpiece.

Crud. I was hoping for a weapon. I didn't need more ticking-ticking-ticking to make my belfry even battier, but this clock was silent at the moment.

"Is that from Ms. Wolff's apartment?" I asked.

Was it from the previous group of missing clocks that had Detective Hawke all shifty-eyed? Or had Mr. Black returned to the apartment lately and grabbed another from the wall? If it were the latter, Hawke was going to be knocking on my door as soon as he returned from his forced leave and had a chance to count clocks.

"*Nein.* This one has been in my possession for many years." He looked over at me. "It will alert you when the hunter has returned. With the help of *das Orakel*, you will have the insight necessary to prepare for retaliation."

I pulled the clock closer, noting the macabre scenes carved into the wood surrounding the face. It was similar to the other clocks I'd seen. I counted eight mutant griffins on the clock. "Is this accurate?"

"In what way?" Mr. Black asked.

"Are there eight of these cat-bird creatures? Or is the number portrayed here arbitrary?" I was curious since I'd recently killed three of them.

"It is my understanding that there are often eight, not to include the hunter. However, the number in stories have varied, sometimes more, sometimes less."

Aunt Zoe ran her finger over the carvings. "So, they're pack hunters?"

"This is so."

Doc snapped his fingers. "It's the Wild Hunt."

"*Ja, die wilde Jagd.*" Mr. Black's ghoulish grin was back. "*Das Orakel* is correct."

I frowned across at Doc. "What's the Wild Hunt?"

"It's an early European myth that tells of a supernatural group of hunters in wild pursuit of their prey," he explained. "If memory serves me right, the hunters are sometimes described as fairies or elves, varying slightly depending on the culture. Periodically, the tale will describe them as ghosts. The leader of the hunt was usually associated with a god, such as the German god of war, Woden."

"But that's a myth," I said.

"Myth, you say?" Mr. Black chuckled. "I have lived enough to witness historical events woven into myths. Often they are not as fictitious as you might believe."

"So this hunter and his pack of nasty-ass creatures are chasing down their prey," I said. "What happens when they catch whatever they are hunting?"

Mr. Black looked at Doc, allowing him to answer.

Doc's brow creased. "It's been awhile since I read about this one. The story I remember best recounted that the sight alone of the Wild Hunt in process was a precursor to some horrible event, such as a plague or war. Another version said that seeing the hunters meant death was imminent for the one who witnessed it."

"It is also believed," Mr. Black said, "that anyone who encountered the hunters would be captured and delivered to the underworld where torture and death awaited."

Doc cocked his head as he frowned at the clock. "Wasn't there something about how being captured by the hunters could result in a nightmare in which the victim would be forced to join the hunt?"

"That is also correct, *Orakel.* However, this nightmare is not the sort that comes in one's sleep. It is in reference not to a nightmare, but to an altered state of reality."

Well, wasn't that just fucking wonderful? I crossed my arms. "To be clear, those creatures I dealt with in Slagton are part of this mythical hunt?"

"They are the hounds, if you will," Mr. Black said. "They will lead the hunter to the prey."

"With Violet being the prey," Aunt Zoe said, her blue eyes lined with worry when they met mine.

"In this instance, *ja. Der Scharfrichter* is now the hunted."

"Why me?"

"You've seen the hunters, Killer." Doc's eyes mirrored Aunt Zoe's.

"There is the probability of another reason," Mr. Black said, drawing all three of our gazes. "Having *ein Scharfrichter* join their hunts would be quite advantageous."

"If they want me to join, why are the mutant griffins attacking me?"

"Mutant griffins?" Mr. Black repeated. "*Ja,* that works, too."

If he approved of referring to the creatures as "mutant griffins," what would he think of "sabertooth turkeys"?

"They attack," he answered, "because they are difficult to control, at best."

"Doesn't their leader need to be here for the hunt?" Aunt Zoe asked.

"Their master is simply the leader of the pack. They are intelligent creatures. You should also be aware that according to legend, they are singularly capable of recognizing enemies, such as *ein Scharfrichter.*"

I thought back to the first creature I killed in the woodshed. "It knew my name," I told him. "I mean what I am—a *Scharfrichter.*"

"But you killed it," Aunt Zoe said. "Before it could tell the others."

"Are you sure?" Mr. Black asked.

I thought back to the scene in the woodshed. "It made a strange sound while it was hiding in the shadows, sort of like a turkey gobble but more screeching."

"It was communicating," Mr. Black said. "Another was nigh."

"So, they all know about me *and* there are five left?"

"Christ." Doc growled in his throat. "This is only one myth out of hundreds passed down through generations. What's yet to come?"

Mr. Black pointed at the clock. "Time will tell."

Doc's dark eyes locked with mine, a troubled expression on his face. "Your nightmares. I can't protect you there."

"Are you certain?" Mr. Black asked Doc. "Your kind have the potential to ward off *ein Mahr*." At our blank looks, he explained, "*NachtMahr*, a troublemaking goblin that sits on your chest while you sleep. A bearer of bad dreams that feeds on your fears."

"*Mahr*," Doc repeated. "You mean a mare, as in nightmare?"

"*Ja*."

"But Violet has been having nightmares since I met her."

I held up my hand. "Wait a second." I thought back to some of my more recent nightmares. Cooper had been there in the last few doozies, but not once had I woken up screaming while Doc was within reach. I sifted back through the months, realizing something Mr. Black had nailed. "I don't think I've had a nightmare when you're next to me."

"You are the key, *Orakel*."

Mr. Black said it as if there were no doubt. I was having trouble wrapping my head around the idea of the whole hunt business, let alone Doc influencing whether I did or didn't see Kyrkozz, Wolfgang, and all of the other monsters in my dreams.

Before I delved into the whole oracle and nightmare business any further, I returned to the clock. "Who is the lead hunter?"

And was this motley hunting crew somehow connected with the horned creature with blue blood we had found in the informant's shack in Slagton?

"I do not know. It varies with every hunt, depending on the prey."

"I thought the clock was supposed to show me what to expect."

"The clock will show you when the leader returns to this realm. Since this is your hunt, only you will know the leader. You must rely on your senses to alert you of danger."

"What are the creatures doing here?" Aunt Zoe asked. "Why are they hunting without their leader?"

"As with many hunts, they have been sent in advance."

"We have company," Doc said, looking out the window.

I turned as the door opened.

Cooper stepped inside, his hand reaching toward his holster when his gaze landed on Mr. Black. "A gunshot was reported in the area. I thought I'd start here with Parker."

"That was me, actually," Aunt Zoe explained. "I slipped on the ice and pulled the trigger by accident."

"So you weren't trying to shoot Parker's pale-faced pal here?"

"Not this time," she answered. At Mr. Black's raised eyebrow, she smiled. "You do cause a stir."

"As does *der Scharfrichter* in Slagton."

"What's going on in here?" Cooper shut the door behind him, his focus still on Mr. Black. He lifted the radio on his belt, giving an "All clear" to the dispatcher, calling the gunfire an accidental discharge.

His eyes narrowed when he saw the clock, his nostrils flaring. "Parker, tell me you didn't steal that clock from Ms. Wolff's apartment. We'll have the police up your ass again if that's one of the inventoried pieces."

"It's not from the apartment."

Cooper leaned closer, inspecting the carvings. "Are those what I think they are?"

"Yep." I looked up to find Doc watching me, his expression shielded again. "Apparently there are five more of them roaming around out in Slagton."

Cooper swore, not even bothering to keep it under his breath. "I suppose you want to drive back out there and kill the others."

"These are just the 'hounds,' Coop," Aunt Zoe told him. "The lead hunter has not arrived yet." She caught him up to speed with a quick playback of what Mr. Black and Doc had explained about the Wild Hunt, ending with, "The leader's return will be shown by the clock. Then Violet will have to defeat that hunter, too."

"Or die trying," I muttered. I turned to Mr. Black. "What happens if I move the clock's arms?"

"You shift the gateway."

"Shift it how?"

"There are known portals between the realms. It is imperative that we know the locations so that we may monitor them as necessary. If you shift a gateway, we will not know where to expect the traveler to enter our realm."

"And that's a problem because why?" I asked, wanting to be clear on this.

"The ability to track a traveler's entry point is crucial. If harm is a probability, the traveler needs to be monitored upon arrival on this realm."

"And this is part of the job of a Timekeeper?" Doc asked.

Mr. Black gave a single nod.

"So, when this clock chimes or cuckoos," Aunt Zoe said, "the lead hunter has returned to this realm?"

Another nod.

"And you already know the gateway it will come through?" I asked.

"I do, but hunters may take many forms."

"Like what?"

Before he could answer, something screeched outside the window. It didn't sound like any bird I'd heard before.

Mr. Black backed away from the worktable. "I must leave."

"But how do I know where to find the hunter?"

"When the clock alerts you to its arrival, contact me. The death dealer knows where I can be reached."

"Death dealer?" Who the hell was that?

"*Herr* Mudder," he answered.

Oh, Eddie.

Mr. Black started toward the door, but then stopped abruptly. He stared at the mirror hanging on the far wall, then stepped toward it.

It was the same mirror with foggy corners that had hung there since I was a child. The one Aunt Zoe had always said belonged to me. She'd even stuck a picture of me in my purple boots in the dented bronze frame that was etched with weird symbols. Doc had noticed the mirror months ago, commenting at the time that he didn't think it was a normal mirror.

Mr. Black reached toward the frame.

"Stop!" Aunt Zoe said, her voice sharp with warning. "You shouldn't touch that."

He lowered his hand, looking at her in the reflection. "You have *ein magischer Spiegel.*" His voice was filled with disbelief.

"A what?" I asked.

"A special mirror. A gateway." He looked over at Aunt Zoe. His eyes had morphed into the snake-like pupils again, his mouth and nose protruding. The mirror must have forced him to change, just as I'd witnessed happening to him once before when I'd flashed one of Aunt Zoe's trigger charms in his face.

"Have you told her how to use this?" he asked, his pupils and face returning to their previous state.

She shook her head, her focus shifting to me. "The time hasn't seemed right yet."

What did she mean by that?

"The time may never be right." Mr. Black stared at me for several beats, and then he shrugged. "Or it may have already come and gone, and it is too late now. Only *der Scharfrichter* will know."

Chapter Nine

An hour later, I sat behind my desk at Calamity Jane Realty pondering the meaning of life. Not life in general—I didn't give a shit about that at the moment. My focus was on the mad, mad world that had cracked open under my feet since I'd moved to Deadwood.

Fortunately, I was alone in the office this morning, unless I counted my old boss, who had been murdered months ago by one of Mr. Black's more nefarious kind. Since I didn't have a ghost radar, the way Doc and Cooper did, I wasn't sure if Jane was hanging out with me in her wispy form. Oddly enough, I sort of hoped so. Her ghost was preferable to some mythical hunter bent on bagging me for future use as an evil weapon.

Groaning, I lay my head on my desk. If only I could find a pause button on this runaway train to Hades.

I'd left for work shortly after Mr. Black disappeared into thin air. At least that's what it seemed like when I raced after him out the workshop door, wanting to know how on earth I was supposed to use Doc to get insight on retaliation in Slagton. I searched the back and front of Aunt Zoe's house, coming up juggernaut-less.

The damned, cryptic, pale-faced pain in the ass. He'd blown in and out of my morning with gale force gusts, leaving me in a tailspin.

To top it off, I now had a whole new dilemma swirling in my noggin. According to Mr. Black, I was Doc's Achilles heel. That tidbit of information grew heavier in my gut by the moment. It was no surprise that Doc would put his life on the line for me—that was old news. He'd proven from the get-go that he'd race into a burning house to keep me breathing. What had me staggering was the fact that helping me made him vulnerable on a whole new level, something beyond his control. And Doc liked having control, especially when it came to the paranormal crap raining down on him. Something he'd almost achieved prior to my entrance into his life. That was one of the hangups early in our relationship, since me plus my kids equaled chaos most days. This morning's breakfast in bed was a perfect example.

I banged my forehead on my desk a few times, cursing my Executioner bloodline. Then again, would Doc have even been attracted to me if it weren't for my hereditary tendency to kill? Had our attraction been fated? If I were just a plain ol' single mom of twins, would *das Orakel* have even looked twice when I'd tripped over his box of books the first time we met?

That seemed like a minor technicality, but call me old-fashioned. I wanted Doc to like me for me, not some genetic anomaly that turned me into a weapon.

I hadn't had a chance to talk to Doc alone about Mr. Black's revelations before he and Cooper had driven off in the detective's police Bronco. While Doc had been upstairs showering, Cooper had informed me that he and Doc were going to Bighorn Billy's to grab some breakfast and compare notes about the clusterfuck out in Slagton. Doc had kissed me good-bye as if everything between us were hunky-dory, but he'd avoided making eye contact.

What did that mean?

I wasn't new to sex. Long-term relationships, however, were still a mystery to me. Communication was key, but how did I go about asking Doc if he were still interested in pursuing this love "connection" we had been solidifying after learning the initial bond might have been an innately strategic move on my part?

"Crikey!" I pushed to my feet, needing more coffee to wash down Mr. Black's bitter pill and its hair-tugging side effects.

Mona had paid a visit to the office before I'd arrived this morning, leaving the lights on for me along with a fresh pot of coffee. According to the note she'd left on my desk, she needed to check out several potential listings and would be out until lunch.

While I poured and sugared up a cup of coffee, I told Jane the ghost about my predicament. The sound of my voice in the empty room made the whole Wild Hunt business seem less goose bump-worthy. Jane had been an ace at writing lists and setting goals. Maybe she could give me some kind of message from beyond, advising me how to proceed with this latest Executioner mess into which I'd stumbled.

I knew better than to ask for her opinion on my love life. Jane had been in the process of divorce number three when she'd been murdered. She'd warned me about mixing business with pleasure, such as my relationship with Doc who'd been my first buying client, in one of our last conversations.

"To sum it up for you, Jane," I said as I lowered into my chair. "I now have mythical hunters trying to make me their bitch, an oracle keeping my heart and bed warm and safe, and a mirrored gateway hanging on the wall in Aunt Zoe's workshop." I took a sip of coffee, leaning back and resting my boots on my desk like Ray the arrogant dickhead so often did. "I'm on a freaking roll today. It has to be all downhill from here, right?"

Jane didn't answer, thankfully.

I pulled out my cell phone and started to text Doc, but then cleared the text and shoved my phone in my desk drawer. I'd made a royal muck of everything over the last couple of days, starting with the situation in Slagton. I didn't need my blundering brain and yap trap creating a Superfund site to evacuate and decontaminate.

But damn it, I needed to make Doc understand that my feelings for him had nothing to do with his Oracle ancestry.

I reached for my desk drawer again.

The bell over the front door jingled. I lowered my feet to the floor without thinking, sitting upright like a good Realtor. The sight of Natalie rushing inside and shutting out the cold behind her made me do a double take.

"What are you doing here?" I asked as she stomped the snow from her boots.

"Coop called." She took off her coat and hung it on the coat rack. She'd changed clothes since she'd left Aunt Zoe's earlier. Now she sported a pair of overalls and a baby blue, long-sleeve thermal that made her look ten years younger than her thirty-six years, especially with her hair pulled back in a ponytail. "Is that coffee fresh? It smells good."

I nodded. "What do you mean, he called?"

"To call—a verb meaning to attempt to contact another person via a phone-like device." Her eyes sparkled.

"Don't make me vault this desk and do a full nelson slam on your smart ass."

She guffawed. "You may be a kick-butt Executioner chick when you have your funky weapons, but I've always been better at wrestling. Just ask Quint."

She was right. My brother had taught us several wrestling moves when we were kids. Natalie was wigglier and almost always able to squirm free of Quint's holds, whereas I ended up pinned every time by the big ogre. Then again, I often wondered if he took it easier on her since she wasn't his little sister.

Skirting my desk on the way to the coffee maker, Natalie grabbed a spare mug from the stack. "Coop called to tell me that I needed to pay you a visit ASAP."

What the—? "Why?"

"How in the hell should I know? The guy isn't known for his candor. All he said was that you'd received some disconcerting news, and Doc thought you might need some company."

Doc. Of course. He was still in protection mode, sending in a backup while he went offline to regroup.

She lowered into the chair opposite me, setting her steaming coffee mug on her knee. "So what's going on? Why am I being called off the bench and sent into the game?"

Doc was right. I needed my best friend to share my burden. Taking a deep breath, I spilled what had happened after she'd left Aunt Zoe's this morning, skipping the bit about the chicken and gerbil sideshow. By the time I'd finished, Natalie's coffee had stopped steaming.

She leaned forward, setting her cup on my desk. "So, according to Mr. Black, Doc and you were predestined to be together?"

"Sort of. He didn't actually say that we were hooked up by unseen forces, only that our union was beneficial to me, as if I'd thought about it and selected Doc for his skills."

"His oracle skills," she said, as if trying to cement it in her head.

"The ability to see what others cannot."

"Gadzooks, girlfriend. This shit keeps getting more screwy by the day."

"Tell me about it." I leaned my elbows on my desk, resting my chin on my hands. "I'm worried Doc will want to leave me now."

She frowned. "Why would he want that?"

"Because being with me puts his life at risk."

"It was already at risk and he was fine and dandy with that. Why would anything change?"

"I don't know. This whole revelation, along with my recent screwups in Slagton, has made me feel like some sort of untouchable."

"Untouchable? You're referring to the lowest group in the Hindu caste system, right? Not Eliot Ness's hand-picked team assembled to stop Al Capone."

I scowled. "Of course I mean the caste thing."

"Don't give me that scrunched face, whiner forty-niner. You've assembled a team of your own for hunting your enemies, just like Ness." She cocked her head. "You know, I kind of like that name for our team—The Untouchables. We should borrow it."

"We are not going to borrow the name of Eliot's team, ya gomer."

She stuck her tongue out at me.

I blew a raspberry back at her.

Her smile brought out mine. "Okay, so being around you is dangerous to Doc's health. You're apparently forgetting an important detail in your pity party celebrations."

"I'm not having a pity party." At her raised brows. "Okay, but it's a small one, more like a pity meeting. What important detail?"

"Being around you is a risk, period."

"Gee, that makes me feel so much better."

She held up her index finger. "Hear me out, Vi. When you love someone, you are weakened. Consider Addy and Layne."

"What about them?"

"You're always fretting something will happen to them."

"For legitimate reasons." I went on the defense. "Do you know how many times Layne has super-glued his fingers together? And I'm waiting for that day when Addy gets bit or stung. She brings all sorts of wild animals home without thinking about the diseases they could be carrying, like rabies or fleas with the plague. I have spent a ton of money on hand sanitizer over the years, especially since Elvis came into our lives. If Addy hadn't potty trained the damned chicken so fast, I would've had to break my daughter's heart and keep Elvis outside where the coyotes probably would've eaten her."

Natalie nodded. "You do remember that I was there with you in the delivery room when those two popped out, right? I'm not new to their antics."

"What's your point?"

"When you love someone, you're willing to take all sorts of risks to keep them safe."

"Yeah, but they're my kids. I really don't have a choice."

"Yes, you do. There are plenty of crappy parents out there who opt out from the get-go, like Rex."

"He's not a parent. He's a piece of shit sperm donor."

She growled in her throat. "Jeez, you're a pain in the ass to talk to this morning."

"Sorry. Finish making your point before I grow old and die."

"Have you considered that Doc feels the same about protecting you as you feel about Addy and Layne? That he's willing to take on the risks that come with loving you, no matter what you're up against?"

"But what if he's not? Or if he changes his mind down the road?"

She shrugged. "I'll take a sledgehammer to his Camaro SS."

I grinned. "God, I'd hate to get on your bad side."

"Nobody hurts my favorite girl," she said with a wink. Then her expression sobered. "I suspect the risks that come with loving another is what scares some people from investing in any sort of romantic relationship. A lack of attachment is the safest bet for the heart." Her tone had grown bitter.

"Are we still talking about Doc and me?" I was ninety-nine percent certain we'd shifted focus.

"I meant in general." She grabbed her coffee and took a drink.

"No, I think you meant a certain detective." I called her bluff.

It was time to talk about what had happened at the Purple Door the other night. I was tired of dancing around the truth, and since it was only the two of us in the office at the moment, now was as good a time as any to find out what was really going on in her head.

Her cheeks darkened. "I was thinking of the many bachelors I've known over the years."

I wasn't going to give up that easily. "But specifically Cooper."

She stared down into her cup. "We're not going to talk about this right now, Vi. We're focusing on you here."

"I'm tired of focusing on me. What the hell is going on with you?"

"Nothing. I'm just sitting here trying to help you make sense of your bizarre life." She gave me a lopsided smile. "And I'm trying to decide what to get your aunt for Christmas. Any ideas?"

"Stop trying to derail me. You have been acting skittish and weird since your birthday, especially when Cooper is in the room."

She stood, walking over to the front windows. I waited as she took another drink of coffee, trying to be patient with her. Natalie was never one to be rushed into any sort of admission, whether it be heart or crime related.

"I can't do it, Vi," she finally said.

"Do what? You can't tell me what has you acting so strange?"

She downed the last of her coffee, returning to set the mug on the corner of my desk. "Coop kissed me on my birthday."

"I know. I was there."

She fell into the chair across from me, rubbing her palms on her thighs. "Do you remember what he said after he kissed me?"

"That's where the scene gets a little fuzzy."

"Damn." She chewed on her lower lip. "I was hoping you'd remember, because I'm fuzzy, too. I'm pretty sure he said something about trying again with me."

I was more than pretty sure of that, but I had to dance across the coals here since I'd agreed to keep my mouth shut. Besides, I wanted to give Natalie the space to work through this whole Cooper attraction on her own. I feared blurting out something that might nudge her one way or the other, and if her world crashed around her in the future, I'd feel terrible.

"What do you think Cooper meant by telling you he wanted to try again?"

"I'm not sure, but he looks at me differently now."

Hell, Cooper had been looking at her differently since before Halloween, she'd merely had her blinders on before.

"Different how?" I pressed.

"Like he's thinking about me in my birthday suit." She kneaded her thighs. "Like he wants to do things with me. Naked things."

"That's nothing new for you. You've had tons of guys undressing you with their eyes before."

"Not tons."

"Okay, a bunch."

"A few," she conceded. "But none of them were Coop."

"I thought you were over Cooper. That you'd put that night at the Purple Door behind you."

She shook her head slowly. "There's no putting that night out of my mind. I've tried to shut it away, but as soon as I see Coop, the door pops back open and there it is again." She sucked air through her teeth. "When he undresses me with those gray eyes ..." She trailed off for a moment, her gaze growing glassy before she blinked back to me. "It's all I can do not to tackle him and finish what we started years ago."

"Maybe you should."

Her forehead puckered. "I'm on sabbatical, Vi."

"I know, but it's not like you signed a chastity contract in virgin's blood."

"Don't you get it? If I go off and sleep with Coop, I'll be right back where I was last summer." She stood, pacing in front of me. "There's no way I can have sex with him and then skip down the road on my merry way. It took me months to get over the burn of his rejection last time."

"Months?" I had my doubts about that. She usually brooded for a week or two after the breakup, but not months in the plural form.

"Months, Vi." She continued to pace. "Around Coop, I'm in serious trouble. If I open the door a little, he'll shoulder his way inside. Then when he grows tired of me, which I have no doubt he will since I'm just a 'local' girl, I'm going to be majorly screwed up in the head. Not to mention what this will do to my heart."

I understood her worries. I'd done some pacing myself in the past about falling for Doc. A lot of good all of those miles on my bedroom carpet had done me, though. "What makes you think Cooper is the love-'em and leave-'em type?"

"Please. The guy is forty-plus and hasn't been married once, let alone even had a fiancée."

"Maybe he's picky."

"He's not interested in long-term relationships."

"How do you know?"

"I ran into him at a bar down in Rapid months after our night at the Purple Door. He had a curvy blonde on his arm."

I remembered her mentioning that blonde back before she knew the truth about Doc and me. She'd been determined to set me up with

Cooper at the time.

"The jealousy bug bit me hard that night," she continued. "After a couple of beers, I dug up the courage to ask Coop if there was a wedding in his future. Right in front of the blonde, he told me he was more of a one-night stand sort of guy."

I winced. Way to go, Cooper. Had the bonehead been drunk, or trying to hurt Natalie even more for some reason?

"Maybe you're different, Nat. Or maybe he's changed his mind."

"I'm different right now only because I'm not giving in to him like all of the other women."

Were there really that many women in Cooper's past? The detective ate, drank, and slept police work. I wouldn't think there was a lot of availability on his social calendar to hook up, at least not since I'd moved to town and filled his desk with unsolved murder cases.

"If I have sex with Coop, I'm fucked."

"Aren't those one and the same?" I tried to joke. When she threatened to sock me, I held up my hands in surrender. "Okay, okay. I'm sorry but I think you're giving Cooper too much power. You are a strong, independent woman, Nat. I highly doubt Cooper's abilities in the sack could turn you into his sex slave that easily."

She stopped, jamming her hands on her hips. "Did you, or did you not, have sex *one time* with Doc and then try to ruin our thirty-plus years of friendship because you wanted to keep having sex with him?"

My neck warmed with guilt. "Touché."

She returned to pacing. "If one night of heavy flirting with Coop messed me up for months, imagine what sex multiple times with the guy is going to do."

"Multiple times? I thought we were talking about one night."

"We are. You've seen Coop's house. That man is overflowing with testosterone. On top of that, Harvey told me that Coop is extra ornery because he hasn't had a woman in a long time. One night allows multiple opportunities to blow off steam, if you get my gist."

I grimaced. "I wish you'd keep your gists to yourself."

"I'm telling you, Vi, when I kissed Coop years ago, it was like falling down a rabbit hole."

"He kissed you the other night and you remained topside." Although Cooper had been the one to pull away first, if my drunken memory was correct.

"I was totally wasted."

"That's never stopped you with men before."

Her eyes narrowed. "I believe we established whose headboard has more notches on it during our tequila shots." My middle-fingered response made her grin for a moment. "The tequila made a good buffer. On top of that, I don't think he was really giving it his all."

"How would you know? You were drunk."

"Because I've previously been on the receiving end of him giving it his all, remember? Trust me on this."

"So, you've been acting weird the last couple of days because you don't want to lead Cooper on?"

"No." She sat back down in the chair across from me. "I've been acting weird because I want to drag him off to the nearest closet and finish what we started."

"I'd avoid my closet. It has chicken feathers and eggs in it."

Natalie didn't appear to hear me. She buried her face in her hands. "I want him, Vi. I want him bad. There are times that I can hardly stand to be near him. This is horrible. Going on sabbatical was supposed to keep anything like this from happening."

I had a feeling Cooper was suffering on a similar level.

"Part of me wants to punch him in the jaw for messing with my head again."

"I'd pay to see that."

She lowered her hands, her expression forlorn. "I'd gotten over the petty jealousy and urge to finish what we'd started way back when, damn it. Why in the hell is he interested in starting up the merry-go-round again? I haven't changed, so why has he?"

"But you have changed. Since you went on this sabbatical, your self-confidence has soared."

"But I don't even wear makeup most days anymore. I don't dress to impress anyone. I've been focusing on myself for months, straightening up the mess I'd made on the inside, ignoring the outside."

"Makeup and clothes are not what make you beautiful." I drew little hearts on my desktop calendar, considering what I was about to say before letting it fly, testing it out in my brain first. It passed muster. "Natalie, whether or not you have sex with Cooper, you need to talk to him and clear the air so that our team of untouchables can continue to work together without all of the awkward friction."

"Really? And how would that conversation go?" She crossed her arms, her chin jutting. " 'Hey, Coop, I can tell by that smoldering look you keep aiming my way that you're interested in some friends-with-benefits action. What I need to know is how many times you're planning to frequent my vagina before you get bored of this local girl and move on to greener, non-local pastures again?' "

I grinned. "I don't think you should use the word *vagina*. It's too clinical. Maybe something prettier sounding, like *flower box*."

"Frequent my *flower box*? Oh jeez, you got that from high school. I remember Trip Mendletain asked you if he could plant his tulips in your flower box, and that's when I punched him in the ear."

I wrinkled my nose. "Oh, yeah. No flower box references. How about your Venus butterfly?"

"No."

"Baby oven?"

"Absolutely not."

"Lady attic?"

"Stop."

"I know. Your tunnel of love." I made some porn music sounds.

"Seriously. If you don't shut it, I'm going to tell Doc that you only want him for his oracle-ness."

"All right, I'll quit, but I was just getting rolling."

"You really need to quit looking up synonyms for bad words when you're bored at work."

"I have to keep up on this stuff. I have kids heading into high school soon, you know."

"Sure, blame your kids for your sick curiosity."

"Anyway, have you considered that maybe Cooper wants more than just a few rounds of sex with you?" I could be wrong there, but the guy wasn't acting like he was only interested in a piece of ass. There was some true pining going on with him.

"Please. I've been with enough men to know better than to start picking out a wedding dress." She sighed. "Plus, I think Coop's kind of broken."

"What do you mean 'broken'?"

"You've seen his scars. The guy has been shot to hell."

"Yeah, but that doesn't mean he's full of holes on the inside."

Wait! What was I doing? Why was I defending Cooper after all of the times he'd bitten me?

"And he sees ghosts now. That's really messing with his head."

I couldn't argue with that, but my head was pretty messed up too at the moment. "He's working through it. Doc is helping him."

Shush! Did I really want my best friend to hook up with a law dog who repeatedly threatened to throw me in jail?

"If I get involved with him and—"

"Fall in love?" I finished.

"No, interrupter. I was going to say that if I let him lean on me for emotional support, I'm going to want to fix him. But there is no fixing that man."

"We can't be certain of that without a psychological evaluation." I covered my traitor mouth before it defended the detective any further.

"It's a doomed relationship," she said with a final nod.

"Maybe so," I said through my fingers. "But what if you have the right tool for him?"

"There is no right tool for Coop." She smirked, making little quote marks in the air. "*End of story.*"

Damn Cooper for saying those three words that were now branded into her brain. Screw it. I'd tried to help him here, but short of love potion number nine, Natalie wasn't willing to get her heart singed again. I couldn't blame her.

The sound of the back door opening made Natalie and me both turn. It was a little early for Mona to be back.

Cornelius strolled into the front room wearing his favorite robe over a pair of flannel-striped pajama bottoms. A neon orange stocking cap topped off his outfit with wires coming down from each ear that joined in the middle and disappeared into a pocket in his robe. What was he listening to? A choir of moaning ghosts? Heavy metal attic chain rattling?

"Have either of you seen my alarm clock?" His cornflower blue eyes seemed droopy at the corners. He pulled out Jerry's desk chair and took a seat.

Natalie glanced around at the other desks. "What's it look like?"

"A small, thin rectangular device with a large digital screen that has numbers on it."

I sighed. "You mean your cell phone?"

"One might call it that."

Most people did. I crossed my arms. "Did you just wake up?"

"Partially."

Natalie chuckled. "Are you sleepwalking?"

"Almost. I haven't officially gone to bed yet."

What had he been doing all night? "Why not?"

"I've been wiring the office. It takes time to set up the mics to receive optimal results. Not to mention my commute time between buildings slowed me down since your ghost boss refuses to let me keep my equipment in her old office."

Set up what mics?

"Between buildings?" Natalie hit me with raised brows. "He's using Doc's office now, too?"

I nodded. "Doc is letting him keep his monitors and other paranormal gadgets in the back room." I frowned at Cornelius, who was scanning the room. "You set up microphones?"

"Correct. I'm going to talk to your boss later tonight when she is usually most active. I'll expect you here to join me after the sun sets."

What? No. It was Sunday. "It's a school night."

"True. We'll be learning about your boss's experiences post mortem."

"I'm not talking about ghost school, Cornelius. I like to be home on Sunday nights with my kids to get them ready for another week in the classroom." It was one of the few ordinary tasks left in my life. I wasn't willing to give it up tonight to chat with a ghost, not even Jane.

"Then we'll wait for your offspring to retire for the evening. Will ten-oh-seven work? I'll make sure the mics are still functioning. Your boss likes to play tricks on me."

"Her name is Jane, remember?" Hold on a second. "Are you talking about EVP mics that pick up electromagnetic activity?"

Natalie's gaze bounced between us. "Is that like ghost airwaves?"

I nodded. "Or are these microphones you planted able to pick up live human voices?"

"Both."

My gaze narrowed. "And they are working already?"

He tapped his ear, the wire below it jiggling. "I have been up most of the night making certain of that."

That explained the earphones. "You're kidding me." I exchanged frowns with Natalie. "Have you been listening all morning?"

"More or less. I dozed off a few times in between your monologues." He stroked his goatee. "Being an Executioner explains the dark clouds I often see swirling in your aura."

"Dammit, Cornelius!" Now I had to add his name to the list of those who knew the truth about me. I stood and strode over to Jerry's desk, leaning over him and his bright orange hat. "Those were private conversations." Especially the one that involved my talking to a ghost about Doc and Slagton—and the Natalie and Cooper song-and-dance. "You better not have recorded anything I said while you were eavesdropping."

"Nothing was recorded," he assured me, clasping his hands together on the desktop. "As I said, I was only partially listening while I was awake. Rewiring a condenser microphone requires considerable concentration, you know."

No, I didn't. I jabbed my pinkie toward his face. "Promise me you'll keep your lips sealed about what you heard."

He looked cross-eyed down at my pinkie, one black brow rising. "Why are you pointing your smallest digit at me?"

I lifted one of his hands and wrapped my pinkie finger around his. "Pinky promise me you'll keep your lips closed about what you heard."

His forehead creased. "Is this another mating ritual?"

Natalie laughed.

"It's called a pinkie promise."

"The entwined digits represent what?" His cornflower blue eyes met mine. "Will you remove my digit if I speak about what I've overheard?"

Jiminy Cricket! Did he seriously believe I would ... "Yes," I said. "If you spill one word, I will chop off your finger and add it to my collection of pickled pinkie fingers."

He didn't even crack a smile. "And how will I win your 'pinkie finger' in this agreement?"

I sputtered, looking over at Natalie.

"If Violet and I don't show up here tonight for your recording session," she said, "Violet will forfeit her pinkie finger."

I gaped at her. "Really?"

She shrugged in response, a grin shadowing the corners of her lips. "Pinkies are a serious wager."

"Good." Cornelius tightened his pinkie around mine. "It's a deal."

I pulled my finger free, wondering how Doc was going to feel about talking to Jane tonight. "What exactly did you hear, Cornelius?" Besides the bit about me being an Executioner.

He pulled out a small recording-looking device from his robe pocket, clicking it off. "First, I need to inform you that Jane didn't respond to you, but I believe reaching out this evening will have more encouraging results with the help of your Tall *Oracle*."

Fudge-a-matic. He'd heard my whole conversation with Jane about Slagton, Doc, Mr. Black, and everything in between.

To Natalie, he said, "Second, I may not have a wide range of experience with live humans, but I have learned that you cannot fix people, only yourself. That being said, the detective isn't broken. He merely becomes cranky when forced to bend."

And now Cornelius knew about that mess. If Cooper found out that Cornelius was aware of his feelings for Natalie, he was going to drag me out to Slagton, tie me to the porch post next to that dead thing's carcass, and leave me for the hunters to gut and eat.

"Do you have any other nuggets of wisdom to share?" I asked, sarcasm dripping. We might as well know the full extent of verbal leakage we'd suffered.

Cornelius's black brows wrinkled, his expression thoughtful. "Yes, I do. I have to agree with Violet." He stuffed his recorder back in his robe pocket, and then gave Natalie one of his crooked smiles. "When you proposition the detective, try using more traditional methods to elicit a gentlemanly response. It has been proven via several university studies that many male humans, especially those over the age of thirty, enjoy a less vulgar style of flirting before mating."

I cringed. Were we really having this discussion with Cornelius? "Thank you for your insight, Professor Curion, doctor of love. I propose we change the subject now to something that won't get me thrown in jail if Cooper finds out we were discussing his sex life."

Natalie silenced me with her hand. "Give me an example of an old-fashioned proposition, Cornelius."

"I've always found the offer to 'take a stroll down Petticoat Lane' with a pretty lady quite titillating. I believe that phrase was used more widely in the early nineteenth century."

"Coop's not exactly old fashioned," Natalie said, her mouth pursed.

"What if he doesn't know what 'Petticoat Lane' refers to?"

"I suppose you could then offer to let him play in your Field of Dreams. That expression conjures many romantic notions, incorporating naked flesh and wild flowers." Cornelius stood. "Now if you'll excuse me, I need to prepare for tonight." He looked at me. "Where do you keep your crowbar?"

Back in Slagton, where I liked to kill hunters from other realms.

"Why do you need a crowbar?" I asked.

"There is a jammed door between me and a particular Hellhole that you and I must explore further."

Chapter Ten

I was going to throw Cornelius down the Hellhole.

"I'm telling you, this damned door isn't going to budge unless Jane wants it to," I said to Natalie, handing her the crowbar.

"Tell him that, not me." She stepped forward to try her hand at it.

I looked up at the video camera Cornelius had installed in one of the corners of Jerry's office. "Did you hear what I just said through your fancy microphone?"

My cell phone chirped. I grabbed it from the top of the filing cabinet and frowned at the words on the screen.

"Who's that?" Natalie asked, wedging the pry end of the crowbar into the jamb next to the doorknob.

"Cornelius."

She pushed on the bar. "What did he say?"

"That the microphone in this office is a state-of-the-art parabolic unit able to hear voices up to 300 feet away." My phone chirped again. "And that I need to stop mumbling and speak more clearly when I'm talking to him."

Natalie chuckled, stretching her neck from side to side.

I walked over to the camera and gave Cornelius a closeup of both middle fingers.

Natalie's phone pinged. She left the bar jammed in the door crease and pulled her cell phone from her overalls, her grin spreading. "He wants to know if you are offering both of your middle fingers in addition to your pinkie in your deal."

Grumbling with more clarity, I strode back to where Natalie stood.

She grunted and pushed on the bar, trying to pop open the closet door that had somehow sealed shut after that first descent through a hole in the floor leading to the musty cellar.

We'd discovered what Cornelius liked to call a "Hellhole" on that trip. Soon after, he'd recorded a screech that he believed was coming from the grate-covered hole. Next thing I heard, the closet door had somehow become stuck closed, refusing to budge.

"It's like someone glued it shut," Natalie said, moving to the other side of the crowbar and tugging on it.

"We need some dynamite or TNT."

Natalie's phone pinged.

"And where are you going to find dynamite, Wile E. Coyote?" She wiped her hands on her overalls and pulled out her phone again. "Are you going to order it online from the Acme Corporation?"

"Maybe I will, just to show you up, toots." I pointed at her phone. "What does Deadwood's great and powerful Oz have to say?"

She read from her phone: " 'Dynamite has a typical maximum shelf life of a year, after which it sweats nitroglycerin and becomes unstable. Trinitrotoluene, aka TNT, has a lower energy density and convenient handling properties.' "She lowered her phone. "Cornelius recommends neither."

Jerry's office door swung open. I looked over, expecting to see Cornelius in his robe. The sight of Mona in a black knit sweater and a rose-colored cashmere scarf that matched her lips made me do a double take.

Her gaze moved from me to Natalie, who was still trying to jimmy the door. Her auburn eyebrows arched. "Doing a little breaking and entering, are we?"

Shoot! I thought Mona would be gone for another hour or two. I frowned over at Natalie. She cringed.

"We are … uh …" My mind was a desert wasteland, not a lie to be found. "This isn't what it looks like."

She crossed her arms, leaning against the jamb. The sweet scent of her favorite jasmine perfume wafted into the room. "You mean you're not trying to get that door open so you can sneak into the cellar?"

My jaw unhinged. I thought Cornelius and I were the only two who knew about the hole in the closet floor. Well, besides Doc and Nat, and Jerry. And Aunt Zoe. And maybe Cooper. "You know about that?"

"Of course. I've worked here long enough to know all about this building's hidden secrets."

"What other secrets does it have?" Did she know about the Hellhole?

She smiled. "Besides an interesting history including a murder, a bootlegger, and two suspicious fires, I suppose the ghost who haunts it is worth mentioning."

"Ghost?" Natalie and I said together.

"Yes, ghost. Isn't that the reason Cornelius Curion is staying in the upstairs apartment?"

"Oh, yeah." Jerry had informed all of us early on so we wouldn't be surprised by Cornelius's appearance throughout the day. "That ghost."

She must be thinking of the one that resided in the building when I'd first started working at Calamity Jane Realty. The one that had kept Doc from stepping over the threshold some days in an effort to avoid its ectoplasmic hug. I'd often wondered where that ghost had gone, because ever since Jane had returned to haunt the place, Doc hadn't sensed it. Had Jane shooed it away, or had she somehow locked it up somewhere? Was that what Cornelius had heard shrieking from the basement that night on his EVP recorder? Was that why Jane had blocked off access to the Hellhole?

Natalie pulled the crowbar free and wedged it into the crease between the door and jamb a few inches further down, closer to the hinge.

"You know," Mona said to her, "unless you have some C-4 hidden in your overalls, you're not going to get that door open."

I looked up at the video camera. "See! We need TNT." I glanced at Mona. "Do you know anyone on the bomb squad? I don't think I should put in the request for it given my reputation at the police and fire stations."

She laughed. "You're funny."

I was sort of serious.

"If you two want to go down in the cellar," Mona continued. "You're going to need to convince Jane to open the door first."

Skirrrrchhhh.

Natalie stopped working the crowbar, her brow creeping upward.

Had Mona just referred to Jane?

"Come again," I said when my brain picked itself up off the floor.

"Jane Grimes, our deceased boss. The one with whom Cornelius is here to make contact." Her gaze held mine, clear and steady. "Rather, her ghost."

"You know about Jane's ghost?"

"Sure."

"For how long?"

She picked some lint off her sweater sleeve. "I had my suspicions a week or so after her funeral when Jerry set up shop in here. I'd come into the office in the morning and things would be moved around on my desk. The placement reminded me of how Jane preferred our desks be set for client visits."

That was the same thing that had happened to Jerry, only on a much larger scale. Multiple instances of furniture moving around on its own in his office were what had spurred him to reach out to Cornelius.

"I didn't think too much of it at first due to our regular ghost. Usually, though, that ghost kept to itself."

"But Jane's ghost is more active?" I lowered myself onto the corner of Jerry's desk, still reeling from the fact that Mona had known about Jane's ghost all along. What else did she know?

"Much more. Especially since Jerry and I ... " She grimaced, looking at his desk.

"Kissed?" I finished.

Her face reddened, her eyes shifting to Natalie. "It was only a friendly kiss."

Really? Because it looked more like a back-bending, hot and steamy lip-lock when I caught them in here.

Natalie's grin had a teasing tilt to it. "Tell me something, Mona. Does Jerry kiss as well as he plays basketball?"

Mona sputtered, her neck turning the same shade as her cheeks.

"I mean," Natalie continued, her eyes twinkling, "does he slam dunk when he gets in close? Live up to his old 'Slammer' nickname? Or does he use more finesse these days when taking it to the hole?"

"Natalie!" Mona chastised, but her smile lit her face for a second before she dimmed it down. "I have no idea to what you're referring."

I pshawed her. "We have eyes, Mona. We've seen the way you sneak glances at him when you think he's not looking."

"Shhh," she said, pointing at the ceiling.

"Cornelius isn't up there. He's over in Doc's office." And probably eavesdropping, to boot.

"I mean Jane," she whispered. "It was after we kissed in here that she really started messing up Jerry's office."

I hadn't put that together before now. "You think she is jealous?"

Mona winced. "I hope not, but the two coincide enough to make me wonder."

"Is that why you've cooled toward Jerry?"

She toyed with the ends of her scarf, lowering her gaze. "Mostly."

"There's another reason?" I pressed.

"Yes, but this is not the place to discuss that."

Did she mean it wasn't the place because of Jane possibly listening? Or Natalie? Or was there another reason?

Natalie's phone pinged. She looked down at the screen. "Cornelius wants you to ask Mona to join us tonight."

I shook my head, pinching my lips tight. Mona didn't know the truth about me. If she sat in when we tried to talk to Jane, there'd be no hiding my *other* job.

Or Doc's.

As it was, I doubted Doc would appreciate my dragging him here tonight with his bruised ribs. Would he think I was using him for his ability to "see" after Mr. Black's revelation? Was I?

"Join you in doing what?" Mona asked, looking from Natalie to me.

"We're going to have a little ... um ... party," I said, cursing Cornelius for putting me in a tough spot. I didn't want to lie to Mona, but the truth had a lot of potholes.

"A party in the office?" she asked.

I shook my head. "Not really a party-party. More like a huddle."

"Round-robin fits even better for it," Natalie said.

"There will only be a handful of us."

Mona's eyebrow arched. "Like who?"

"Nat and me, of course."

"And Cornelius," Natalie added.

"What about Doc?" Mona asked.

"Probably." I tried to play it cool, my expression schooled. "He'll want to ensure I make it home safely on the snowy roads."

"Anyone else?" she pressed.

Besides Jane's ghost? "Probably not."

Another ping came from Natalie's phone. "Uh, Vi?"

"Not now, Nat," I said, figuring Cornelius wanted to argue his case for inviting Mona. Tonight's list of attendees wasn't up for discussion.

"I think you might want to read this, though."

"Tell Cornelius—"

"It's not Cornelius." Natalie handed me her phone.

Harvey's name was at the top of the screen: *Tell Sparky we got us a fox in the henhouse.*

Where are you? I wrote. Why was he texting Natalie instead of me? *Next door watching you on the boob tube.*

I looked up at the camera. What was Harvey doing at Doc's? And what fox? Was he talking about Cornelius?

"We know about Cornelius," I told the camera.

The phone in my hand pinged. *Do you know about your sister?*

My sister? The Bitch from Hell? Red flashed behind my eyes at just the thought of Susan and the many wounds her claws and sharp teeth had caused since we were kids. From burning my favorite teddy bears to seducing my boyfriends, my half-sister had been doing her best for over three decades to steal anything that was mine and stomp on it with her spiky heels.

What about Satan's bride? I typed.

She's in town.

Damn it! I'd rather face off with another one of those mutant griffins. I tried to decide if I had any give-a-shit left to deal with Susan right now.

I wrote my reply while snarling: *As long as she stays away from me, I couldn't care less.*

Is next door far enough?

Susan was in Doc's office? *What is she doing there?*

Waiting for your stallion.

"Jezebel!" I shoved the phone back at Natalie. It turned out I still had a good helping of give-a-shit after all.

"Cover for me," I told Mona, racing past her.

I didn't bother with my coat, blasting out the front door. I barely felt the rush of cold air as I flew to Doc's office.

The sight of Susan sitting in the chair behind Doc's desk brought me to a hard stop. "Get out of his chair," I ordered in greeting.

"Hey, *big* sis," Susan said, her lips extra red this morning. She must not have wiped her mouth after finishing off her last victim.

"Get out of that chair now, Susan!" I planted my hands on my hips. "Or I'll drag you out of it by your hair."

"Wow," she chuckled, flipping her long brown hair over her shoulder. "You're extra tense this morning. Did you forget to eat? I'd forgotten how grouchy you get without your plate of carbs."

I reached across the desk for her, but she dodged my hand.

"Okay, I'm getting up." She rose from the chair like a snake from a basket, her hands raised in surrender. "Relax, Violet."

For once she wasn't dressed like a pole dancer. Instead, she'd donned her black snow-bunny ski pants and a puffy white coat. Her gazelle legs seemed extra long in the knee-high faux fur boots with beaded leather tassels. She looked ready for the star-filled slopes of Vail, not the brick streets of Deadwood.

I swallowed a lungful of fire, facing the man-stealing harlot across Doc's desk. "I'll relax when you've permanently relocated to Antarctica."

She snorted. "There are only research stations there."

I was thinking more along the lines of a deep-sea submarine stuck underneath the ice.

Her gaze traveled down my dark green sweater dress, her smile smug. "Oh, honey." Her tone had a razor-sharp cutting edge. "You really should stick to ankle boots and leave knee-high leather to those of us with long legs. Those just make you look chunkier."

Forget shipping her off to winter with the emperor penguins. I was going to cram the bitch in a rocket and blast her to Neptune.

Movement behind Susan caught my attention. Harvey was inching his way toward us along the back hallway. He held his index finger to his lips, mouthing something to me. Unfortunately for both of us, I sucked at reading lips, especially when said lips were surrounded by a bushy beard.

Focusing back on Susan, I pointed my thumb behind me at the door. "Leave. Now."

She crossed her arms, pouting. "But I just got here."

"This office is off-limits to you from here on out, got it?"

Her chin lifted. "What if I don't 'got it'?"

As much as I'd love to sit on her and pluck her nose hairs out one by one, I couldn't touch her. It'd break my mom's heart, and I'd promised my dad not to do that again. But … "I'll sic Natalie on you."

Susan's kohl-lined eyes narrowed. "You keep that psycho away from me." She touched her hair. "She cut off a piece of my hair last Saturday when I came up here for our family dinner. I didn't realize it until I got home that night and she texted me."

This was news to me. "Oh, really? What did her text say?"

"She was making a voodoo doll with my hair and asked if I thought ten needles were enough to do the trick, or if burning the doll over an open flame would be more painfully satisfying."

God, I loved Natalie and her warped sense of revenge. "I can try to keep Nat close, but she slips her leash every now and then. I can't be held responsible if you are within reach when she's loose. She does like to bite."

"You have rotten taste in friends."

"Ah, Susan. Jealousy is such an ugly color on you." I pointed at the door again. "Don't let it hit your skinny ass on the way out."

Her nostrils flared. "Mom has a message for you. I'm not leaving until I've delivered it."

"You know there are telephones made for the sole purpose of communication. You should use one next time. Better yet, pencil, paper, and a stamp."

"She also wanted me to drop off some goodies at Zoe's."

Susan had stopped using the "aunt" prefix with Aunt Zoe's name when she found out she was not my dad's kid, but rather the child of a man whom our mom had briefly dated when she and my father were separated for several months. Aunt Zoe told me that Susan's omission didn't bother her. That she'd long ago learned not to allow my sister's games to affect her. I wish I had Aunt Zoe's strength on that front, because right now I was thinking about poking Susan with a bunch of pins, and I meant the real flesh and blood woman, not the voodoo doll version.

"Neither of these reasons explains your presence in Doc's office."

She pulled a pair of fur-lined gloves from her coat pocket. "I want to see your boyfriend. Mom won't shut up about him. Call it a case of curiosity."

"I call it a five-gallon crock of shit. Mom was drunk that night. I doubt she remembers much about Doc."

"Ah, but that's where you're wrong." She slid on one glove. "She's quite enamored with him."

"And you're not here to *see* anything," I continued. "You're here to touch, steal, and destroy. That's what you do. It's what you've always done to anything that mattered to me."

She wrinkled her nose. "Really, big sis. Your flair for the dramatic could burn this building to the ground."

"Take an English class, tart monkey. Flair with an 'i' doesn't mean the same thing as F-L-A-R-E."

Her face pinched into the sneer I'd glared at across the dinner table too many times to count. "Sticks and stones, my li'l potbellied piggy."

My fists clenched at her favorite childhood insult.

The door behind me opened. A gust of cold air washed over my backside. Oh, shit. My gut blanched. I hoped like hell that was Natalie and her voodoo doll and not Doc.

Harvey joined us in the front room, but Susan didn't see him since her back was to him. Half of his face was scrunched in a big cringe.

Susan froze in the midst of pulling on her second glove, her gaze moving north. Her eyes widened for a fraction of a second, and then the ski-bunny shifted into street-corner-ho mode. "Well, hello Mr. Tall, Dark, and Handsome."

My ears started ringing, blocking out everything but the sound of her sultry voice. I watched the man-stealer lick her lips, making them extra shiny, and then bat her fake lashes several times. "You must be the one and only Doc Nyce." She tossed her long, straight hair over her shoulder, mimicking shampoo commercials. "I've heard a lot about you, but my mother left out a few …" Her gaze trailed south, her lips parting ever so slightly. "Stimulating details."

My stomach cramped. Nausea bubbled up my esophagus, burning the back of my throat. Sweat beaded my brow.

"I'm Susan, by the way." She held out her hand like a princess, waiting for a kiss on the knuckles. "Violet's much *younger* sister. "

Chapter Eleven

Y ou're Violet's sister?"
Stop the presses! That wasn't Doc's voice.
A wave of nausea steamrolled over me. I gagged a little, clutching my
stomach, and looked over my shoulder.

Dominick Masterson closed the door behind him. He hit Susan
with one of his mega-watt smiles as he took her hand, dropping a kiss
on her gloved knuckles. "Hello, beautiful."

I stumbled toward the far corner of Doc's desk, putting the visitor's
chair between Dominick and me. I needed more distance from the
charming devil, or I'd be spray-painting Susan's faux fur boots with the
contents of my stomach.

Harvey dropped into Doc's leather chair, leaning back with a shit-
eating grin on his bristly cheeks. "Looks like I showed up just in time
fer some good ol' honky-tonkin' fun."

"You should leave," I told Harvey, swallowing another swell of
queasiness. He wasn't invulnerable to Dominick. I'd seen the slick son
of a bitch lure men as well as women. Harvey was at risk as much as
Susan of falling under the rogue's spell.

"And leave you standin' in the middle of this stampede?" Harvey
shook his head. "I've been wantin' to see what all the fuss is about,
anyhoo."

Dominick glanced in my direction as he released Susan's hand.
"Your sister is such a lovely flower. A delicate blossom ready to be
plucked."

Delicate blossom? Susan? Ha! She was more like poison ivy.

"But she doesn't have your scent," he added.

What scent was that? My Executioner scent? I decided not to ask him to clarify in front of Susan.

"Leave her alone," I said half-heartedly. As much as I'd like to watch Susan be manipulated by a man for once, she was my mother's child.

Susan let out a lovesick sigh that had me feeling the urge to hurl once more. "You are as handsome as Mom said."

Harvey snorted. "She's lassoin' the wrong steer again."

I squeezed the bridge of my nose. Over the last month, Cornelius, Cooper, and Harvey had all been mistaken for Doc. I thought I'd cleared the air on his identity after my family's disastrous dinner party a week ago. Apparently not.

I debated on telling Susan the truth, but decided to focus on the bigger problem at the moment. "What are you doing here?" I asked Dominick.

He was dressed in biker garb today—black leather jacket, jeans, boots, and gloves. Quite a shift from his usual Armani suit, long wool coat, and expensive Italian shoes.

His wicked smile fit his bad-boy guise. Fortunately, I was immune. "You've been avoiding my calls, Violet."

"Only one." I'd missed a call from him yesterday while I was back in Slagton. After returning to signal-civilization, I'd been too busy trying to figure out what the hell I'd stumbled into back there to call him back. "How did you know to find me here?" Rather than at my office.

"I was driving past when I saw you rush over here."

Susan's moony-eyed expression was similar to Aunt Zoe's when Dominick had her wrapped around his finger weeks ago at Bighorn Billy's Diner. "I'd never avoid your call," she said, running her fingers down his leather coat sleeve.

He scowled down at her hand, and then stared at her for several seconds. His dark gaze returned to me. "How is it you two are sisters? I can't see any …"

"Their mouths are both heart shaped," Harvey pointed out. At my glare, he shrugged. "It's a natural-born fact."

"Ah, now I see it. It makes one wonder if you kiss the same."

Rex would have an opinion about that, but I wasn't interested in hearing the bastard's answer. "My sister is of no concern to you."

"Don't listen to her," Susan said in an exaggerated whisper, then leaned into Dominick, sniffing his collar. "You smell delicious. I want to lick you all over."

Dominick patted her head. "She'd make a cute pet."

I'd be tickled pink to have him teach Susan how to roll over and play dead. "I thought you wanted my aunt for that."

"My plans for Zoe are much more stimulating. She has depth that I will enjoy exploring with infinite patience."

My molars ground at his use of the future verb tense, as if it were a fact that would come to be. Whether or not I could catch a *lidérc* would be answered in time. Until then, I'd appreciate a little bolstering of my abilities from the cocky cheeseball who hired me for the job.

"I do believe yer saddlin' horses that don't belong to you, Masterson." Harvey spoke up, looping his thumbs in his suspenders.

"According to whom, Mr. Harvey?" Dominick lowered his head slightly, staring at Harvey from under his brows.

A fresh dew of sweat coated my upper lip. I looked over at Harvey, waiting for the ol' boy to start spouting sonnets in Dominick's honor like the other victims I'd witnessed falling under the scoundrel's spell.

"Accordin' to Zoe, fer one." Harvey scratched his bearded cheek as he held Dominick's gaze. "I can see how ya might be thinkin' you can charm the skin off any ornery rattlesnake with yer knee-wobblin' good looks, but Zoe's stubborn enough to make a mule back down. That girl can whip her weight in wildcats, 'specially when her horns are out."

I did a double take. How was Harvey resisting Dominick's magnetism? I thought I was the only one impervious to it.

"I appreciate your attempt to warn me off Zoe, Mr. Harvey. Like you, I prefer my courtesans feisty. It promises great fervor in bed." Dominick stroked his finger down Susan's cheek, drawing a cooing sound from her. "This one is a paltry comparison to Zoe, but she could be useful as a plaything while I wait for my prize." His focus shifted to me again. "As well as incentive for her sister to return my *lidérc* with haste."

Was he seriously trying to use Susan as a means to inspire me? A voice inside my head cackled with laughter. Schooling my expression in the face of his challenge made me sweat anew. "Let me get this straight," I said, wanting to savor this moment a bit longer. "You want to ensnare my poor, sweet little sister with your merciless love spell, turning her into an amoral sexual slave in order to motivate me to hurry up and catch your pet?"

He beamed with confidence. "Exactly."

I must be dreaming? I pinched my leg. Nope, it was the real deal.

Crossing my arms, I leaned my hip against Doc's desk and pretended that I actually cared about Susan's feelings. All the while, I tried to think of the ways this situation in which I'd found myself might come back to bite me in the ass. Besides my parents' opinion on the matter, which held a lot of weight, why did I care if Dominick exploited Susan?

I had a notion of his game plan. He figured if he had my sister by the scruff of the neck, he had me on a leash, too. Oh, what delightful irony. I fought down a gurgle of giggles.

"Stay away from Susan," I said, trying to sound like I meant it. Harvey's throat-clearing told me how woefully short I fell from the mark. Robots showed more emotion in their tone.

"Your sister is not part of our original deal," he said. "Only Zoe. That makes her fair game." Apparently, Dominick was too taken with his plan to control me to notice my half-hearted objection.

An idea struck, sobering me. "Maybe we should make another deal, then," I suggested. "An addendum to the original."

"Careful, Sparky." Harvey leaned forward, resting his elbows on Doc's desk. "Yer wadin' into quicksand here."

Dominick's eyes narrowed. "I'm listening, *Scharfrichter.*"

"I've run into a situation back in Slagton."

"So I've heard." Dominick chuckled. "You really should try to be more discreet when you hunt. Although some are of the opinion that staging an execution in the middle of town demonstrates extreme confidence."

"Or she has a big gap in her hedge." Harvey added his two bits, sounding like his nephew. He scowled at me. "I say let yer sister go and focus on tamin' one wild mustang at a time."

I respected Harvey's opinion, but he hadn't heard Mr. Black's news about the not-so-mythical pack of hunters and the new target on my back. "I need information, Dominick."

"What makes you think I can give you what you need?"

"You have the air of one who gets answers when he wants them."

He crossed his arms. "If I acquire the information you need, what do you have in exchange?" He glanced at Susan, who was still clutching his arm, her eyes wide and starry. Was she even hearing this discussion through the heart bubbles popping in her head? "Your sister?"

Tempting. Very tempting. But no. "I'll bring you a pet from Slagton."

Harvey shook his head at me. "That there's a leaky boat yer climbin' into, girl."

Dominick snorted. "What would I want with a *Drakona Ragana?*"

Come again? It sounded like he said *draw-cone-a raw-ganna*, with a trill at the beginning of that *raw*-word. "A what?"

"*Drakona Ragana*," he repeated more slowly.

"Does that mean 'mutant griffin'? Because that's what they look like."

His sigh was edged with derision. "Let me use a word you might understand, *Scharfrichter*. They are a breed of chimera."

"A chimera, ya say." Harvey finger-combed his beard. "Isn't that one of them fire-breathin' critters from Greek mythology with a bunch of mixed animal parts?"

"Your description does injustice to a magnificent predator, but yes."

"Chimeras are supposed to be big ol' monsters," Harvey said. "These critters' heads are only about chest high."

"They are obviously a sub-species," Dominick clarified.

"Whatever the dang name is," I interrupted. "It would make a great pet, and you could teach it to hunt."

Dominick's gaze narrowed. "I accept. What knowledge are you seeking?"

"My informant is missing." Well, actually Cooper's informant, but I'd rather conceal the detective's connection to the matter as a precautionary measure. "When I visited his place in Slagton yesterday, there was a headless beast hanging from the porch." I wasn't going to open a can of worms about the official name of the decapitated thing with blue guts. "My informant was nowhere to be seen. I need to know where he is."

"Why does this matter to you? You are a *Scharfrichter*, not a detective."

"The reasons for my curiosity are no more your business than your motives for wheeling and dealing are mine."

He nodded slowly. "And if I give you what you want, you will deliver a *drako*—a chimera to me?"

"Correct, as long as your information is timely and satisfies me."

"Satisfies?" One dark eyebrow lifted. "And if you fail to deliver on your end of the deal?"

"I won't fail." That sounded far more certain than I felt.

"You might." He toyed with a strand of Susan's long, straight hair. "I want to play with your sister until I tire of her."

I held his stare. How many times had Susan done that very thing with a man? It would be sweet justice to see her being used and manipulated at someone else's will for once.

But I couldn't allow that, dammit. I couldn't face my parents, nor could I live with myself. If anyone were going to mess with my sister and treat her like a pet, it was going to be me. "You can't have Susan. I don't deal in humans anymore."

He'd burned me before with his slick trick of finagling Aunt Zoe into the deal. I wasn't going to let him double up on my family members. Not even with the Bitch from Hell.

"We'll discuss forfeiture penalties *if* I fail to deliver," I told him. "Until then, the deal is one chimera in exchange for information on the Slagton resident's whereabouts, and that's it."

His smile gave me the chills. "And when will you be part of a deal, *Scharfrichter*?"

"You'd regret that deal. I don't think you can handle me."

What Dominick hadn't realized yet is that I couldn't be within touching distance of him without feeling the need to toss my cookies. Something about him set off my internal alarms. But that was my secret, and I'd rather he not know.

"But trying to corral you would be exciting."

"Or deadly."

He sobered. "Possibly. I accept your addendum." He dropped Susan's hand, the wolf in sheep's clothing gone and plain old handsome Dominick back. "Now, back to the reason for my phone call. I need to talk to you about a property in Lead."

The gears in my brain ground as we shifted back to normality. "Something you want to sell?"

"A piece I want to purchase."

I pointed at the door. "If we're going to discuss real estate, we should return to my office and leave Harvey to finish his work here." I needed to get everyone out of the place before Doc decided to stop in for a book or a file and found out about our little party.

"What of your sister?"

I frowned at Susan, her expression similar to a mannequin I'd seen dressed in a red velvet holiday dress down at the mall. "I'd appreciate it if you'd release her from your hold so she can be on her way."

"Her will is weak, especially compared to Zoe."

"I'm not surprised." I suspected that was because Susan was game to his seduction, whereas Zoe fought him tooth and nail while he held her under his thumb. "Now free her."

Dominick shrugged.

And in a blink, Susan stumbled backward, her hand moving to her chest. "What did you two do to me?" she asked, her gaze accusing when it landed on me.

I held up my hands. "I'm innocent, I swear."

She squinted, her face pinching. "You're up to something." She turned back to Dominick. "You and your so-called boyfriend. And before you go and tattle to Mom that I'm trying to steal another one of your lovers, you should keep in mind the way he's been looking at me. It's immoral."

Please. As if that word wasn't tramp-stamped above her ass.

Dominick chuckled, low and velvety. "She thinks I'm your lover."

"Susan is often easily confused, especially by homonyms and simple fractions." She'd been too busy in high school mastering the art of flirting and manhandling to focus on her studies. "That's not Doc," I told my sister.

"It's not ... but I thought ... then who is he?"

Wow. I hadn't seen Susan flustered like this since she was being arrested for possession of stolen jewelry back before my kids were born.

"Susan, meet Dominick Masterson, an associate of mine."

"Ohhhhh, you are such a shit!" She shoved past Dominick. "You can't hide your boyfriend from me forever," she snapped at me as she yanked open the front door.

She was right. I was going to have to get the introduction over with sooner or later, and the scene needed to happen under my conditions, not hers.

"Good-bye, Susan. Give Mom a hug for me."

After a parting middle finger, she slammed the door behind her.

"So spirited," Dominick said. "You share that as well as the shape of your mouth. Shall we?" He ushered me toward the door.

"Give me a minute with Harvey."

"What shall I do while I wait?"

"Twiddle your thumbs and try not to seduce someone for once."

"Where's the fun in that?" Dominick stepped over the threshold. "Don't make me wait long. I have information to acquire and a chimera to name."

As soon as the door closed, Harvey said, "How in tarnation are ya gonna catch one of those Slagton critters?"

"With your help."

He cringed. "Coop's gonna be pissed."

Harvey's nephew was in a permanent state of pissed-off-ness. "He should be grateful. I'm going to help him find his informant."

"But at what cost? Ya should have run this by Doc first."

Maybe, but he wasn't here, and I'd been shooting from the hip when the idea hit. "I'll explain it to him later. Where's your phone? You need to warn Natalie that Dominick is on his way and she should stay away from him."

"I already did. She said to tell you she was headin' home for lunch."

"Good. What are you doing here, anyway? I thought the front door was locked." Cornelius only had the key to the back door. "Did Doc send you over?"

"No, I came looking for yer stud, but found ol' Corny when I knocked on the front door."

"Where is Cornelius?"

"He's in the back room playin' with his expensive ghost toys." He frowned. "Why are ya tryin' to get that closet door open, anyway?"

"Cornelius wants to see what's down in the Hellhole under the building."

"That's a downright foolish idea, right up there with catchin' a sharp-toothed critter. Some holes are better left plugged."

"I agree, but Cornelius has a plan tonight involving Jane's ghost."

"Ya best keep yer nose out of trouble, especially with the way yer luck has been runnin' these days."

Right. Avoid trouble. I tried not to scoff too loud. "Listen, if you need to talk to Doc, find out where your nephew is. I think the two of them are together talking about the shit that hit the fan this morning."

"What shit?"

"I don't have time to explain right now. I want to get next door before Dominick seduces Mona into having sex on her desk."

"I'd pay to see that show. The sight of Mona in her sweaters makes my ticker bounce around like a young pup."

"You and most of the other males in this town." I remembered Cooper's visit last night. "Oh, Doc had Cooper drop off his laptop at home yesterday. I think he might be planning to work from Aunt Zoe's dining room table later. You can wait for him there if you don't get hold of Cooper."

Harvey stood, stretching his back. "In that case, I'll go pay a visit to Zoe and her cookie jar while I wait."

Dominick knocked on the front window, making me jump. He pointed at his watch.

Jeez, as if he didn't have several lives' worth of time to kill.

"Damn, that devil won't fly away, will he?"

"That's what scares me about him." I blew out a breath. "I'll talk to you later tonight," I told Harvey and stepped out into the frigid air, closing and locking Doc's front door behind me.

I kept my distance as I led the way into Calamity Jane's. "What's with the urgency on this property, Dominick?"

Mona wasn't at her desk when I arrived. The light in Jerry's office was still on, the door half closed. Maybe she was in there trying to convince Jane to open the door for us.

"I've recently learned that it has something that I thought I'd lost," he answered.

"What's that?" I pulled out my chair.

"A ghost."

I slid into my seat. "Most of the buildings in Deadwood and Lead are supposedly haunted. What makes this ghost so special?"

"She took something from me a long time ago." His jaw hardened. "I want it back."

* * *

I spent the afternoon struggling to play real estate agent while my thoughts bounced around like Mexican jumping beans. Mona was there with me, her nails clacking on her keyboard in between phone calls to several clients.

Jerry called in once to check in on his "favorite girls." Mona and I gave a brief recount of the day's slow going, including virtually no foot traffic except for Dominick Masterson and one of Mona's appointments. Jerry informed me I'd had five more calls thanks to my latest billboard in Spearfish, but only one was actually interested in real estate. I didn't want to know what the other four had said they wanted from me, but I could hazard a guess based on that stupid pen between my bright red lips up on that dang billboard.

Shortly after Jerry's call ended, Mona grabbed her purse and told me she was heading out for the day. She planned to drive by a Deadwood residence that she'd heard was going to be available for sale soon—a century-plus old Colonial Revival cottage with rounded canopies over the windows and columns framing the front entrance on upper Main Street. I expected her to question me again about tonight's get-together here at the office, but she didn't say a peep before heading out the back door.

An hour later, the outside world had gone dark. I was packing up to head home when my phone chirped. I looked down at the screen as I slipped on my coat.

Doc had texted me: *We need to talk.*

My chest tightened. He hadn't used any nickname for me. No *Boots*, no *Killer*, no *Tiger*, not even a *Sweetheart*. Something was wrong, and I had a feeling it had to do with an ornery ol' coot squawking about a new deal I'd made with a charming devil.

I texted back: *When and where?*

Wookie? Doc texted back.

Frickety-frack! My dumbass smartphone had automatically changed the word "where" to "wookie" when I'd hit the send button. What in the hell was wrong with my phone? Harvey thought it was possessed. I was beginning to buy into his theory.

I typed the word: *WHERE*, using all caps and then added a frowning face emoji.

Now. Come pick me up at my place. Alone.

I grimaced at the last word, but typed: *On my way.*

I locked up the office, but left Jerry's office lights on since Cornelius would probably be over soon to set up for tonight's shindig.

Five minutes later, I pulled into Doc's drive. He stepped outside several racing heartbeats later, moving more slowly than usual down his porch steps, his upper body stiff. Guilt washed over me again. I didn't care what he said, those bruised ribs were my fault. I needed to stay focused while hunting, especially if I were going to catch instead of kill next time.

Doc climbed in my SUV, bringing in the scent of fresh air along with the cold, and closed the door with a grunt.

"Hey, Wookie," he said, settling into the seat.

A nickname. Whew! My shoulders loosened several clicks. I waited for him to fasten his seatbelt before shifting into reverse. "Where to?"

"I don't know, but I don't want to be interrupted for a little while." When I pointed at his house, he added, "Cooper is home catching some shut-eye after a long shift."

Eek! I agreed—no Cooper in the vicinity. I backed out of the drive.

"Zoe knows we'll be running late," he added.

How late? "What about supper for the kids?"

"Harvey's feeding them."

I nodded, trying to think of a place for us to sit uninterrupted on a freezing Sunday evening. Both of our offices were out thanks to Cornelius. The Purple Door might have someone hanging out that one of us knew. The library was closed.

I glanced down at my gas gauge. Half a tank. Maybe we could just hole up in my Honda somewhere, but if any of the local cops saw my vehicle idling in a parking lot, they'd come knocking. My reputation preceded me these days, thanks to Detective Hawke's paranoia.

We needed to get out of town, somewhere I could pull off the main drag and … I knew the perfect place for a dark, cold night. I headed toward Lead, taking a left on US Highway 385 before I started up Strawberry Hill. Snow flurries drifted through the air, swirling around as I drove.

"Where are you going?" he asked.

"Someplace where we can park without one of Deadwood or Lead's boys in blue finding us. I have a bit of a reputation for troublemaking around town, you know."

He chuckled. "Yeah, I know."

Near the top of Strawberry Hill, I took a right on a snowplowed road. It was the same tree-lined gravel road I'd visited months back when I'd found out Rex was back in my life. I'd taken out my frustration on a pine tree branch that day. Not much had changed on that front. I still wanted to beat the hell out of something at the thought of the no-good bastard—preferably knocking around Rex himself.

A short distance off the main road, I pulled off to the side and hit my hazard lights, leaving plenty of room for the local residents to pass.

"I'm surprised they plow this road," Doc said, staring out into the dark forest.

"Aunt Zoe told me there are a couple of hoity-toity Deadwood business owners with big log homes back here. They pay extra to have one of the plows drive up here and clear the road when it snows." I killed the headlights, but left the engine idling for heat.

"Enough small talk, Doc. Let me hear it."

He leaned his head back against the headrest. The glow of the dashboard made his face look rugged, his eyes dark pools. "I believe we have a few complications to address."

My chest fluttered, like there was a chicken flapping around in there, squawking about the sky crashing down on its head. "I know." I smiled at him, wanting to lessen the tension in the cab. "Christmas is a little over a week away and I don't know what to get you." No lie.

He glanced my way, his gaze lowering. "Yes, you do."

Sexual innuendos. That was a good sign, wasn't it? "I've already given you *that* a bunch of times."

"I always want more from you, Boots." His focus returned to my face. "Harvey told me about Masterson's visit."

"I figured." The buzzard had no patience anymore, claiming he was too old to wait around for others to spill the beans. "Let me guess, you're pissed at me for making another deal with Dominick without talking to you first."

"Pissed? No." His forehead wrinkled. "You're a grown woman, Violet. An Executioner, for crissake. I have as much to say about what you do in your arena as you do in mine."

Did that mean we were still a team or not?

"In case you haven't noticed," he continued. "This thing between us is not a normal relationship between a guy and a girl. Mr. Black made that crystal clear this morning."

"Right. Me, Executioner; you, Oracle." The wedge between us had been sledgehammered deeper thanks to Mr. Black's words. My angst from earlier about where Doc and I stood post-enlightenment came flooding back tenfold. "So now what?"

Doc shifted, turning toward me. "I can tell by your tone that your take on what this revelation means is different from mine. Tell me what's swirling around behind those eyes."

"You being an Oracle changes things between us," I said.

"Yes and no."

"Yes and yes," I disagreed.

"How do you think it changes things?"

"Do you love me, Doc?" I held my hand up to stop him before he could answer, clarifying with, "I mean *me*, the single mother of two children who does a rotten job of selling real estate for a living. The woman who can barely get her shit together enough most days to wear matching shoes. The *me* that spends each day battling jealousy, incompetence, doubt demons, and crazy hair. Not the Executioner you are compelled to help because of your bloodline, but the woman who makes numbskull mistakes that end with an accidental pregnancy and trips to jail. Do you love that version of me?"

Doc stared at me, his expression unreadable. "I don't like it when you put yourself down."

I shrugged. "It's one of the few things at which I excel."

"That's not true. You excel in multiple areas of everyday life."

"Cooper would disagree with you."

He shook his head. "Coop may not like how you go about your life at times, but he understands where your strengths lie. He's even mentioned that."

"No way. When?"

"Behind your back."

I snarled. "He's a butthead."

Doc looked out the windshield for several beats, the vertical grooves in his forehead returning. "Violet, since the first day I met you, I've felt this overwhelming need to protect you."

"And here I thought you just wanted to get into my pants."

A smile flitted over his face. "That, too." He took my hand, meeting my eyes. His smile faded. "There was something different about you from the start. Something compelling that tugged at me. I couldn't get you out of my head, no matter how hard I tried. Now I understand why."

"Because you're an Oracle. It's in your genes to help others."

"But it's not in my genes to fall in love."

"Maybe you're blurring the lines."

"On the contrary, several things have come into focus since this morning's disclosure. The ghosts, the feeling that I don't fit in, the ability to see occurrences from the past, the knack of guessing what's to come." He lifted my hand to his mouth, brushing his lips over my knuckles. "The inability to retain any measure of control around you."

I held his gaze. "How can you be sure that you're not being tricked on some subconscious level into having sex with me?"

He let out a bark of laughter and then flinched, holding his ribs. "Boots, even if I were being tricked, I'm happy as hell to be the recipient of your duplicity."

When he stilled, I said, "I'm serious, Doc. I don't want to sound like a needy girlfriend, but I have a shitty history with men."

"So you've said. What are you looking for from me, Violet?"

"Some sort of proof, I guess. That if we stripped away the Executioner and Oracle roles, there'd still be something between us."

"But those roles are part of who we are, key to our makeup. You have only recently come into your *Scharfrichter* responsibilities, so I understand why the concept might be harder for you to blend in your head, but I've been dealing with this shit for almost four decades. I've always been in a hybrid state of mind."

I pulled my hand from his, gripping the steering wheel. "This whole Executioner gig is such a big pill to swallow. It keeps getting stuck on the way down." I rested my forehead on the wheel. "I'm sorry you are being forced to deal with my inadequacies. Give me time and I'll stop grinding gears about it, same as I did with the notion of being a single mother of twins."

"Violet, look at me."

I crossed my arms on the top of the steering wheel, resting my cheek on my forearms. "What?"

He shifted to face me more, a pinch of pain coming and going as he moved. "From the time you found out the truth about my ability to interact with ghosts, you stayed by my side. You struggled to believe at first, which is ironic considering what you are, but never once did you push me away because of what I am. You opened your arms to me—both the man and the medium. You shared your bed at first, and then your heart, and now your family. I don't believe you love me only because of my abilities to see what others can't."

I let his words soak in, considering the way I felt when I thought of him. Did I distinguish between the man and the medium? If we could no longer play in the paranormal world, would I still want to spend the rest of my life with him?

There was no question, really.

He ran his hand down my bowed back. "Personally, I find it even more of a turn-on that we have a connection far deeper than human emotion. Call me sentimental, but I like the idea that we were made for one another. We just had to find our way to each other first."

My heart pitter-pattered. "We do fit together well, Oracle."

His gaze moved to my hair and then headed south. "It's like you were designed in a lab for me, with the perfect amount of curves, wild and wonderful hair, and sharp wit. Not to mention your come-hither look and that mouth." He groaned. "That sweet, soft, sexy mouth." He gave me a smolder that stole my breath. "How about you hop over here and sit on my lap for a few minutes?"

I leaned back from the steering wheel. "If you call yourself Santa, I'm going to start giggling and ruin the moment."

"How about an early Christmas present, Mrs. Claus." He wiggled his eyebrows at me. "What are you wearing under that dress?"

I chuckled, moving closer. "One kiss and that's it. You're not fit for extra sugar tonight, Mr. Kringle. Those ribs need to heal."

He took my face in his hands. "Heal schmeal. Kiss me, Boots."

Obeying, I tasted his lips, making myself hungry for more. But now was not the time or the place, so I pulled back before his hands convinced me to crawl over the console and show him what I wanted for Christmas.

He pointed his thumb at his window. "It's getting hot and steamy in here. Maybe you should take off your dress and get more comfortable."

"Nice try, Romeo." I shucked my coat, trying to cool down. "Tell me, honestly. Are you upset about me making a deal with Dominick to help find the missing informant?"

He adjusted his inseam, lifting his gaze from my chest. "I'm concerned, of course. Mainly, though, I'm suspicious about Masterson's motives. Harvey said you had an opportunity to offer up your sister to Masterson on a silver platter but you didn't. That's impressive will power."

I smirked. "Well, I want to take you to my parents' for Christmas." It would be Doc's first family-filled holiday since he was a kid. "Handing over Susan to the charming devil for use as his sex toy seemed like it might result in our invitation being revoked."

"I've met your parents, remember? With your history, I'd bet they'd take that in stride."

I stuck my tongue out at him.

"Tell me truthfully," he said. "Was it your parents who held you back, or do you really love your sister under all of the hurt and anger?"

Love her? After all of her backstabbing over the years? I pondered that. "She's blood. I take offense at someone else doing her wrong, especially when it's in order to manipulate me." I pulled my lip gloss from my purse. "Although I'm perfectly okay with Natalie making a voodoo doll of Susan and poking it five hundred million times."

"How are you going to catch a chimera?" he asked.

Harvey had obviously told him about the name game we'd played with Dominick, too. I flipped down my visor, coating my lips as I looked in the mirror there. "I haven't thought that through yet. If you have any ideas, I'm open to them." I rubbed my lips together, uncomfortable with the next item I needed to share. "Cornelius wants to have a séance tonight to reach out to Jane." I closed the visor and frowned at Doc. "He's determined to check out that Hellhole again."

Doc raised one eyebrow in response, but said nothing.

"We need your help, Oracle."

"But it's Sunday night," he said. "The kids have school tomorrow, and I told Addy I'd listen to another episode of *The Cinnamon Bear* with her."

Addy had a soft spot for that old-time radio program that Aunt Zoe had introduced to her years ago.

"I didn't realize Addy had lassoed you into listening to it with her."

"There was no lassoing, Violet. In case you haven't noticed, I'm smitten with your kids."

My heart swelled, clogging the back of my throat. I gulped around it and blinked silly tears from my eyes. "Damn, you're good."

"I'm hooked on the whole package, Boots." He wrapped one of my curls around his finger. "You sure you don't want to come over here and sit on my lap?"

I did. I very much did. "What about your ribs?"

"I don't care about my damned ribs." His focus lowered to my mouth. "I want to find out what you have on under that dress."

Headlights blared in the back window. A yellow light flashed, bouncing off the trees.

I squinted in the rearview mirror. "It's a snowplow. We have to move."

Doc cursed. "Bad timing. The driver must be related to Coop."

I rolled my window down and waved at the driver, then made a sharp U-turn, heading back down to Deadwood.

When we hit the city limits, I rested my hand on Doc's thigh. "How about I kiss those ribs better later tonight?"

"Will you be wearing my favorite lip gloss?"

"Sure, but it will make you sticky."

"I hope so. What about the séance?"

"We agreed to meet at the office after the kids are in bed asleep."

"So." He covered my hand with his. "If I agree to this late-night rendezvous with a ghost, you'll reward me with your lips?"

I puckered up and blew him a kiss. "And more."

He squeezed my hand. "Then I'm your huckleberry, Killer."

Chapter Twelve

I t was a dark and snowy night," I said in a Vincent Price voice
several hours later as Doc steered my Honda into the parking lot
behind Calamity Jane Realty.

"It's only spitting snow," he said, parking in the middle of the
empty lot, close to the back door.

A swirling cloud of snow whipped in front of the headlights. "Well,
it's definitely cold and blustery."

"Promise me something, Killer." He handed me the keys. "Don't
go down into the Hellhole tonight."

"Trust me, that is the last place I want to visit, especially tonight."

"You say that now," he started, his smile teasing. "But then off you
skip, leaving me clutching my poor ticker."

I patted his chest. "I give you and your little ol' heart my word.
Tonight is about finding out why Jane is blocking off the hole, that's it.
No exploratory mission to be made."

"Good, then let's get this over with. I have a date later with a sexy
blonde and her sticky lip gloss."

Earlier, Cornelius had sent Doc a message saying he'd be set up in
Jerry's office tonight, so we rushed to the back door of Calamity Jane's
instead of Doc's building.

Once inside, we stomped the slush off our boots and hung up our
coats. The lights were off up front where our desks sat in a circle,
except for the one fluorescent bulb over Ben's desk that was always
left on so the police could see in the office when they did their rounds.
Doc sniffed, earning a raised brow from me.

"Is Jane here?" I whispered.

"If so, she's not within my range." He sniffed again, this time near my neck. "All I can smell is your peach pie–scented soap."

I'd taken a shower when we returned home, wanting to scrub off some of the day's frustrations—Susan, Dominick, Mr. Black, and everything in between. The peach pie soap was one of Doc's favorites, so of course I'd used it without putting together how it might act as a distraction for a medium who used his olfactory senses to find ghosts. "Sorry about that. I wasn't thinking."

"It's okay, Boots." He winked at me. "But don't be surprised if I try to bite you at some point tonight."

"So long as it's your teeth doing the biting and not the fangs of something that crawled out of that Hellhole hunting its next meal."

"You have horror movies on the brain tonight."

"Yeah, well, warped thoughts come with the job." Taking hold of his wrist, I led the way into Jerry's office. Natalie sat behind the desk in my boss's extra-large leather chair. She wore the same getup from earlier: overalls and a thermal shirt. The only difference was she'd added a fuzzy black stocking cap.

She gave me a toothy smile while spinning a pencil around on the desktop. An odd glint in her eyes made me do a double take. Her gaze lowered quickly when I peered closer—too quickly. Three-plus decades had taught me a few things about my best friend, and my instincts wagered that she was hiding something.

"What's going on in here?" I approached the desk.

Taking a line from Doc, I sniffed the air. The room smelled normal enough, including hints of Jerry's cologne mixed with leather and floor varnish.

"Nothing, Ms. Paranoid." There was a defensive tone underlying her response. "Cornelius and I were just chatting while we waited for you two to join us. How are the kids?"

And now a diversionary tactic. "They're sleeping."

What could Natalie and Cornelius have been talking about that made her all shifty eyed? I knew better than to think it was anything risqué. Natalie was too busy pining over Cooper, and Cornelius didn't mix ghost hunting with sex, at least not in my experience with him.

I focused on Cornelius, trying to see if he was playing the same game as Natalie. Dressed all in black, he held some gadget out in front of him while walking from corner to corner. It made a slight crackling sound, but was otherwise silent. No buzzing, no beeping, no humming to be heard from either him or his toy. He moved up next to me, running his toy down the front of me from head to toe. One green light in a range of green-yellow-orange-red stayed steadily lit. Below the lights, digital numbers flittered quickly with his movement.

"What are you doing?" I asked him.

"Making sure you're human."

"The verdict is still out on that one," Natalie teased.

"I'm leaning toward her being part Wookie," Doc added from where he squatted next to Cornelius's briefcase, checking out the array of gadgets inside.

Natalie chuckled. "Did you forget to shave your legs again? Poor Doc. If you're not careful, you'll scar him for life."

"Too late. I'm damaged goods now." Doc lifted a banana from the case. "Uh, Curion, are we trying to catch a monkey tonight?"

I looked from the banana to Abe Jr. "Did somebody tell you Jane likes bananas?" He'd used favorite items to lure ghosts out of hiding in past séances.

"No, Violet. You are going to talk into the banana," he answered.

"Are you serious?" Speaking into a banana was going to make me feel just plain dumb and stupid.

He lowered his toy. "In Malay folklore, banana plants are associated with the pontianak, a female vampire-like ghost. I'm surprised you did not know this."

"A vampire ghost? How is that even possible? Vampires are undead. Don't they turn to ash when they die? Do these ghosts walk around with stakes in their hearts?"

"And we're back to horror movies," Doc said, setting the banana back in the case.

Cornelius's lips twitched. "The banana is for me to eat, Violet. I have difficulty focusing when I'm low on potassium. But if you'd prefer to use it as a microphone to reach out to your old boss, I'm sure we'd all find it quite entertaining."

"I'm going to stick that banana where the sun doesn't shine," I warned him.

"If you are referring to the Hellhole," said Cornelius, circling his toy a couple of inches above the desktop, "that is not a good idea."

"Why not?" Natalie pushed her chair away from the desk so he could check the drawers.

He frowned down at the steady green light. "Banana peels are notoriously slippery," he said without even cracking a grin.

"Damn, Corny," Natalie said. "You're on fire tonight."

"I am feeling more flammable than usual in this cotton fabric." He hit several buttons on the side of his doohickey.

I crossed my arms. "What is that toy you keep playing with?"

"It's his brand-spanking-new EMF meter," Natalie said, beating him to the punch. "It's supposed to be ten times more sensitive than his other ones."

EMF meters were used to detect electromagnetic frequencies. Something I'd learned from hanging out with Cornelius and his bag of tricks. "Why are you using it already? Did you sense Jane's presence?"

"I'm taking baseline readings of the electromagnetic energy in the room now that all of us are here. This will help me determine after we start the séance if a spike in my readings is due to some ordinary source of natural, electrical, or magnetic energy, or if your boss has entered the room."

Doc walked over to Cornelius, checking out the meter. "You're not picking up anything unusual yet, are you?"

"The energy increases I've noticed are due to currency flows from typical AC and DC sources. It could be a meter error, though. I haven't tested it before now." Cornelius looked up from his EMF meter. "But I don't hear anything in the walls. Are you sensing Violet's dead boss?"

Doc shook his head. "But if Jane is keeping her distance on purpose, she'll be off my radar until we seek her out." He scanned the room, frowning. "We could use Coop's eyes in here, but he's on duty again tonight."

Natalie growled low in her throat. "Coop is always on duty. Work comes first for him, remember?"

"Miss Bitter, your table for one is ready," I said, nudging her leg with my boot.

She lifted her chin. "It's the truth and you know it."

"Maybe, but what else does Cooper have waiting at home for him these days besides an ornery ol' uncle and his mangy mutt?"

Wait! Was I actually making excuses for Cooper again? Sheesh, did

I have a fever? Had the stress from the Slagton hunting trips cracked my melon?

"Besides," I added before I could stop myself. "He said the police station is running on a skeleton crew right now because of the upcoming holidays. Have you considered that maybe Cooper is being generous with his time so that others can be home with their families?"

My heart panged a little at that idea, the fickle traitor feeling sorry for the gigantic pain in the ass.

Natalie stared up at me as if a rainbow-colored horn was growing from the center of my forehead. "Do you really believe any of this pro-Coop hot air spilling out your pie hole?"

"The part about the skeleton crew, yes." I also believed that if Cooper could swing a moment to join us, he would. At the least, he'd want to help Doc, but the main reason he'd be here was because of the frowny-faced woman sitting here complaining about him. "I also think he's working because he's single without a wife and kids waiting at home for him. Whether he's enjoying the extra time on the job or not, I haven't a clue. Since he's no longer sharing a house with me, we don't talk like we used to."

I kind of missed our middle of the night talks, too. Dang Cooper for finding my soft spot. I didn't want to like the bristly butthead.

Natalie snorted. "Who are you and what have you done with Violet Parker?" She poked me in the leg. "Are you Deadwood's new robot cop? Did Coop program you himself?"

I poked her back. "Trust me, I still feel like hurting Cooper when I see him. Didn't I just give him a black eye last week?"

"By accident," she said. "And it's mostly gone, so next time try harder." She searched my face. "If he still bugs you, why are you being his biggest cheerleader lately?"

That was a good question. The guy locked horns with me whenever he had a chance, yet here I was defending him to the girl who'd been my best friend for decades through thick and thin.

"I guess because it seems like you're being extra tough on him lately." I shot a frown in Doc's and Cornelius's directions and then leaned closer, whispering. "It's your heart's self-defense mechanism kicking in."

"Really? When did you become a love expert?" she whispered back.

"I've seen you do it before when you're getting too close to a guy."

"It's you who sabotages a relationship before it takes flight, remember? Not me. I'm the one who dives in headfirst and ends up crashing and burning."

Shoot. She was right. I glanced over to make sure Doc was still preoccupied with Cornelius and his gadget. "Maybe we've switched places," I whispered even quieter. "I'm diving in headfirst with Doc and you're jumping ship."

She moved closer, her voice barely audible even to me. "There's no ship to jump from yet, though."

"Yeah, but taking a card from my deck, if you can make Cooper into a villain in your head, you'll find him less desirable, like I did with that insurance salesman I dated years ago."

"You only went on three dates." She held up three fingers and shook them for emphasis.

"That's because the creep announced on our third date that he wanted to take out life insurance on *me*. Do you know how weird that is? Why was he already thinking about me being dead?"

"Maybe he liked to insure things he found valuable," she said under her breath.

I harrumphed. "Or he planned to kill me and collect the dough."

"Doc's right," she said a little louder, leaning back in the chair again. "You're running some kind of horror movie marathon in your head tonight."

"Hey, you two," Doc interrupted our whispering. "When you were trying to break into this door earlier with this …" He held up the crowbar. "Were you able to budge it even a little?"

"No." Natalie stood and joined him, pointing out where she'd wedged the crowbar in her attempts. "Short of tearing a hole in the door—no easy task with a solid piece of oak—I only managed to dent the jamb."

"Interesting." He grabbed the doorknob, twisting it and pulling a couple of times. "Jane must be using psychokinesis," he said.

"That's where people use their minds to move things without actual physical contact, right?" Natalie asked.

"Precisely," Cornelius answered her.

"But how is a ghost able to make a door stick like it's been superglued shut?"

The sound of the back door opening made me hop to my feet. I frowned toward the hallway, my fingers crossed I wouldn't see Ray or Jerry appear in the doorway. I wasn't ready to exchange blows with the former tonight or play any kind of "ball" with the latter.

The sight of Cooper made me take a step back. His black police coat and wool cowboy hat were dusted with snow. His scrutiny of the situation in Jerry's office started with Natalie and ended at Doc. Before I could ask why he was gracing us with his surly self this cold and dark evening, he said, "Guess who I found sneaking around outside?"

Mona took center stage, waving in at us with her gloved hand. "Hi, everyone." Her eyes sparkled between her mint green scarf and matching stocking cap, her cheeks and nose bright pink from the cold.

"She wants to join your party."

Doc aimed a wrinkled brow my way.

I held my hands up, showing my innocence. Turning to my real estate mentor, I asked, "What are you doing here? I told you it was only going to be the four of us in here tonight, nothing for you to worry about."

She opened her mouth, but Cornelius moved over to her and started scanning her with his EMF meter. "I invited her," he said over his shoulder. The light stayed a steady green as he checked her out. "It's as I figured," he said, lowering his toy.

"You mean Jane's attached to her?" Natalie offered.

"No. She's real."

I scoffed. "Of course she's real."

"You can never be sure when you're in active locations."

I muttered a few choice words about socking him in an active location.

"Violet," Cornelius said. "I told you before that you need to speak more clearly for us to pick up your voice on tape."

I crossed the room, jabbing him in the forearm with my finger. "And I told *you* earlier that having Mona come was not a good idea. Don't try to tell me you didn't hear me say that either."

"I heard you, but this one already knows." He lifted his EMF gadget again, inching over next to where Doc and now Cooper stood by the closet door. Natalie had returned to the safety of Jerry's chair, keeping plenty of distance from Cooper.

I planted my hands on my hips. "What does he mean you already know, Mona?"

"He's probably referring to Jane's ghost," she answered vaguely.

"We covered that." Something about the way she was slowly pulling off her gloves, as if it took concentration for each finger, gave me pause. "What else do you know?"

Setting her gloves on the corner of Jerry's desk, she unzipped her white, puffy coat. "Merely a few things that I've gleaned while observing life around the office over the last few months."

"Give me an example."

She smiled. "For one, your boyfriend is a medium."

Doc's mouth tightened, but he didn't deny it.

"Why in the world would you think that?" I tried to make her declaration seem absurd.

"Please, Violet. Enough with the theatrics." She unwound her scarf, her jasmine perfume freshening the stale office, and dropped it next to her gloves. "Don't worry. I haven't told anyone else that he's seen Jane's ghost."

Doc hadn't really seen Jane's ghost, mostly just sensed her. At least that was what he'd told me.

"How do you know about that?" Natalie's worried expression probably mirrored mine.

"Jane told me."

My lower jaw bounced onto Jerry's floor. "What? You said you hadn't actually seen Jane's ghost, though."

"I haven't, but she's been leaving me notes."

"What kind of notes?" Cooper prodded, unzipping his coat. Apparently he was sticking around for a bit. He shot another glance in Natalie's direction, holding steady on her face for a couple of beats before focusing back on Mona and his interrogation.

"Mostly short to-do lists here and there around the office. You know how Jane loved her lists."

Yes, I remembered well. Until Jerry showed up, the office was run by lists—from sales and pending sales to marketing and yearly goals.

"Are the lists in her handwriting?" Doc spoke up for the first time since Mona had shown up.

"When they are handwritten."

"What do you mean 'when'?" Natalie pressed.

"Sometimes, when I'm alone at work, she types notes on my computer."

"Like when you're typing away during the day?" Was that what Mona was doing when she was clackety-clacking on her keys day after day? Writing back and forth with Jane's ghost?

"No. She does it when I step away from my laptop for a few minutes to grab some coffee or use the restroom. I'll come back to find a document open with a short note typed on it. Those are usually typical of her to-do notes she used to leave on my desk, requesting I order more office supplies or run out to pick up more coffee."

"Sounds like she's still playing boss." Doc shot a raised brow at Cornelius, who nodded once in response.

Cooper crossed his arms, his gaze narrowed on Mona. I'd been on the receiving end of that interrogation stare too many times to count. "She leaves you other types of notes, though?" he prodded her to continue.

"Yes. Several times she's drawn a word or shape in the zen sandbox on my desk—those messages are tough to decipher though and more cryptic than not."

"Cryptic in what way?" the detective continued.

She shrugged. "They're random. I get the feeling she was sitting at my desk pondering something, doodling in the sandbox."

"Has she ever left you a message on the bathroom mirror?" Natalie asked. "Cornelius told me mirrors are sometimes portals between realms."

"Not to date, at least not that I've noticed."

"You mentioned that some messages are actually handwritten," Doc said.

Mona nodded. "Every now and then, I'll find a couple of words scrawled on the whiteboard first thing in the morning when I arrive. At first, those messages were very hard to read, as if her hand was trembling as she wrote each letter. However, her penmanship has improved, and now the writing is similar to when she was still with us."

"Does that mean she's gaining strength?" I asked Doc.

He scratched the thick stubble on his jaw. "Or perfecting her aim, if you will."

I turned back to Mona. She'd been hiding these hair-raising incidents for months. What kind of a friend was I not to have realized something was going on behind the scenes? I'd been so caught up in my wacky world full of asshole detectives, jerkoff exes, and deadly *others* that I had missed the signs. Then again, I had noticed more tension in her, but I'd figured it was due to her attraction to Jerry, not because her dead friend was sending her ghostly messages from the other side.

In the future, I needed to pay more attention to signals I detected, watch more closely for obscure clues. "How come you didn't say anything before about these notes from Jane?"

Her brows pinched. "At first I thought that maybe I was seeing things. I was still pretty upset about losing my good friend, her funeral only days past. But when the messages continued, I started researching messages from beyond. I read an article written by a paranormal investigator about a woman who thought she was being haunted by her recently deceased husband. She talked of similar events—cryptic love notes carved on her headboard, a bouquet of her favorite flowers left on the kitchen table, the scent of his cologne on the pillow next to her in the morning. You know, ghostly activities similar in some ways to what I was experiencing here with Jane."

"Damn, that's so sad," Natalie said. "It reminds me of the pottery wheel scene from *Ghost*."

"It was heartbreaking to read about the poor widow," Mona agreed. "Upon further investigation, though, it turned out she was responsible for all of the so-called paranormal activity in her house."

"A form of poltergeist activity," Cornelius clarified.

"That was the investigator's theory. Their hidden cameras showed the woman moving around the house in the night as if in a catatonic state." Mona clasped her hands together. "Anyway, for some time after that, I wasn't sure if I was doing these things myself, acting out in a grief-stricken, zombified state. The feeling of losing one's mind is not something you openly share with your coworkers." She looked at me, a hint of sadness in her eyes. "Not even when they are your friends."

Boy howdy! I knew what she was talking about, having been in the same sinking boat myself with Prudence and Wilda Hessler, and then this Executioner gig. "You came clean with Cornelius, though."

At her nod, Cooper asked, "What changed?"

"First, Jerry started seeing things, too. He wasn't as apprehensive about the sightings, talking openly to me about the items Jane was moving around in his office. Then he called in reinforcements."

She focused on our upstairs neighbor, who was now fiddling with one of his hand-held recorders. "One morning last week, Cornelius and I were sharing coffee out front. He told me there'd been a lot of electromagnetic energy spikes during the night, especially near my desk. He mentioned noticing a floral-scented perfume in the air. The next day, I brought him the bottle of perfume I'd taken off Jane's dresser after her funeral, something to remember her by. One sniff and he declared it a match."

"Why didn't you tell me about this last week, Cornelius?" I asked.

"Ms. Hollister requested I remain quiet about her spectral interactions."

"Does Jerry know about any of this other stuff you've been experiencing?" Natalie asked. "The notes and messages?"

"No. He is only aware of her tendency to mess up his office."

I paced in front of Jerry's desk. "Do you think Ray or Ben knows about Jane?" More worrisome, did they know about Doc?

"Ray is too obsessed with trying to muck with your career and bolster his, especially after you made the hotel sale. He doesn't want you to outsell him. Unfortunately, the feud between you is personal now in his distorted fantasyland."

Cooper grunted. "Parker has a special talent when it comes to stirring up hell with a long spoon."

I wrinkled my nose at him.

"If Ben noticed anything, he hasn't mentioned it," Mona continued. "I've done my best to erase all evidence of Jane's notes prior to his arrival at the office each day."

Cooper's radio spurted static-filled gibberish, making Mona and me jump. He turned a dial down without even looking. "Why were you sneaking around outside tonight? Was it only to see what these four were up to? Or did you have an ulterior motive?"

"Cooper," I sighed. Once a cop, always a cop. "Why would Mona have ulterior motives?"

"I have an ulterior motive," she told him. "And I wasn't sneaking."

The smirk he aimed at me was overflowing with gloat. "Any other questions, Parker?"

"Nobody likes a know-it-all," I shot back and then turned to Mona. "What ulterior motive?"

"Earlier this evening, I stopped back here to grab some paperwork I'd forgotten in the printer. You'd already left, but Cornelius was in

Jerry's office setting up another camera. When I checked my laptop before heading home, there was a new note from Jane."

"She'd accessed your laptop while it was closed?" Doc sounded surprised.

"No. She carved two words into the cover."

Chills peppered my arms.

"What did it say?" Natalie pressed.

" 'Stay out,' " Mona said. "With several exclamation marks."

"The carvings are rather disturbing," Cornelius added. "They are reminiscent of the scrawls I saw inside a haunted prison in Missouri years ago."

"She must mean the cellar," Natalie said.

"When Cornelius saw the carvings, he insisted I join your séance tonight. He thought I could help, acting as a lure since I have a previous connection with Jane's ghost. So here I am. However, Coop's right, I have an ulterior motive. I'm tired of being on the receiving end of all of Jane's notes. I want to talk to her and find out why she is sticking around, leaving me notes, and harassing Jerry." She focused on me. "I know you don't want me here, that you're probably trying to keep Doc's medium abilities a secret, but I give you my word." She turned to Doc. "Both of you. I will not say a thing outside of this circle about what happens here tonight."

"What's the plan, then?" Natalie glanced from Doc to Cooper, pausing on the latter long enough to size him up and down and all around. "Are you guys going to have Mona sit in the center of the room, like Vi did in Harvey's barn?"

"You guys held a séance at Willis' ranch?" Mona hit me with raised eyebrows. "Violet, you and I need to have a long talk about some of your properties."

Mona had heard enough for now. It was one thing for her to think I could see ghosts. Finding out I was a killer might not make her eyes light up quite so much. Besides, Harvey's barn dance was nothing compared to the galas I'd had at Prudence's place.

I glared at Natalie. "Way to spill the beans, bucket mouth."

"It's a dangerous idea to include Mona in this operation." Cooper took his wide-legged cop stance, shooting a scowl my way. "With Parker in attendance, there's always the possibility for shit to go sideways on us and somebody end up hurt."

"Are you going to start whining about your black eye again?" I shot back, patting my pockets. "Dang, I left my teeny-tiny violin at home, or I'd play you a sad song."

Cooper and I locked glares until Doc waved his hand between us. "Come on, you two. Kiss and make up. We have work to do."

Mona looked around the room, rubbing her hands together. "Now, what do you need from me to get things started? Should I get the candles we keep under the bathroom sink for power outages?"

"I really don't—" I started to say.

"Parker, shut up," Cooper said.

"Rude," I snapped back. "You need to take a lesson on—"

"I'm serious, be quiet." He cocked his head to the side, taking a step toward the doorway. "Do you hear that, Nyce?"

We all stilled, listening.

Something was beeping. Cooper eased out into the hallway. "It's coming from out front."

We filed out of Jerry's office, following the sound. In the front room, my computer screen flashed on and off like a beacon.

Mona lowered into my chair. "That's weird. Have you been having any problems with your computer lately, Vi?"

"No." I looked at Doc. "Is it Jane?"

He sniffed, searching the room. "I'm picking up traces. Coop, do you see her?"

I sniffed, too. The room smelled normal to me, a combination of varnish, stale coffee, and old building.

Cooper scanned the lowly lit room. "No, everything looks cl—" His gaze snapped back to the hallway. "There's something moving at the edge of the shadows past Jerry's office door."

Why was Jane keeping her distance? Was she shy? Or was there something more ominous behind her avoidance?

My screen stopped flashing, staying lit.

"Jesus, Parker." Cooper took a closer look at the screen. "Your desktop is as messy as your hair in the morning."

I held my fist out toward him. "Keep it up, Cooper, and I'll give your buddies down at the station another reason to poke fun at you."

My screen was filled to the edges with icons representing file folders, documents, and applications. I liked to have everything spread out in front of me, not tucked away all neat and tidy like the anal detective probably did.

"Look," Doc said, pointing at it. "The icons are disappearing."

We all leaned in, watching over Mona's shoulders. The buzz of the one fluorescent bulb lit over Ben's desk seemed especially loud, the atmosphere charged.

One by one, the icons on my screen faded away, until there was only one folder icon left. It had no title.

"Should I open it?" Mona asked.

"Yes," I whispered.

She moved the cursor over the icon and double-clicked. Inside the folder were two image files and one video.

"Do you want to do the honors?" she asked me. "It's your computer."

"You do it. She was your friend a lot longer than she was my boss. Besides, I have a feeling this message is for you as much as it is for me."

"Okay," Mona said. "Here goes."

She viewed the first image. It contained a slightly blurred, grainy image of a symbol that appeared to be carved into a stone. Or was that a wall? It was hard to tell from the photo alone. The symbol was a long skinny diamond with two lines crossing in the middle, looking like a kite, giving the diamond a 3-D appearance.

"Is that a pagan symbol?" Natalie asked. "Or something witchcraft related?"

I looked to Doc for an answer.

He stared at it with a wrinkled brow. "I'll have to look it up."

"Can you print it?" Cooper asked Mona.

Mona obliged and then opened the next image file.

I cocked my head to the side. "Is that the same symbol taken at a different angle?"

"I think so," Mona said, moving the cursor over it. "Although the scarring on the surface behind it looks different."

"Let's see the video," Natalie whispered, holding onto my shoulders as she watched.

Mona double-clicked on the file.

It took a moment to buffer, and then everything was a moving gray blur for a couple of seconds, reminding me of watching the wall outside of elevator doors as it dropped. The camera's descent came to a stop and a grainy picture of the symbol we'd seen in the other files came to life. The video was shaky as the camera slowly spun in a circle. Actually, there were multiple copies of the same symbol carved into the walls. The shadows were heavy at the edge of the screen, the light eerie and bright, whiting out some of the symbols as the camera turned one way and then back the other. I watched with my breath held, waiting for something to jump out at us. Something not human, or worse—something that was human at one time. But the video ended without a jack-in-the-box finale.

Doc was right. I needed to lay off the horror movies.

"I don't understand," Mona said. "Where was this video taken?"

"Your boss was a clever lady," Cornelius said, walking over to the printer. He held up the image she'd printed, nodding, and then turned it for us to see. "It appears she managed to get a camera down in the Hellhole before she died."

"How can you ... ?" I started to ask as I watched the video play again. Then I saw the giveaway clue at the bottom edge of the screen. "Oh. Now I see it," I told Cornelius. "The old mining carbide lamp."

Cornelius flipped the printout back over to view for himself. "She must have used a rope and lowered her camera down through the grate with the flashlight and video running."

"It was probably her cell phone," Cooper said.

We all watched the video again, as if hypnotized by the spinning.

Then my computer screen went dark.

So did the fluorescent bulb over Ben's desk.

"What the hell?" I whispered.

Natalie shushed me, grabbing my wrist. "Listen."

I heard several soft squeaks. I knew that sound. I'd heard it day after day when Jane was still alive. I sniffed, knowing that sharp smell, too—a marker.

"Coop," Doc said. "Your flashlight."

"On it." A beam of light pierced the darkness.

"Look." I grabbed Cooper's wrist and directed his light at the whiteboard. "Jane left us another message."

Scrawled diagonally across the pending sales list in large black capital letters were two words written in Jane's handwriting: *STAY OUT!*

Chapter Thirteen

Monday, December 17th

I woke up at too-flippin'-early-o'clock feeling chewed up, spat out, and stepped on.

And then I rolled over and fell out of Addy's bed.

Picking myself up from the floor, I limped to the bathroom and stared into the mirror. The reflection of the toilet made me grimace.

After the past six hours, I'd sooner face off with whatever had Jane's bobbin wound up tight than see one more speck of vomit.

I splashed my face with cold water. Leaning over the sink, I let my thoughts return to last night, water dripping from my chin.

Jane had refused to play. Period. The séance hadn't made it off the ground because all signs of her ghost—sight, sound, scent, as well as fluctuations on Cornelius' EMF meter—had disappeared soon after she'd left us her whiteboard message. Cornelius speculated that her demonstration with the computer and whiteboard might have sapped her energy. I figured she'd said her piece, dropped the mic, and floated away.

While we were regrouping in Jerry's office, discussing whether to try to reach Jane anyway, Cooper received a call about a possible hit-and-run at the south end of town. He tipped his hat and left us to head to the scene of the crime.

Natalie watched him go with a small scowl at his backside. I didn't bother touching that hot mess. I'd dabbled in their business enough for one night. Besides, I'd probably end up defending the detective again to Natalie, and frankly, I was getting sick and tired of hearing that dingbat cheerleader's voice spell out G-O C-O-O-P in my head.

Not long after Cooper took off, Aunt Zoe called me. Addy had woken up soaked in sweat and sick to her stomach. Before my aunt could even finish informing me of the situation, Addy had raced past her into the bathroom.

So, that was that. I had to go tend to my sick child, and Doc insisted on driving me. The séance was a bust. Yet it wasn't, because Jane had made contact with us, if only on her terms.

I grabbed a towel and patted my face dry, wondering how Doc had slept. When I checked on him after Addy's second tango with the porcelain prince, he'd been sound asleep under my covers. Rather than risk waking him if and when there was another upheaval from Addy's stomach, I took one of my pillows and crawled into my sick kid's bed.

I sized up my teeth and hair in the mirror. Both were fuzzy, especially my curls, but the smell of coffee lured me downstairs before I did anything about either. If Doc truly loved me like he said yesterday, then he'd understand that caffeine comes before beauty after a night with a vomiting child. Besides, if we were going to keep playing house, he needed to see me in all of my morning glory.

Cooper was standing in the kitchen when I stumbled in. His bloodshot eyes were at full squint when they locked onto me.

I stopped and blinked—twice.

Turning to my aunt sitting at the table nursing a cup of coffee, I pointed at the detective, who leaned against the counter next to the coffee maker wearing jeans and a black long-sleeve T-shirt. "Aunt Zoe, do you see a crooked-nosed, cranky cop standing between me and my coffee?"

"Hell, Parker. Did you stick your toothbrush in a light socket this morning? You could hide a chicken in that nest."

I glared bullets at him. "Really? You want to do this dance with me pre-caffeine, Detective Dickwad?" Without waiting for his answer, I shouldered him aside. I was in no mood to play patty-cake with Johnny Law after facing off with the contents of Addy's stomach displayed in full technicolor multiple times throughout the night.

Aunt Zoe chuckled. "I know you're a tough son of a gun, Coop, but Violet turns borderline rabid after pulling all-nighters with sick kids. You might want to keep your tail tucked this morning."

"Addy or Layne?" he asked me.

"Addy." I filled the mug to the rim. I was going to need straight up high octane to get through today. According to Mona, Jerry had scheduled Rosy to come to Calamity Jane's for some website vlog prep with each of us. If I didn't jump-start my brain, my vlog would consist of me with my head down on my desk, singing a chorus of zzzzz's for the viewers.

"Is she okay?" Cooper asked.

I took a sip of black coffee, cringing a little. "She'll live."

"Is it the flu?" Aunt Zoe asked.

"I believe it's a common case of too-much-sugar-itus." I carried my coffee over to the table. "The candy fiend ate a bunch of Mom's peanut butter fudge along with several Christmas cookies before bed."

"What?" Aunt Zoe frowned. "When did she get into the fudge? I put it away as soon as Susan gave it to me."

"According to Addy, dear diabolical Aunt Susan let her take a couple of handfuls to her room before delivering the tin to you."

The tin of fudge was what the Bitch from Hell had driven up to Deadwood to drop off yesterday. Feeding my little sugar addict's habit was yet another reason for me to want to stick gum in Susan's stringy hair the next time I saw her. After the third trip to the bathroom with Addy, holding her trembling body while she emptied the last drops of her stomach contents, I considered calling Dominick and telling him I'd changed my mind—he could have Susan for free.

"It's no wonder you look like hell," Cooper said.

My chin swung in his direction. "Strike two. One more, *Coop*, and I'm going to shove my foot so far up your ass that my toes will tickle your uvula."

He almost cracked a grin, but not quite. "I'm going to steal that one. And it's 'Cooper' to you, Parker. Always."

"Criminy. After all we've been through, why won't you bend even a little on that 'Coop' rule?"

"Because I don't bend."

Cornelius had that right. "Whatever. Why are you here in my face at oh-dark-thirty and what have you done with Doc?"

"Your boyfriend is at the Rec Center," he said. "I saw the green Ford in the lot."

I sighed. Doc had a morning appointment over in Spearfish and had wanted to get up and out early, but dang. "He's nuts. Who in their right mind goes to the gym at this hour, let alone with bruised ribs?"

"Bruised isn't broken." Cooper finished his coffee and set the mug in the sink. He smirked at me. "Besides, he needs to keep up his strength. Taming his shrew and her wild hair is hard work."

Aunt Zoe laughed.

"That's it." I set my cup on the table and stood, fists clenched. "Aunt Zoe, call my lawyer. I'm going to assault Deadwood's current top-ranking town clown."

A laugh escaped Cooper's locked lips. Then another. And then a bunch more.

I sat back down, frowning at him. Uh-oh. I'd witnessed this rare event once when he was forced to share quarters with me. It was the equivalent of a pressure cooker valve releasing steam. I aimed a worried brow at Aunt Zoe. "I think he's stressed out again."

"When has he ever not been?" she asked.

When Cooper quieted, wiping the corners of his eyes with the back of his hands, Aunt Zoe asked, "What's wrong, Coop?"

He sighed. "I got a call early this morning."

How early? Hell, the sun wasn't even up yet.

"Eddie Mudder requested I come over to the morgue and take a look at what he called a 'bit of a situation.' "

The garage behind Mudder Brothers Funeral Parlor, which was located down the hill from Aunt Zoe's house, acted as the town morgue, temporarily storing bodies for the Deadwood Police Department. For minor county autopsy needs, Eddie Mudder filled the bill. If the state needed to get involved, though, they shipped the corpses off after getting them nice and frosty for the trip.

"What sort of a situation?" I asked, wondering if one of Eddie's corpses up and walked away again like the faceless guy that Harvey, Natalie, and I had found out at the old buzzard's ranch months ago.

"You remember the partially eaten, burnt corpse discovered on the Michelson Trail a couple of weeks back?"

Aunt Zoe crossed her arms. "The one I said could be the result of a *Nachzehrer*?"

He nodded.

"What's a *Nachzehrer* again?" I asked, needing more coffee before I'd be ready for this conversation.

"Think of it as a ghoul and a vampire mixed," Aunt Zoe said. "A human that's reanimated after death. Only it's not a blood drinker. It eats human flesh—living or dead."

I shuddered and took another sip of coffee.

"We were storing the body at Mudder Brothers' morgue for the time being because the county coroner is out of town for the upcoming holidays and this case is a little advanced for Eddie." He crossed his arms, looking both pissed and tired at the same time. "When Eddie went into the morgue around three this morning, the freezer door was busted open."

"Why was Eddie in there in the middle of the night?" I asked.

"That's not important."

"It is to me." I'd grown to like Eddie Mudder, in spite of his love of eccentric organ music and his somewhat creepy resemblance to Lurch from the old black and white *Addams Family* television show.

"He likes to work on the dead in the middle of the night," Cooper explained. "He claims most of the bodies are less active when it comes to de-gassing at that time, because it's when they were normally in sleep mode while alive."

I cringed. "That's an unsettling observation about the dead." It figured Eddie was the source.

"Can I continue?"

I waved him onward. "You were saying the freezer door was open," I helped him return to where he'd left off.

"When Eddie looked inside the freezer, the body from the Michelson Trail was gone."

Aunt Zoe rubbed her eyes. "That could be a big problem."

"That's not the only issue," he said. "There was another body in there—another of the older Haskells passed a couple of days ago."

"I heard." Aunt Zoe ran her finger around the rim of her cup. "I ran into Eloisa at the store. She told me her uncle Elliot, the hoarding bachelor she was named after, had finally kicked the bucket. There's a rumor that he had a lot of money hidden under his chicken coop."

"Good ol' penny-pinching Uncle Elliot," Cooper said, staring out the back door into the darkness for a moment. When he turned back, he scowled in Aunt Zoe's direction. "While Uncle Elliot was on ice, something gnawed on his corpse."

"Oh, jeez," I muttered, covering my eyes since it was too late for my ears. "Please tell me it was a hungry raccoon or coyote."

"From what Eddie and I can determine, the bite marks are human." He grimaced. "Well, made by something that used to be human, anyway."

I lowered my hands, looking across at Aunt Zoe. "What now?"

Cooper answered for her. "I'm going to need both of you to join me at Mudder Brothers' morgue to inspect Mr. Haskell's remains."

"Right now?"

"I'll give you an hour to eat and get dressed. I'll meet you down there."

"Are you serious?"

He pointed at his face. "Do I look like I'm joking?"

* * *

Cooper wasn't joking.

Forty-five minutes later, Layne was up, fed, dressed, and reading his library book on weapons while he waited for me to drive him to school. I'd called Doc and left him a message about my morning's field trip to the morgue thanks to Cooper. I knew it wasn't really the detective's fault that I needed to go look at a dead body first thing on a Monday, but after my sleepless night, I needed to curse and rant about somebody. I probably should have called Natalie instead of Doc. For once I wouldn't be defending the object of her sexual frustrations.

Harvey showed up a few minutes before we had to leave dressed in a fancy blue western shirt, new-looking jeans, and silver-toed cowboy boots. He'd agreed to come over and keep an eye on Addy while Aunt Zoe and I hung out with Cooper at the morgue. My little sugar junkie was still sleeping after her eventful night. School wasn't going to happen for her thanks to their 24-hour puke-free rule.

I stepped back to let him inside, picking up a whiff of his spicy cologne. "Wow, you didn't need to dress up for Addy. She's not even awake yet."

"I had a breakfast date scheduled fer this mornin'."

I pulled on my pea coat, which I'd brushed and beaten thoroughly to get rid of the majority of the chimera's ash, adding a final spritz with a deodorizer to finish the job. I'd have to drop it off at the dry cleaners sometime this week to do it justice.

I waved Layne over and held the door open for him, saying to Harvey, "We'll hurry so you can still get your chuckwagon on."

"Who said anything about food?" he winked. "The sweet buns I ordered were supposed to be pre-glazed, warm, and waitin' fer me. Ya owe me big fer this, girlie. Like two dinners out on the town big."

"Put it on my tab, horny toad." I headed out the door after Layne with Aunt Zoe on my heels.

The ride to school was quiet, with Aunt Zoe and I exchanging angst-laden glances several times along the way. The last time I'd started my day with a visit to see a body at Mudder Brothers I'd inspected a decapitated guy with a black wart in his bellybutton. Having learned my lesson before, I'd skipped breakfast today in preparation for what we were about to inspect. Throwing up in front of—and partially on—Cooper had been one of my all-time low points since moving to Deadwood. I didn't want to give him an encore performance.

After Layne kissed me good-bye and hopped out of the SUV, I steered toward Mudder Brothers. I needed to focus on something normal for a few minutes and lower my blood pressure several notches. Something that didn't include gnawed-on bodies, flesh eaters, and otherworldly hunters.

"What are you getting Reid for Christmas?" I asked Aunt Zoe.

She huffed. "Why would I get that man anything?"

"Because he has amazing bedroom eyes that you love staring into."

"Shut it, child," she said without conviction. "You know not of what you speak."

"Please. All Reid has to do is look your way and your bloomers catch on fire, which in turn makes the sexy fireman reach for his hose." That made her grin. "Now what are you getting him?"

She stared out her window as I turned right onto Sherman Street. "I made him a new watch band. It's leather with several different silver charms."

"Decorated armor. I like it." I gave her a teasing smile. "He's going to think you're going steady when you give it to him, you know."

"It's for his protection."

"Sure it is."

She jabbed my shoulder. "Quit trying to play cupid, Violet Lynn."

"I can't help it. I like Reid."

"So does my heart, and that's a problem for my head."

"Are you going to invite him to Christmas dinner?"

"No. You saw your father's reaction last weekend. If Reid shows up on Blake's doorstep, he'll probably belt him in the breadbasket next."

Over a week ago, my dad had tackled my ex on Aunt Zoe's front lawn, landing a few punches in Rex's midsection before Cooper managed to separate them. It was not one of my family's finer moments, but at least nobody ended up in jail this time. Well, except for Doc.

"That's probably a good idea. Although I bet Doc would appreciate having Reid there to help take the heat."

"Doc has you, me, and the kids."

"Yeah. I wish I could figure out a way to have this first Christmas without the potential for another mushroom cloud."

"What are you getting Doc for Christmas?"

I groaned. "You tell me."

Eight days left until Santa made his run and I had no idea what to give Doc. My shopping for the kids, Aunt Zoe, Nat, my parents, Harvey, Mona, my boss, Cornelius, and Reid was complete. Hell, I'd even ordered something for Cooper in the midst of my online shopping adventures at work last week—a new tie with police handcuffs and "Do Not Cross" tape zig-zagging down it to replace the one I'd ruined months ago by accidentally throwing up on it ... and Cooper.

When it came to Doc, though, the perfect gift eluded me. Natalie suggested a fur-lined teddy, but that seemed too cliché. I wanted it to be something that didn't have to do with sex for once. Something that showed I was nuts about more than just his body. Something heartfelt but not too mushy.

"What about two tickets for a weekend getaway to somewhere warm and tropical?" Aunt Zoe suggested. "No kids, no family, just you and him."

"That sounds like heaven, but I'm afraid to leave my kids with all of these weird killers on the loose. Not to mention Dominick Masterson stalking you."

She growled, enlisting a multitude of curse words to describe her situation with Dominick. Before wrapping up, she threw Reid into the mix as well.

I was still chuckling a short time later when we pulled into the parking lot at Mudder Brothers Funeral Parlor. I rolled around the side of the century-old, two-story house with its white neoclassical columns. Eddie Mudder was waiting with my favorite Deadwood detective in front of the morgue-slash-garage.

I parked and pulled out the key. "You ready for this?"

"No," Aunt Zoe said and hopped out.

Eddie smiled when he saw me climb out of my SUV. "Violet, how is your son doing?"

Months prior, Eddie had been dragged into my messy world, acting as a liaison between Mr. Black and me before I realized we were on the same team. Layne had been the main subject the three of us had in common, or rather my son's picture that had been stuck in a mirror in Ms. Wolff's apartment around the time of her death.

"He's doing well, thanks." I jabbed my thumb at the big house where he held funerals in the parlor and performed autopsies in the basement. "How's the business of death treating you? You have a lot of stiff competition for your attention?"

The glare Cooper gave me said plenty about the non-sunny location of his funny bone this morning.

Eddie chortled. "People are dying to get in here these days. I've been thinking about writing a novel."

"Really?" I imagined Eddie had a lot of macabre stories to share. "About what?"

"An overcrowded cemetery. Unfortunately, there's no plot."

I giggled. "Good one." I looked at Cooper, whose lips remained in a flat line. "You need to have Eddie teach you how to be funny."

"I've already had my big laugh for the day, remember?" He turned to Eddie. "Let's get this over with. I need to write up a report and then try to catch some sleep before my next shift starts."

His next shift? How many hours was Cooper putting in these days? His red-rimmed eyes made me feel guilty about giving him a hard time this morning. Although he'd started it with that crack about my hair when I'd joined him in the kitchen.

Eddie led us into the open front room of the garage where he kept the stretchers and dry goods needed for taking care of his clients. The building was heated enough to take the chill out of the room, but I swore I could smell a hint of formaldehyde in the air every time I visited. To the left an interior door opened into a small crematorium with a furnace that gave me the willies to even think about most days.

In front of us was a wide freezer door, a chain and padlock wrapped around the handle to keep it secure. I didn't remember seeing a padlock or chain when I was in here last, nor the convex crinkle in the center of the stainless steel slab. Then again, I'd been with Cooper and Detective Hawke that day. The former had been busy grinding his molars while the latter tried to pin another murder on me, so I'd been plenty distracted.

"I haven't been in here in years." Aunt Zoe frowned toward the crematorium room. "Not since my grandmother died."

I shivered at the thought of my great-grandma, her gnarled fingers, and the constant clacking of her rune stones.

Jamming my hands in my pockets, I hunched my shoulders. This place gave me the heebie-jeebies every time I stepped inside of it ... or snuck around outside of it with an ornery old goat. Thinking of the night Harvey and I discovered the Mudder family's collection of antique mortician tools reminded me of a question I had for the owner of the funeral parlor.

"Eddie, do you know anything about a female undertaker that lived and worked in Deadwood in the late 1800s?"

Cooper's eyebrows drew together. "Uncle Willis must have put a bug in your ear. He keeps bringing her up, nagging me to scour the police archives for information on her. What the hell is going on with you two? What's with the sudden interest in this woman?"

I shrugged. "I was inquiring on Harvey's behalf. He brought it up when we were waiting for you in Slagton on Friday. When I mentioned it to Doc, he remembered reading that there was a female undertaker, but he hadn't come across much information on her at the library."

"Let me scour our storage room and get back to you," Eddie said. "My father kept all of the old books that came with the parlor when he bought it. My brother, George, made sure to store them in a dark, dry area. He took pride in being one of the town's historians, serving on the city council and advisory board of the local history group. Maybe there's something in one of those record books on this female undertaker."

"Thanks." I pulled my hand out and skimmed my palm over the cold, bent steel. "Is this bulge new, Eddie?"

"Yes." He took a key from his pocket and unlocked the padlock. After removing the chain, he hit the light switch next to the freezer and then pulled open the door. He pointed at a large concave dent on the other side. "Something wanted out last night and this door was in its way."

The inside of the door was peppered with shallow dents, with the one in the center by far the deepest.

"Holy shit." How strong was a *Nachzehrer*? I glanced at Aunt Zoe.

Her worried gaze held mine.

Eddie led the way inside the freezer. Aunt Zoe followed and then me, with Cooper bringing up the rear. The freezer reminded me of a butcher's freezer. I covered my nose, not wanting to smell anything, especially with what I was about to see.

Only one of the long shelves held a body. "It's been slow," Eddie explained. "Apparently nobody is in a rush to die over the holidays."

"Yeah, me neither," I whispered through my fingers.

He walked over to the body. It was wrapped in a layer of opaque plastic, reminding me of another body I'd seen when I was standing alongside Cooper in Lead back in November, only that one had my war hammer sticking out of its chest.

"You can see here where the plastic was chewed on."

Chewed? I cringed, gearing up for the task in front of me.

Cooper extracted his flashlight, shining the beam on the plastic to give us a better view. It looked like a big rat had been working on it.

Eddie took out a utility knife and sliced along the plastic, pulling it apart to expose the lower leg. "You can see the chew marks here on the outside of the calf. They go all of the way down to the ankle." He took a pencil from his shirt pocket and pointed down the leg.

In the flashlight's beam, I could see where something had worked on Mr. Haskell's leg like it was an ear of corn, leaving a mangled fleshy mess.

I recoiled, my stomach hitching in spite of my mental preparation. "Jesus," I said and turned away.

"Is Mr. Haskell embalmed?" Aunt Zoe asked.

Eddie shook his head. "His will specifically requested that no embalming be done."

I stepped back, glancing at Cooper. "You really need to start taking me to nicer places for breakfast."

His mouth tilted at one corner. "I thought you were a meat eater." He pointed toward the body. "You haven't seen the ear yet."

"What about the ear?" Aunt Zoe asked.

"It's gone," Eddie said. "This is going to make an open casket viewing impossible."

The black coffee swishing around in my stomach was threatening to play geyser and erupt via my esophagus.

I didn't need to see anymore. I'd take Eddie's word for it. "I'll wait outside for you guys to finish." Without giving anyone a chance to stop me, I rushed out of the freezer.

Cooper joined me a short time later as the sun crested the hills, zipping up his thick cop coat. "Did you tell Nyce about this?" He jabbed his thumb toward the morgue.

"I left him a voicemail."

He nodded, frowning toward the funeral parlor. "I don't know how to write this up. I can't say there are chew marks on the body. The chief will give me a week off for mental stress leave like Hawke, and now is not a good time to turn in my badge and gun."

"Especially with your informant missing."

His gray eyes swung back to me. "Nyce told me you made a deal with Masterson regarding Slagton."

I cringed. "I suppose you're going to bitch at me for that."

"I don't bitch. I bite, remember?" His lips twitched.

Cooper picked the oddest times to joke. "Too well, detective."

"How in the hell are you going to catch one of those nasty fuckers?"

I squeezed the back of my neck. "I'll let you know when I figure that out. In the meantime, keep your fingers crossed that Dominick gives us something helpful on your missing informant."

Aunt Zoe stepped into the pale morning sunshine, shielding her eyes as she approached.

"What do you think?" I asked her.

"We're going to have to bone up on how to hunt *der Nachzehrer*."

Shit criminy! I was a little busy being hunted myself at the moment. "My dance card for the hunters' ball is already full."

"Make some room, baby girl."

"Let me get this straight," Cooper said, extra heavy in the scowl department. "You think there's some kind of flesh-eating ghoul roaming the area?"

"No." Aunt Zoe scanned the trees on the hillside behind the morgue. "I think there are at least two flesh-eating ghouls roaming the area now, and if we don't stop them, the two will become four, and then eight, and so on."

My stomach sank. "Please tell me you're kidding."

"I wish I was." Worry lines fanned from her blue eyes when she turned back to me. "Let the hunt begin, *Scharfrichter.*"

Chapter Fourteen

Going to work was a welcome change from monster hunting. After I dropped off Aunt Zoe at home and made sure Addy was feeling okay, I put on my real estate agent hat and dragged my tired ass to my desk.

The normalcy of everyday office life inside Calamity Jane's helped me come to grips with what I'd learned at Mudder Brothers this morning. Mona clacked on the keyboard as usual, pausing only to send me an insider's smile, along with a "Good morning, Vi," as I settled in at my desk. Jerry and Ben returned from the Rec Center showers shortly after I arrived, their hair still damp and their surplus testosterone spent on the ball court. They both shared small talk for several minutes before focusing on their computer screens.

Ray came in last, crowing that his breakfast meeting was a success. He dropped into his chair, kicked up his boots, and aimed a wrinkled upper lip my way. If his goal was to upset my applecart, there was nothing left to tip over. Learning that I had to figure out how to hunt down a party of *Nachzehrer* before they grew into a colony of flesh-eating ghouls pretty much blew my cart into teeny-tiny pieces. Ray could go fuck himself as far as I was concerned, and he could take Tiffany along for the ride.

"Ray," Jerry said, interrupting Ray's glower. "Don't forget I need your month-end expenses early."

I looked at Jerry. That was odd. Usually he requested our month-end paperwork after the first of the next month. Maybe Ray was taking a couple of weeks off. Could I be so lucky? Santa must have read my wishlist. If only I could convince Tiffany to relocate to the North Pole.

Rosy walked through the front door around the time I'd started my second cup of coffee since arriving at the office. She carried a stainless steel case and a big smile.

"We need to huddle up for a moment," Jerry said, standing in the middle of our circle of desks. "I asked Rosy to join us today to begin filming."

Son of a mother trucker! After a night full of Addy's technicolored yawns and a morning staring at a nibbled-on corpse, I did not want to try my best to look good for the flippin' camera.

"I can tell by some of your expressions," and with that his gaze zeroed on Mona for a moment, "you're not thrilled with smiling into the camera lens. However, this is just a practice run. The footage Rosy captures will be used as a game tape to see where we need to improve."

Rosy set her case on Jerry's desk. From it, she extracted an expensive-looking video camera and microphone.

"I'll start the filming, working with Rosy to test her equipment and get things ready for the rest of you. I've written some scripts, but feel free to try something new. Remember, this is practice. We're figuring out your comfort zone and shooting for warm-up purposes only."

I didn't love the idea of watching myself on film, but Jerry's passion for perfection and his determination to achieve the top real estate ranking in western South Dakota left no doubt in my mind that I'd be going along with his plans.

I shared a frown with Mona. She pointed at my computer. I looked down right as an email from her hit my inbox.

Opening it, I read: *There was another note on the whiteboard this morning.*

I looked over at the board. Of course it was empty. At my raised brows, Mona clacked on her keys again.

The next email read: *Ray is not alone.*

I read that again, then replied: *What do you mean?*

She typed: *That's what the message said.*

We both turned to look at Ray, who was leaning back in his chair, talking on the phone. When he noticed Mona was staring he winked at her. She looked away, as did I before he caught me watching him, too.

I sent her an email: *I'll let the others know.*

She nodded and then Jerry leaned over her, cell phone in hand with somebody on the line, asking her about one of her listings.

Rosy sidled up to my desk. "How about I film you before lunch?"

"That works for me." I took the script cards she handed me.

"Are you busy today?" she asked. "I mean for lunch."

"Not that I know of. Why?"

"I want to take you out and shower you with food."

I smiled. "Food showers are my favorite kind."

"Great, because I love my new house and you were a big part in making my dream to live here happen. Will you let me take you out for burgers?"

After my morning, a greasy burger didn't appeal.

Jerry hung up his phone, joining Rosy at my desk. "A happy customer is like a game-winning three-pointer. Way to go, Violet." To Rosy, he said, "Why don't you two take some extra time at lunch? That way you can celebrate without rushing. Besides, it's plenty slow here. That's why I scheduled the vlog prep for today."

It was a done deal now. Jerry had spoken.

The rest of the morning crept by as I tried to bury my head in some of the new real estate regulations that had recently been handed down by the state for the upcoming year. I went through my script cards a few times in front of the camera, smiling so wide at first that Rosy stopped filming and asked me to tone it down a few notches so I didn't scare the others.

A quick phone call home right before lunch confirmed that Addy's stomach issues were sugar-related only, as no other flu symptoms had occurred since she'd come downstairs. That was a relief. Battling the flu over Christmas would have sucked. Aunt Zoe added that my child had eaten almost half her weight in toast and scrambled eggs after waking. Apparently her stomach was making up for lost contents.

Finally it was time to go eat and be merry. Rosy drove us up to Lead, swinging by her place first so I could do a walk-through to see all she'd done to what I'd formerly liked to think of as Fort Cooper.

Gone were Cooper's monochrome furnishings and leather accessories. Rosy preferred flowers, especially those like her namesake and mine. The man cave had been overhauled, turned into a garden cottage flush with flower prints on the furniture and walls. I couldn't help but smile at the cringing and cursing Cooper would have done had he been standing next to me.

I wouldn't have figured Rosy for such femininity in her decorating due to the size of her biceps and daily uniform of old T-shirts and jeans, but the house felt warm, comfy, and cozy. Or maybe it was just the lack of artillery that gave it that illusion.

After admiring Rosy's handiwork, I stared at the Georgia O'Keefe "Black Iris" print over the fireplace that Cooper had grudgingly hung when I was prepping to show his house to potential clients. Harvey would be happy to see it was still there. That print had reminded him of some good times he'd spent with a dark-skinned *señorita* from some brothel down in Nevada.

The iris painting was gorgeous and now fit the décor to a T, but to be honest, I missed Cooper's framed print of dogs cleaning their guns around a poker table. This admission made me realize that I might actually think of Cooper as a friend now, even with his rough edges and sharp teeth. That must be why I kept defending the crabby monkeybutt to Natalie.

With the tour over, Rosy and I headed to Lead's main drag. She parked behind The Golden Sluice Bar. I hadn't been in the place since my lunch meeting last summer with a philandering asshole, who currently resided at Cell-block C in Prison, USA.

"You want to eat *here*?" I asked. My experience with the food was not nearly as exciting as that with my last lunch companion. The chicken was overcooked, the floors were grimy, and the air was hazy and filled with a multitude of nose wrinkling odors.

"Yeah, I ate here the other night. The food's pretty good."

Since Rosy was paying, she got to pick the place, so I smiled in spite of my previous experiences and followed her inside. At least, this time my companion would be much easier on my nerves, saving me the worry of being felt up under the table by the town's notorious playboy, and then being overly self-critical afterward about why the creep hadn't even tried to play footsy.

The first thing I noticed was the Grizzly Adams look-alike still tending the bar. However, the place was lit up with some fancy new lights dangling from the tin ceiling that reflected off a shiny wood floor. The original planks must have been sanded down and then sealed with several fresh coats of varnish since my last visit. Also gone was the haze and rank in the air, replaced by the scent of charbroiled meat and fried goodness.

"This is a lot different from when I was here back in August," I told Rosy as we slid into a corner booth across from each other.

"According to your coworker, Ben, the previous owner passed away last month," she said. "Since then, her son has taken over the place, using some capital and elbow grease to spruce up the joint."

"It's certainly a lot nicer." I glanced around the room, pausing on the polished bar and lighted shelves that made the bottles of liquor seem to glow.

My cell phone rang. I looked down at the phone, seeing Zelda Britton's name.

"Do you mind if I take this?" I asked.

"Not at all."

"Thanks." I slid out of the booth. "If the waitress stops by, please order me a chef's salad, a side of fries, and an iced tea."

I took the call as I stepped outside the front door. "Hello?" I shivered in the cold, steady wind blowing up through Lead.

"Hi, Violet," Zelda said. I could hear her perky smile in her voice. "I'm sorry to bother you, but Prudence really needs to see you."

Since when had Zelda become Prudence's personal assistant? And how could I get one? Those minions Detective Hawke always accused me of having kept refusing to show up for work each day.

"Prudence needs to see me right now?"

"As soon as possible. She's quite agitated. I don't know that I've seen her like this before."

Prudence could join the dang club. I frowned in the direction of her house. "I'm sorry, but today is not going to work for me, Zelda. Let Prudence know that I'll see if I can find some time to swing by tomorrow afternoon." I'd need to remember to take my purse inside when I showed up. I had the tooth from that thing in Slagton sealed in a pill bottle, waiting to be handed off to the dead woman.

Zelda's voice was muffled for a moment as she repeated my message. I could imagine her standing in her kitchen, talking to empty air, looking plumb nuts. I'd done the same thing in her house myself several times.

"Violet, she insists upon seeing you immediately."

I growled in my throat. Who in the hell did Prudence think she was? I didn't care if she used to be some badass killer, I had some shit to work through today. I had no desire to look into the whites of Zelda's eyes while being threatened and told how worthless I was at my Executioner role.

"I can't come right now."

"She can't come now," Zelda spoke again to her invisible boss.

A jacked-up truck rumbled past.

"Prudence wants to know where you are."

Why did that matter? I wasn't coming to her house, not even if I was parked next door to it. This was quickly becoming a matter of pride. I was not Prudence's lackey, waiting for her next order.

"I'm at The Golden Sluice with a client." Well, someone who used to be a client, anyway.

"Prudence says to bring the client here with you."

"Zelda …" I blew out a breath, not wanting to shoot the messenger. "Please tell Prudence that I'm not coming to see her today. Period. I need to return to work when lunch is finished and cannot fit her into my schedule at this time. She will have to be patient and wait."

The door opened behind me. "Howdy, Sparky," an older guy said as he walked past me.

Frowning after him, I wondered how he knew me and who'd told him my nickname. I suspected it was another old-timer who had a weekly dinner deal with me until I sold his ranch. A smart move on Harvey's part, since it would probably take a decade to unload that property what with all of the body parts that kept popping up there.

I focused back on my phone. "Zelda, I need to go. I'm sorry to put you in the middle like this, but Prudence will have to wait until I can fit her into my schedule. I'll be in touch."

I doubted that would go over well with the uppity ghost, but too damned bad. She could take a number and get in line for my freaky-shit show.

Returning to the warm bar, I shucked my coat and slid across from Rosy. "Sorry about that," I told her. "Now, where were we?"

"About to eat pretzels," she said as the waitress appeared with two big soft pretzels on a plate with cheese dipping sauce.

I practically drooled all over the waitress when she set them down between us.

"And we were about to toast to my new house and to you soon becoming a reality show superstar."

I groaned at the superstar bit. "I'd settle just for being a successful Realtor living a regular old happy life these days."

"To plain ol' life, then," Rosy said, holding up her glass of water. I clinked it with my glass of iced tea.

We dug into the hot pretzels, dipping them in melted cheese. I basically inhaled the salt-covered, carb-laden goodness while I listened to Rosy talk about her idea to make Cooper's garage into a recording and editing studio. Not only could she tape commercial footage in there, but she could also work on the freelance film work she did on the side, including additional vlogs as Jerry continued to build the Calamity Jane website.

Shortly after the waitress delivered our main course, I glanced toward the bar and stopped listening to Rosy's plans for the upcoming holiday. Was that Zelda staring back at me through a pair of dark sunglasses?

I lowered my fork. Her black stocking cap and thick, quilted coat were covered in daisies. Yep, that was Zelda. We shared a love of the happy-faced flower. What was she doing here? If Prudence sent her to lobby for a visit to her house today, she was wasting our time.

I waved Zelda over.

Rosy paused, looking over her shoulder. "You know her?"

"Yeah."

The petite librarian wore black sweater tights under a knee-length corduroy skirt. She walked toward us in her yellow snow boots, but she seemed to have a slight limp. Upon closer inspection, Zelda was dragging her left foot a bit. Had she twisted her ankle recently?

"What's with the dark sunglasses?" Rosy asked. "The lights aren't that bright in here."

Zelda reached our table before I could answer.

"Hi." I could see my frowning reflection in her glasses. "What are you doing here? I thought we'd agreed that I'd contact you tomorrow to set up a meeting with you and your friend."

Her jaw taut, Zelda leaned down and spoke next to my ear. "When I request your presence, Executioner, you will heed my bidding!"

Prudence!

I recoiled at the sound of her mid-Atlantic Eastern accent, which I'd come to associate with humiliation and pain. How in the holy rollers was Prudence the ghost standing in a bar in Lead?

A ghost walked into a bar ... a voice said in my head. A cackle of panicked laughter echoed after it. This was like the start to a lousy joke.

"Wh-what are you doing here?" I whispered.

I knew Prudence had been growing stronger by the fact that she was able to use multiple people as her puppets at the same time she was interacting with me, but that was in her own house. I'd assumed the house acted as a cage, keeping her trapped for as long as she continued to roam this plane of existence.

Apparently, I'd assumed wrong.

"Since you did not come to me, I came to you." She pushed the sunglasses on top of her stocking cap and glared down at me with the whites of Zelda's eyes. "Do not make me seek you next time. You will regret such insubordination."

The fury lining Zelda's face would have made a newer Executioner cower, but I'd faced off with plenty of crazy crap over the last few days, let alone months.

"Violet?" Rosy croaked. "What's going on?"

Oh, crud. I'd forgotten about Rosy. I looked her way, grimacing as her burger slipped from her fingers and plopped onto her plate, knocking the top bun loose. Her face was pale, her mouth gaping as she stared at Zelda's rigid profile.

"Put the glasses back on, Prudence," I said quietly. "You're making a scene in front of my client."

Prudence's white eyes shifted to my lunch companion. "This is of no concern to her."

Rosy's eyelids dropped, making her look as if she were meditating across from me. Then, in turntable fashion, she swiveled slowly away from us and faced the wall.

"There is much to prepare, Executioner." Prudence focused on me. "Yet you insist on causing upheaval among our enemies by killing openly. What were you thinking? Such blatant foolery!"

Her chastising made my cheeks warm. How did she know about what had happened in Slagton already? I could buy Dominick having caught wind of it, but Prudence was a ghost, for crissake. Was there some underground ghost gossiping network? It wasn't like they could call each other up and blab about my dirty laundry. Or could they? What did I know about ghosts? Hell, most of the time I couldn't even see or sense them, Prudence being the exception.

I glared up into the whites of her eyes. "The hunters attacked me. What was I supposed to do? Turn the other cheek?"

"Draw them into the shadows. An Executioner's power is in part derived by obscuring her skills from her enemy. What cannot be seen is immeasurable and unpredictable. You would do well to keep that in mind in the future if you want to keep breathing."

My gaze darted around the bar. A couple of the other patrons were looking our way. I leaned closer to her, speaking low in case anyone was eavesdropping "Let's go outside and talk about this in private."

"No. We shall speak of this right here." She jabbed the table with her finger. "Immediately."

"Fine, but put those damned sunglasses back on. Nobody wants to look at the whites of Zelda's eyes." Especially me.

With a jerky movement, she lowered the sunglasses to her nose, hiding those unnerving eyeballs.

"And quit standing over me." I pointed at the seat across the table. "You're drawing unwanted attention, Ms. We-Must-Remain-Unseen."

She dropped onto the bench seat, pushing Rosy closer to the wall as if she weighed no more than a doll.

"You better not be hurting Rosy."

"She is merely diverted until I release her."

"What about Zelda?"

"What of her?"

"Is she okay inside there?" I aimed my fork at Zelda's forehead.

"I would never harm Zelda. She is an uncommonly clear channel, and her heart is kind and generous. I regard her as a friend."

If taking control of Zelda's body represented how she treated her friends, I'd hate to see what Prudence did to anyone she perceived as an enemy. Oh wait, I'd already witnessed it. Ray had lost a tooth and Hawke now barked on command.

"What is so urgent that you had to risk exposure to talk to me?"

"You are in dire straits."

I guffawed. "You raced down here to deliver that news? Tell me something I don't know."

Her nostrils flared. "You may still be of the flesh, but I have the experience and knowledge to lead where you continue to stumble and create disorder."

If I wanted to be insulted over lunch, I would have asked Ray or Tiffany to tag along today. "You know, Prudence, when you talk to me like that, it doesn't motivate me to try any damned harder. It just pisses me off."

"What is your fascination with vulgarity?" She picked up one of Rosy's French fries, taking a nibble from it, and then dropped it like it bit her.

"Vulgarity is the name of the game for my Executioner line. It blends well with my stumbling disorder." She snorted, perhaps in agreement. "How do you know what happened back in Slagton, Prudence?"

"I have my ways, not unlike you."

Yeah, but my ways involved eyeballs that actually belonged to me. "What ways?" And whose side was she really on? She'd made no pretense on how she felt about Team Violet, what with her constant critiquing.

"My means of acquiring information are not your affair." She linked Zelda's fingers together on the table. "I need you to seek out the Timekeeper who bound you to another."

"It's too late," I said, poking at my salad. I took a bite, grinning at her through a mouthful of lettuce. "She's gone."

She reached across the table and slapped my cheek. "Do not talk to me with your mouth full. It is repulsive and uncouth."

I swallowed, holding my cheek. "Dang it, Prudence. Just once, could you not hurt me when I'm in your presence? I'm supposed to be your associate."

"You are not my associate. We merely share an occupational hazard."

I lowered my fork. "If we're not comrades in arms, then why did you wait around all of these years for me to show up in Deadwood?"

"Who said I was waiting for you?"

"You did." Right after she handed me Ray's tooth. "And then you told me I needed you because I couldn't succeed on my own."

She'd ended that conversation by telling me not only was I wasting precious time, but I reeked of death. I stabbed another forkful of salad. It was no wonder I had on-the-job confidence issues.

"You do and you will not."

"Why did you say you were waiting for me if you weren't?"

"I was waiting for another of our kind. You were the first to arrive." She pushed away Rosy's plate of half-eaten food, disappointment in her voice. "What do you mean, the Timekeeper is gone?"

"I mean she is no longer of this world." Well, no more of *my* world. What did I really know about other possible worlds? "Ms. Wolff—or rather Ms. Hoont, as you called her—is no longer on this plane or in this realm or whatever you want to call it."

"How do you know this?"

I leaned forward and whispered, "I executed her."

Prudence stilled. "You *what*?"

Stabbing another forkful of salad, I said, "You heard me." I wasn't real proud of the fact, either. I preferred killing the bad and the ugly, leaving the good alone.

"Another of your blunders," she accused more than asked.

"Wrong. It was her will."

"And what of the *other* Timekeeper?"

I shrugged, dipping a fry in the pool of ketchup on my plate. "Mr. Black has contacted me. We are working together now." I stuffed the whole fry in my mouth, wiping my hands on a napkin. It tasted just fine to me, not too greasy. What was her problem?

"Together?" Her hand snaked out and captured mine. She tugged me across the table and ran the pads of her fingers over my palm like there were braille letters stamped on it. "Oh, my stars. You are a Timekeeper."

I pulled my hand free, frowning down at my sweater sleeve that now had ketchup on it. "Dang it all! Look what you did." I sat back in the booth seat. "Just once, it would be nice to have a normal conversation with you."

She crossed her arms. "Do you have a tooth for me?"

"See, this is what I'm talking about." I dabbed my napkin in Rosy's glass of ice water and tried to get the worst of the ketchup off my sleeve. "If we're going to work together, you need to stop hurting me all of the time and threatening to take my teeth."

"And what will you offer in return for my benevolence?"

"What would you like?"

She drew something on the table with her fingertip. "You cannot provide what would please me."

Maybe not, but I dug into my purse and pulled out something that might warm her up a little. "Will this suffice for today?"

I opened the small pill bottle and dumped the tooth Doc had pulled from the head of the creature back in Slagton on the table between us.

Zelda's mouth fell slack as Prudence stared at the tooth. Slowly, she reached out and picked it up, sniffing it. "Do you have any idea what this is?" She held the tooth between her thumb and index finger, admiring it.

"A tooth for your collection, delivered as promised."

She pocketed it in Zelda's coat. "You are a dolt. You take ostentatious risks."

"Yeah, well, you're welcome and keep your fingers out of my mouth, thank you." I took another bite of salad. "What's with you and all of those teeth, anyway?"

"Teeth are unique to the individual," she said, as if it made her odd fetish seem natural. "The same can be said of the tongue."

"Then why don't you collect tongues?"

"Do not be absurd."

"And collecting teeth is more rational?"

"What you do not understand could fill an abyss." She pulled Rosy's glass of ice water toward her. "The hunters will not cease until you are dead."

I stuck a French fry in my mouth, frowning across at her as I chewed. "Which hunters are we talking about?"

"All of them." She stuck Zelda's hand in the glass and fished out an ice cube, dropping it onto Rosy's plate next to the burger. "Are you prepared?"

"For what?" I watched as she fished out two more ice cubes, tossing them aside as well. What was her issue with ice? "The mythical hunter after my hide or *der Nachzehrer*?"

She stopped mid-fish. "What? What did you say?"

Ah-ha. Something she didn't know. How was it she knew about Slagton but not the flesh-eating ghouls? Was it because it was too soon for her ghost radar to detect them?

"*Der Nachzehrer.*" I mumbled more this time, since I wasn't sure I was pronouncing the name correctly.

"Has it consumed the flesh of another?" At my nod, she pulled her hand from the glass, drying it on Rosy's napkin. "How many are there now?"

"Two, maybe more."

"This is not good. They are exceptional at subterfuge."

"Are they tougher to catch than a *lidérc*?"

"Why would you bother to catch a *lidérc*? You need to execute it."

"I sort of made a deal with a devil." Two deals, actually.

She threw down the napkin. "Must you complicate what should be a simple task? In our line of work, it is slay or be slain. There is no catching, not with these fiends. One misstep and they will slice your throat."

I glanced down at Zelda's throat, grimacing. Was that what had happened to Prudence? She made a mistake and had her throat sliced open because of it? While in her ghostly form, she still wore the dress she was murdered in, the blood staining the high collar.

"I didn't intend to complicate things. Not everything is black and white in my world, Prudence. Sometimes I have to work in the gray."

"With whom did you make a deal?"

I took a sip of iced tea, looking down at my half-eaten salad. "I'd rather not tell you."

"Why not?"

"Because you'll just insult me again."

She leaned over the table. "Who?"

"Someone non-human."

She reached for me, but I dodged her hand. "Tell me!"

"Stop trying to hurt me and I will."

Folding her hands together, she lowered them into her lap. "Who?"

"He currently goes by the name of Dominick Masterson."

She sat back, inhaling her gasp. "That coxcomb? You *Dummkopf*!"

"See, I knew you'd insult me again."

"Do you understand the ramifications of dealing with a guardian?"

Obviously not, because … "What's a guardian?"

"They take pride in their ability to appear gallant when they are truly knaves, a peccant larcener of souls."

Peccant? I was going to need to look that word up if it meant something other than what Addy's chicken did to my coat buttons.

"What is this deal you made?" she asked.

"Information on who killed the Timekeeper in exchange for catching his *lidérc*."

"But you said that you slew the Timekeeper."

"I did, but this was before I knew it was me."

Zelda's mouth opened and closed a couple of times before she spoke, as though Prudence was oiling her jaw hinge. "How could you not know it was you?"

I chomped on another fry. "There was a time loop. I had to complete the second loop to see the whole replay of events."

"You are like a child with a delicate flower, crushing and tearing it apart before you realize what you have in your hands."

I pointed the last half of my French fry at her. "Oddly enough, your words aren't helping." I shoved the rest of the fry in my mouth, pushing aside the plate. "If you insult me one more time, we're done talking."

"I will tell you when we are finished conversing."

"Fine, insult away, but answer me this—how do I catch a *lidérc* alive?" With Aunt Zoe's future on the line, I needed to figure this out fast.

She sat quietly for several moments, long enough for me to finish my iced tea.

"You need to devise a trap."

"And use a human as bait," I finished for her.

She sighed at what was apparently a stupid answer. "No."

"Why not? They attach to human hosts."

"Had you been locked in a cage for over a century, what would tempt you more? An innocent bystander or the one who jailed you?"

"The jailer."

"Precisely. You want to lure the *lidérc*? Offer up the one who sealed it away in the dark long ago."

I let that settle in my thoughts before moving on to my next question. "How do I catch one of those mutant griffins in Slagton?"

"Mutant what?"

"Chimeras," I said, using Dominick's word to see if that worked better for her.

"Must I do everything for you?" Zelda's mouth moved several times with no words following. Then Prudence appeared to regroup. "I am tired now. I must rest." She reached across and clasped my wrist, squeezing hard enough to make me squirm. "Remember, do not let them see your strengths. Distract them with your weaknesses."

"But what about …" I trailed off when Zelda's head drooped forward. Her grip on my wrist slackened. "Prudence?"

Zelda lifted her head, looking around. "Why is it so dark in here?"

"You're wearing sunglasses," Rosy said.

I looked over at the camerawoman, who was staring at Zelda like she'd seen her somewhere before but couldn't place her.

"Hi, Violet," Zelda said, lifting her sunglasses. Her beautiful green eyes stared back at me. "Did you have a chance to speak with Prudence?"

I nodded. "I'm sorry you had to come down here on my account." Actually, it was on Prudence's account.

"Oh, it's no problem." She waved me off. "Prudence is always gentle with me. In fact, when I come back from my little Prudy naps, as I like to call them, I feel extra energized. I probably won't be able to sleep tonight." She smiled, her usual bright and sunny self again. "Maybe I'll make a batch of Christmas cookies for Zeke. He'll be pulling in tomorrow afternoon." She turned to Rosy and held out her hand. "I'm Zelda, by the way. What's your name?"

"Rosy." She shook Zelda's hand. "I work with Violet."

"So you live around here?"

"Yeah." Rosy pulled her hand free, frowning down at her plate. "Did I spill my water?" She lifted her burger. The bottom bun fell apart in her hand, waterlogged from Prudence's ice fishing.

"We should have coffee together sometime," Zelda said to her and then slid out of the booth. "If you two will excuse me, I need to run to the post office and mail some last-minute Christmas gifts." She slid on her gloves. "Stop by sometime, Violet. Prudence is always much happier after your visits."

Happ-*ier*? No way. That would require the haughty ghost to actually be happy first.

Zelda bebopped toward the door, waving at the bartender on her way out.

I turned back to Rosy. "Are you okay?"

"I think so." She rubbed her forehead. "What in the hell happened? Did I pass out?"

I wasn't sure where to start, but I was relatively certain that leading with her being temporarily possessed by a ghost was not the way to go.

"Uhhhh, what do you remember?"

"Your friend standing over our table. Then it all went dark."

I debated how much to spill, not wanting to go into the long version of Prudence's ghost story. "Zelda has an entity attached to her.

It tends to draw energy from others in the vicinity, leaving them feeling like they've awoken from a deep sleep."

"A parasitic ghost?"

Prudence would be offended by that description, I had no doubt. That made me smile. "For lack of a better word."

Rosy touched her fries. "My food is cold. How long was I out?"

"A little while. How about I order you a fresh plate of food. We still have another half hour before I need to return to work."

Shaking her head, she pushed her plate away. "I don't really feel like eating anymore."

Another side effect of temporary possession, I imagined. Cooper hadn't mentioned feeling sick to his stomach afterward, but he'd rejected going to lunch with his uncle and me.

She sniffed. "I keep smelling blood." She lifted her burger, sniffing it, and then dropped it. "It's weird. Can you smell it?"

I shook my head.

"When I blacked out, it was really strong, like I was lying in a pool of it." Her eyes widened. "Wait!"

"What?"

"I remember something else from the darkness. I was gagging."

I cringed. I'd had enough gagging for a month after my adventures with Addy last night. "On what?"

"Blood, I think." She touched her neck. "Someone had slit my throat, and I was drowning in my own blood."

Prudence.

Chapter Fifteen

Rosy returned to the office long enough to grab her camera case. On her way out, she told Jerry she would be back tomorrow to film Ben and Ray. She claimed to be feeling under the weather, but I knew it was from being under Prudence's thumb.

I walked her out, apologizing for our lunch interloper.

"It's okay, Violet. It wasn't your doing." She placed her case in the back seat of her Subaru.

"I'll bring you a coffee in the morning." I knew her favorite.

Her smile was a shadow of its usual self. "It's a deal." She slid in behind the steering wheel, frowning up at me. "Can I ask you something?"

"Sure." I cringed in anticipation of a Prudence question.

"Why did my house's previous owner install a lock on the inside of the walk-in closet?"

Whew! That was an easy one. "He's a cop."

"A safe room. That makes sense." She started to ask something else and then stopped. "I'll see you tomorrow morning."

"You will." I stepped back, watching her drive out of the lot.

I'd been back at my desk for twenty minutes when Cooper walked in the front door in plain clothes, no firearm or radio. At least not as far as I could tell. I didn't doubt for a minute that he carried concealed 24/7.

He didn't dilly dally with conventional greetings to my coworkers, barging straight at my desk. "Parker, I need you to show me a house."

I stared up at him. His eyes were still red rimmed, tired around the edges. What was with this sudden need to see a place? Last time I'd asked him about going house hunting, he'd told me that he wanted to wait until after the holidays were over and his work schedule returned to normal.

Aware that my boss was sitting two desks away, I pasted on a cheery smile. "How about we go tomorrow, Detective Cooper?" I was dragging ass myself and didn't feel like walking through a house while he listed everything that was wrong with it.

"Tomorrow is no good," he said without hesitation. "I'd like to go right now."

What in Sam Hill? Had Coop been taking lessons from Prudence? Why was he being so pushy about doing this right now? Wasn't our breakfast date looking at a chewed leg enough of my company for one day? Usually he preferred to take twenty-four hour breaks from me.

"I just returned from lunch." That sounded feeble as soon as it left my lips, but damn it, a long night filled with a sick kid followed by an early morning at the morgue made me dig in my heels. Not to mention spending my lunch hour getting reamed by a pompous dead woman.

A muscle in his jaw twitched. "Perfect, then you're available," he said. "My truck is out back."

What truck? He didn't have a pickup. Maybe he meant one of the Deadwood police vehicles. I turned to Mona, who was watching the two of us closely, especially Cooper. Was she seeing what I was seeing? A pushy detective who wouldn't take no for an answer?

"Jerry?" I looked at my boss. "How do you feel about me stepping out for the afternoon to show Cooper a house or two?"

I tried to use mental telepathy to make him reject the idea and insist that I stay and go over my "game tape" with him.

He glanced my way, gave me the thumbs-up, and then went back to his computer.

I sucked at thought transference. I'd have better luck knocking Jerry over the head with my war hammer next time.

"Grab your coat, Parker," Cooper ordered, leaving no room for discussion. "We need to hit the road."

I bristled, mumbling, "Yes, Detective Bossypants," as I collected my purse and coat. I followed him out the back door. As soon it was closed, I put my foot down, splashing slush on my suede ankle boots and cashmere leggings, which only made me snarl louder. "What's the deal, Cooper? I'm not in the fucking mood to drag you around empty houses all afternoon and listen to you bitch and moan about how shitty they are."

"You need to work on your customer service skills." He grabbed my elbow and pulled me over to Harvey's idling pickup. "I'll tell you what's the deal when you get your ass inside of Uncle Willis' pickup."

I climbed into the back seat. Harvey was waiting for me with his hair slicked back. He smelled ripe with cologne. He must have convinced his lady friend to join him for brunch after I messed up their breakfast date.

"Hey, Sparky." He gave me a thorough once-over. "Yer eyes look a little buggy."

"Well, it's been a buggy kind of day so far." After Cooper belted himself in behind the wheel and backed out of the parking spot, I said, "What's going on, Cooper? Why is it so important that we go look at a house together right now?"

"We're going out to Slagton again," Harvey answered for his nephew, sporting a gold-toothed smile in the face of my scowl.

"No." I was not going to add a trip to Hell to my itinerary today. "Take me back to work."

"You're going to Slagton with us. It's not up for discussion," Cooper said, glaring at me in the rearview mirror.

"Are you kidnapping me, Detective?"

"Now you're being ridiculous," he replied.

Maybe I was, but I really was not in the mood for whatever Slagton had to offer today. "I'm not dressed for a hunting trip. The snow out there will ruin my suede boots, and I don't want to get a tear in my cashmere leggings."

"We're not hunting today, we're scouting." Cooper turned onto Sherman Street. "As for your clothes, Uncle Willis stopped by your house and grabbed something more appropriate for the trip."

I shot Harvey a wary look. "You picked out my clothes?" That meant he'd gone into my closet, which looked like a tornado had torn through it, leaving a dusting of chicken feathers behind.

"I've seen cleaner chicken coops than yer bedroom."

"My bedroom is clean." Mostly. I made a point of trying to keep it semi-clean because Doc was sleeping in there with me now and I didn't want to scare him away with my lousy housekeeping. "My closet is simply a little untidy."

He snorted. "Yer not shootin' square. Why on Earth do ya have so many frilly bloomers?"

I gasped. "What were you doing in my underwear drawer?"

"Lookin' fer yer war hammer."

"Why would it be in my underwear drawer?"

"Most skirts tend to hide things in with their unmentionables."

He was right. I did tend to hide things in with my underwear. "Not a war hammer."

"How was I to know that?"

"And for the record, my underwear is not frilly." Doc preferred lace and satin in a multitude of colors, the skimpier the better. "And what I wear under my clothes is none of your beeswax, old man."

Harvey glanced down at my pea coat, chortling. "I reckon we know now why yer stallion gets hot to trot and already a-saddled when yer in heat."

I leaned forward and tugged on his beard. "Keep it up, you old goat, and I'll pull you through a knothole and back out again."

"Hey, that's my line."

I held up my fist. "Come and get it, crybaby."

" 'Crybaby'?" Harvey looked at the back of his nephew's head. "Watch out, Coop. Sparky's huntin' trouble with a big gun again."

"Good," Cooper said. "I like big guns."

"Why am I being kidnapped and dragged to Slagton?" I asked, wondering why Cooper had turned into the Presidential district instead of heading out of town toward Strawberry Hill.

"Because I got a call about my missing informant."

"A call from whom?"

"A concerned citizen of Slagton."

"Real funny. Who really called?"

Cooper pulled into Doc's driveway and let the pickup idle. He turned in his seat. "He wouldn't give me his name."

Doc's front door opened. He walked out, dressed in jeans, snow boots, and a thick winter coat. His movements were still stiff from the waist up, so his ribs must still be tender. Rounding the front of the pickup, he climbed into the passenger seat with a small grunt of pain. He clicked on his seatbelt and then lowered the visor, looking at me in the mirror there. "Hey, Killer. I hear you had a hair-raising morning."

I had to think back to what had happened before my lunch with Prudence. Oh yeah, the chewed-on dead guy. "My morning was relatively tame compared to my lunch."

Cooper shifted into reverse, backing out of the drive. "What happened at lunch?"

"Prudence took Zelda out for a walk."

"What in tarnation does that mean?" Harvey asked.

Cooper glanced at me with a wrinkled brow in the rearview mirror. "That doesn't make any sense, Parker."

Doc made the effort to turn in his seat so he could look me eye to eye. "Out where?"

"The Golden Sluice."

"The ol' gal just moseyed inside The Golden Sluice?" Harvey asked.

"Well, officially Zelda's body walked up to the table. I believe she drove down to the bar, but somewhere between exiting her car and stepping inside The Golden Sluice, Prudence took over the controls."

"Were the whites of her eyes showin' again?"

"She was wearing sunglasses, but after she got to the table, she raised her sunglasses, which I'm pretty sure freaked Rosy out."

"Rosy who?" Cooper asked.

"Rosy, the woman who bought your house."

"What were ya doin' out to lunch with her?" Harvey combed his beard. "Was she videotapin' you eatin'?"

"Why would she record me eating?"

"They tape people eatin' all the time on those reality shows."

"We were at The Golden Sluice because she'd wanted to show me all she'd done to Cooper's place and then take me out for a celebratory lunch for helping her buy it. She really girlie'd up your place," I told Cooper, and then looked over at Harvey. "You'd like it, dirty bird. She still has that print with the black iris on it over her fireplace."

A grin filled Harvey's cheeks. "I might have to get me one of those prints when I get my own place and hang it over my bed."

"Back to Prudence entering the bar," Doc said. "How was it she ended up visiting you there instead of you going to Zelda's house?"

As we headed out of town, I told them about the phone call I'd received from Zelda, insisting that I drop everything and come to her house to see Prudence at once. Then I described how Zelda had been there in the bar, but yet she wasn't really Zelda; how Prudence had manipulated Rosy without even moving a hand; and then all of the stuff we'd talked about in between. Well, the bits of conversation I could remember, anyway. I ended with how Rosy smelled blood and then remembered that she'd been choking on it while she was under Prudence's spell.

By the time I'd finished, we were almost to the turnoff leading to Harvey's ranch, aka the road to Slagton.

"How long ya reckon Prudence has been able to fly her coop?" Harvey asked.

"She might have always been able to leave the house, but chose not to," Doc said. "Prudence has told Violet repeatedly that Zelda is a remarkable channeller for her. My guess is she hitched a ride down to the bar and then took over once inside the door."

"But how did she know about what has been going on in Slagton the last few days?" Cooper asked. "Was she reading Parker's mind?"

Harvey squinted at me. "Did she do anything funny to ya? Like reach inside of yer chest again?"

"No. She grabbed my wrist and slapped me in the face, but that was it."

"She slapped you again?" Doc frowned.

I nodded. "I think she's jealous."

"Of what?" Cooper asked.

"That I'm breathing and she's not."

"So she takes it out on you?"

"Every chance she can."

"That," Doc said. "Or she was very aggressive when alive."

Harvey hooted. "I'll bet that ol' girl was roadhouse rowdy and mean enough to bite through horseshoes back in her day."

"She's mean enough to do that now," I grumbled.

"She does tend to leave a mark on ya that won't rub off."

"So does Parker," Cooper said, hitting me with a squint in the mirror.

Doc chuckled. "Like I mentioned before, I don't think Prudence can get into Violet's head. If she could, she would've already, but she continually uses other people to communicate with Violet."

I thanked my lucky stars for that! If Prudence got into my head, she'd probably smack my subconscious around, too, the bully.

"Do you think Dominick Masterson contacted her?" Cooper asked

Doc. "He's the only outsider who knows what Parker has been up to in Slagton."

"No," I answered first. "Prudence is not a fan of Dominick's. She's spoken negatively about guardians twice now." I frowned out my window at the snow-sprinkled pine trees. "Whatever a guardian is."

"Maybe she has some non-human contacts, same as Dominick," Cooper suggested.

"That could be," Doc said.

I pondered that possibility for a moment and then moved onto Slagton. The pickup was silent all around. I don't know what they were thinking, but I was wondering what in the hell we would run into back here today and worried that it would be dark before we could escape.

"How was Spearfish?" I asked Doc, wanting to get my mind on to lighter subjects.

He nailed me with one of his smoldering stares. "Lonely without you, Tish."

Cooper groaned. "Don't start that lovey-dovey shit when I'm trying to get my mind wrapped around what we're heading into back here, or I might end up not-so-accidentally shooting both of you before the day is out."

"Why the big hurry to do this today?" I asked him. "Couldn't we wait until tomorrow morning?"

"You don't wait around when dealing with a missing person, Parker." He spoke to me as if I was one of his rookies on the force. "If you don't act immediately, the window closes and you're back to square one. Or worse."

"Lesson learned, Detective," I said.

"Also," he said in a less bossy voice, "I have to do a twelve-hour shift starting tonight at seven, and I might need to shower before heading in. Going to Slagton with you tends to get me coated in shit."

"Didn't you just work a twelve-hour shift?"

"I've worked several since the day after Natalie's birthday party. Until Christmas is over, this is the norm."

"All work and no play makes Cooper a snarly wolf," Harvey said.

Outside, the Slagton town sign came and went. The mood inside the pickup cab grew heavy with tension, silence reigning. I watched out my window as we eased into the rusty old town, creeping along between the rundown shacks and dark shadows.

As we passed the informant's place, I noticed the body of that weird creature was gone. No hide, no blue guts, nothing to show that it had been there just two days ago. I wondered if the head was still inside on the freezer.

"The thing hanging from the porch is missing," I said.

"Yep," Harvey said.

"Aren't we stopping here?" I asked as Cooper rolled by the driveway and kept going.

"Not today," Cooper said.

"The messenger gave him instructions," Harvey told me.

The sun disappeared behind a cloud as the snow tires crunched along on the slush and gravel road. I stared into the shadows under the trees, looking for any signs of the chimeras or their leader, not that I had a clue what the leader would look like. My heart pitter-pattered as a chunk of snow fell from high up in a tree, the branches below bobbing from the blow.

We slowed to a creep in front of the two-story, boarded-up company store.

"You're stopping here?" I asked.

"No," Cooper said. "I saw something in the upstairs window."

"I saw it, too," Doc said, leaning over so he could peer out the driver's side window. "But it was more of a moving shadow."

I hadn't seen anything, nor did I want to. That building gave me the willies, especially with the warning about being gutted spray-painted on the front. I slinked down in my seat, willing Cooper to hurry up and hit the damned gas so we could hook up with whoever called, find out about his informant, and then get the hell out of Dodge.

After one last look, Cooper moved along.

I ran through several nail-biting what-ifs until he stopped in front of that woodshed with the old bullet hole–filled 1941 Plymouth Fastback behind it.

Please let him be pausing to give his gas foot a break.

He shut off the pickup.

Damn it. I grimaced out the window at the eerie woodshed that I knew from a previous glance was filled with lumberman's tools—handsaws, sharp hooks, and a long bench with a table saw sticking out of one end.

"Shouldn't you turn the pickup around?" I asked. "You know, have our getaway vehicle ready to bust ass out of here?"

"You've seen too many movies," Cooper said.

"What if we get stuck turning around?"

Harvey smirked. "I got a shit-ton of weight in the back end, brand-new snow tires, and four-wheel drive. Short of drivin' into a mud-filled gulch, we ain't gonna get stuck."

Doc looked at Cooper. "Did you bring anything for Violet's protection?"

"Yeah, I brought you," Cooper said. "And my gun."

"I couldn't find yer war hammer," Harvey said. "But I got my crowbar under the seat, snuggled up next to Bessie."

The crowbar again. I frowned down at my hands, crossing my fingers I didn't need to use it this trip, especially since I was supposed to try to catch one of those things. "Do you still have those illegal traps in your barn?" I asked Harvey.

"Nah. Coop's buddies confiscated 'em, which pisses me off because those belonged to my grandpappy. They were family heirlooms."

"I told you that I'm working on getting them back for you," Cooper said.

How did I go about catching instead of killing? Would traps even work? Or were these creatures too smart for those?

"What's the plan?" Doc asked Cooper.

"There's supposed to be a message for me in the old Plymouth. Since there are potentially five more of those *things* out there waiting for us, we hightail it back into this pickup as soon as I find the message."

"Who's leading?" I asked.

Cooper looked around at me. "I am. Parker brings up the rear."

I'm in the rear? "Don't you think I should lead?"

"No, you'll have a clearer view of anything coming at us from the back of the line."

"You need to change yer duds," Harvey said, handing me a plastic bag. Inside it was a pair of my black jeans, a sweatshirt, socks, my purple boots, and a pair of pink underwear.

"What did you bring my underwear for?" I asked him.

He dug around for them in the bag and held them up in front of Doc. "I thought yer stallion might wanna pocket 'em fer good luck."

I snatched them from his hand and stuffed them in my coat pocket.

Doc chuckled. "They're certainly more fun than a rabbit's foot."

Cooper scowled at me in the rearview mirror. "Hurry up and get your clothes on, Parker. The longer we sit here, the better the chance something might see us and come shooting first and asking questions later."

"Fine, but you all need to close your eyes, because I'm not getting dressed out there in the cold."

Doc refused to obey, watching me struggle to change in a tight spot, his grin flirty. To his credit, he helped me pull my arm free of my coat and folded my wool skirt and sweater so I could stuff them in the bag. I kept my cashmere leggings on under my jeans, using them as long underwear.

That left my feet. I held up my purple boots, frowning across the seat. "Harvey, why didn't you bring my other boots? These cowboy boots aren't any good in the snow. I'll be slipping and sliding like a baby deer on the ice."

"I couldn't find yer others and Coop was in a big hurry, so I grabbed what was near the door."

Thankfully, I'd semi-recently taken my purple boots to have the leather cleaned and coated with water and stain repellent for the winter, but tromping through ankle-deep snow was pushing it. I frowned down at my suede half-boots, which would be completely ruined if they got wet, not to mention even less helpful in the snow.

Minutes later, I had my cowboy boots on and pea coat buttoned, along with the stocking cap and gloves Harvey had grabbed for me.

"You missed a button," Doc said.

"No, Elvis stole that one." Damned chicken. "Let's do this," I said, and opened my door. I extracted the crowbar I'd used before from under the seat.

The four of us gathered in front of the pickup. The sun was back reflecting off the snow, blinding me. The air seemed too still, the silence cottony. A rustling in a nearby pine made me turn. More snow had fallen victim to the sun's warm rays and gravity's pull. The pine tree branches bounced back into place, causing the white stuff to sprinkle to the ground, sparkling as it fell.

It was a beautiful wintry day in the Black Hills, the air fresh, the sky blue. I frowned, glancing back at Harvey's pickup. Why did I want to climb back into the cab and hide under the seat? I shook off my unease, focusing on the task at hand. All we had to do was trudge through the snow to that old car and back. How hard could that be?

Cooper held out a handgun to Doc. "It's loaded and ready."

Harvey rested Bessie on his shoulder. "Try not to aim at my backside," he said to Doc.

"Maybe you need to be carrying some pink underwear," Doc joked.

I held up the bar. "It's not fair that you three get guns and all I get is this stupid crowbar."

Cooper smirked. "You're the one who always says that guns won't work on these things. Besides, in those boots, you'd slip while pulling the trigger and shoot one of us."

"You leave me no choice but to clobber you instead." I shifted the crowbar from one hand to the other, trying to find the best hold. Neither worked. The gloves were too thick with no leather grippers to stick to the steel.

"You give me another broken nose, Parker, and I'll leave you back here with your hunting pals."

Doc put his arm around my shoulder. "I won't let him leave you, Killer. But try not to hurt Cooper this time."

"I give no guarantees."

"You ready?" Cooper asked his uncle.

Harvey guffawed. "I was ready before you were born, boy."

"Good. You'll be following me. Don't fall behind." Cooper stepped into the unmarred snow, moving cautiously around the side of the woodshed to where the old Plymouth sat in the snow.

"Violet," Doc said as Harvey followed Cooper, leaving us alone.

"Yeah?"

"I don't like this. Something isn't right."

I felt it, too. But I wasn't sure if it was only a side effect of being in Slagton. "What do you mean? Are you sensing something?"

"Yes and no. Somebody or something is watching us, but it could be ghosts of Slagton's past lurking back here. Just stay close, no more than a step behind me."

"I'd prefer to ride on your back and bury my face in your neck."

"Even better." He gave me a quick kiss. "Your lips are cold. How about I carry you up to bed and warm us both up when we get back to your aunt's place?"

"Deal. We better get moving or Cooper is going to yell at us."

Doc looked around, scanning the tree line for another breath or two, and then he followed in Cooper's footprints.

I stepped down off the edge of the road into Doc's tracks and my boots slid out from under me. I landed on my ass right out of the gate. "Damn it."

"Are you okay?" Doc asked, holding out a hand to help me up.

"What're ya doin' down there?" Harvey asked. The old buzzard stood at the corner of the shed, shielding his eyes as he looked back at us. Cooper was out of sight around the other side.

"Making sure gravity is still working," I said, taking Doc's hand.

He brushed the snow off my backside. "You want me to hold onto you?"

Yes, forever would be almost long enough. "I'm good now. That drop was a little steeper than my boots could handle." I waved toward Harvey. "Let's go catch Cooper before he starts shooting at us."

I slipped and slid along behind Doc through the snow. He kept glancing back, making sure I was not laid out flat on my buttinski. Off to my right, I heard more snow plunk down as another pine tree dropped some of its load, but I was too busy navigating each footstep in the slippery path to look around.

As we rounded the corner of the weathered shed, I stopped, bracing myself against the sun-warmed wood so I could stand steady on my feet for a moment. Wearing my cowboy boots in the snow reminded me of my first time ice skating back when I was a kid. I'd had to hold onto the wall all of the way around the rink.

Scharfrichter.

I thought I heard my other name spoken softly next to my ear.

My fingers tingled in the gloves. I looked around for any signs of the chimeras, seeing only glistening snow, dark pine trees, and weathered wood. Sunlight glinted off the round saw blade hanging on the outside of the shed. Shielding my eyes, I sniffed the air, but my nose was too cold to do anything more than drip.

Up ahead, Cooper stood next to the rusty Plymouth full of bullet holes, frowning down into the front seat. Harvey was squinting toward the trees beyond, his head cocked to one side, Bessie half-raised. Had he heard something, too?

Doc looked back at me, holding out his hand. "You coming?"

"*Scharfrichter,*" I heard again.

This time it was louder, coming through the planks of wood next to me. There was a knothole in the wood about chin level. I bent and peered in the hole. It took a second for my eye to adjust to the darkness after the bright snow. I blinked, squinting.

A yellow eye stared back at me.

I gasped and jerked back, my boots sliding, my arms whirling as I tried to catch my balance. I fell again, landing on my side this time.

Before I could get my bearings, a gunshot boomed from over by the car. I'd heard that blast before. It was Bessie's call sign.

Scrambling to my feet, I took several sliding steps in the snow.

Another shot rang out, this one higher-pitched. That must be Cooper's handgun.

To my right, something fell out of the tree. I glanced over to see a black chimera push to its feet and stalk toward the car.

"Shit!"

Before I could take a step, something fell out of another tree, this time up ahead on the other side of the old Plymouth.

Boom! Bessie exploded again.

More of Cooper's shots rang out.

"Parker!" Cooper yelled. "Get your ass over here!"

I skated and slid toward the car, crowbar flailing as I tried to keep my balance.

All around me, hulking and snarling beasts dropped from out of the pine trees, where they'd been hiding and watching.

Harvey stood at the back fender of the old Plymouth, reloading Bessie as his gaze darted here and there.

I skidded to a stop beside him, holding onto the open driver's side door. Snow and dead weeds were drifting in behind the steering wheel.

In the thick shadows under the pines, I counted five, six, seven creatures on our side of the Plymouth alone. Shit, I thought there were only supposed to be eight total.

"They set up a trap," I said between huffs.

"This ain't no trap, girl." He finished loading, lifting Bessie's double barrels and aiming toward one of the chimera that was slinking under the trees. Its jaws opened in a toothy snarl. "It's a doggone ambush!"

Chapter Sixteen

Fire in the hole!" Harvey yelled.

I covered my ears as Bessie boomed next to me.

"Violet!" Doc shouted from the other side of the Plymouth through the open windows. "To your right!"

I turned in time to see one of the chimera charging at me from about twenty yards away. I raised the crowbar in prep to swing. The damned piece of metal flew from my gloved hand, sailing high into the air.

"Heads up!" I yelled, turning back to see my attacker closing the distance.

I heard the crowbar hit the Plymouth's roof and looked over in time to see it ricochet toward the other side of the car.

A grunt followed, and then, "Son of a—Parker!"

Oops!

Weaponless, I faced my foe, planning to dodge at the last moment, using the open driver's side door like a matador's cape. But when I took the first step, my boot slipped out from under me. I fell backward into the snow in front of the door, cringing as the creature sailed over me. Its jaws snapped downward as it tried to adjust course in mid-air, and then it slammed headfirst into the door, ramming it closed.

The loud creak of rusted hinges made Harvey glance around from his position at the back fender. The chimera lay in the snow near his boots, its tongue hanging out.

"It knocked itself out cold," I said, sitting up. Or dead. "The car wins round one."

Harvey strode over and jammed his shotgun barrels into its open jaws. "Here's a good-bye kiss from Bessie."

"Wait!" I yelled, scrambling backward through the snow while shielding my face.

He pulled the trigger. *Boom!*

Fur, black blood, and shards of bone spattered against the rusty car, as well as my jeans, upraised arm, and neck.

"Dammit, Harvey!" I wiped the wet, furry mess off my neck with my gloves, grimacing at the foul stench. "You got it all over me."

Several shots rang out from the other side of the Plymouth.

I scrambled to my feet. "I need to catch one of them alive."

"Quit yer caterwaulin'. Ya got plenty left to pick from." He stuffed more shells into Bessie. "Why'd ya go and throw yer weapon away?"

"I didn't. It slipped." I yanked off my useless gloves and threw them on the ground. "I really need to get me some fighting gloves."

"What we need is to get the hell outta here," Harvey said. "We're outnumbered."

"Unless you have a helicopter on call, we're screwed." I searched around us. "I need something to hit with." Near the back fender, a rusted leaf spring stuck out of the snow. I tried to pull it out, but it wouldn't budge.

"You can't swing that thing, Sparky. It's near on fifty pounds."

I let go of the cold metal, rubbing my hands on my jeans to keep them warm. When I looked up, I locked gazes with a big burly bastard of a chimera with a white mane ringing its thick neck. It stood not twenty feet away with its head lowered, sizing me up. Before it finished its assessment, another chimera joined it. This one stood a couple of inches shorter, its muzzle gray with white dots.

"Harvey," I said, backing toward my bodyguard.

"I see 'em, but I got me a bit of a prickly situation over here myself." A low growl rumbled from the trees beyond him.

"I sure wish you had a cannon in your pocket," I said, keeping my focus on the two beasts still watching me, making those throaty gobble-growl sounds back and forth.

"I'm gonna start carryin' dynamite under my seat when I come to Slagton," Harvey muttered. He glanced over his shoulder, doing a double take. "Doc! Two o'clock."

"Got it," Doc shouted. Two rapid shots rang out from the other side of the car. My blood pressure lowered at hearing Doc was still in the game. What about Cooper?

"Parker!"

Speaking of the law dog …

"I'm a little busy right now." I frowned down at my hands, trying to think of what I could do if both of the toothy bastards came at me at once.

"Look at me!" Cooper barked from behind me.

"I said I'm busy."

"Now!" Two rapid shots whined past my head, scattering the two creatures into the trees.

I flinched, turning to glare at him over the top of the Plymouth. "Damn it, Cooper! You almost took off my ear."

"Take your fucking weapon." He shook it with every other syllable. *Oh!*

He tossed the crowbar to me.

I noticed a cut on his forehead. A drop of blood was trickling toward his eye. "You're bleeding." I pointed at my own forehead to show him where.

"I know!" He wiped it with his sleeve, smearing the blood. His face scrunched up tight. "Someone threw a goddamned crowbar at me."

I grimaced. "Sorry about that."

"If we get out of this alive, Parker, I'm gonna—"

Boom! Boom! Bessie went off twice next to me, rattling my eardrums. I turned to see what Harvey was trying to blow to smithereens.

"Coop!" Harvey shouted, loading Bessie again. "Git over here. I'm gonna need ya to cover me."

"Where do you think you're going?" I asked.

"I'm gonna make a run fer my rig. We need to split these cocksuckers up so you got a chance."

"How fast do you think you can run with your trick hip?"

"A helluva lot faster than you in those fancy shitkickers."

He had a point.

"I'll go," Cooper said, jogging around the front of the Plymouth. "You're too slow, Uncle Willis."

"I'll move faster than a prairie fire with a tail wind when those critters are bitin' at my heels. Watch and see."

"No, you stay here and cover me."

"Where's Doc?" I asked Cooper.

"Right here," Doc called from the other side of the car. "If you guys are going to do something, then hit it. We have a situation brewing over here."

I looked over the top of the Plymouth. Across the way, four of the creatures were lining up with us in their sights. They waited at the tree line, the creek winding between them and us. Meanwhile, another chimera was stalking toward Doc from the trees to the north, taking one slow step at a time, snout down, mane bristling. I had the feeling it was trying to distract him from the other four.

Shit! There were too many. "We can all make a run for it," I said.

"Runnin' is what ya do when all else fails," Harvey said. "I got me an escape plan. Cover me, Coop."

He took off across the snow.

"Dammit!" Cooper said, taking aim at one of the predators that sped off after his uncle. "I got the fucking keys!" he yelled after Harvey. As soon as Cooper fired off two shots, he frowned at me. "Hold on tight to that damned crowbar, Parker." Then he took off after his uncle, aiming and shooting as he ran.

I heard a garbled hoot from one of the beasts under the trees to my left. The hooter and several more of the chimera, including the one that had been stalking Doc, rushed after Cooper as if on command, their jaws snapping as snow flew from under their three-toed feet.

Gripping my bar tight, I skirted the back of the Plymouth, almost falling in my haste.

"Harvey has a plan," I told Doc, squatting next to him with the old car at our backs.

"I hope to hell it works." He glanced my way. "You hurt?"

"No, but I could use a shot of tequila."

His grin was pained. "I'll buy you a big bottle if we make it out of this in one piece, Killer."

"Look." I pointed at the four lined up to attack. "What are they waiting for?"

A volley of shots rang out from the other side of the woodshed, followed by a surprised bellow and then: *BOOM!*

My heart pounded in my ears. Criminy! Just this morning I was sitting at my desk worrying about some flesh-eating ghouls. Now here I was facing off with a shitload of mutant griffin-like creatures intent on ripping out my throat. I shook my head. To think I once worried that life in the hills might be too slow paced for my liking.

"Do you see those two over there under that big half-burned pine?" Doc pointed the handgun to our right.

I shielded my eyes. "Yes."

"I think they're running the show."

"You mean they're the alphas in the pack?"

"Alphas? I don't think so. They are calling the shots, though. Commanders, maybe. Every so often, they make that gobble-growl-hoot noise, and then the others will shift positions."

"You mean the—"

"Shhh." He held up his hand, quieting me. "You hear that?"

I tuned in, picking up a low guttural rumble coming from the four holding in position across the valley. Goose bumps peppered my arms.

"Check out those three," he said, pointing to the north.

Damn. I hadn't even noticed them hiding in the shadows.

As I watched, they lined up, spacing themselves so that two were out front and the other was about ten feet behind. A call from one of the commanders rang out in the quiet. The three to the north switched so that the biggest one was out front, with two falling back several feet behind it.

"See," Doc said. "This is like a pack hunt on steroids."

"Wonderful. If only we weren't the prey."

"Counting the two commanders, we're looking at nine that we can see." Doc squinted into the distance. "I have a feeling there might be more hidden back in the trees, the sneaky bastards."

"I thought there were only eight beasts in the Wild Hunt, plus the leader."

"It's a myth, Violet. A tale based on truth." Looking through the passenger window, he peered into the car. He reached across the front seat and grabbed the steering wheel, tugging. Something creaked and snapped in the cab, a puff of rust and dust billowing.

"What are you doing?"

"Buying us more time for Harvey's plan to work." He scanned the enemy line, frowning. "Stay here," he said, and ran around the back of the car.

I watched through the window as he wrenched open the driver's door. The hinges screamed, echoing in the cold still air. Doc kicked the steering wheel several times, bending it in my direction as rust rained down onto the blanket of snow covering the seat and floor.

I looked back toward the line of predators. Two more stepped out of the trees and joined the other four in the line.

"Hurry, Doc," I said.

He grunted and kicked again. Flakes of rust flew. The steering wheel wilted forward. One more kick broke the sucker clean off.

Boom! Bessie went off again, only she sounded farther away.

Several gunshots blasted in quick succession, also in the distance.

I peeked over the car toward the woodshed. Harvey and Cooper were nowhere to be seen. As I searched, two more of the damned chimeras trotted around the woodshed from the north, pausing at the edge of the shed, watching Doc.

"Coop and Harvey are gone," I said. "Should we follow them?" The south side of the woodshed was the only open path, which was the way Harvey and Cooper had run.

"We can't," Doc said, skirting the rusted remains of the front of the car. He handed me the old steering wheel. "Take this."

I took the wheel in my left hand. It was a big circle with a Y in the center. "Why not?"

A high-pitched yapping noise made me scan the tree line. Including the commanders, I now counted thirteen total of the bastards setting up for what I surmised was their final attack.

"Because I have two bullets left in Cooper's gun and only one Executioner." He stepped into the snowy weeds where the Plymouth's motor used to hold court long ago. "And we're surrounded."

"We could make a run for it."

"Not in those boots, you can't." Doc reached down and yanked on a thick, rusted steel bar coming out from the engine side of the dashboard.

"I'll take them off and run in my socks."

"It's too late to run, Killer." He wrenched on the corroded joint near the end of the bar, then kicked it a couple of times. "I just need to free this damned steering shaft before they rush us."

My gut sank. Doc was right. To flee now was inviting a frenzied chase to the death. We needed to stand and fight.

I frowned out at the six facing us. They'd moved closer, now lining the far edge of the creek. The predators to the north had moved nearer, too. "They're tightening the circle," I said out loud.

Something clanked in the engine compartment. "Got it!"

In the trees, the two commanders made a growling-clicking sound, followed by a piercing yowl.

"Time's up," I whispered.

As soon as the words left my mouth, everything slowed around me. Something inside of me opened wide, like a daisy in the sun, cranking up my senses.

I could hear the huffs of breath and gnashing teeth from the beasts surrounding us as they prepared to pounce. On my left, there was a thump-thump as snow fell from a pine tree branch. Behind me, near the woodshed, a branch snapped. A truck door slammed.

Without turning my head, I could pinpoint in my mind's eye all six chimeras in front of me, the two commanders on my right, and the five others scattered to my left. It was as if I had finally grown the eyeballs in the back of my head that the kids always joked about.

I smelled the pine trees, the musky scent of the creatures, Doc's fabric softener, the musty remains of the old Plymouth's interior, and the foul stench from the blood and pieces of brain and flesh splattered and smeared on my coat from the bastard Harvey had blown to pieces.

My fingers and toes tingled, adrenaline pulsing through me. The rush of sensations made me dizzy for a blink or two. Shaking it off, I took a deep breath and tightened my grip on the crowbar and steering wheel.

"Let the dance begin." I stepped away from the car, digging in with my heels as I cut through the snow to keep from falling on my ass.

"Where do you think you're going, Killer?" Doc grabbed my arm.

I stopped, frowning at him. "I need to lure them away from you."

"No, you don't."

"Two bullets will only slow them for a second."

He raised the nearly three-feet-long rusty steering shaft. "I'm armed with more than two bullets."

I scanned the area. The circle of predators was cinching tighter. "Doc, if I can get them to come for me, you can take the offensive and pick them off one by one while I try to keep them busy in the middle of the pile."

"There are too many for that to work."

"You have a better plan?"

"Damned straight. We work as a team."

"Doc, I don't—"

"Yeah, but I do." He looked over my shoulder. "Here they come!"

Like a swarm of ants, they attacked.

Doc lifted Cooper's gun.

"Aim for the head," I yelled, and raised the crowbar, using the steering wheel as a half-assed shield.

A shot rang out next to me at the same time two of the suckers on my left sprung, catching air with those flaps of skin on their sides. I swung hard, the bar connecting hard with the skull of one, sending it tumbling as the crowbar vibrated free of my hand. Before I had a chance to blink, the second creature slammed into the steering wheel. I lost my footing, and we both rolled through the snow.

When we stopped, the chimera's head was wedged in the metal Y while I held the wheel with two hands, keeping it at arm's length. Its teeth gnashed, spit flying, while I cringed back into the snow. I twisted the wheel hard and fast, snapping the beast's neck. Its body went limp on the ground next to me.

Clambering to my feet, I scooped the crowbar out of the snow. "To Hell with you," I said and gripped the cold wet bar with both hands, thrusting it through the predator's chest. It exploded, filling the air with ash.

Coughing, I picked up the steering wheel. Now where was the other one I'd clobbered? Black blood covered the snow where it'd landed.

I heard heavy breathing behind me and whirled, wheel and bar at the ready. The creature stood on the roof of the old Plymouth. It leapt through the air toward me. I ducked at the last minute, shoving the crowbar up into its belly as it flew over me. It hit the ground at my feet and didn't move, black blood spilling into the snow. I stabbed it clear through the neck. The damned thing blew up in my face before I could pull the crowbar free, coating me with another layer of ash.

A second shot rang out behind me. I started to turn to see if Doc needed help, but three more chimeras rushed me at once, clawing at the snow in their haste to chew me to pieces.

Crap! I tried to dart to the left, my stupid boots losing traction out of the gate. As I started to fall forward, I planted the crowbar in the snow and let my momentum spin me while holding onto the outer ring of the steering wheel. I clocked one beast hard enough to send it flying into the remains of the Plymouth's rusted engine bay. I kicked another of the three in the head with the toe of my boot, knocking the sucker into the third. As they righted themselves, I pulled the crowbar from the snow. The metal was cold and wet in my hand, the snow cleaning most of the blood off. I wiped it off on my jeans and tightened my grip on the bar.

One of the chimeras lunged for me. I slammed the steering wheel and crowbar together, playing cymbals with its head. Its eyes rolled back as it slipped to the ground. The third leapt over the downed predator, lunging straight for my chest. I sidestepped, snaring it in the steering wheel like I had the other, but its momentum tore the wheel from my grip. It landed headfirst, plowing a path through the snow with the wheel. When it turned back to charge at me again, snow blocked its sight. I rushed it, bringing the crowbar down like a sledgehammer on its head. The gray ash flew in my eyes, making them water and burn.

I heard something racing through the snow toward me and swiped at my eyes, trying to clear them. The beast's breath caught as it pushed off the ground, springing toward me. Through a blur of tears, I saw it coming for my throat. "Shit!" I raised my arm to block it.

A bar swung down fast and hard from my right, nailing the creature in the middle of the back.

I heard the crunch of its spine and lowered my arm. It twitched at my boots.

"That was close," I said.

"Too close." Panting, Doc wiped sweat from his temple. He double-gripped the steering shaft, swinging it down again, putting the beast out of its misery. It didn't explode like those I'd killed, merely lay there bleeding out.

"You have two more behind you," he said in between gulps of breath, and turned to face off with another predator rounding the back of the Plymouth.

I spun and faced my hunters, planting my feet. I played Frisbee with the steering wheel, sending it flying through the air. It nailed one in the snout, knocking it to the side. The second chimera caught my crowbar upside the cheek as I hit it with a two-handed, solid whack. The bar shuddered in my hands. The bastard rolled like a tumbleweed, slamming into the Plymouth, and was impaled on the rusted grill.

A gunshot sounded. The bullet whizzed past me.

What the hell? I thought Doc was out.

The bullet hit something solid behind me. I turned to see a dark gray predator stumble as it charged me. I had time to veer right at the last second, striking with a crowbar uppercut. The chimera flipped backward into the snow. While it struggled to roll back onto its feet, I spun the bar around and stabbed it through its side.

Poof!

Before the ash cleared, another lunged at me. I sidestepped and my boots slid out from under me yet again. The chimera winged me as I fell, its claws slashing through my coat.

I pushed to my feet, my breath hitching in my chest, my mouth gritty from the ash in the air. A growl behind me made me cringe.

Another shot rang out to the left. I looked over my shoulder in time to see the bullet slam into a predator with a gray and white snout. I swerved, escaping its sharp teeth and claws.

A loud rumble thundered from over by the woodshed, but I didn't dare turn because not thirty yards away, the hulking bastard with the white mane was charging straight at me through the smattering of trees to the north. To the left, I saw another beast kicking up snow as it raced toward me, its teeth bared and ready for battle.

Hell's bells! Two at once. I took several steps backward. My arms ached, my shoulder burned, my lungs needed more oxygen. I tried to take off running toward Doc, who was swinging at the gray and white snouted beast, but my boots lost traction again. I fell onto my hands and knees. When I looked up, the two predators had joined each other, coming for me in tandem.

With seconds to spare, I scrambled upright, crowbar raised.

They sprang at me in unison.

A horn blasted.

The front of Harvey's pickup filled my vision. The burly steel grill rammed both beasts, sending them flying toward the trees.

Harvey yanked the wheel and slammed on the brakes. The pickup skidded in an arc, facing the way it'd come when it finally stopped with the driver's side closest to me.

"Violet!" Doc raced through the snow, the chimera with the gray and white snout scrambling to its feet behind him. "Get in!" He grabbed me by the arm and sprinted toward the pickup, half-carrying me when I skidded and stumbled behind him.

"Move your asses!" Cooper stood in the bed of the truck with his Colt .45 firing behind us as we dashed through the snow.

Harvey rolled his window down as we drew near. Bessie's double barrels pointed straight at us. "Get down!" he shouted.

Doc pulled me to the ground.

Boom!

Bessie's sweet song made my ears ring again.

A black furry body slammed into the front quarter panel of the pickup. I looked over. It was the relentless sucker with the gray and white snout.

I stood, raised the crowbar, and jammed the wedged end through its chest. Ash billowed in the air.

Harvey coughed and cursed, rolling up his window.

"Let's go!" Doc tugged on my arm, dragging me around the open back door. He shoved me inside the cab and crowded in after me.

"Go! Go! Go!" Cooper yelled, climbing into the passenger side.

Harvey hit the gas, the tires spinning in the snow as Cooper hauled his door closed.

Something thumped against my door. The back of the pickup bounced as the tire rolled over what I guessed to be another beast.

I sat up, holding onto the seat in front of me as we fishtailed around the woodshed, which now had a collapsed corner. Broken boards were scattered in the snow. Harvey skidded sideways when he hit Slagton's main drag, steering his way out of the slide before hitting the gas again.

Looking back, I watched through the dirty window as several of the chimeras ran out onto the road, giving chase. I counted five.

My heart pounded as they gained ground. But suddenly the chase ended, the five turning back toward the woodshed, where a creature twice the size of the others strolled out into the road and stared after us. A ray of sunlight hit the back window, glaring through the dirt and dust, cutting visibility in half.

"What in the fuck is that?" Cooper asked.

"If I had to guess, I'd say it's their alpha," Doc said.

Harvey didn't slow to see what we were talking about. He sped past the informant's shack and barreled out of town, not taking his foot off the gas until Cooper touched his shoulder. "We're clear. You can let off the gas some."

"Christ," Doc said, leaning his head back against the headrest. He clutched his side, grimacing. His cheek and coat were splattered with black specks and smudges. The knuckles on his right hand looked raw, red with his own blood. "They just kept coming at us."

"You called it from the get-go, Oracle," I said. He'd mentioned things didn't seem right when we started toward that Plymouth. Next time he told me that, I was running home and hiding under my bed.

I frowned down at my pea coat. It was so covered with ash and black blood that I couldn't even tell it was red anymore. My left shoulder stung where that one bastard had caught me with its claws.

Doc looked at me. "Are you okay, Killer?"

"I'm still breathing."

Sitting up, he touched the tear in my coat. "What happened here?"

"I slipped." I inspected the shredded material. There'd be no patching it up.

"Let's get this off of you," he said, unbuttoning my coat. He helped extract my arm from the sleeve, his touch gentle as he assessed the sliced skin under the torn sweatshirt.

"Well?" I asked. "Will I live?"

"Yeah, but it's going to be tender for a while." He glanced up at me. "You might need stitches."

I wasn't going to the hospital. "I'll be fine." I pulled my sweatshirt aside to see the scratches for myself. "A few Band-Aids and I'll heal in no time."

His eyes narrowed. "I'll tell you what you need after I clean it up."

"Are we going to play doctor?" I teased, trying to lighten the mood for my own sanity's sake after slaying Lord knew how many of those creatures.

"Maybe." Doc grinned. "Or we could go back to my place and study some anatomy."

"Only if you promise to skyrocket my dopamine levels."

Harvey snorted. "Is that an epi-pen in yer pants, Doc? Or are ya just happy to see Sparky still alive and kickin'?"

Chuckling, I looked toward the front seat and slammed into Cooper's scowl. I sobered. "What now, Cooper? Are you going to give me a debriefing on what I did wrong back there?"

Another snicker came from Harvey's corner of the cab. "Yer debriefing is a job for Doc, not Coop."

I leaned forward and flicked the old boy's ear, making him laugh.

"You didn't do anything wrong, Parker," Cooper said, his focus moving to my bloody shoulder. "I almost got you three killed today."

"It's not like that," Doc said. "It wasn't your fault."

"Yes, it was." His scowl moved to Doc. "I should have known better than to take the bait."

"Who would've guessed they were capable of setting a trap?"

Cooper shook his head. "I left Parker standing there beside that Plymouth." His scowl deepened. "I left her with one lousy crowbar to fight off all of those fuckers."

"No, Coop. You left an Executioner while you went to get something to help us escape," Doc said. "Violet comes from a long line of fighters, remember? Besides, she wasn't alone."

"Are ya forgettin' what Sparky can do with a plain ol' crowbar, boy? How many of them critters did you turn to dust today, girl?"

"I don't know, maybe five or so." I'd lost count while trying to stay alive. The haunted look on Cooper's face tugged at me. "Hey, you got us out of there alive. Harvey wouldn't have made it to the pickup without your help."

"Darn tootin'," his uncle added. "That one snaggletooth woulda torn out my throat if you hadn't filled its brain bucket with holes first."

"This is all so screwed up." Cooper scrubbed his hand down his face. "Parker has kids. If anything had happened to her ..."

"It's a different world now, Coop," Doc said. "A whole new game with no instructions."

"We're a long way from ordinary these days," Harvey added.

"Cooper," I said, grabbing the back of his seat. "Look at me."

He turned and focused on me, too many days of long hours showing on his face. "What?"

"Knock this guilt shit off. You've been working twelve-hour shifts night after night. Your instincts were snoozing when that call came in. How were you to know it wasn't legitimate? That the caller didn't have information about your missing informant?"

"Parker," he started, but I held up my hand.

"I'm not done. As for my children, our job is to rid the hills of deadly vermin so that Addy and Layne can live to see another day. And when I say 'our,' that means you, me, Doc, Harvey, and whoever else steps up when duty calls. So suck it up and go back to being the pain in the ass I've grown to respect and like ... sort of ... when you're not being a dickhead to me."

Harvey hooted. "Ya hear that, Doc? These two curly wolves are finally tuckin' in their teeth. Did ya ever think ya'd see the day? Let's go to town and shoot out the lights."

After a nod at me, Cooper faced forward again. "You've done enough shooting with Bessie for one day, Uncle Willis."

"Yer right. Next time, I'm bringing my new cannon."

"What?" Cooper gaped at his uncle. "I told you not to order that."

"And I told you I wanted a cannon." Harvey eased onto the main road and then hit the gas.

Doc leaned his head back again, closing his eyes. "Somebody set us up. Someone who knows the truth about Violet." He reached out and found my hand, lacing his fingers though mine.

Who would have set us up? I thought of the possible players who might make the lineup—Dominick? Prudence's contact? Cooper's informant? Someone else hiding back in Slagton?

"But why?" I asked. "To catch an Executioner?"

"Maybe," Doc said.

Cooper rubbed his neck. "Looked more like the goal was to kill one, if you ask me."

Chapter Seventeen

Home was where my heart was—or rather were, since I had twin hearts waiting there for me. However, I didn't want my kids to see me fresh from battle. There'd be too many questions from Addy and several fibbed answers that Layne wouldn't believe. So, we swung by Doc's place first, dragging our sorry, stinky, wet, and dirty carcasses inside.

We took turns showering in Doc's two bathrooms. I volunteered to go last, because my hair did not like to be rushed. Not to mention that I was in the worst shape by far, coated with multiple layers of ash, blood, saliva, and many other parts of dead creatures that I didn't want to think about until I was scoured pink.

The guys were all quick, even Doc, who had to do some scrubbing himself after his batting practice with Slagton's motley crew. Since everyone was done when my turn came, I opted to use Doc's master bathroom. I wanted at least two doors between me and the outside world while I assessed the emotional stability of the wild woman with a blood- and grime-covered face staring back at me in the mirror.

"Executioner." I spoke the name aloud, trying it on for size.

The role still fit like a boot that was too big—loose and clunky, rubbing me wrong, causing blisters in my tender spots.

"*Scharfrichter,*" I whispered, thinking of that yellow eye I'd seen through the knothole in the woodshed. Who'd spoken that? One of the chimeras? Maybe, but the hole was pretty high up on the wall. My gut told me it was the leader. The creature that had stood in the middle of the road as we drove away.

I leaned closer to the mirror, peering into my eyes. They looked the same as always. Did they change when I went into killing mode? Did my pupils narrow during that moment when I could suddenly see beyond my normal spectrum, sensing my enemies? Like Mr. Black's?

I touched the tip of my nose, moving it around. Did my nose grow so that I could pick up scents I normally couldn't? Caly's face had grown a snout when she shifted into attack mode. Was I similar to her kind? Or was mine more internal, like a switch flicking in my brain—Executioner On/Executioner Off?

A knock sounded on the bathroom door.

"Hey, Tiger." Doc's voice came through the wood. "I have some clothes for you and a garbage bag for that sweatshirt."

"Come in," I said, turning away from the mirror.

Doc closed the door behind him. His cream-colored thermal made his hair and beard stubble look even darker than usual. I'd never really cared one way or another about guys having facial hair, but this new look of Doc's had me staring extra long. Too bad my body ached too much to do anything about the X-rated ideas he spurred in my head. Did executing always take such a toll, or was I pathetically out of shape? Probably the latter.

He placed the yoga pants and T-shirt I kept at his place on the counter next to the sink. From his front jeans pocket, he pulled out the "lucky" pink underwear Harvey had packed with my Slagton clothes. "Turns out Willis was right, you could use these after all." Doc lowered them on top of my other clothes.

"Don't tell Harvey. He'll start fishing in my underwear drawer for 'lucky' panties each week before playing poker with you guys."

"Can't say as I blame him." Doc's grin was flirty. "I like fishing in your drawers, too."

I faked a groan at his pun.

"Come on," he said. "That was a good one."

"Good? That's reaching." I slipped my uninjured arm out of my sweatshirt. "I guess it could've been worse."

"How's that?"

"You could've waxed eloquent about the length of your fishing rod, ending with a limerick about your fondness for skinny-dipping in my fishing hole."

He laughed. "You need to quit spending so much time with Willis."

"You don't know the half of it." I tried to tug off my sweatshirt with heavy arms and a sore shoulder.

His hands stopped me. "Let me help."

"Thanks." I played rag doll as he carefully freed my other arm and pulled the sweatshirt over my head, stuffing it in the garbage bag he'd brought.

He grimaced at the sight of my shoulder. "We'll come back to these wounds in a minute. Let's get the rest of your wet clothes off."

"It's not that bad." The claw marks stung, but they didn't ache.

"Maybe not, but it doesn't look too good."

I unbuttoned my jeans, starting to push them down and pausing to take a breath. "Maybe I can just shower in my pants."

Doc stepped in again, easing my jeans down over my hips. Then he helped me up onto the counter. After he tugged off my boots and set them by the door, he peeled my jeans and cashmere leggings the rest of the way off. My socks came next, leaving me sitting in my unmentionables.

"Will you hand me that?" I pointed at the thick terry cloth towel hanging from the bar next to the shower.

"Why?"

"Because I want to cover up a little."

"Are you cold?" He grabbed the towel.

"No. I'm shy."

"Shy?" Creases appeared at the corners of his eyes. "Boots, I've seen your body from head to toe and I'm totally smitten, I assure you."

"Yeah, but you're fully dressed right now and I'm mostly naked."

One dark eyebrow lifted. "You want me to get naked, too?"

"Of course." Doc naked was great eye candy, and I had one hell of a sweet tooth. "But I'll get you dirty again."

"I like getting dirty with you." He handed me the towel. "However, we need to get you cleaned and patched up first."

"My modesty thanks you." I took the towel and draped it over my lap, like when I sat on the doctor's examination table.

"Now," he said, grabbing a washcloth from under the sink. "Let me take a better look at that shoulder."

I didn't feel like fighting him, so I sat quietly like a good patient as he ran the washcloth under warm water and began cleaning off the mostly dried blood.

"Does this hurt," he asked as he dabbed at the claw wounds.

"It stings, but not too much." I closed my eyes, letting him work his magic unsupervised. The intoxicating scent of his cologne filled me, making me want to burrow into his chest, wrap his arms around me, and hide away from the world for a week ... or ten.

"It's looking better already," he said.

"My blood clots well."

He chuckled. "You should add that to your Executioner résumé."

"I've always healed pretty quickly." The water ran again, and then the warm washcloth returned, feathering over my skin. "But not as fast as Quint. He's kind of a freak that way. My mom claims it's due to the herbal, meat-free diet she was on while pregnant with him."

The washcloth paused. "Your brother is your father's son, right?"

I opened my eyes. "Yeah, why?"

"Nothing." He went back to cleaning my wounds.

Nothing my ass. "Cough it up, Doc."

"I was just wondering if there's a connection between his quick healing and you being an Executioner, but I'm probably way off."

I chewed on the idea of Quint having a part in this "other" world business for a moment. Wouldn't he have mentioned if he were experiencing some of this bizarre shit?

"How many of those things back in Slagton did you take out?" I asked, changing the subject.

"Not nearly as many as you, Killer." His breath was cool on my damp skin. "Those chimeras were strong and fast."

Chimeras? Harvey must have told Doc what Dominick called the creatures.

"And relentless," I added. "Thanks for coming in swinging and saving me."

"You're welcome." He lowered the washcloth, inspecting his work.

I checked out the scratches. I'd had worse before and skipped the stitches then, too. The scarring would be minor.

"You're hard on a guy, Violet."

I looked up into his eyes. "Why's that?"

Doc draped the washcloth over the faucet. "You were incredible out there, moving unnaturally fast, belting and stabbing like a killing machine, working that crowbar with the strength of two men. If you'd been wearing boots with tread on them, you would've probably taken out twice as many as you did."

A killing machine. That gave me pause. I was a mom with two kids who had struggled for the last decade to provide for them and not screw up their heads in the process. I frowned down at my palms. With these hands I had killed not one or two chimeras back in Slagton today, but so many that I'd lost count in the thick of battle. How had it come to this?

"It was all I could do to fend those things off one at a time," Doc continued. "When I looked over in the midst of the chaos, there you were, mowing down one after another with only a damned crowbar and a steering wheel." He lifted my chin so I could meet his teasing gaze. "A man with a small fishing rod might suffer from a jarring blow to his ego after watching you in action, Tish."

That snapped me out of my reverie. I chuckled, playing along. "Gomez, dear, what's a poor girl to do? You know how wreaking havoc in lethal doses makes my heart pitter-patter."

"*Mi querida.*" He leaned down, giving me a soft kiss. "I've been wanting to do that for the last hour."

"What took you so long?"

He turned my head so I could see my reflection in the mirror. "I was waiting for some of the dust to clear."

I picked some black fur and feathers from my hair, grimacing as I dropped them in the garbage bag with my sweatshirt. "Did any of them explode when you killed them?"

"No."

"When Harvey shot that one by the car point-blank, it didn't explode either. But every time I killed one, it blew up in my face. Why do you think that is?"

"If I had to guess, I'd say it's part of the Executioner package deal."

I scowled. "There is so much of this I don't understand."

"Neither do I, but together we'll figure it out."

"Or die trying."

He stared at me in the mirror, suddenly serious. "That's not an option."

"I'm not saying I want to die."

"Good. I've grown kind of fond of you and have plans for us."

"Like what?"

He shrugged. "You. Me. Your underwear drawer. Fishing."

"Dang. And here I thought you were going to say something about your hands, hot oil, my naked skin, and a deep-tissue massage."

"Well, that's certainly another way of saying what I'd like to do after you shower."

"After I shower?" I smiled extra wide in the mirror, batting my eyelashes at him. "You mean I'm not irresistible now in all of my post-Executioner glory?"

"Oh, you're still tempting." He took my hand, raising it to his lips for a kiss. "To prove it to you, I'm willing to strip down and help you shower."

I considered that scene for a few seconds, but practicality won out. "I'll take a rain check on the shower. Cleaning off this mess isn't going to be very sexy."

He helped me down from the sink and then turned on the shower.

"I want it extra hot this time," I told him.

"Sweetheart, we've been together long enough that I know how hot you like it—both in and out of the shower."

Yes, he did.

He pulled the curtain back and hung a fresh towel over the rod. "I'll be back when you're finished to bandage those wounds." He opened the door. "Do you need anything else?"

Yes, but I didn't know how to ask for it. "No, thanks." He started to shut the door behind him. "Hey, Doc," I called out.

He looked back. "Yeah?"

"I love you."

His mouth curved slowly upward. "You don't say?"

I nodded. "Will you stay with me at Aunt Zoe's again tonight?"

"There's no place I'd rather be than in your bed, Boots."

After the door shut behind him, I stuffed my bloodstained jeans in the garbage bag. Then I stripped off my bra and underwear and rolled them in a ball with my socks and cashmere leggings to wash later at Aunt Zoe's.

In the shower, I stood under the hot water with my eyes closed, letting it wash away the layers of death coating my skin. The day's battle scenes flashed through my thoughts. I analyzed what I'd done wrong, rehashed what I'd done right.

After scrubbing from head to toe with shampoo and Doc's soap, I shut off the water. With the towel wrapped around me sarong-style, I stood in front of the steamed mirror. A swipe with the hand towel showed the girl I knew. I smiled, touching my cheek, my nose. It was all the same as before. Who knew a "killing machine" had been hidden under my skin all of this time? I sure hadn't.

"Violet?" Doc said from the other side of the door.

I opened it, noticing the first-aid kit in his hands. "Do you want to play doctor in here or on your bed?"

"My bed. It's less steamy out here."

"I don't know." I moved over to his bed, sitting on the corner. "The last time we bounced around on this puppy, we got very steamy."

He pulled a bandage from the kit. "Quit flirting with the doctor."

"How about I play with your thermometer while you work?"

"Keep your hands to yourself, vixen, or you might get more than you can handle."

"Promises, promises."

A few minutes later, my shoulder was bandaged and my arms were covered with chills.

"You're cold," Doc said, bringing my clothes from the bathroom. "Get dressed and come downstairs. I'll make you some hot buttered rum. It won't be as good as your aunt's, but it will warm you up inside and out."

"You sure you don't want to stay and heat me up some other way?" It was rare we had time alone together in his bedroom, and it seemed a shame to waste an opportunity.

"If you're asking if I'd like to unwrap that towel and inspect your skin inch by inch with my mouth, the answer is 'Hell yes.' However, you're dead on your feet and my ribs are killing me after today's fun and games. Not to mention, we have company downstairs."

I'd forgotten about Cooper and Harvey. "I'll be down shortly."

He started to walk toward the door leading to the back stairs that exited into the kitchen, but then strode back over to me.

"I just need to do one thing," he said, unfastening my towel. He pulled it open, his gaze sliding down over my peaks and curves as he sucked air in through his teeth. "Damn."

His obvious admiration made my libido purr. "It's all yours, Doc." I meant that, too, with every cell of my body, and mooned up at him like a shrieking Elvis groupie.

Doc wrapped the towel around me again, hitting me with a pulse-pounding smolder. "I love you, too, Violet."

He pulled me against him, leaning down to hit me with a slow, tender kiss that nearly made my towel catch on fire.

"Jumpin' Jehoshaphat," I whispered when he stepped back. "Your kisses are like crack cocaine."

"You inspire me, Boots." He patted my bottom through the terry cloth. "Cookies and hot buttered rum will be waiting in the kitchen."

After he disappeared down the back stairs, I slid my clothes on. Since Harvey had only grabbed a pair of underwear, not a bra, I had to borrow a sweatshirt from Doc to hide my bare fun-bags poking out through my T-shirt. I took the back stairs, joining Doc and Harvey in the kitchen.

Doc was leaning against the counter next to the stove, drinking a glass of water. His gaze raked down my front side. "I like my clothes on you better than on me." He lifted the bottle of liquor sitting on the counter next to him. "You ready for some rum?"

I nodded. "Where's Cooper?"

"He got a call from the station," Harvey said. He was sitting at the bar eating cookies—dark chocolate with butterscotch bits by the look of them. "Something about a hit-and-run."

My stomach pawed the ground, growling about those cookies. I perched on the stool next to Harvey and stole one from the plate in front of him. "That's like the second one in days."

"It's a might slippery out there fer the tourists."

I guess that might explain it, but for a small town like Deadwood, it seemed odd.

Taking the mug of buttered rum from Doc, I blew him a kiss. The sweet, warm liquor coated my tongue, heating my throat all of the way down the hatch.

"Thanks for sharing," I told the old buzzard and bit into a cookie. Rich chocolate and creamy butterscotch coated my tongue. My eyes fluttered closed for a moment as a burst of flavor drew a low moan from my chest. "Oh my God, Harvey." I grabbed two more from the plate, cramming the rest of the first in my mouth. "Did you buy these at the store?" I asked through gooey, chocolate heaven.

He snorted. "Bite yer tongue, girlie. That's one of my momma's recipes."

"Damn. You'd make a helluva catch for a hungry lady."

He scowled at my goofy grin. "Now don't be gettin' any notions about you and me unitin' in holy bedlock. I'm allergic to bein' bridled and tied to any female."

I giggled. "Can't blame a girl for trying."

Harvey pointed a cookie at Doc. "There's yer huckleberry. Young stallions like him ain't against being roped and ridden."

My cheeks warmed at the hint about marriage to Doc. Recently, he'd made it clear that wedding bands might be an option someday, but we hadn't taken things any farther than that baby step.

Doc grinned. "Are we talking about riding bareback or saddled?"

"Well, saddles tend to chafe, leavin' ya raw in all the wrong ways. Bareback will make ya bounce around like a colt in clover."

"You would know, dirty buzzard." I took another bite of cookie, keeping my moans to myself this time. It was time to change the subject before Harvey said something that made me squirm enough to slide off my barstool. "Seven," I told my bodyguard after swallowing a mouthful of cookie.

"Seven what?"

"I added my kills while I was showering. I remember seven of those things blowing up in my face, and I think five or six were injured."

Doc set his empty glass on the counter. "You were counting kills while you were taking a shower?"

Harvey snickered. "Seems like a waste of a wet female and hot water, if ya ask me."

"Nobody asked you." I snapped one of his suspenders. I took another sip of warm rum, chasing away the chilling memories of all those pointy teeth. "I was trying to figure out how many of them had been waiting for us, and what we have to face when we go back."

"Go back?" Doc frowned.

I nodded. "We have to finish this."

"Is that Violet the Executioner talking?" Doc asked.

Chewing on another cookie, I considered his question. Was this a matter of my Executioner pride being injured? Was it a need to kill no matter the cost because that was what I was programmed to do now? I looked from Harvey to Doc, lingering on the latter who'd stood next to me in the face of death, putting his life on the line to protect mine once more.

"No," I answered. "This is the mother of two kids speaking. The girl who doesn't want to risk the lives of those she holds dear when those toothy bastards come looking for her." I broke the cookie in half, eyeing Doc. "You're partially right, though. The Executioner has a say in this, too. She's pissed as hell about how close she came to losing two people very near and dear to her heart in that ambush."

"Only two?" Doc asked.

"Okay, Cooper, too. But you need to tell him to stop yelling at me in the midst of battle."

"You hit him in the head with a crowbar," he reminded me.

"Not on purpose."

Harvey chortled next to me. "Coop's gonna take a ribbin' for that gash on his forehead from his buddies in blue."

I winced. "Is he still pissed at me for that?"

"No." Doc leaned his elbows on the bar. "He was too busy feeling guilty for the rookie mistake of taking us back there today."

"We're all rookies when it comes to this Executioner business."

"Explain that to him."

I would, the next time we had a moment alone and weren't ramming our horns together. "Any idea how many you two and Cooper took out of the game permanently?"

The three of us spent the next ten minutes replaying the scene, adding up the dead and injured with Doc and Harvey estimating Cooper's take since each of them had fired shots alongside the detective. In the end, we came up with Cooper taking out two for sure with his Colt .45, Harvey and Bessie blasting three to pieces, and Doc killing three with the steering shaft, which included the one he'd stopped from taking me out. With my seven ash clouds, that made fifteen confirmed dead and around ten more injured to some degree.

"Christ." Doc looked at me. "And you want to go back?"

I nodded. "There's another reason I haven't told you."

Shaking the cookie crumbs from his beard, Harvey's eyes narrowed. "Daylight's burnin', girlie. Spit it out."

"I need to go inside that woodshed next to the old Plymouth."

"Why?"

"There was something hiding in there, and it knew my name."

* * *

As soon as I finished my hot buttered rum, we packed up and returned to Aunt Zoe's for the night. The kids were watching a Christmas special on television and barely looked my way as I kissed them each multiple times on top of the head. Ahhhhh, normal life.

I ran upstairs and put on a bra under my T-shirt, but I kept Doc's sweatshirt on because it made me grin like a silly ninny when I looked in the mirror. Maybe I was being juvenile, but it'd been a long time since I'd had a man in my life, and getting to wear his shirts made me feel cherished, especially after the way Doc kept eyeing me at his place.

The smell of baked cheese and potatoes lured me downstairs. According to Harvey, supper tonight was going to be ham steaks with Aunt Zoe's hearty, three-cheese scalloped potatoes. Just the thought of one cheese with my potatoes had me drooling, let alone three. Those cookies I'd inhaled at Doc's place didn't even put a dent in my hunger.

When I joined Harvey and Doc in the kitchen, Aunt Zoe looked over at me from where she was cleaning mushrooms and tomatoes at the sink. A bowl of green leaf lettuce sat next to her on the counter.

Her gaze dipped to Doc's sweatshirt and then climbed to my damp hair. "Did you have a fun afternoon with Doc?" Her eyes twinkled.

I thumbed at Doc's sweatshirt. "This isn't what it looks like."

"It's not your boyfriend's shirt?" she joked, her smile wide as she glanced at Doc, who was getting plates down from the cupboard.

"Sparky got into a bit of a pickle today at work," Harvey said, grabbing one of Aunt Zoe's aprons from the pantry.

"A pickle, huh?" She scowled. "What's your sexist boss having you do now to promote his damned business? Whipped-cream dunk tanks? Bikini mud wrestling down at the Prairie Dog Palace?"

"I was referrin' to her other job, the one where she kills trouble-makin' critters." Harvey finished tying the apron and opened the refrigerator, as if he hadn't dropped a truth bomb on Aunt Zoe.

"We need to buy some whipped cream, Boots," Doc whispered in my ear as he passed, carrying plates to the table.

She lowered the knife, her face becoming serious. "What happened?"

I checked to make sure the kids were still immersed in the Christmas show before answering. "We took a trip back to Slagton this afternoon," I said in a quiet voice. "Shit kind of blew up in our faces."

"Blew up how?"

"We were ambushed," Harvey explained, grabbing a big chunk of ham from the fridge and setting it on the cutting board.

Doc walked over and nudged Aunt Zoe aside, handing her a dishtowel. He grabbed a knife and begin cutting up the tomatoes she'd cleaned.

For the next few minutes, Harvey and I took turns telling her about the Slagton fiasco, while Doc added tidbits along the story trail.

When we finished, Aunt Zoe came over and wrapped me in a tight hug. Then she cupped my cheeks and kissed my forehead. "We need to make sure you're better prepared."

"For what?" I asked.

Her blue eyes held mine. "Next time."

"Next time?" Doc frowned over his shoulder. "You're okay with Violet going back there again?"

After planting another kiss on my forehead, Aunt Zoe let me go. "Of course. She needs to finish what she started, or the retribution will be worse." She started collecting silverware from the drawer.

"Retribution," I repeated, lowering into my usual chair. She'd confirmed my earlier suspicions.

"It's personal now, kiddo." She closed the drawer with her hip. "We need to put together a battle plan, though."

Harvey hooted while cutting thick slices of ham. "Now we're talkin'. This is gonna be more fun than rubbin' belt buckles at a Saturday night barn dance." He pointed the butcher knife at Doc. "Didn't I tell ya it was a good thing I didn't listen to Coop and ordered that cannon?"

Doc cringed visibly.

"You'll have to surprise them next time to gain the upper hand," Aunt Zoe continued, setting silverware around the table.

The front door closed. "Howdy, pipsqueaks," I heard Natalie say to the kids. She strode into the kitchen carrying a paper grocery bag. Her cheeks were pink from the cold, her hair pulled back in a ponytail. "Hey, guys. It smells amazing in here." She turned to me. "Guess what?"

"You saw a ghost?"

Being that Natalie lived in a haunted boarding house, it seemed like a viable guess.

"No." She set the bag on the table and pulled a bottle of tequila from it. "Try again."

I tipped up the bottle, checking out the label. It was a different brand from our regular. I was ready to drink some now, but I'd wait until the kids went to bed. I held up the bottle. "Am I going to want to drink shots about it?"

She shrugged. "Maybe."

"Does it have anything to do with Cooper?" I asked with a wink.

That brought out a scowl. "No, but I did run into him afterward."

"Did Coop tell ya about our trip to Slagton?" Harvey dropped a slice of ham in the cast iron skillet on the stovetop.

"No. He asked if I could give Violet a message for him."

Doc turned, his gaze narrowing. "What message?"

"He's going to stop by tonight. He needs to talk to her and Zoe."

Groaning, I leaned on the table, resting my chin on my knuckles. "Now what?"

Was this going to be about what happened in Slagton? Was he still feeling guilty? Because if so, I needed to set him straight so that we could get back to insulting each other on a daily basis. This sad teddy-bear side of Cooper made me want to give him a hug and assure him everything would be okay, which was a bad idea. I'd undoubtedly be bitten by the rabid law dog and end up snarling back at him from the end of my chain with frothy saliva flying everywhere.

"He didn't clarify." Natalie smirked. "Because if he did, then Coop wouldn't be nearly as maddening, would he?" I had to agree with her on that note. "What happened in Slagton?" she asked me.

"You tell me your news first."

"Okay. Since I was up in Lead, I swung by your ex's work to see if he was able to get a new hood ornament yet." She grinned. "I was merely curious, of course."

"Did he?" Aunt Zoe asked, leaning against the counter.

"Not yet."

Doc chuckled as he rinsed off the knife.

"But while I was there, I noticed Dominick Masterson's rig in the parking lot."

That made Aunt Zoe do a double take. "What was *he* doing there?"

Natalie pulled a six-pack of Corona Extra out of the bag and carried it over to the fridge. "Stirring up some trouble, I'm guessing."

"Why's that?" I asked.

"Because he came walking out with Rex by his side."

"Rex?" I followed Natalie, placing the tequila on top of the fridge. "That's weird. I didn't think Rex interacted with the locals outside of Ms. Geary."

Harvey cursed, flipping a sizzling slice of ham steak. "That ex of yers is lower than a cockroach's belly."

Ms. Geary, Aunt Zoe's neighbor across the street, had kicked Harvey to the curb last fall in order to let Rex start parking his Jaguar in her garage, so to speak. Weeks later, the truth came out that Rex was using Ms. Geary so that he could spy on us off and on for months.

I patted Harvey's back on my way to the table. "You'll get no argument from me on that one."

"No matter how many times a snake sheds its skin, it's still a snake," Aunt Zoe said.

"Anyway, Dominick and Rex looked as thick as thieves in the parking lot," Natalie said, joining me at the table. "But maybe they were strangers before today. We all know how Dominick can charm the pants off his victims with those dreamy eyes of his."

Aunt Zoe muttered something very unlady-like under her breath.

What was Dominick up to now? The chances of his randomly befriending the father of my children were slim. How had he figured out who Rex was? What angle was he going for by looping Rex into the chess game Dominick and I were playing?

I looked over to find Doc watching me with a pinched brow as he dried his hands on a towel. "You need to pay a visit to your ex."

"Or I could just execute him."

His eyes creased. "If you need help, I'm your huckleberry."

So Harvey had confirmed earlier. I winked at my stallion.

"You need to get in line behind me on that score, Doc," Natalie said, pulling a small white box from the paper bag.

"Please tell me those are chocolate truffles." I reached for the box.

She snatched it away. "They're for dessert." She put them on top of the refrigerator next to the tequila. "You have to share."

"But I don't like to share," I said, folding the paper bag.

Doc brought the bowl of salad over, setting it on the table. "That makes two of us, *cara mia*." He ran his hand over my hip.

I beamed up at him, hearts undoubtedly pulsing in my eyes like a lovesick cartoon cat.

Natalie made a gagging sound in her throat. "Save it for the bedroom, lovebirds."

"I don't trust Dominick," Aunt Zoe said, still snarling about the shifty charmer.

"None of us do, Zoe." Natalie nudged her aside to get to the cupboard with drinking glasses. "Now, I've spilled my news, so it's your turn. What happened back in Slagton today that Coop neglected to tell me about?"

I told her the story, focusing on the highlights of the trip rather than the details we'd shared with Aunt Zoe.

When I finished, Natalie gaped at me from the open fridge door, two bottles of Corona in her hands along with a bottle of salad dressing. "Holy castration clamps!"

"Hey now," Harvey said. "Watch yer language. Yer gonna scare my giggle berries into cryin' raisins."

Doc carried over bowls of sliced mushrooms, tomato wedges, and chopped bacon, setting them next to the salad. "Willis, you have a true gift when it comes to painting pictures with your words."

"A gift? Right." After wrinkling my nose in Harvey's direction, I turned back to Natalie, who handed a bottle of beer to Doc before returning to the table with her own. "We were just planning our next trip to Slagton when you got here."

"You're going back there again?" She twisted the top off her bottle. "What the hell? Did you eat a loaf of dumbass today?"

I flipped her off. "No, and that's not how the saying goes."

"I'll say it the way I want to, and my version works perfectly well when it comes to any nutty-ass plans to go back and face off with those things again."

Doc lowered into the seat next to me, offering me a drink of his Corona. "I'm glad to see I'm not the only one questioning a return trip."

"What does Coop have to say about it?" Natalie asked.

"He doesn't know yet." I took a hit from Doc's bottle, handing it back. "That needs a squeeze of lime."

"Well, when Cooper gets here," Natalie said, "I bet he'll have plenty of hot air to share about why that is a bad idea."

"Harvey approves," I said, throwing the old boy under the bus.

"That's because Harvey likes to blow holes in things with Bessie."

"You can borrow money on that," Harvey agreed, flipping two of the ham steaks over.

He stepped aside while Aunt Zoe pulled a casserole dish from the oven. She carried the cheesy potatoes over and set it next to the salad.

Man, oh man. I almost drooled right on the casserole.

"What do you think, Zoe?" Natalie asked.

Aunt Zoe grabbed the bowl of bacon crumbs and sprinkled half of them over the top of the scalloped potatoes. "There's a Winston Churchill quote that I believe applies to Violet's situation." She set the bowl down. " 'If you're going through hell, keep going.' "

Raising his bottle of Corona in a mock toast, Doc said, " 'Hell is empty and all the devils are here.' "

Harvey harrumphed. "Leave Shakespeare and his wagon of words outta this." He pulled another slice of ham from the cast iron pan.

"Addy and Layne!" Aunt Zoe called out. "It's time to eat."

"Wash your hands," I added.

Minutes later, Addy joined us in the kitchen as Harvey placed a plate full of browned ham steaks next to the scalloped potatoes. "Something smells yummy," she said.

"You ready to eat some grub?" Harvey asked, taking off the apron.

"You bet! I love your grub." Addy rubbed her hands together as she slid into the seat next to Natalie. "It's way better than Mom's."

I stuck my tongue out at her as I dished her up some potatoes.

Layne took the chair next to Doc. "I like your cooking best, Mom."

"Liar, liar, pants on fire," Addy sang. "You're just kissing up."

"Am not!"

"Are so!"

"Stop it," I said, handing Addy's plate to Doc to add some ham. "Or I'll send you both to bed with gruel for supper."

"Is Harvey making the gruel?" Layne asked, handing me his plate.

Aunt Zoe laughed. "Your children remind me of you at their age."

"Cheeky li'l brats," I joked, smiling at my two pint-sized hearts in turn while I filled Layne's plate and handed it off to Doc.

As chatter filled the air, focusing on the upcoming holiday and what gifts Santa might leave under the tree, a memory of that yellow eye looking through the knothole flashed through my thoughts. A shadow darkened my happy little moment. How many more family dinners were left in my future? What if I didn't return from Slagton next time?

What if …

Doc squeezed my thigh under the table.

I turned to him, blinking away silly tears.

The warm glow in his eyes lit the darkness of my thoughts. Leaning closer, he whispered in my ear, "Looks like good ol' St. Nick needs to give us a 'Gone Hunting' sign for Christmas, *cara mia*."

Chapter Eighteen

Doc and I were almost finished cleaning the supper dishes when Aunt Zoe's doorbell rang.

"I got it," Layne called out from the living room.

"Layne, wait!" I looked at Doc. "I don't like him answering the door at night." There were too many boogeymen roaming the Black Hills these days for my comfort.

"I'll go," Aunt Zoe said, pushing away from the table.

She returned a minute later with a blue-eyed fire captain. Cooper followed behind Reid, the gash on his forehead bandaged. He scanned the room, pausing when his gaze ran into Natalie's narrowed glare.

What was with the dirty look she was sending his way? Hitting the Deadwood detective with an angry scowl was part of my repertoire, not hers.

Natalie took a hit of her beer, not taking her eyes off Cooper the whole time. He turned to me, his eyes squinty, brimming with unspoken accusations.

What did I do?

Shaking my head at the soap opera brewing in that corner of the kitchen, I let the water out of the sink and focused on the much less prickly of the two men. "Hey, Reid. What are you doing here?"

I hadn't seen him since the night of the Deadwood Chamber of Commerce Christmas party when he and Dominick had gone head to head over Aunt Zoe.

"I brought something for your aunt."

"If it's a tired and bitchy detective," I said, "you can leave him on the front porch." I borrowed a corner of the dishtowel from Doc to dry my hands.

"Ease up, Killer," Doc said for my ears only, planting a kiss on my cheek. "Coop's worn out."

Reid chuckled, socking Cooper's shoulder. "You hear that, Coop? You'd better buck up or Sparky will give you another lashing." His teasing grin swung my way. "By the way, nice try on knocking sense into Coop with your crowbar, but I don't think it did much good. His head is too damned dense."

Cooper's upper lip wrinkled. "Keep it up, chicken shit." He focused on Aunt Zoe. "Martin called me, requesting a police escort to enter the premises."

A snort of laughter came from Harvey. "Zoe, yer firebug has rawhide wisdom, I tell ya."

"He's not *my* firebug." She crossed her arms. "What did you bring me, Reid?"

He pulled something from his pocket, holding out a closed fist. "You left this in my truck."

She took the bait, palm up. When he dropped a jeweled hair comb into it, her cheeks darkened. "Oh. Right. Thanks." She stuffed it in her sweater pocket.

"That's odd," I said to her. "Since your hair is so thick, I mean," I suspected someone had pulled it free, hoping it was Reid while kissing her senseless. But maybe I was reading too much into her blush. "Your hair combs don't usually succumb to gravity."

"Drop it, Violet Lynn," she shot back.

Harvey and I exchanged grins. I was sticking with that kiss notion.

"How have you been, Reid?" I asked the fire captain.

"Cold and hungry." I didn't miss the heated look he sent Aunt Zoe.

Hungry for what? Or should I say for *whom*? I played dumb for Aunt Zoe's sake, waving toward the leftovers sitting on the counter that I hadn't put away yet. "If you're hungry, we have plenty of leftovers."

"Is that Zo's famous three-cheese potatoes dish?"

I nodded. "Grab a plate and load up."

Aunt Zoe glared at me as Reid took the clean plate Doc held out. I gave her a toothy smile back. She could pretend she was unhappy about Reid being in her kitchen, but I knew better. If she hadn't wanted him to join us, she wouldn't have let him cross the threshold.

"Coop," she said, "you're welcome to have some supper, too."

He massaged the back of his neck, wincing. "I'm on duty."

"So take a break and eat up, boy," Harvey said. "Yer gettin' too skinny from workin' so many hours. You keep this up and yer drawers will fall off."

Doc handed Cooper a plate. "You want some coffee, too?"

"Sure," Cooper said, following in Reid's wake.

Natalie stared at Cooper's backside as he dished up a plate of food. When she caught me watching her, she wrinkled her nose at me.

Before he settled into Doc's chair, Cooper spoke into his radio, rattling off a couple of codes and reporting he was on break—at least I think that's what he said. I never understood how cops could comprehend the static-filled gibberish.

A dull thumping overhead made me frown up at the ceiling. While Cooper and Reid dug in, and Doc finished putting clean dishes away, I went upstairs to check on the kids. They were supposed to be finishing their homework that should've been done as soon as they got home from school, but they'd made a deal with Aunt Zoe to do it after supper so they could watch the Christmas special.

When I opened the door to Addy's room, she had her back to me while jumping up and down on her bed, swinging a plastic bat around like a ninja princess. I stood in her doorway, watching her take swings at invisible enemies, using impressive evasive strategies to dodge unseen return blows. Holy crap. Where had she learned those moves? Layne was the one into weapons and superhero movies. Was it innate for Addy? Had I started out that way? I'd first played softball in fifth grade. Swinging the bat had felt natural out of the gate.

I shook out of my stupor. "That doesn't look like homework to me, Adelynn Renee."

She squealed in surprise and landed on her butt on the mattress. "You scared the Parcheesi out of me, Mom."

That was one of my mother's favorite expressions. "What were you doing?"

"Nothing." She slid to the floor, shoving the bat under her bed. "Just messing around."

"You know how I feel about jumping on the bed."

"Sorry."

"You're supposed to be finishing your homework."

"I'm done." She held up her sheet of math problems. "See?"

I took the paper, checking her work. "Good job. How about you get ready for bed?"

"Ah, Mom. Do I have to go to bed already?"

"No, I said to get ready for it, that's all. And make sure you take your time brushing and flossing those furry fangs of yours." I left to check on Layne.

"They aren't furry," Addy called after me.

"Brush for two minutes anyway," I called back.

I knocked twice on Layne's door and then walked inside. The place was empty. His science book lay on his bed.

"Layne?"

A shuffling sound came from his closet. I walked over and pulled open the door.

He sat with his arms around his knees, smiling wide up at me. A flashlight lay on the floor beside him.

I didn't trust that smile for a second. "What are you doing in here?"

"Just sitting, Mom."

"Do you think I was born yesterday?"

"No. You're way too old for that. You were born like over ten thousand yesterdays ago."

Lately, it felt more like twenty thousand. I crossed my arms. "What are you doing in your closet, Layne?"

"My homework."

"So, you're having an out-of-body experience?"

"What?"

"Your science book is on your bed. How else would you be finishing your homework from in here?"

"Oh. I was taking a break."

"And doing what?"

He sighed, his smile slipping away. "You're not going to let this go, are you?"

"I'm your mother. My job duties include extreme probing in an effort to uncover all of your secrets." At least until after he moved out on his own, but I suspected I'd still be plenty nosy even after that.

He pulled a book out from behind his back, handing it to me. "I was looking at this."

I took it, reading the title aloud. *"Medieval Sword Combat—A Learner's Guide."* I lowered the book. "Don't you think you're taking this new obsession with weaponry a little too far?"

He shrugged.

"Come out of there, Layne."

He joined me on the edge of the bed. "Is there something you want to tell me about this?" I held up the book. Something about his discovering that his mother was an Executioner?

"Yes."

I waited, brows raised.

"I'd like a dusack and a rapier for Christmas."

"A dusack?" I parroted.

"It's a practice weapon. Sort of like a saber."

"Layne, Christmas is a week away. Santa already has your presents picked out."

"Come on, Mom. I know how Santa really works."

"You do?"

He patted my leg. "It's okay. I've known the truth for a couple of years now."

I got up and closed his bedroom door, returning to his side. "What? How?"

"I had to use the bathroom one Christmas Eve, and I saw you putting presents under the tree."

I frowned. "Does your sister know, too?"

"I don't think so."

"So, you just play along with her each year?"

He nodded. "Why ruin her fun?"

"Sheesh, you're growing up too fast for me, kid." I gave him a sideways hug. "Why do you want these particular weapons?"

"I told you I'm going to protect you."

"Ah." Of course. My little man of the house.

"And Harvey says I'm too young to have a 12-gauge like Bessie."

Alarms went off in my head at the thought of Layne swinging those double barrels around the place. Not to mention that Bessie's recoil would knock him on his keister. "Harvey's right."

"Then I need a sword."

I stood. "Let me think about it." I wanted to talk to Doc about this, see if Layne's sword request was normal for his age, or if this was a sign of something else—something to do with our bloodline.

"It doesn't have to be a big one," he said as I opened the bedroom door.

"I said I'll think about it, Layne."

"But—"

"No buts. While I appreciate you wanting to protect me, you're still a kid—*my* kid. I get to make this decision, not you."

He sighed. "Fine."

"Brush your teeth, King Arthur. If your homework is done, come downstairs and hang out with us."

"Is Doc spending the night again?"

"Yeah, why?" I cringed, waiting for what was to come next.

"Just curious. I want to ask him about something in that sword combat book."

Whew! "Don't forget to floss."

I left his room and headed downstairs. I figured I'd given Cooper plenty of time to eat in peace. It was time to find out the real reason he was here.

"Cooper," I said when I joined the kitchen crowd. I took the chair opposite him. "Nat said you have something you want to talk to Aunt Zoe and me about."

The detective swallowed, chasing his bite with a drink of coffee before answering. "We had a hit-and-run today."

"Harvey mentioned that earlier. What are the chances of two so close together in a small town like this?"

He stabbed several potatoes. "It's odd, especially since it's not tourist season, but the bigger concern is the story behind both."

"What do you mean?" Aunt Zoe asked, taking the seat between Natalie and me. The fresh cup of coffee in her hands steamed as she sipped it.

"Both incidents were reported by the drivers of the vehicles, not the victims."

"You're saying that the 'runner' was the victim?" Natalie clarified.

"Correct." He looked her way, holding her stare until she lowered her gaze. His focus returned to Aunt Zoe. "This afternoon, the driver actually came to the police station to report the incident."

Reid paused in the midst of washing his plate in the sink. "For insurance reasons?"

"Partly, but more because what he experienced scared the hell out of him."

"How so?" Doc asked, leaning against the counter.

"According to his statement, he was heading out of town toward Sturgis when someone came running out of the trees and crossed the road right in front of him. He slammed on his brakes, but he was unable to avoid hitting the victim. He said the body flew several feet through the air, landing in the ditch."

I cringed. I bet he was going to relive that scene in his head for a long time to come.

Cooper finished his potatoes. "That wasn't the worst part," he explained after he swallowed. "He swears the victim stood up within seconds and wandered back out onto the road. At that point, the driver assumed there was alcohol or some other substance abuse involved. What struck him as odd, though, was that the victim's body appeared to be severely burned."

Aunt Zoe and I exchanged worried glances.

"The driver opened his door and stepped outside, intending to offer a ride to the hospital. Before he could get the words out, one of the victim's arms fell off."

"What?" Natalie said, her jaw lowering. "It just dropped to the ground?"

"Apparently."

"What happened next?" Aunt Zoe asked.

"The driver said the victim made a horrible screeching sound, unlike anything he'd ever heard, and charged toward him. He returned to his car and locked the doors, but that didn't deter the victim, who tried to bite and head-butt his way inside the vehicle."

"Oh my God," I whispered, holding my pounding chest. "What did he do?"

"He shifted into reverse, whipped the car around, and got the hell out of there, straight to the police station."

Aunt Zoe sighed. "Damn."

"My thoughts exactly." Cooper finished off his ham steak. "What do you think, Parker, is this one of your flesh-eating creeps running loose? Or do we have another problem to deal with now on top of everything else?"

All eyes turned to me. I pointed at Aunt Zoe. "Ask her. She's the expert on bizarre species. I mainly kill the troublemakers."

"I believe it's a *Nachzehrer*," Aunt Zoe said. "However, until I see it for myself, I can't be sure." She frowned at Cooper. "Although I really don't relish the idea of looking at this one-armed, crispy ghoul."

"Me neither, especially if it's gnashing its teeth at everything that moves." He pushed his empty plate away. "Will I be able to stop it with a gun, or is this going to take Parker and whatever blunt instrument she can get her hands on at the moment?"

"From what I remember reading about them, the only way for a human to kill one is to decapitate it and then place a copper coin in its mouth."

"You're kidding me," Reid said, drying his hands.

"Or was it stick a coin in its mouth first and then cut off the head?" Doc cursed, rubbing his beard stubble. "Who makes these rules?"

"Not the Executioners." Aunt Zoe patted my arm. "This method of elimination for *Nachzehrer* will most likely not apply to Violet and her kind. They dance to a different tune than you and me. If she is to kill it, she'll have to use the tools of her trade."

"I wonder what Mr. Black knows about this *Nachzehrer*," I said to nobody in particular.

"Mr. Black?" Reid asked, looking to Aunt Zoe for the answer.

"He's a new friend of Violet's." She frowned at Cooper. "Have you checked on Mr. Haskell's body since we were there?"

"No, but that was just this morning."

Holy horse pucky! Had that only been earlier today? It seemed like days ago. It was no wonder my eyes were starting to feel droopy after all that had gone down since sunrise.

"I know, but he was most likely bitten by a *Nachzehrer*. I don't know how long it takes to turn a body into one of their kind, nor if he'll escape that fate because he was dead when bitten."

"I'll stop by Mudder Brothers on my way back to the station." Cooper scooped up his plate and stood. "Thanks for supper. Those potatoes were delicious, Zoe."

"You need to start making a habit of joining us," she told him.

The idea of Cooper being here for supper each night made my shoulders tighten, but I held my tongue because the thought of him eating alone made my heart twinge a little for him, damn it. Somehow, the detective had squeezed his way into my inner circle, and I wasn't sure yet whether that was a good thing or bad thing.

"What about me, Zo?" Reid asked, stabbing another forkful. "Can I make it a habit, too?"

She threw her napkin at him and stood. "Shut up and eat."

"Hey, Doc?" Layne walked into the kitchen, waving "Hello" to Reid and Cooper. "I need your help with something."

"What do you need?" I interrupted.

"I need Doc," Layne said firmly, giving Doc a sly look that made me squint back and forth between the two of them. What was Layne up to now?

"Will you come up to my room for a minute?" Layne asked him.

"Lead the way." Doc gave me a two-fingered salute and then followed my son out of the room.

Cooper's radio made some static noises, which sounded like a mix of gibberish and a math story problem. He grabbed the radio and muttered something back. "I gotta go."

Aunt Zoe reached for the box of truffles on the table. "Do you want a truffle for the road?"

He looked down at the box, hesitated, and then shook his head. "No, thanks."

"I'll eat his," Harvey volunteered, reaching for the box.

Aunt Zoe playfully swatted his hand away. "Be careful out there tonight, Coop," she said. "Especially at Mudder Brothers."

"Will do." He headed for the door.

I remembered something Doc had mentioned earlier and pushed back my chair. "Cooper," I called, catching him at the front door. "I need to talk to you."

"What?"

"Outside." I grabbed my red padded vest while stepping into my boot slippers and followed Cooper out onto the porch, closing the door behind me. The porch light bathed us in a soft glow, keeping the darkness at bay.

"Make it quick, Parker. I need to check on a prowler."

The air was crisp and still. I jammed my hands into my vest pockets to keep them warm. "I hope it's only a stray dog."

"Me, too. I've had enough of your crazy shit for one day."

I let that one go. "About what happened back in Slagton," I started, shuffling my feet. I wasn't used to having heart-to-heart talks with

Cooper. Snarling and teeth gnashing were my usual go-tos. "A little birdy mentioned that you're still, uh, bothered about today."

Cooper scowled, glancing toward the street. "It was a rookie mistake. I should've known better."

"You said that already on the way home. What's this really about? Usually you cuss at me a few times, and then I call you several not-very-nice names, and we move on. Why are you so stuck on this?"

He stared down at me. "I could have gotten you killed, Parker."

I shrugged. "This is how it works now, Cooper. It's life and death every time for me. For you, too. Hell, for anyone along for the ride."

"Maybe, but I knew better than to race in like that. I've been trained on proper procedure. I've experienced multiple situations involving gunfire exchanges. I should have stopped, listened, looked, and tried to set a basic perimeter before waltzing into that mess and dragging you three with me."

"You do realize that you are human, right?" I pinched his shoulder through his coat. "See, flesh and muscle, no robot parts in spite of my previous suspicions."

His taut expression didn't crack, not even one little hairline fracture. "I was so bent on finding out what happened to my informant that I didn't think to treat it like a hostile setting."

"Which is totally understandable."

"No, it's not, Parker." He tore his hand through his hair. "Mistakes like that lead to fatalities. Quit letting me off the hook, damn it."

"Jeez Louise, cut yourself some slack, Cooper. You're exhausted. You have a missing informant. You're dealing with a flesh-eating ghoul or two. You're seeing ghosts all over town."

He jammed his hands on his hips. "Thanks for the reminders of my current version of Hell. What's your point?"

"My point is that you're allowed to be human and make mistakes." When he started to talk, I held up my hands. "Let me finish."

He crossed his arms, huffing, waiting impatiently.

"You're allowed to screw up, you hardheaded bozo, especially considering that you have a huge distracting crush on a woman who is *pretending* she doesn't remember what happened the other night at the Purple Door Saloon."

Cooper stilled, his head cocking to the side as if he wasn't sure he'd heard me right. "She's pretending?"

"You heard me." I pulled my arms tighter against my sides, blocking out the cold. "And that's as much as I will say, being that I'm her best friend and confidante." Actually, that was probably too much, but I felt bad for Cooper after hitting him with my crowbar earlier.

"Damn." He rubbed the back of his neck. "Is her pretending good or bad?"

"I don't know. It probably changes depending on the day."

"Damn," he said again.

I frowned. "I probably shouldn't have told you that."

"Don't worry. I'll keep my mouth shut."

"It's not that. You're going to need a clear head when you go to Mudder Brothers."

"Right. Shit. Just once I'd like a dead body to be only that."

"You and me both. Do you want Doc and me to come with you?"

"No," he said. "But thanks for the offer."

"Just remember, decapitation."

"Fuck," he growled, pulling out his keys. "Is there anything else you need to tell me?"

As a matter of fact ... "I want to go back to Slagton, and I need you there with me."

"Why?"

I assumed he meant the Slagton part, not why him. "We have to finish what was started."

"And what if we don't find any of those things when we go back?"

"Then we have to hunt them—or haunt them. Either verb works in this case, so long as I execute them in the end."

The front door opened behind me. We both turned as Natalie stepped outside, pulling on her faux sheepskin coat in the process.

"Did you tell him about your big plan?" she asked me.

"Yeah. He hasn't officially agreed to anything yet."

"Good." She turned to Cooper. "Because I have a bone to pick with him first."

She did?

He frowned at the index finger she had aimed at him. "You do?"

"The next time you take Violet on a little day trip into a deadly arena and arm her with only a fucking crowbar, I'm going to kick your ass from here to Terry Peak." She poked him in the chest. "She might be a killer, but you put her at risk today on a level that would endanger even a trained Executioner."

"Natalie," I started, "Cooper already apolo—"

She covered my mouth. "I'm not done, Vi."

Removing her hand, she focused on Cooper again. "I know you're used to throwing yourself in harm's way day in and day out, not giving a damn about those who care for you, but she isn't like you in that way. Nor can you take care of her enemies with a mere bullet."

"I fucked up, Natalie," he said, catching her finger and holding it. "I'm sorry."

"It's not that big of a—" I tried to get out.

" 'Sorry' isn't going to cut it," Natalie interrupted. "Not if my best friend is bleeding to death with her throat ripped out."

I grimaced at that image. Did she have to be so graphic when she was making her point?

"I can't lose her, Coop. Do we have an understanding here?"

"Yes," he bit out.

"Great." She grabbed Cooper by the coat lapels. "Then get your head out of your ass and back in the game, because this shitstorm is only going to get worse." She pulled him down to her level. "And I don't want to lose you either, damn it."

Natalie went up on her toes and kissed him. From my front row seat, she went in hard and fast, steaming up my eyeballs, ending with a tug on his lower lip with her teeth. Then, in a blink, it was over.

She licked her lips, not meeting his wide eyes. "Be careful out there tonight, Detective." Without another word, she walked inside, closing the door behind her.

Cooper and I stared after her.

"Sweet shnookerdookies!" I looked at Cooper. "What was that?"

He ran his fingers over his lower lip. " 'Pretending,' you say?"

I shrugged. "Nat was never very good at holding her cards close to the chest when it came to men." Which explained why she was currently supposed to be on a year's sabbatical after numerous, spontaneous relationships that ended in ugly disasters.

His radio crackled to life, shaking us both out of our stupor.

"I have to go. Tell Nyce I'll stop by the gym in the morning."

"Keep your head low, Coop. We need you and those damned guns of yours with us in Slagton."

"That's 'Cooper' to you, Parker," he said, giving me a rare smile that showed his teeth.

I watched him stride across the lawn to his police rig, keeping my fingers crossed that Mr. Haskell's body was still chilling at the morgue.

Chapter Nineteen

Tuesday, December 18th

"It is time," Addy whispered in my ear.

Opening my eyes, I blinked several times in the dark quiet. Time for what? School?

I turned my head, searching my bedroom for her. My door was open a crack. Light from the hallway spilled inside, brightening the room, thick shadows in the corners the only hiding spots for boogeymen.

I didn't see Addy. Unless she was hiding in my closet, some other female had whispered in my ear. But who? Maybe I'd dreamed it. Maybe I was dreaming this, too. I pinched my arm. Nope, awake.

I sat up, listening for the creak of a floorboard on the other side of the door, the swishing of a slipper or bare foot on hardwood, or any other clue that might explain that voice. I could hear Harvey's snores rumbling up the stairs, but all else was silent.

Next to me, Doc slept quietly. His breathing was slow and steady. I debated on waking him, but we'd both been exhausted last night, so I hesitated.

Natalie had left shortly after Cooper, refusing to talk to me about that kiss. After putting the kids to bed for the night, I came back down to find that Aunt Zoe had sent Reid on his way. I joined Doc and my aunt on the couch, while Harvey kicked back in the recliner. *White Christmas* filled the television screen, a favorite of mine since childhood. Harvey fell asleep halfway through the film, and Aunt Zoe went to bed before the final song, leaving Doc and me to watch the end credits.

After she left, I had spread out on the couch, my cheek pillowed on Doc's lap. The local news crew made promises about more snowy weather coming our way, just what we didn't need. Doc trailed his fingers down my arm while we watched, his caresses making my eyelids heavy. Later, he'd helped me up the stairs, lowered me into bed, and crawled in next to me. I couldn't remember anything after that.

It is time.

Easing out of bed, I grabbed my robe and slippers. A glance Doc's way found him still sleeping. I stole out of the room into the hallway, pausing to slide into my slippers and tie on my robe before tiptoeing to Addy's room. Inside, I found her curled up under the covers. She moaned and shifted when I straightened her comforter, settling back to sleep as I watched.

It definitely hadn't been my daughter whispering in my ear.

I checked on Layne and Aunt Zoe next. Both were snoozing away, making me envious. My bed called to me, but I hesitated in the hallway, chewing on my lower lip. That voice had sounded so real. Could it have been my imagination? Some voice in my head screwing with me?

Truth be told, I'd rather it have been my imagination than a ghost … or worse.

I started toward my bedroom. Several steps from my door, I froze.

What was that?

I moved to the top of the stairs, listening.

In between Harvey's snores, I heard recurring notes. They were faint but steady. I edged down the stairs. Christmas lights gave the living room a warm, blinking glow. My bodyguard slept like a snoring baby. I grabbed another blanket from the back of the couch and covered him to help ward off the early morning chill.

The tree lights hypnotized me, spurring memories of Christmases gone by when I'd played Santa for the kids. How many times had I sat alone late on Christmas Eve, eating the cookies they'd left on a plate for Ol' Saint Nick? Or wished I had someone to snuggle up to in the morning while watching my kids tear open their gifts? This year would be different. This year, I had Doc … and Susan. Oh, nuts. I crossed my fingers that Christmas evening at my parents didn't end in disaster.

The rhythmic notes grew louder, intruding on my holiday reverie. Chimes. Something was chiming.

I looked toward the dining room. The clock in there was ticking, but not chiming.

Damn. There was only one other explanation.

I headed for the kitchen, opening the basement door. I stood at the top of the stairs, listening. The chiming was loud enough now to block out Harvey's snores. I hit the light switch and stepped carefully down the stairs. My slippers were almost as worthless on the smooth concrete steps as my boots had been on snow.

The fluorescent lights buzzed overhead down in what I liked to think of as Layne's mad scientist lab. An old dresser filled with his lab equipment sat in the opposite corner from Elvis's pen. A row of crates lined the far wall, butting up against one of Aunt Zoe's old workbenches.

Elvis clucked at me when I passed her cage, not bothering to climb out of her roost to greet me.

I crept over to the two clocks from Mr. Black that lay on the old workbench. I hadn't bothered hanging them up, since they functioned on their own with or without batteries, or winding for that matter. The newest one depicting the Wild Hunt was as silent and unmoving as the day Mr. Black had given it to me. The other clock—the one I'd received weeks ago that had a large hellhound-like beast with a long snout and pointy ears with opened jaws and claws reaching toward the cuckoo door—was chiming repeatedly, but not cuckooing.

Why was it chiming? A couple of weeks ago, it had cuckooed and then started up, keeping time until this last weekend when Layne had noticed it'd stopped. Was chiming the same type of alert as cuckooing?

I leaned closer, trying to open the little door where the cuckoo bird hid. The wood wouldn't budge, reminding me of the closet door in Jerry's office. I needed a paper clip to pop it open. Better yet, Harvey's handy screwdriver.

Running my fingers over the beast's snout, I marveled at the craftsmanship. Who was the clockmaker? Dominick had refused to tell me when I'd asked, recently. Was it someone in town? In the Black Hills? There was so much I didn't understand about this clock business. Hell, about all of this Timekeeper stuff.

Maybe the clock was chiming because I'd broken it somehow when

I'd moved the arms, back before I realized messing with time was bad juju. Or had the kids fiddled with it? I'd laid down the law about touching these clocks, but my kids were curious like so many others, dangerously so at times.

"Hi," a familiar voice said behind me.

I whirled, my hand on my chest. Addy stood next to Elvis's cage, her hair mussed, her face puffy with sleep. She clutched a stuffed-animal version of Elvis that my mom had given her.

"Hey, baby," I said, stepping sideways to block the chiming clock from her view.

She padded closer, her gaze on the workbench behind me. "What's going on down here?"

"Nothing. I was just ... uh ... checking on Elvis."

She stopped a couple of feet away from me. "Those clocks creep me out," she whispered.

"Me, too. You want some breakfast?" I tried to distract her, adding a dose of sugar to sweeten the deal. "I can make you some French toast with powdered sugar on it."

She moved closer, standing next to me. "How come these clocks hardly ever work? Are they broken?"

"They're antiques. They kind of run on their own time."

She put her stuffed chicken on the workbench next to the clock that was chiming. "I wonder what is hiding behind the cuckoo doors."

"Just a little bird, like any other clock." I wasn't sure this was true of the newest clock, because it hadn't woken up since Mr. Black handed it off to me. "Addy, you know not to touch these clocks, right?"

She didn't answer me. My chest tightened. Something was off with my daughter. For one thing, she wouldn't meet my eyes. For another, she hadn't mentioned the constant chiming. "Sweetheart, do you hear any noises coming from these clocks?"

Elvis released a loud series of squawks that drowned out her answer, if she gave one. I glowered at the chicken, watching her fluttering about the cage, banging against the wire repeatedly. Chicken feathers floated around her. What was wrong with that dang bird? "Elvis, stop!"

When I turned back, Addy was pulling open the cuckoo door that had been stuck moments before.

I gasped. "Addy, no!" I reached for her, but my arm went right through her, like she was a ghost.

What the hell?

I tried again. The result was the same.

"Oh, look," Addy whispered. "It's a little girl."

She was right. Instead of a cuckoo bird that I'd witnessed popping out of the clock before, a little blond girl crouched behind the door. I stepped closer, noticing her tiny hands were painted red, along with the neckline of her shirt. Was that supposed to be blood? Was she bitten in the neck by the beast? I needed a brighter light to see for sure.

Addy reached toward the little wooden girl. The air between Addy's finger and the girl-cuckoo seemed to ripple. A tendril of black smoke snaked out from the clock, wrapping around Addy's finger.

In the shadowed alcove behind the wooden girl, something moved.

"Addy, get back!" I tried to grab her wrist to no avail. Panic welled in my throat. The chiming started to clang so loud it rattled my teeth.

The little girl popped out from the clock, her mouth forming a teeny black O. A high-pitched scream blasted up at us.

"Addy!" I shrieked, taking a step back in surprise. I tripped over my own feet, falling on my ass on the hard cobblestone floor. Pain throbbed in my hip as tears streamed down my face. "Addy, no," I cried again, reaching for her.

"Mom!" Layne yelled in my ear. "Stop it!"

A hush of silence filled my head.

I blinked at my son, whose face now filled my vision. His blond eyebrows were pinched together.

"Layne?" I lifted my hand toward his face, touching his cheek. "You're real."

"Of course I'm real." He covered my hand with his.

I pulled him into my lap, squeezing him hard, covering his face with kisses. He smelled like his bed, his skin still warm from it.

"Mom! Come on! Stop already." He pushed out of my lap, resting on his knees beside me. "What are you doing down here?"

I looked beyond him at the workbench with the clocks. A clucking sound drew my gaze to the other side of the room. Elvis watched me from her cage, her head tilting one way and then the other.

"I don't know," I said. "Help me up."

He pulled at my arm, tugging me to my feet. I walked over to the clocks, my hip still throbbing.

"Look at that." Layne joined me at the workbench. "That wolf one is ticking again."

The clock with the snarling beast was ticking away, not a chime to be heard, or a cuckoo for that matter.

"But the time's wrong," he continued. "We need to fix—" He reached toward the clock.

"No!" I snagged his arm, pulling him back. "No touching!"

"I was just—" he started.

"I mean it, Layne. These clocks are off limits. Look with your eyes, not your fingers."

Heavy footfalls sounded overhead in the kitchen. Doc took the steps two at a time. "Violet." He was slightly winded when he stood next to us at the workbench. His hair reminded me of Cooper's shark fins. "What's going on?"

His shirt was missing. The bruises on his ribs were beginning to fade, his skin colored a dull bluish green now instead of vivid purple and black. He'd managed to pull his jeans on before coming downstairs, although they were zipped only, not buttoned.

Layne gaped at Doc's side. "It looks like you were hit with a battering ram."

That was one way to describe what happened.

"Addy woke me," Doc said, rubbing his eyes. "She told me you were down here screaming. Are you okay?"

Was I really screaming? I wasn't sure what was real and what wasn't. "I think so."

"What happened?"

I looked around, trying to piece it all together. "I'm not sure."

"Mom was down here sitting on the floor yelling at Addy," Layne explained, eyeing the clocks.

Just then Addy came down the stairs, making a beeline to her true love. "Poor, poor Elvis. Did Mom scare you?"

Screw the chicken, I scared myself.

I covered my mouth with a trembling hand, watching my daughter pull the chicken from its cage and stroke its feathers. My gaze returned to Doc's. "Maybe I was sleepwalking."

His gaze dipped to my toes. "You're wearing your robe and slippers."

"Yeah." I glanced down. The belt on my robe was even tied. "I remember putting them on, too. Is that normal for a sleepwalker?"

"Have you ever done something like this before?"

I shook my head. "Not that I know of."

"Look, Doc," Layne said. "This wolf clock is ticking again."

The lines in Doc's brow deepened. "It sure is."

"What time is it?" I asked.

"Almost six."

"Layne," I said, snapping back to mom-mode. "Go upstairs and start getting ready for school."

"Ah, Mom. It's too early."

"Do as I say, please." I glanced over at my chicken-lover. "You, too, Addy. Get dressed and I'll make you both some French toast."

"Fine," Layne snapped, stomping up the stairs.

Addy put Elvis back in her cage. "No offense, Mom." She paused on her way up the stairs. "But I'd rather have Doc make us French toast. You can pour our orange juice, though."

How generous of her. I narrowed my eyes. "Go, Adelynn Renee."

When the kids were out of earshot, I turned to Doc. "I heard a clock chiming," I said in a lowered voice in case anyone was eavesdropping from the top of the stairs. "That's what brought me down here."

"Another nightmare?"

"No. I don't have nightmares when you're near me."

He crossed his arms. "Okay, start from the beginning."

I leaned against the workbench. "Somebody whispered in my ear, waking me up."

"Whispered what?"

"The words, 'It is time.' I thought it was Addy at first, because the voice sounded female. I checked on her, but she was asleep in her bed. Then I visited Layne and Aunt Zoe. I even came downstairs and peeked at Harvey. Everyone was sleeping, including you. That's when I heard the chiming and followed it down here."

"Did it feel like you were awake at that time or were things hazy?"

It was all very clear. "I'm pretty sure I was awake."

"What happened after you came down here? What spurred your screaming?"

"I was looking at this clock with the wolf-like beast on it." I stared at the ticking clock, replaying the scene in my head. "It was chiming non-stop. I tried to open the cuckoo door at the top, but it wouldn't budge." Out of curiosity, I pulled on the door again. It still wouldn't open. That didn't seem normal, but then what did these days?

"I heard Addy's voice behind me," I continued. "She started talking to me, and then …" I trailed off.

"And then what?"

I held up my index finger. "There was something off about Addy. She didn't look at me or answer my questions. Then, when I tried to touch her, my arms went right through her like I was a ghost."

One of Doc's eyebrows lifted. "Or she was."

"How can that be, though? If I were dreaming, it would make sense. But everything seemed so real—sights, sounds, smells. Things were too solid feeling not to be."

He rubbed his jaw. "I'll need to think about this more after I've had some coffee. What made you scream?"

"Addy opened the cuckoo door on the one that's ticking. Something about her touching it frightened me. I had the notion that her making physical contact with it put her at risk. Inside the door, instead of a cuckoo bird, there was a little blond girl with blood on her hands and around her neck. I thought she'd been bitten by the beast. Addy reached out to touch the girl. I tried to stop her, but she wasn't listening and I couldn't grab her. When her finger brushed over the little girl, a black wisp of smoke came out and wrapped around her finger. Then the girl popped out of the door, shrieking at us instead of cuckooing."

Concern lined his face. "So you screamed back."

My cheeks warmed. "Yeah, something like that. Then I stumbled backward, tripped, and that's when Layne came into the picture."

Doc moved next to me, his focus on the clock. "And now it's ticking again."

"What do you think, Mr. Oracle? What do you see that I can't?"

He put his arm around my shoulder. "You're a Timekeeper."

"That's not very enlightened 'seeing' on your part."

"This experience with the clocks is new for you. Maybe the voice you heard comes with being a Timekeeper."

"But why was Addy pulled into it?"

"I don't know. It could be as simple as you being worried about her messing with the clocks when she's down here taking care of Elvis."

I had repeatedly warned her and Layne not to touch them.

"It also could have been a premonition," Doc added.

"Like a vision of something that is going to happen in the future."

"Or a warning."

I rubbed my eyes with the heels of my palms. "Well, if that's the case, I know how to keep this sort of thing from happening for real."

"How?"

Blinking the last of the sleep from my eyes, I grimaced at the two time bombs. "I'm moving these clocks out of here today."

"Moving them to where? Zoe's workshop?"

"No. That's too accessible for my kids. I'm taking them to work."

"Calamity Jane's?"

"Actually, the apartment above my office."

"You're going to delegate timekeeping to Cornelius?"

"More like trust him to watch over the clocks and keep me updated on their status."

"What makes you think he'll be willing to be your timekeeping lackey?"

"He loves eccentric, haunted stuff. These clocks are right up his spook-filled alley."

"But *you* need to keep an eye on them. You're the Timekeeper."

"So far, this aspect of my job includes waiting for a clock to start ticking or stop ticking. Until Mr. Black teaches me some of the finer details of timekeeping, Cornelius can handle clock watching. It's along the same lines as ghost spying with the fancy cameras and microphones he's planted throughout Calamity Jane's."

Doc pulled me closer, his chest warm as he hugged away my chills. "I'm not sure this is what Ms. Wolff intended when she handed off the baton."

I smirked up at him. "Yeah, well, Ms. Wolff didn't have curious children who like to explore with their fingers."

"You do see the bigger problem going on here, don't you?" His gaze was on the clocks.

"Bigger than my kids getting caught up in some kind of trouble with magic clocks?"

"Yes." He turned me around, pointing at the clock depicting the Wild Hunt. "This one isn't ticking when you'd think it should be after what we saw standing in the road on our way out of Slagton yesterday."

Which meant that the leader of the hunt wasn't even here yet. How pissed would the hunter be after finding out I'd executed so many of the pack?

Doc aimed his finger in the direction of the other clock. "And this one *is* ticking, which means you have someone to worry about in addition to the rowdy crew in Slagton, the *Nachzehrer*, and the *lidérc*."

I laced my fingers through his, careful not to bump his bandaged knuckles. "Santa's naughty list is getting long."

"Yeah. I have a feeling we're going to have to do something about that sooner rather than later." He kissed my temple and then led me toward the stairs. "Tell you what, Killer. While you get ready for work, I'll box up the clocks and make breakfast."

Upstairs in the kitchen, Harvey was pouring himself a cup of coffee. I left Doc to explain this morning's scream-queen festivities while I headed for the shower.

Last night, Jerry had left a message that he wanted to meet with all of us employees at Bighorn Billy's this morning for another emergency team huddle. I hoped it had something to do with determining who was covering the office over the holidays and not a new marketing idea that involved me, more makeup, and another idiotic pose.

According to my cell phone, I had an hour and a half before my meeting. I'd need to hustle if I wanted to take a side trip to drop off the clocks with Cornelius first.

After a speedy shower, I pulled my hair back in a chignon, jamming a few of Aunt Zoe's charm-decorated hair combs in the snarl of wet curls to corral some of the loose ends. The fancy combs reminded me that I needed to catch her alone and find out if something happened with Reid after the Christmas party. Nosy Parker wanted to know the juicy details.

The kids were chattering away with Aunt Zoe and Doc when I returned to the kitchen. Their plates were half-empty.

"Where's Harvey?" I asked, grabbing a mug. I poured a cup of black coffee, took a sip to check the temperature, and then gulped half of it down. I needed a solid kick-start after this morning's sideshow.

"He went home to shower and trim his beard," Aunt Zoe said.

"Does he have a date today with a hot babe?"

"Doesn't he always?" Doc stood by the empty griddle, munching on a piece of French toast. "You want me to fix you up a plate?" He indicated toward the serving dish on the table.

I shook my head. "Jerry wants us to meet at Bighorn Billy's this morning." I moved over next to him. "Thank you for taking the kids to school today."

"Doc's taking us to school *and* picking us up?" Addy asked.

Layne cleared his throat, glaring at his sister.

What? Doc getting the kids after school was news to me. "You don't have to pick them up," I said. "I can do that."

"The kids and I have plans."

"We're going to the Rec Center," Addy blurted out.

Layne threw his napkin at her. "Way to blab our secret, big mouth."

I started to reprimand him, but Aunt Zoe beat me to it.

"Layne," Aunt Zoe chastised. "You know how I feel about you two throwing things at each other, especially at the table."

"Sorry," he said. When she pointed at Addy, he apologized to his sister, ending with, "But it's supposed to be a secret, remember?"

She pinched her lips together, staring down at her plate.

I turned to Doc. "All right, spill. What are you guys doing at the Rec Center today?"

"It's none of your business," Aunt Zoe sang.

I harrumphed at her, and then took another swallow of coffee.

Doc tugged on one of my curls that had escaped the chignon and combs. "If you want to know what we're doing, you should join us there this afternoon."

"Really?" He was finally going to let me be a part of their secret Rec Center meetings?

"Are we sure we want her there?" Layne interjected. He didn't sound too thrilled about it, which spurred me to glare in his direction.

"I believe the time has come," Doc answered.

It is time, I heard in my head. According to the voice that had whispered sweet nothings in my ear this morning, Doc was right.

"Do I need to bring my bathing suit?" I said those last two words with a curled upper lip. I didn't relish squeezing into my tankini and waltzing around in public. Public pools were breeding grounds for large-scale outbreaks of embarrassment in my past.

"No suit. Just a T-shirt and some yoga pants will do."

I finished my coffee, setting the mug in the sink. My smile spilled out before I could stifle it and play it cool in front of Doc. I couldn't help it. Going to the Rec Center felt like something a family would do, and for once it was *my* family, not some other happy little mother-father-kids group that I'd be watching while green with envy. "Sweet! It's a date."

Layne groaned. "It's not a *date*, Mom. That means you and Doc will get mushy and kissy again. A boy can only see so much of that before it melts his brain."

"Coop would agree with him," Doc said, chuckling.

"Well, I think it's neat that Doc likes to kiss Mom," Addy piped up.

"Why's that?" Aunt Zoe asked.

"She went a long, loooong time with no boys wanting to kiss her. I was starting to think we'd have to find her a frog to kiss."

My face heated. "You make me sound like a leper, child."

"Leopards are fast."

Layne rolled his eyes. "She said 'leper,' not 'leopard,' you bozo."

"Layne, knock off the name calling." I kissed his head, then moved to his sister and did the same. "Addy, don't forget to turn in your library book today or you'll have to pay the fine with your allowance."

Aunt Zoe gave me an "ahem," and tapped on her cheek. I obliged with a quick kiss. "Don't shoot any fire captains today," I ordered.

"I give no guarantees." She squeezed my hand. "Be careful out there, baby girl."

"Why? What's going to happen?"

"Knowing you, probably something that will require tequila to fix."

Doc walked me to the door. "The clocks are in your back seat. Do you want my help dropping them off?"

"No. I can do the rest. Thanks for taking the kids to school today. Are you serious about me joining you three at the Rec Center?" I opened the hall closet, fingering through the coats, searching for a replacement for my red pea coat. "I don't want to impose on whatever you guys are doing."

"I am serious, and you're not imposing. We can show you a few things that might help."

"Help with what?" I pulled out a knee-length, blue wool trench coat with a matching belt that my mom had bought me years ago for Christmas.

"You'll see."

I pulled on the coat. "Will you bring my T-shirt, sports bra, and yoga pants for me?"

"Only if I'm allowed to fish in your underwear drawer while I'm at it," he said with a glint in his eye.

I wrapped my arms around his neck. "Mr. Nyce, you can frolic in my underwear anytime you want." I made a face at the image that popped in my head. "Wait. I think that came out wrong."

He laughed.

"What I mean is—"

His kiss stopped the rest of my words, warming me clear to my toes. He tasted sweet, like maple syrup with a side of happily-ever-after. I wanted the tingling sensation he was stirring deep inside of me to go on and on until I keeled over and joined Prudence in the wispy world, but reality prevailed, butting its ugly head into our business.

"You have to go," he said, his lips sliding to my ear, searing a path across my skin.

"Yeah," I breathed in his scent, hungry for more of his touches.

He stepped back and tightened my belt. "Stop by my office today if you have a chance." He opened the door for me.

I licked my lips. They felt swollen, along with my other throbbing parts that wanted Doc to finish what he'd started. "Okay. Why?"

Did it have to do with Cornelius and his ghost monitors?

He ran his finger down my sleeve. "I have an idea about you, this coat, your boots, and something from your underwear drawer."

"Oh! Tell me more."

"I'd rather show you, vixen."

Another lip-tingling kiss later, I was on my way to hand off the troublesome clocks.

Chapter Twenty

The parking lot behind Calamity Jane Realty was empty except for an SUV and two pickups—none of which I recognized. I was halfway across the snow-plowed parking lot when the door to Doc's back entrance opened a crack. Cornelius's head popped out.

"Violet," he called, waving me over.

What was he doing in Doc's office this early? He opened the door wider, giving me a glimpse of his robe and striped pajama pants. Was he sleeping in Doc's back room now, while curled up next to his camera monitors?

He held the door wide, making room for me and the two boxes I was carrying. "It's about time," he said as I neared.

His words stopped me. "How do you know I'm here about time?" Had Doc called and told him I was bringing him the clocks?

"Because time is nothing if not constant." A frigid blast rippled my coat hem and tore at his robe. He pulled me inside, shutting out the cold.

"I don't think we're on the same page." I stomped the slush off my boots onto Doc's doormat.

"You mean you actually read?"

I glared up at him. "Of course I can read. I went to college."

"I know you *can* read, but I thought you preferred moving pictures to printed words."

He was right, which made me grind my molars. "What gave you that idea?"

"You quote movies, not books."

"Stop analyzing me and take these damned clocks."

He glanced down at my armload. "Those look like boxes."

"The clocks are in the boxes." I shoved them at him.

He tucked them under his arm. "Why are you bringing me clocks in boxes or rather boxes of clocks? And why don't I hear any ticks or tocks coming from these boxes of clocks?"

I jammed my hands on my hips. "Do you hear yourself, Dr. Seuss?"

"Of course I hear myself. I can hear you, too. In fact, I can often hear those who go *boo*."

"Son of a nutcracker! I might kill you today if you don't stop talking like a character from a children's book."

"Ah ha! So you prefer to read young adult fiction."

"You know what, I don't have time for this. I have a breakfast meeting this morning and I need to grab something from my desk before I head over there." I reached for the doorknob.

He blocked my path. "You can't go over there yet."

"Why not?"

"Follow me." He handed the clock boxes back to me, leading the way into Doc's back room with all of his monitors.

The place smelled of warm computer guts. I set the clock boxes on the floor inside the doorway and then joined him at his bank of computer screens now sitting on several folding tables.

He pointed at one of the monitors. "This is why I was waiting for you at the back door. The Tall Medium told me you were on your way when I called him."

"Why didn't you call me?"

"Because the potential that you were still sleeping was high."

"It was nice of you to be considerate."

"It was self-preservation." He hit a few letters on the keyboard. "Your early morning temperament leaves much to be desired."

That was his fault for all of the times he'd called me at the butt crack of dawn, asking for me at the top of his lungs. "Ah, bite me."

"My point proven."

I snarled at him, and looked over his shoulder. A colored image of Calamity Jane's front office filled the screen in front of him. The picture was much clearer than I'd expected. He must have forked out some serious dough for his equipment. The camera was positioned in the corner behind my desk, looking toward the dark hallway. I leaned closer, staring into the shadows, waiting for a ghost to float past. "What am I supposed to be looking at?"

"Your desk."

My gaze lowered, zeroing in on my computer. "Why is my monitor lit up?" I crossed my arms. "Was Ray messing with my computer?" It would be like that jerk to dig through my emails, searching for some dirt to smear on me this morning at our meeting.

"No one has been in your office today to my knowledge."

I frowned, leaning down again. "It looks like a document is open."

"It is."

"What's going on?" I asked him.

"Your monitor came to life about ten minutes ago."

"Did we have a power surge?"

"No, we have a ghost."

He was being purposely ambiguous, one of his specialties. "Spell it out for me, Cornelius."

"G-H-O-S-T." When I threatened to clobber him, he frowned. "My attempt at levity was apparently misguided. You're even tenser than usual this morning. Did you have a quarrel with your Tall Medium?"

He was right about the tension part. "Doc and I are fine and dandy. I had an issue with those clocks."

"The clocks in the boxes."

"Yes, those damned clocks," I snapped before catching myself. "Sorry. I need you to do me a favor and keep an eye on them."

"This sounds mysterious. To what end?"

"If they stop or start, you need to let me know immediately."

"That does not seem particularly stimulating."

"I'll explain more when one of those changes occurs. Until then, do not touch the hands of the clocks. Simply take them out of the boxes and observe them."

He stroked his goatee. "I'll watch your clocks if you do me a favor in return."

"What favor?"

"Go next door and read what's on your computer screen."

Focusing on the monitor, I asked, "Read it?"

"Yes, we did establish that you can read, correct?"

I poked him in the ribs. "Why do you want to know what's on the screen?"

"When I zoom in, you can see that someone is typing." The camera view enlarged, my computer dead center.

"Typing? As in present tense?"

"Correct. I believe your old boss is writing a list."

My jaw dropped as I watched blurry letters pop up one by one on my screen. "Holy shit."

"I need you to go over to confirm."

"Me?" I took a step back, almost tripping on a tangle of cords. "Why don't you go?"

"She hides whenever I step in the office. I suspect she knows I'm trying to interact with her."

"How do we know she won't leave when I go?"

"We don't. However, we will once you make an attempt."

"But ... but I can't see ghosts. What good will it do if ... Hold on. I might not be able to see ghosts, but I know someone who can."

I pulled out my cell phone.

Cooper took his time answering. "What do you want, Parker?" He sounded more weary than angry.

"Where are you?"

"That's a stupid question."

"Just answer it."

"If you've found another dead body, then I'm in Mexico."

"I didn't find a body."

"It must be a fucking Christmas miracle."

"Cooper! Where are you!?"

"I'm at my goddamned desk, who needs to know?"

"Me. Get off your stubborn ass and come over to Doc's office."

"I'm a little busy here. You may not realize it, Parker, but my world does not revolve around you."

"Now, Coop!" I yelled in the phone and hung up on him. "That should piss him off enough to come chew me out in a hurry."

Cornelius gave me one of his half smiles. "Has anyone ever told you that your relationship with the constables in this town is dysfunctional at best?"

"They started it."

"Why mustn't I touch those clocks?"

"They're cursed." That was the best I could think up on the fly.

"Cursed time pieces? Intriguing."

It turned out I had long enough to visit the restroom before Cooper showed up, pounding on Doc's front door.

"Parker!" I'd barely flipped the latch when he barged inside, his horns leading the way. "This had better be worth my fucking time."

"Come with me." Grabbing him by the forearm, I tugged him back outside. I stopped out of view of Calamity Jane's plate-glass windows. "I need you to peek in at my desk and tell me if you see anything."

Cooper scowled. "I don't have time for games. Unlike you, I've been working all night and have things to wrap up before I go home this morning."

"Dammit, Cooper. Just do it. You owe me after yesterday."

His gaze hardened. "Ohhhh, now you're going to play that card?"

"That's right, Buster Brown, so get peeking."

"That's 'Detective' Buster Brown to you, and don't you forget it." He nudged me aside, giving me one last glare before doing as told.

I counted to five. "Well?" I whispered.

The bewildered expression on his face when he stepped back told me plenty.

"It's Jane, isn't it?"

"You know damned well who it is." He rubbed his red-lined eyes.

A twinge of guilt hit me at how tired he looked. I should let him go home to Doc's place and get some sleep, and I would shortly. But first, "What's she doing?"

"Sitting at your desk."

"I already knew that."

He growled. "Then why did you call me over here?"

"Because Cornelius and I can't see her, only the letters showing up on my screen. We wanted to be sure it was Jane, which required your ghost-detecting eyes. Can you see what she's typing?"

"I can see her, not through her. Besides, I didn't know you wanted me to read your damned screen."

"Quit being so pissy, Cooper. I'm on your side, remember?"

"I'm not pissy. I'm just ... tired." He squeezed the back of his neck. "Sorry." His apology was gruff, but I accepted it.

"I want to know what she's typing, but I'm afraid if I go inside I'll scare her off."

"Let me look again."

I peered around him but saw only an empty office. My computer screen was impossible to read from this distance without a bionic eye.

"It's too far away," he said.

"Do you have any binoculars?" I asked.

"Sure. They're hanging next to my secret decoder ring on my utility belt."

I ignored his sarcasm, lifting my cell phone.

He frowned. "What are you doing with that?"

I took aim at my screen, zooming in on the words typed there. "Trying something." I clicked the picture button, and then enlarged the photo. "Dagnabbit. It's still too blurry."

My cell phone chirped. A message from Cornelius popped up.

"Uh-oh," I said.

"What?"

"Cornelius says my computer screen just went dark." I looked up at Cooper. "Is she gone?"

He peeked again. So did I, leaning into him, using his shoulder to keep from falling face first into plain view.

I felt his shoulder tense under my hand. "Oh, shit," he said.

"What? Is she gone?"

"No, she's still in your chair."

"That's good."

"Maybe. Maybe not. She's staring at me."

"Are you sure?"

"Yes, I'm sure, Parker."

"Do you think she can see you?"

"I know she can see me."

"How do you know?"

"Because she's giving me the 'come here' motion." He stepped into view, dragging me by the wrist with him.

"What are you doing, Cooper?"

"Going inside."

"Great. I'll wait for you back at Doc's with Cornelius." I tried to yank free, but he held tight.

"Nope. You're going in with me." Before I could object, he towed me over to the front door.

"But I left my keys back at Doc's in my purse." That was no lie.

"I have a feeling we're not going to need them."

He was right. The lock clicked. The door swayed on its hinges, as if a small breeze was trying to blow inside—or out.

Cooper opened the door and led me into the office. His grip on my wrist remained ironclad.

"What is she doing now?" I whispered, stepping closer to him.

"Staring at me."

"What does she look like?"

"You don't want to know." His grip tightened further.

Unfortunately for Cooper, ghosts appeared however they'd looked at death. In Jane's case, I wasn't certain what he might be seeing, since she'd been killed with a fist-sized barbed hook before being chucked over the edge of the Open Cut, Lead's huge open pit mine. Rumor was, Cooper had been the one who'd had to pick up the pieces of Jane after her body was found. I bet he'd never figured on running into her again after that grisly task. Irony could be a real bitch.

"Cooper." I tried to pull free again. "Loosen your grip a little." A flashback of his crushing grasp on my thigh up at Prudence's place weeks ago made panic flutter in my chest.

He let go, but didn't move from my side. "She's standing in front of me now."

I stared hard at the empty air, trying to see a ripple or blur or any evidence of spectral energy without success. "What does she want?"

"To touch me, I think."

Goose bumps peppered my skin. I clutched his elbow. "You need to let her do it."

"Why?"

"That's what they do in the movies."

"This isn't a fucking movie, Parker." He cringed, but held steady. "She's touching my badge."

"Maybe she wants your badge."

"Why would she want that?"

"Maybe she always wanted to be a cop."

"Really, Parker? Is that the best you can come up with?"

"Well, how am I supposed to know why she likes your badge all of a sudden? It's shiny. Maybe she likes shiny things now."

"Just shut up."

"Okay." I pressed against his side, my heart pounding loud in the quiet office. "What's she doing now?"

"She's pointing at your computer."

"Look! The screen is lit up again."

We walked over, Cooper leading the way while I held onto him. We leaned over my desk together. I read the list of words on my screen aloud. "Greenborn, Dunken, Booth, Porterson, Tarrow, Belldirk, Stevendale, Yarbrow." I squeezed Cooper's arm. "Ask her what these names mean."

"I can't. She's gone."

"Gone where?"

"How in the hell should I know?" He looked at my hand still holding his arm. "You can let go of me now, you big tough Executioner."

"Cram it, law dog." I let go and hit the print button on my keyboard. I grabbed the paper from the printer, reading through the names again and then held the printout high in front of Cornelius's camera. "Got them," I said loud and clear, no mumbling this morning.

Cooper sat on the edge of my desk. "Jesus, I could use a drink."

"Call Jane back," I told him. "We need to find out about the names on this list."

"I'm not calling for Jane's ghost."

"Why not? If you're scared, I'll hold your hand this time," I teased.

"You're not half as funny as your hair looks first thing in the morning."

"Don't you start with the hair jokes, Cooper. I will hurt you even if you are Doc's best buddy."

He rubbed the back of his neck. "I don't need to ask Jane about the names on that list because I already know who they are."

"You do?" I lowered the paper. "Are they more dead people?"

"Yes and no."

"How can they be dead and not dead?"

"They're dead men whose names are carved on several old buildings in Deadwood and Lead."

* * *

"I don't have time for that shit," Cooper said, pointing at the list of building names in my hand.

We stood on the sidewalk in front of Doc's office while cold morning air and exhaust fumes swirled around us. In the weak rays of winter sunshine, Cooper looked rundown, run over, and wrung out.

"Do you want me to ask Doc to look into it?" I offered.

"No." He grabbed the paper from my hand, stuffing it in his pocket. "Where is Nyce, anyway?"

"He's taking my kids to school and then heading to Sturgis for a meeting with a client." At least that was what he mentioned was on his agenda while we were watching the news last night. That reminded me of another agenda. "Hey, was Mr. Haskell's body at the morgue when you checked?"

"Yep. Still dead." He shot me a quick frown. "Did Natalie spend the night at your place?"

"No. She left soon after you."

"She say anything else about ..." he trailed off, focusing on a passing pickup instead of finishing his question.

I grinned. Dang, Cooper sure had a bad itch when it came to Natalie if he was thinking about her in between flesh-eating ghouls and list-making ghosts. "Did she say anything about what an anvil-headed, pain in the ass you are?" I completed his inquiry for him.

My smile widened at his scowl.

"Remind me why I don't arrest you, Parker?"

"Because we made a deal—I share truths about dead people and other creepy stuff with you, and in exchange you stop threatening me with handcuffs."

"Right. I should have included a no-insult clause in that deal."

"What would we have left to talk about if you had?" A chilly breeze ruffled my coat. I tightened my belt and decided to throw him a bone. "After you left, I asked Nat about that kiss she gave you, but she refused to discuss it and went home."

His brows pinched together. "I'm not sure where to go from here."

Wait an ass-freezing minute! Had I woken up in a parallel universe? Was that what my crack-of-dawn clock premonition had been trying to tell me?

"Why, Detective Cooper. Are you asking li'l ol' me for advice about a girl? Have the planets stopped circling the sun?"

His nostrils flared. "This is turning into my worst nightmare."

He should try living in my head for a day. This shit was child's play.

"Easy there, law dog. I'm just funnin' with you." I crossed my arms. "Before we go any further, I need to know what your intentions are."

"To go home, crawl into bed, and forget I ever brought this up in front of you."

I rolled my eyes at his ruffled feathers. "Quit being such a wuss."

"Call me a wuss again and I'll leave you behind the next time we're in Slagton."

"Ha! Doc and Harvey wouldn't let you. Answer the question, Cooper. What are your intentions with my best friend?"

He scratched the blond beard stubble on his jaw. "How in the hell should I know this early in the game?"

I wasn't going to let him off the hook that easily. It was interrogation time and I wanted some answers, damn it. "Fine. See if you can dance to this tune then—are you just looking for a roll in the hay with Nat?"

"No."

His quick response gave me pause. "Are you sure about that?"

"Parker," he growled, his threatening glare warning me to back off.

Screw backing off. My best friend's heart was on the line. "Don't you 'Parker' me. You didn't even take a moment to think about my question."

"I didn't need to."

We exchanged gunslinger glares. It was high noon in Deadwood and I hadn't even eaten breakfast yet.

Was I reading him right? Was this about more than only being hot for her bod? Even if that were so, it didn't mean he wouldn't do as Natalie feared and dump her after she'd traveled a few miles in his bed.

"You do remember that Natalie is on a much-needed sabbatical from men, of course."

He cursed. "Whose bright idea was that?"

"Not mine." When he hit me with a raised eyebrow, I explained, "Her last boyfriend screwed around on her with another woman. He was one of several philandering pricks in a long history full of dickweeds and scoundrels. She needed a break to catch her breath and build a fortress around her heart."

His face hardened. "I wouldn't do that to her."

"You say that now."

Steely eyes stabbed mine. "I'm not like those other assholes."

"You hurt her once before."

He groaned. "That was different."

"How?"

Jamming his hands in his pockets, he glanced down. His jaw muscles worked, as if he was trying out answers before speaking. "Something spooked me."

Had I heard that right? "You got spooked?"

"That's what I fucking said. Are your ears broken?"

"No, but keep giving me lip and your nose will be—*again*."

A hint of a smile flitted over his features. "It's no wonder Hawke goes apeshit over you."

I made a cross with my fingers. "Don't say that name aloud. It will conjure the big nincompoop and mess up my day even more." I checked my cell phone. "I have a meeting soon. What do you mean, you got spooked?"

"Christ. Are we really going to do this here? Now? On the sidewalk in broad daylight?"

We were alone and I was curious. "Yes, yes, and yes, so quit stalling if you want my help."

He grimaced. "I had no intention of getting involved with Natalie that night at the Purple Door Saloon."

"You mean years ago, right? Not last week on her birthday."

"Yeah."

"You didn't plan to kiss her, but you did. So what?"

"Local girls are taboo in my book."

"So I've heard." As in a million times from a certain woman who still gnashed her teeth about Cooper and his no-local-girls policy. "Why are they taboo?"

"I had a bad experience with one. It almost cost me my job."

That must be the girlfriend story Reid had told me about the night Aunt Zoe had rejected his proposal. The tale involved a woman who'd used Cooper while committing crimes behind his back. "Okay, so Nat is a local girl and you broke your own rules and kissed her. Is that what spooked you?"

He opened his mouth to speak and then frowned instead. "Why in the hell am I telling you this? Jesus, I'm beat." His fingers tore through his hair. "Forget everything I said, Parker."

I grabbed his sleeve and held tight when he tried to walk away.

"Dammit, what spooked you?"

He exhaled, his breath steaming around his lined face. "How do I know what I tell you won't end up on the front page of the *Black Hills Trailblazer*?"

"Nobody gives a crap about your love life but you, Cooper." Well, him and Natalie. And me too, since I was the one hanging on his every word at the moment. "I promise to keep my lips sealed."

"Even around Natalie?"

"Yes."

"And Nyce?"

"Yes!"

"And—"

"Just tell me, for crissake!"

I didn't think he was going to continue, but then he snorted. "This is going to sound stupid."

"Criminy! Just pop your damned corn already."

His eyes crinkled. "You sound like Uncle Willis."

"Cooper!" I balled my fist, holding it under his nose. "I swear I'll leave another mark."

"Calm down, Rocky Parker." He pulled me nearer to Doc's front door, glancing around before speaking in a low voice. "I lost control that night. I had no intention of kissing Natalie, only talking."

"You saw Natalie and her killer lips and you only wanted to chit-chat? Quit trying to sell me snake oil, Cooper."

"Okay, maybe I decided to engage in a little flirting after she let me buy her a drink. What can I say? I needed to take my mind off some shit I was dealing with at work and she looked like a pinup girl with feet. But that was it."

"Seriously?"

"Yes. I've known Natalie since we were kids. The last thing I wanted to do was muddy the waters between us."

"But then you kept drinking," I said, moving his story along with what I knew about the evening.

He nodded. "Alcohol was only part of the problem, though." He squeezed the back of his neck. "We started playing pool, joking around, flirting. I lost sight of the line in the sand at some point."

I held up my hands. "Timeout. You can skip the physical stuff." I couldn't handle hearing the play-by-play again, not while I was sober.

"I wasn't going to give you any damned details, Parker."

Thank God for that. "You still haven't said why you got spooked."

Another glance at my cell phone made me huff. Was he dragging this out on purpose? Ray would make sure to rub my nose in my tardiness if I was late for Jerry's huddle.

He shrugged. "I got spooked because I wanted Natalie that night."

That was it?! Talk about a lame finale. "No shit, Sherlock."

"You don't get it, Parker."

"Apparently not. Why don't you explain?" And hurry up about it.

His mouth thinned. "I've had sex plenty of times."

"Okay." Where was this going? Maybe I shouldn't have pushed him so hard for an answer. "And?" I pressed anyway, squirming on the inside.

"One woman served as well as another. I wasn't particular."

"FYI, Cooper, this cynical recount of your previous sexcapades isn't helping you to win my approval for a place in my best friend's bed."

"Let me finish," he ground out.

"Fine. Go."

"I wanted Natalie."

"You already said that."

"Yeah, but you're not hearing what I'm saying. She wasn't just another random female I'd chosen to bed."

Oh. Was this what locker room talk was like? I wondered what Doc would say if he were here. Would he tell Cooper how easy it had been to 'bed' me? Harvey would undoubtedly share the details of his latest one-night stand, crowing about how limber his hot flame was, sharing the intimate particulars on what body jelly he'd spread on her …

"I wanted Natalie," Cooper continued, hauling me back from the cringe-inducing catacombs of Harvey's sex life. "I wanted her in my bed all night. I wanted her to still be there with me at the breakfast table the next morning. Do you get what I'm saying, Parker?"

"Got it."

"I wanted her in a way that scared the hell out of me."

Yeah, but … "You left her hanging high and dry that night?"

He glanced away. "Work called."

"You were off duty."

"Let me put this another way." His gaze snapped back to mine. "I left before things went too far so that we could look at each other the next day without regrets."

"Bullshit, Cooper." I jabbed him in the shoulder. "You left because when push came to shove, you chickened out."

His face solidified into a slab of granite, all sharp angles and rocky edges. "What the fuck do you know about me?"

"You and I are peas in a pod. Like you, I had a history of random men who didn't matter. I made a habit of leaving before shit got too real. The one time I'd let my guard down and tried to build something with a guy, the dickhead screwed my sister."

"Rex Conner?" he asked.

"The one and only. Then Doc came along and scared the shit out of me." Truth be told, deep down I was still a bit of a nervous Nelly even now. Investing in games of the heart was not for the lily-livered.

He straightened his shoulders. "I'm not a chicken, Parker."

"Why did you pull away without even giving Natalie a chance?"

"I'm a cop. My profession comes with a high rate of relationship casualties."

"So you were protecting her?"

He nodded.

That was hogwash, but I let it go. "Fine. If that was true then, what's changed? You're still a cop. Why are you pursuing her now?"

He took awhile to answer. "I'm tired."

"I know, I know. You're working long shifts and worn out. You look like hell, by the way. Maybe you should try some sleeping pills to really knock yourself out for a solid eight hours."

"No, jackass. I mean I'm tired in here." He tapped his temple. "I'm tired of battling the voice that says I need to keep my hands to myself. I want Natalie as much as I did that night at the Purple Door."

"Really?"

"No, that's not true. I want her even more now."

I pursed my lips, weighing his words. "What if you take what you want and then break her heart?"

"What if she breaks mine?"

I held his gaze, my chin high. "That would require you to actually have a heart, Tin Man."

A cough of laughter escaped from his lips, followed by several more before he could contain the rest.

"Uh-oh. You're cracking up again," I said. "You need to go home and get some sleep, Cooper."

He sobered. "Yeah, I do."

We stared at each other for a few more seconds.

"I won't say anything," I told him, and I meant it.

"If you do, I'll throw you in jail, no matter our previous agreement."

I had little doubt that he meant that, too. "Understood. I also won't sabotage your efforts."

"Thanks."

"But I won't overtly steer her in your direction either."

"Good. If she comes my way, I want it to be her choice alone."

"In the meantime," I said, "you should treat me nicer."

"Why in the hell would I want to do that?"

"It might help warm her up."

He smirked. "Good try, Parker, but I'd rather heat her up without you in the picture. Now go to your meeting." He started to walk away and then stopped. "Oh, and Parker, one more thing."

"What?"

"Don't call me until I'm back on duty tonight. I need some sleep, and your problems screw up my beauty rest."

"I'm not sure even a week's worth of sleep will fix that mess." I pointed at his face.

"Said Medusa's blond twin."

I flipped him off.

He grinned and crossed the street without a backward glance.

"Dang," I said, watching him go.

Natalie was about to get slammed by Hurricane Cooper. I had a feeling his sustained winds might knock her back a few steps, but that'd be nothing compared to the storm surge of lust and emotion that would sweep her off her feet.

I pushed inside Doc's office, locking the door behind me. Cornelius had texted earlier that he was heading back to his apartment to shower, so I grabbed my purse from where I'd set it next to the boxes of clocks, which were now gone. Cornelius must have taken them to the apartment above Calamity Jane's. Slinging my purse over my shoulder, I zipped out the back door, making sure it was locked, too.

Halfway across the parking lot, I snapped out of the highlights reel replaying my conversation with Cooper and realized someone was leaning against my Honda. Someone dressed in an expensive black wool coat, mirrored sunglasses, and leather gloves.

"Good morning, Dominick. What can I do for you today?" I kept my distance. Dry heaving before breakfast didn't appeal to me.

His smile would have charmed the skin off a snake. Good thing I didn't have a head full of them in spite of Cooper's claim.

"You look stunning in that shade of blue, Violet."

"As do you in your black duds." I gave him a dismissing smile. "As much as I'd like to stand here and exchange pleasantries, I have an appointment for which I'm on the verge of being late. Can you get to the point of your surprise visit?"

He clucked his tongue. "Life is so short for you human hybrids, and yet you insist on rushing through it, wasting precious time with puerile obligations."

Of all the condescending ... I was going to sic his damned *lidérc* on his uppity ass. "Dominick," I said in a warning tone. "State your case."

"I have information on your missing informant."

Crap. I was going to have to call Cooper before he clocked out. There went his day of beauty rest.

"What did you find out?" I asked.

He shrugged. "He is no longer with us."

"What's that mean? He moved to another state?" Or was it another realm?

"It means your informant has been permanently taken out of commission. He will snitch no more. Ever." He laced his gloved fingers in front of his coat. "Now about your end of the bargain ..."

Chapter Twenty-One

Bighorn Billy's was dead, much like Cooper's informant from Slagton, damn it.

The whole drive to Jerry's emergency huddle, I'd plucked daisy petals in my head. Only instead of debating whether somebody loved me with each petal, I vacillated between calling Cooper now or later this afternoon after he'd had some much-needed rest. By the time I'd parked my Honda beside Jerry's Hummer in the diner's gravel lot, I still hadn't decided what to do.

I could text Cooper. He'd told me not to call, but he hadn't said anything about texting.

Nodding to myself at that brilliant plan, I thumbed a quick message to him: *FYI—Your informant is dead.*

No, that was too blunt.

I erased it and typed: *Sorry to bother you, Detective Cooper, but I received news that your informant has met his demise.*

I read my text aloud. Nah. Too wordy.

How about: *Got information on your informant. Call me.*

I pondered that. It was kind of redundant with both *information* and *informant* in such a short sentence. Was there a better word for information?

I deleted and typed: *Good news—I know what's up with your informant. Bad news—He's dead.*

Ugh, that was pretty cold and harsh. I cleared that message. For all I knew, the informant had been a nice guy who happened to live like a hermit in the boonies, unaware that deep freezers were not normally considered dining room furniture.

Jeez, how did one tell a cranky detective that his snitch would breathe no more, let alone inform anyone of anything?

I glanced at the time. Shit, I was now two minutes late. I opened the door and pulled up my speakerphone texting option, jogging across the parking lot while I used the talk-to-text feature. "Talked to Dominick. Your informant has been compromised. Call me when you wake up."

After I hit the send button, I silenced my phone and stuffed it in my purse. One step inside the diner, the smell of fried bacon and eggs filled my lungs, nudging my stomach awake. Dolly Parton was singing through the overhead speakers about being fine and dandy for her "Hard Candy Christmas." I could relate to good ol' Dolly when it came to barely making it through each day and took her words to heart about not letting my problems get the best of me.

Jerry waved me over to the corner booth.

A sprinkling of locals were enjoying brunch along with us in the diner, but I didn't recognize anyone.

"Hey, Sparky," said a skinny Santa look-alike with a red plaid hat and earflaps as I walked by the table where he sat with two of his cronies.

I slowed to a stop, doing a double take. Who in the hell was he? "Uh, good morning," I said to him and his grinning pals. That was the second old guy in a week who'd called me Sparky. Was Harvey spreading my nickname around town?

"Have a nice Christmas, boys," I told the three musketeers and joined Jerry, Mona, and Ben. "Where's Ray?" I asked, scooting onto the booth seat. Jerry bookended the other side of the half-circle bench, with Mona and Ben the monkeys in our middle.

"How about some coffee?" Jerry asked instead of answering. He motioned the waitress over.

Mona and I exchanged quizzical looks across the table as Jerry ordered coffee for all.

"Do you need to look at the menu, Violet?" he asked.

"No, I know what I want." I gave the waitress my order, and around the table she went collecting the others' requests.

As soon as she left, Jerry cleared his throat. "I called this huddle because we're a man down."

We were? He must mean Ray. That was why he wasn't here. Had the horse's ass gotten hurt? Slipped on the ice? Or was it something to do with his top-secret dealings with that troublemaking juggernaut back in September? Had those mysterious shipments Ray used to make for George Mudder come back to haunt him somehow? Whoa, I'd gone from zero to paranormal in seconds. Ray could be sick with the flu, not being tortured by a one-horned demon fiend.

"Is Ray okay?" Mona asked.

I glanced at Ben, who sat next to me. He lowered his gaze, fiddling with his spoon. I'd expected him to look concerned, not guilty.

"Ray is fine physically," Jerry said. He laced his big fingers together on the table. "Unfortunately, I had to fire him yesterday."

My eyes nearly popped out of my head. "Say what now?"

Mona took the news a fraction better than I did. Her face paled, her eyebrows climbing halfway up her forehead. "Why?"

Ben fiddled some more, frowning.

"For good reason," Jerry said. "As you all know, Violet recently lost a customer to a competing Realtor."

"Jeff Wymonds?" I asked, trying to piece together how my losing Jeff to Tiffany had turned into Ray getting shit-canned instead of me.

"Yes, Mr. Wymonds." Jerry's square-cut jaw jutted. "I have since come to learn that Ray had a hand in this customer firing Calamity Jane Realty in favor of the competing agency."

Holy shitballs of fire! Jerry must have found out about Ray working behind the scenes with Tiffany. I sat back, still trying to grasp the fact that Jerry actually fired Ray, one of Calamity Jane's longtime, top-selling agents.

"Ray was scheming with Tiffany Sugarbell?" Mona asked.

Jerry nodded once.

While it wasn't news to me, apparently Mona hadn't realized how low Ray would sink in his effort to eliminate me from the competition.

I shot another glance toward Ben. How did he feel about this? His uncle had helped him land his position with Calamity Jane after Jerry took over as boss. Where did Ben's loyalty sit? At the moment he was here with us, but was this temporary for him as he searched for another position somewhere else? Jerry had sunk a lot of marketing money into Ben, same as he had me. Did that count for anything in Ben's head? Or did Ray being blood trump everything else?

"How did you find out about this?" Mona pressed Jerry.

His chiseled face hardened. "I have my ways. Let's leave it at that."

I tried to, but my brain had its own plans. It flashed back to Friday, after my first kill in Slagton, when Cooper and I had gone in Doc's office to tell him about the chimera in the informant's woodshed. Harvey had come in a short time later and told me about a parking lot meeting between Jerry and Tiffany. I'd been worried at the time that they were talking about exchanging me for Tiffany, but maybe—as Cooper often told me—not everything was about me. Although this sort of had to do with me, so take that, Cooper!

Had Tiffany been ratting out Ray that day? The timing was right. Jeff Wymonds had contacted me a few hours later, right after lunch, and fired me.

I took a sip of coffee, trying to nail down the possible timeline of Ray's demise in my head.

"The point is," Jerry continued. "Ray played dirty, turning on one of his own teammates for personal gain." His gaze settled on me. "That's unacceptable in my game book. While I want us to be the number one selling real estate office in western South Dakota, I want to do it playing a clean game."

I nodded. Point taken. It was a good thing I'd been too busy hunting juggernauts and a *lidérc* when I wasn't channeling spine-chilling changelings to plot against Ray.

"When you return to work today, his desk will be cleaned out. There will be no good-bye party for liability reasons."

Damn. Ray was gone. No more staring across the office at his stupid sneer day after day. No more putting up with his nasty comments behind the boss's back. No more insult matches in the parking lot. What was I going to do with all of my free time now?

"Ben," Mona said. "Are you okay with this?"

Ben stopped fiddling. "I am sad to see Uncle Ray go, but Jerry has done the right thing." His focus turned to me. "I'm sorry you had this happen, Violet. You're a good agent. I wish my uncle had been able to see that and appreciate what you bring to the team."

I blinked in surprise. "Ben, you don't need to apologize for Ray. You've been kind since the first time I met you. But thank you for saying that."

He nodded, frowning down at his spoon again.

Mona reached over and squeezed Jerry's arm. "Now what, coach?"

His hand rested on hers for a moment before she pulled her hand back. "Ray's absence leaves a big hole in our team. He and Mona shared the top spot for both sales and clients. I won't lie to you—not having Ray in our lineup will make us scramble for a while, but I have faith that Ben and Violet will continue to build their clientele and sales to make up the difference. I'll be taking on more clients, too, until we have our feet back under us."

This had to really suck for Jerry. He'd been so close to landing that number one real estate agency spot on this side of the state.

"I can put in more hours," Mona offered. "Maybe pick up some extra brokerage work to help with the loss of income."

"Thanks, but let's see how our *Paranormal Realty* debut goes and what sort of upswing we get after the show." He looked around at each of us. "I expect each of you to put your heart into the website vlogs, giving it one hundred and ten percent."

I nodded, accepting my fate, but feeling guilty for Mona and Ben having to step up to help replace Ray's sales. If I'd been able to keep my mouth shut around the asshole, maybe it wouldn't have come to this. But his constant harassment spurred the fighter in me, so I'd stood toe-to-toe and swung back instead of cowering in the corner. I stirred my coffee, staring down into it like I was reading tea leaves. Then again, Ray hated me out of the gate because Jane hired me instead of Ben. There probably wasn't much I could've done to derail him short of accepting his crass proposition for lewd sexual acts in exchange for his support back in the very beginning. Lucky for him, I'd walked away from the table without ripping off his dick and cramming it down his throat that day.

So, fuck Ray. Well, in a metaphorical sense, anyway. He'd made his own bed when he'd decided to come after my job. I'd warned him more than once to back off, promising I'd knock him off his king-of-the-mountain perch. I just hadn't figured Jerry would act as my muscle when it came to the blow.

The rest of our brunch huddle passed in normal fashion, with each of us giving a verbal report on how sales were going and what we thought might be landing in our pipeline soon. I shared the printout I'd grabbed from the office after Jane's ghost had disappeared. The sheet listed more upcoming changes to real estate laws that Jerry had wanted me to research, additions that would possibly add more red tape to our job.

It was almost noon by the time we finished eating and filed out of the diner into the parking lot. I checked my phone for messages, taking it off silent mode.

"Violet," Jerry said when we neared our vehicles. "You have a minute?"

I nodded, my pulse speeding up. Here it came, the result of Tiffany's attempt to screw me over like she did Ray. I wondered what the red-haired spider had whispered in Jerry's ear about me last Friday during their parking lot meeting. The fact that I'd slept with a client, aka her ex-boyfriend, was old news in our office, so it probably had to do with Jeff.

"I want to apologize to you," Jerry said.

Why? What was the catch? "Apologize for what?"

"When I talked to Ben last night about having to fire his uncle, he told me about some exchanges he'd witnessed between Ray and you when I wasn't in the vicinity."

Yikes! "He did?"

Jerry nodded. "I knew that Ray had said some inappropriate things to you, but I had no idea how bad things had become. I should have paid more attention sooner."

It took me a moment to find my tongue. "Jerry, my battle with Ray started long before you came into the picture." How was he to know the depth of depravity? "Ray played a good game when you were around, and the boost his sales gave Calamity Jane Realty was worth overlooking some silly name calling in my eyes." I patted him on the arm. "Besides, my skin is pretty thick."

He gave me a lopsided smile. "You're a good agent, Violet. I see a bright future for you. I know you don't love some of my marketing tactics, but I think that together, you and I can increase your sales to Ray's level within six months."

Wow. He had more faith in me than I did.

"I like the sound of that." That was if I didn't end up dead first. "Thanks for believing in me, Jerry."

He clapped his big hands together, marking the end of our little talk. "I'm going to take the rest of the day off. I didn't get much sleep this weekend. Tell Mona she's in charge of holding down the fort."

"Will do." We headed to our vehicles.

For several seconds after Jerry drove away, I sat behind the wheel staring out the windshield while the sky spit snow.

"Ray got fired," I said aloud. I pinched myself. "Ouch." I rubbed my arm. I really needed to find a new way to prove I wasn't dreaming.

My cell phone rang as I keyed my Honda to life. I stared down at Eddie Mudder's name, my heart skipping a couple of beats. Oh, crap.

I accepted the call. "Please tell me Mr. Haskell is still chilling in the morgue," I said in place of a greeting.

Eddie chuckled. "Mr. Haskell is actually in my basement getting prepped for a viewing this evening."

"I thought you were going to keep the casket closed thanks to that missing ear."

"I attached a fake one for now."

Really? "You can do that?"

"I can do a lot of things with dead bodies, Violet."

An awkward pause filled the line.

Eddie cleared his throat. "I didn't mean that the way it sounded."

I chuckled in relief. "You had me a little nervous there for a moment, Eddie. What can I do for you today?"

"I have a visitor here who is requesting your presence."

"Is the visitor alive or dead?" I joked but was kind of serious.

"I believe he's alive, but I'd have to search for a heart to be sure, and I wouldn't assume the organ is where mine is located."

Were we talking about Cooper? Or had Detective Hawke returned to Deadwood to resume pestering me, his favorite number one suspect? "Intriguing. Who's come calling for me at a funeral parlor?"

"Mr. Black."

Another pause, this time inspired by my surprise. "Mr. Black is at your place looking for *me*?"

"He's actually waiting out behind the morgue for you. I hope you're nearby. He makes my hands shaky, and I need steady hands while working on Mr. Haskell. The poor man has had enough post-death trauma already."

"I'll be there in under five minutes," I told Eddie.

"Great. Head straight back to the garage. I'll leave you two to your business."

After he hung up, I pulled out of the lot and dialed Mona's desk phone, leaving her a voicemail about Jerry's absence this afternoon, claiming I had to make a side trip before returning to work.

True to my word, I pulled around the back of Mudder Brothers Funeral Parlor not quite five minutes later, cutting the engine. Mr. Black stood half-hidden in the trees off to the side of the building, his long white coat and pale skin blending in with the snow. He stepped into the sunshine as I approached, his expression grim, and held open the door to the morgue.

"Do we have to talk in there?" I asked.

"I cannot risk being seen with you, *Scharfrichter.*"

Dang. I led the way into the morgue, stopping inside the doorway. If he wanted to hang out in the dead body cooler, that was too damned bad. This was as far as I was going.

"What's going on?" I asked the pale-faced juggernaut. "Do you have another clock for me?"

"*Nein.*" He leaned against the door, his huge body blocking my escape. "I have a task for you."

"A task?" Was this going to become a thing? *Others* hiring me to clean up their messes?

"*Ja.* You must go to Slagton."

"I was planning to head back there later this week."

"You must go now."

"You mean right this moment?"

"*Ja.*"

"I can't."

"You must."

"It's not possible."

He raised his thick white eyebrows.

"I need to go back to work." That came out sounding pretty lame.

He scoffed, confirming the trivialness of my excuse. "This is far more important than you realize."

"Why do I have to go right now?"

"I received word this morning that a battle is about to erupt. That territory in the Black Hills has remained neutral for centuries. As of late, however, there have been several factions striving for control."

"What's that have to do with me?"

"You have slain multiple enemies in broad daylight for all to witness."

"None of those killings were my fault." Okay, maybe they were a little bit my fault, but they'd started it.

"That is no matter. You have shown you are a competitor in the battle for leadership in Slagton. You must finish the job. Establish control."

"And if I don't?"

"Control will fall into dangerous hands. This cannot happen. *Der Scharfrichter* must intercede to ensure neutrality is maintained."

I crossed my arms. "Let me get this straight. I need to go back to Slagton and do what exactly? Stand in the middle of the road and declare I'm the new queen?"

"That is one option, but I do not recommend it. Your demise would quickly follow. I would suggest a more subtle approach."

"Such as?"

"Executing the opposing leader."

"But the Wild Hunt clock hasn't started yet."

"Are you certain?"

I was until a second ago. "Maybe."

"You must leave at once. It is time."

I froze at the sound of the three words that had been whispered in my ear first thing this morning. "What did you say?"

"It is time. You must go now. We cannot risk delay."

"Are you coming with me?"

"*Nein.* If I am seen with you, the truth about my allegiance would be discovered."

The truth? "What are you? Some kind of double agent?"

"I am a Timekeeper."

"What else are you?"

His dark eyes narrowed. "There is no time for discussion. Go to Slagton and finish what you started. Many are there who need you to save them from a fate far darker than you can imagine."

Crappity crap. I wasn't dressed for another trip to Slagton, nor was I prepared mentally for that shit. "Fine. I'll go." But I'd need to go home and change first, and then gather the troops.

"Excellent. Here," he held his hand out.

I opened my palm, frowning at what he dropped into my hand. One end was shaped like a heart, the other a small tube. "What is this?"

"A key."

"Will it open a gateway to another realm?"

A smile flitted over Mr. Black's face. "*Nein.* It is for the first clock I gave you. I forgot to give you the key."

"I didn't think these clocks could be wound."

"They can't. This key is for accessing the inner compartment."

"What's inside the inner compartment?"

"You must use the key to find out. It is unique to each Timekeeper."

I pocketed the key. "Do you have any advice for Slagton?"

"*Ja.* Try not to die."

"Gee, thanks."

One white eyebrow inched upward. "I detect sarcasm."

"You think?"

"What could I possibly have to say to a *Scharfrichter* prior to battle? I am not of your kind."

"I don't know. You're hundreds of years old. Don't you have some words of wisdom stored in your big ancient brain?"

He tapped his pale chin, his face wrinkling in thought. "*Ja.*"

"I'm all ears."

"You are capable."

Sheesh! That's it? "Did you get that off one of those motivational posters with a kitten on it?"

"*Nein.*" His lips curved upward. "There was no kitten. I believe it had a chimpanzee wearing a tie and reading glasses."

Cursing, I started to leave.

"*Scharfrichter,*" Mr. Black called when I opened the door.

I looked back. His expression was downright gloomy. "What?"

"Take *das Orakel* with you. He will be able to see when all is dark."

Chapter Twenty-Two

Step One—Rally the Troops

I called Doc on the short drive back to work, putting him on speakerphone as I pulled into the parking lot behind Calamity Jane's.

"Hey, Tish."

"I need you," I said as I parked near the back door. The Picklemobile sat in its normal parking spot.

"A man likes to be needed. What kind of need are we talking about and what are you wearing?" He reverted to our usual flirting game. "More important, what are you *not* wearing?"

I would love to sneak over to his office and hand him my underwear in a paper bag again, but I had sharp teeth to face off with in Slagton ASAP. "I have a problem."

"I do, too, after thinking about you in nothing but that blue coat and your boots."

"Hold that thought," I told him, stepping out of my Honda into the cold breeze. "And let me talk to the Oracle."

Silence filled the line as he switched gears. "What's wrong?" All flirting was gone from his tone.

"I just met with Mr. Black in Mudder Brothers' morgue. It seems I have to make an emergency trip to Slagton."

"What's the emergency?"

"Oh, nothing much." I shut my door. "Just a tiny turf war taking place this afternoon that will cause unspeakable doom if I don't slay the opposing leader and declare myself the queen of Slagton."

"What?" His chair creaked. "Did you drink tequila at work?"

"I wish." I crossed the slushy lot, heading for Calamity Jane's back door. "I need to stop by the office, then I'm going to Aunt Zoe's to change into battle gear. Can you cancel any afternoon appointments?"

"I have none."

"You want to join me for a fun-filled, hunting trip to Slagton?"

"Lead the way, Killer. Pick me up at my house after you change."

"We need Cooper and Harvey."

"On it." I heard the sound of papers shuffling. "Don't forget your war hammer."

"I won't. See you soon." After hanging up, I stepped inside Calamity Jane's, not bothering to take off my coat. What I needed to do would only take a minute.

I followed the sweet scent of Mona's jasmine perfume to the front office where she was clacking away at her desk while Ben stared at something on his computer screen. Both of them looked up when I walked into the room. I clasped my hands together.

It is time, I heard in my head.

"I have to leave for the day," I announced.

Ben leaned back in his chair. "Is everything okay?"

It would be so easy to lie. I glanced over at Ray's empty desk, steeling my resolve. Mona and Ben had stepped up to help me multiple times. They deserved honesty in return. "Not really."

"Vi, what's going on?" Mona took off her reading glasses.

I frowned at my good friend and mentor. "I have a problem I need to take care of out of town this afternoon. I need you two to cover for me if Jerry calls in to check on the office."

"Please tell me you're not going to confront Ray," she said, rising.

"This has nothing to do with him."

"What do you want us to tell Jerry if he calls?" Ben asked, apparently already on board.

"Tell him that Detective Cooper and I are out looking at some properties." At their narrowed gazes, I added, "That's not a lie. I will be with Cooper the whole time."

Mona crossed her arms. "Is this police business? The kind that ends with you behind bars again?"

"No. I have a problem that Cooper is going to help me fix. Doc will be there, too," I hinted to her.

Understanding widened her eyes for a moment, and then she nodded once. "We have your back."

"Thank you." I pointed at Ray's desk. "I realize that I played a part in pushing Ray over the edge. While I'm not sorry for standing my ground in the face of his harassment, I *am* sorry that you two have to help make up for the loss of his financial contributions. I owe you both for your support throughout this ordeal."

"We're a team." Ben smiled. "We'll get through this together."

Mona lowered back into her chair. "Be careful, Vi."

"Will we see you tomorrow?" Ben asked.

"I hope so." I said my good-byes and left before I blubbered all over them for being such wonderful friends through thick and thin.

My phone rang halfway to my Honda. It was my clock-watching buddy, Abe Jr.

I took the call. "I'm a little busy, Cornelius."

"Do you want that trident?" he shot back.

I slowed, trying to remember what trident he meant. Oh! Layne's Christmas present request. "I'm not sure."

In the background, I heard a familiar sound that made me freeze in my tracks. I did an about-face, staring up at the building's second-story windows.

"Let me know soon. The seller will need to ship it overnight."

"Cornelius, do you hear that?"

"Hear what?"

"That cuckooing sound?"

"Is this a trick question?"

"Where are you?"

"Currently?"

I growled. "Yes."

"The planet Earth."

Sometimes I doubted that. "Are you in the apartment above Calamity Jane's?"

"Not if the CIA has contacted you recently."

I was taking that as a yes. "I'll be at your door in ten seconds. Get dressed." I hung up and jogged to the door leading to the upstairs apartment, climbing the steps two at a time.

Cornelius opened the door before I even knocked. "You're late."

I rushed past him, following the cuckooing sound into his small kitchen. The clock boxes sat on the table, both lids off.

"Shit," I said, staring at the one depicting the Wild Hunt. How had Mr. Black known? Could he hear the cuckooing clear over at Mudder Brothers? Or had something else alerted the Timekeeper?

"What is it?" Cornelius joined me.

"This one is cuckooing." I pointed at it.

He leaned closer. "I don't hear anything."

"Why aren't your arms moving yet?" I asked the clock.

Was the leader of the pack stuck at the gate? Unable to get through? Or was the hunter hesitating for some reason?

"How would you like me to make my arms move?"

I looked up at my channeling buddy. "You're dressed."

"For the time being."

"Grab your coat and one-horned Viking helmet." I picked up the box's wooden lid.

Cornelius raised one black eyebrow. "Am I going somewhere?"

"Yes." I closed up the box, muffling the cuckooing sound.

His cornflower blue eyes held mine. "Will I need clean underwear?"

I thought about the chimeras' sharp teeth. "Definitely."

* * *

Step Two—Gear Up

"What to wear? What to wear?" I chanted while standing in front of my closet.

What did one wear to battle if no armor or chain mail was available? I needed something that wouldn't hamper me if I were swinging my war hammer ... or fleeing for my life. Whatever I chose would likely end up in the garbage when—or if—I made it back to Deadwood.

In the end, I went for comfort, choosing a pair of jeans and a long-sleeve thermal shirt.

I grabbed my war hammer and a foot-long tapered candle, along with a spare set of clothes, and headed downstairs where I'd left Cornelius with Aunt Zoe.

Only Aunt Zoe was missing when I entered the kitchen. I set the bag of clothes and war hammer on the table next to Cornelius, who was enjoying a molasses cookie.

"You should eat some protein," Cornelius said, seeming to channel my aunt. "You'll need your strength from the sounds of it."

I'd talked fast on the way to Aunt Zoe's, explaining the situation into which I was about to drag him, filling him in on recent events in Slagton and my conversations with Mr. Black about the clocks. To his credit, he did not leap from the SUV and make a run for the hills. Instead, he stroked his goatee and suggested I bring a candle and matches along with us, which reminded me that I needed to grab a lighter from the kitchen junk drawer. I hadn't asked why I should bring a candle, merely nodded and told him to explain what was going on to my aunt while I changed.

"Where's Aunt Zoe?" I stuffed the lighter in my pants and then walked to the refrigerator, grabbing the last piece of ham steak. The bottle of tequila on top of the fridge called to me, but I resisted. I'd need my brain crystal clear for what I was about to do.

"She exited stage left."

"Yours or mine?"

He pointed a cookie at the back door. "You are not to leave until she returns."

"You want some ham?" I held out a forkful toward him.

He shook his head. "I don't eat swine before a performance."

But cookies appeared to be okey dokey.

I chowed down the ham, chasing it with a glass of water. Aunt Zoe arrived as I finished off the last bite.

"Here," she said, handing me a silver ring and a small sachet tied with gold floss.

"What are these?" I held the ring closer, trying to make sense of the design carved into the flat oval face of it. "Are these entwined letters?"

"It's a symbol. Or rather a crest, if you will."

"Meaning what?"

"*Scharfrichter*. It's on several of the pages of our family history book, which you'd know if you'd bothered to read it when I told you to." She took the ring from me and slid it on my right middle finger. It fit like it was made for me. "This ring has been passed down through our line over the ages from one executioner to another."

"Why didn't you give it to me before? Did I have to prove myself to you as some kind of certifiable killer?"

"No, I couldn't find it. Turns out it had slipped into a pocket in the trunk where I keep our family heirlooms."

I held the ring up in the light from the window. "What will it do?"

"It won't do anything, but you will while wearing it."

That earned a scowl from me. "Don't you go turning cryptic on me, Aunt Zoe. I have enough trouble figuring out what Prudence and Mr. Black mean most days."

"I have several suspicions about what wearing this ring will do for you, but you'll have to test it out first to confirm them. Is that better?"

"Not at all." I held up the sachet, which was about the size of a tea bag. It smelled like tea, too, only with a musky undertone that made me wince. "What about this?"

"Stuff it in your bra."

"You're kidding."

"Nope. You need to carry it on your person, and by that I mean touching your skin."

"Like a gris-gris bag," Cornelius said. "Only the Haitian voodoo sort that brings good luck, I hope, not the Cajun black magic bags."

I sniffed the sachet. "What's in it?"

"That's not your concern."

"How is a tea bag stuffed in my bra going to protect me from those toothy bastards in Slagton?"

"You need to trust me on this," she said and hugged me tight. "Be careful out there, baby girl. Stick close to Doc."

"Hug my kids," I said, my voice thick, choked with worry that I might not return. "Tell them Doc and I will take them to the Rec Center another day."

She nodded. "You'll be back, Violet. I know it in my heart."

"Yeah, but will I be in one piece?"

* * *

Step Three—Plan the Attack

I knocked on Doc's door, hesitant to waltz inside since Cooper and Harvey were living there. The sight of either of them in their skivvies would haunt me for months, making me want to scour my eyes out with a pumice stone.

"Parker!" Cooper barked as he opened the door. Tufts of blond hair stuck up on one side of his head. Both eyes were red rimmed, the left one twitching. His T-shirt was on backward, the tag sticking out at his neck. "What in the hell is this text supposed to mean?" He shoved his cell phone in my face, almost ramming it into my nose.

I snatched it from him, shoving the grumpy bear aside so Cornelius and I could step in out of the cold. "What are you talking about?" Looking down at the phone, I read, *Tall kid to Dominatrix. Your uniform nation has income as promised. Call me in you wacko.*

Huh. I could swear I'd left a message in plain old, eighth-grade level English. My phone was cursed, dang it.

Cooper shut the door, leaning against it. "That message makes no fucking sense at all. Do you even know how to spell?"

"She knows how to read," Cornelius supplied. "At least children's books, anyway."

I wrinkled my upper lip at both of them. "I know how to read and spell, thank you very much."

"Then explain your message."

Cornelius took the phone and read it. "I saw secret code language like this once on the back of a cereal box."

I grabbed the phone back. "It says your informant is dead, Cooper."

"What?!" I could have sworn the detective's hair stood up all over for a few seconds before returning to its lopsided state.

Doc descended the stairs. The lines on his face told me he'd overheard what I'd told Cooper. "Who told you the informant is dead? Mr. Black?"

"No. Dominick was waiting at my SUV this morning before I went to my brunch meeting. He informed me that Cooper's informant was no longer with us."

"Jesus." Cooper followed that with a litany of swear words before yanking his phone away from me. "Why in the hell didn't you call me and tell me that?"

"You said not to bug you until later this afternoon."

"I meant don't bug me with inane shit. *This,*" he said, shaking his phone at me. "This was worth an immediate call."

"Well, how am I supposed to know what you do and do not deem as important? The guy is dead. Waiting a few hours for you to get some much-needed sleep wouldn't change that fact." I crossed my arms. "Besides, I was a little busy immediately after I received the news and sort of forgot about the dead guy."

"How in the hell could you forget about a dead informant?" Harvey strolled out from the kitchen with crumbs in his beard. "Busy doin' what?"

"I had a brunch meeting with my boss and coworkers."

"Oh, I get it now," Cooper said, crossing his own arms. "Real estate pow-wows are much more important than someone's life. That makes complete sense."

He could shove his sarcasm up his patootie. "For your information, Cooper, I received some news of my own today that blew me out of the water along with all thoughts of you and your damned informant."

"What news?" Doc asked, leaning against the newel post.

"Jerry fired Ray."

Doc's eyebrows hit his hairline. "It's about damned time."

Cooper's eyes narrowed into slits. "This isn't going to end well."

Harvey grinned so wide his ears almost caved inward. "Well, what do ya know? Pecos Bill has got somethin' inside his head besides nits."

"That reminds me," Cornelius said from where he was inspecting a framed map of old Deadwood on Doc's dining room wall. "You should throw your coffee cup away, Violet."

"Why?"

"My eye in the sky recorded your ex-coworker taking it into the bathroom with him this morning before he left with his box of personal belongings."

"Ewww." I wasn't going to touch that mug with a ten-foot pole.

"What spurred Jerry to fire Ray?" Doc asked.

"Your ex. It appears Tiffany tattled on Ray, who was working with her behind my back to steal Jeff Wymonds. Jerry doesn't condone playing dirty like that and kicked Ray off the team permanently."

"Apparently your boss's ethics outrank his billfold." Doc slid his coat on. "But why would Tiffany turn on Ray?"

Good question.

"After I finished choking down that nugget," I said, turning to Cooper, "Eddie Mudder called to tell me that Mr. Black was waiting at the morgue to talk to me about something urgent. Which leads to why we are going to Slagton today instead of after Detective Whineypuss gets his beauty rest."

Cooper's mouth tightened. "What exactly did Black have to say?"

I repeated the juggernaut's message, what I could remember of it, anyway.

"Damn, Killer." Doc stepped closer, dropping a kiss on my forehead. "You've had a busy morning."

He didn't know the half of it. I hadn't filled him in yet on Jane's ghost leaving a laundry list for Cooper. "I could use a vacation from this Executioner gig."

"You and me both." Cooper rubbed the sleep from his eyes. "So, what's the plan? We return to that old Plymouth for another showdown?"

"I hope ya can stay upright in yer boots this time," Harvey said.

"These puppies won't let me down." I held up one of my thick-treaded snow boots. "Neither will my war hammer." At least my fingers were crossed that was the case.

"Are we leaving Curion here?" Cooper asked. "Or dropping him off somewhere?"

"He's coming with us."

Cooper's mouth hardened. "That's a mistake, Parker. This isn't a skip through the woods with a picnic basket."

"I know that, law dog," I shot back, bristling. "So does Cornelius."

Doc searched my face, his head tipping to the side. "What are you doing, Violet?"

"I'm stacking the deck." I looped my hand through Cornelius's arm and tugged him over to the group. "We need a wider channel than I can offer on my own."

"Why?" Cooper asked.

"Because the Wild Hunt clock won't stop cuckooing, and I have a feeling that the hunter is waiting at the gate to come through."

Harvey snorted. "Waitin' fer what? An invitation?"

"Waiting for me, and we're going to need help to sneak up on this son of a bitch before it gets the jump on me."

* * *

Step Four—Charge into Battle

The trip up Strawberry Hill in Harvey's pickup went way too fast. I sat in the back between Harvey and Cornelius, still working out a plan of attack for Slagton while a certain hard-headed detective vetoed most of my ideas before I could finish my sentences.

"Do you have a better idea, Cooper?" I groused, glaring at the back of his head.

His hands white-knuckled the steering wheel. "I have at least five better ideas than you standing in the middle of the road like a damned sitting duck."

"She'd be a standin' duck," Harvey said. "We need to stop at my ranch fer a few minutes, Coop."

"Why?" Cooper asked.

"I need to grab some ammo for Bessie."

"Violet." Doc's tone was meant to calm me, along with the look he gave me from the passenger seat up front. "Let's hear what Coop has to say."

I pinched my lips together, meeting Cooper's glower in the rearview mirror. "I'm waiting."

"If we stick together and secure one area at a time, our chances of getting out of this without casualties is far greater."

"And what area do you propose we secure first?" I asked.

"We start at my informant's place. It's at the edge of town and provides us with a starting point. Then, we can decide if your idea of splitting into two teams is worthwhile, or if we should continue together."

I looked at Cornelius, who had remained quiet throughout most of the drive. "What do you think of Cooper's big plan?"

"I prefer the plan involving the least chance of dying."

"Stick with me and Bessie." Harvey leaned forward and told him around me. "Sparky here will land you deep in trouble without a shovel."

"Hey," I said, elbowing him. "That's not always true."

"In this case," Doc said, "it probably is." He faced forward again.

Cooper turned onto the road leading to Harvey's place and Slagton.

"I'm going to need to keep one of those chimera things alive," I told Harvey.

"How in the hell are we supposed to do that?" Cooper butted in.

"I'd tell you, but you'd actually have to listen to my idea for once."

"Shut up, Parker."

I looked at Harvey. "Do you have anything that might help me catch one of them in your barn? Or did Cooper's pals clean you out?"

"The only traps I have left are too small to do ya any good."

"How about one of those big burlap bags I saw stacked in a stall? If I knock one out, we can stuff it in there and tie it down in back."

"With those teeth?" Cooper interfered. "It would chew its way free in a heartbeat."

I crossed my arms. "Yeah? Well, maybe I'll tie you up with it so it can chew on you, too." I nudged Harvey in the knee. "Grab me a bag."

He nodded.

Cooper steered onto the gravel drive leading to Harvey's place. He hit the brakes a moment later in front of the barn, leaving the pickup idling. "Make it quick, Uncle Willis."

"Help me out, Sparky."

After exchanging a quick frown with Doc, I followed Harvey to the barn. I held my old fleece-lined parka tight at my collar while he fiddled with the lock and chain on the barn doors. The temperature was dropping by the minute, I could swear. The sky seemed darker, more chilling even. Or maybe my gloomy mood was distorting my view.

A few seconds later, we filed inside. The musty smell of hay and dust reminded me of the night we'd had a séance in here. That thought led to a flashing image of the dead guy we found in Harvey's old safe. Shaking off the memories of that mess, I followed the ornery buzzard over to an upright refrigerator that looked to be a leftover from the 1950s. He pulled open the door. Several green steel boxes lined the dark shelves.

He hauled one out and handed it to me. "Hold this."

The steel box was as heavy as a watermelon. "What is this?"

"It's an ammo can."

"Why's it so heavy?"

"Because it's full of ammo." He shut the refrigerator door. "Shotgun shells for Bessie."

"Are those other ammo cans full of shotgun shells, too?"

"Nope. They have ammo for my other guns, along with a few hand grenades I've bought off the Internet."

Criminy. I took a step away from the fridge, putting distance between the grenades and me. "Are we done?"

"I wanna grab two more things."

I trailed after him into a corner of the barn. Shadows made it hard to see. He lifted a rusted steel door in what looked to be a grain storage bin and pulled out a wooden box from the dark chute. I heard something scuttle across the beam along the wall next to me and stepped closer to Harvey. He pried off the lid of the box with his handy screwdriver and pulled out two long candles with curling black wicks.

"Here we go." He handed one to me. "Keep that some place safe."

I held it up in a shaft of light coming through a crack in the wall, trying to get a better look at it. "Why is there waxy cardboard wrapped around this candle?"

"That ain't yer typical candle. Be careful with that stick, Sparky."

Stick? I frowned at him. "Please tell me this isn't what I think it is."

"Okay, it's not what ya think it is."

I held it out toward him. "I'm not carrying this."

"Don't be such a baby." He grabbed the stick, pulled my collar open, and stuffed it inside of my coat. "Don't let Cooper see it. He gets persnickety around dynamite."

I held completely still, barely breathing. "Can you blame him?"

"What're yer eyes all buggy like that fer?"

"Are you kidding me? How old is the dynamite you just crammed between my boobs?"

His face scrunched in thought. "I'm thinkin' not more than twenty years or so."

Hadn't Cornelius said after a year, the nitroglycerin in dynamite can start to sweat through the wax-coated paper, making it unstable as hell?

I gulped. Fuck. I was now loaded down with an ammo can full of shotgun shells and an old stick of dynamite. One wrong move and I'd be nothing more than a black spot on the ground.

Harvey left me standing there sweating. When I didn't scurry after him, he turned back. "Come on, girl. We got us some huntin' to do."

Back at the pickup, he took the can of ammo from me and placed it in the bed of his pickup, along with a couple of burlap bags he'd grabbed.

"You don't want to shove your ammo under the seat?" I asked.

"Yer clock box is takin' up too much room."

"What about the dynamite?" I whispered.

"Hold onto it in case ya need it in a jiff. I'll carry the other one." He tucked it inside his heavy-duty winter coat.

"Would you two move your asses!" Cooper said out the driver's side window. "Daylight is wasting."

"I'm going to shove this fancy candle up your nephew's ying-yang if he doesn't stop snarling at me."

Harvey snickered. "That will open his channel plenty wide."

We piled into the backseat ... well, eased inside was more like it since we each had an old stick of dynamite keeping us warm and worried. I felt every single bounce on the road to Slagton, holding my breath half of the time, fingers and toes crossed I didn't go *ka-boom* before I even reached the old mining town's sign.

Sleet peppered the windshield and roof of the pickup, the small pebbles of ice ricocheting off, sounding like static in the cab. Meanwhile, Cooper filled the time by telling Doc and Harvey about Jane's appearance in the office this morning and her cryptic list, agreeing to give Doc the names of the buildings sometime soon to research. I told them about the other message from Jane regarding Ray not being alone and let it sit out there for all of us to ponder.

Cooper slowed the rig as we neared the informant's shack.

"Do you see anything?" I asked Cornelius.

"Living or dead?" he replied.

Cooper slammed on the brakes. "Holy shit."

My heart rocketed off the ground. "What?"

"That's not good," Doc said, frowning out the windshield.

I leaned forward, peering through the sleet. Up ahead on the right, where the informant's house had been, was a pile of charred, wooden remains with a crooked stone chimney rising from the middle of the burnt mess.

Was that how Dominick knew the informant was dead?

"Somebody threw a sprag in yer wheel," Harvey said to his nephew. Tapping his coat where his stick of dynamite was hidden, he gave me an exaggerated wink. "Looks like we're gonna have to go with Plan B, Sparky."

Chapter Twenty-Three

The stick of unstable dynamite wedged between my boobs had my heart feeling a mite twitchy.

"What's Plan B?" Cooper asked, squinting at his uncle in the rearview mirror.

"Sparky has a notion," Harvey answered, throwing me to the wolves—or in this case, to the law dog.

Cooper's glare shifted to me.

"We need to split up," I told him, returning to an earlier idea I'd voiced that he'd promptly shot down.

"Parker, I don't—"

"She's right," Doc interrupted. He pointed out the windshield. "Take us to the old store building."

Cooper's shoulders tightened, but he didn't argue with Doc. I resisted the urge to rub my "rightness" into Cooper via a noogie on his hard head and peered out Cornelius's side window instead. I searched the trees, looking for falling snow or any other sign that the chimeras were hiding somewhere in the shadows, and then did the same out Harvey's window. It looked clear, but my gut said otherwise. Those bastards were hiding out there somewhere, watching, waiting to pounce. I just knew it.

When Cooper slowed to a stop in front of what was left of the mining company store, Doc held up the handgun Cooper was letting him borrow. "The Glock has fifteen rounds in the magazine, right?"

"Yep. It's loaded and ready. Remember, aim for the head."

"Right." He scratched his jaw. "We need a distraction. You think you and your uncle can come up with something?"

"What do ya got in mind?" Harvey asked.

"I don't know. Something loud. Maybe try to draw them toward that Plymouth we fought next to yesterday. You need to keep them busy long enough for Violet to go inside and make it back out again. Cornelius and I might not be able to fend them off if they come while we're helping her."

"Inside where? The store?" I asked.

His gaze shifted to me. "Inside the darkness. You need to figure out why that clock keeps cuckooing."

"It's still cuckooing?" Cornelius asked. At my nod, he stroked his goatee. "Intriguing."

Annoying was more like it. The constant cuckooing would make me pull my hair out soon if I couldn't make it stop.

"I reckon I can come up with a big distraction fer ya," Harvey said with a snicker.

Cooper glanced from Doc to me. "I packed extra heat. But if the shooting stops, you need to be ready for trouble."

"I hope you can shoot," Doc said to Cornelius.

"My ability to discharge a firearm is not the problem with which you need to concern yourself, Oracle."

"Why's that?" I asked him.

"If I understand our current situation, what lurks in the darkness is far more dangerous. Firearms will do us no good there."

I grimaced. He'd hit that nail on the head. "I hope you brought your lucky cannon."

Cornelius kept an abundance of talismans in his coat pockets, his miniature cannon being one of his favorites.

"On that cheerful note," Doc said, handing Cornelius the 9mm pistol, grip first. "Violet, grab your war hammer and the crowbar. I'll get the clock. We need to move fast as soon as we open these doors."

"Maybe I should go in alone," I said.

He scoffed. "That extra backbone you lug around is cute as a button, Killer. Now shush up and get out."

We all moved at once, including Harvey and Cooper, who switched places behind the wheel so Cooper could put more focus on unloading bullets at a rapid rate. I grabbed the ammo can out of the back and handed it to Harvey before he closed the driver's side door.

"Be careful," I told him.

Harvey's eyes twinkled when he grinned back at me. "Don't ya fret about me, Sparky. Coop and I are gonna have a knee-slappin' time, aren't we, boy?"

Cooper grunted in reply.

"You get yer tail feathers in and out of that coyote den, ya hear?" The old coot sobered, patting my cheek. "Don't be ridin' any tornados bareback while yer foolin' around in the dark."

"Move your ass, Parker." Cooper pissed on our tender moment while checking the rounds in his Colt .45. "And don't fuck this up."

"I love you, too, *Coop*," I said and then jogged after Doc and Cornelius, who were waiting under the sagging awning of the old store.

Doc led the way around the side of the building through the snow.

"What are you going to use as a weapon?" I asked him.

"My girlfriend." He raised his hand in the air, stopping us. After a finger to his lips, he stepped carefully to the corner of the building, peering around the back. After a couple of seconds, he waved for us to join him.

Cornelius nudged me. "Did you bring the candle?" he whispered.

I'd brought two—one made of wax and one made of nitroglycerin. "Yes. Will it help us see in this darkness that Doc is talking about?"

"Not through our eyes."

Doc gave Cornelius the clock box to hold and then held out his hand to me. "Crowbar."

I handed it to him, gripping my war hammer with both hands as I searched the thick stand of trees growing on the hillside behind the store. I tried to focus inward, attempting to sense if there was anything out there. Something was blocking me, though, making it hard to hear and smell anything beyond the whisper of the pine trees in the breeze and the musky scent of Cornelius's aftershave.

Where was everyone? Were the locals all hiding behind barred doors? Or had they left town due to the chimeras? Or were they all dead?

The screech of a rusty nail made me wince and turn.

Doc levered the crowbar between the side of the building and one of the long planks of wood covering the entrance into the back of the store. Another screech filled the air as he popped the board free of another nail.

A familiar gobble-squawk-yip pierced the air up the hillside.

"Doc," I whispered, tightening my grip on the war hammer.

"I heard it."

"Hurry."

"I know."

Cornelius nudged me aside and grabbed the corner of the board as Doc buried the end of the bar into the crease between the wood and the doorframe further down.

Where was Harvey's damned distraction?

"On three," Doc said to Cornelius. "One."

I set my war hammer down and gripped the edge of the board midway between Doc's and Cornelius's hands.

"Two," Doc said, adjusting the crowbar.

I heard a tree branch crack from up the hillside. Something was coming to see what we were up to.

"Three."

We tugged as one, ripping the board almost free. It hung by one loose nail overhead yet, giving us enough room to squeeze into the building.

"You guys ready?" Doc asked.

I stepped back, reaching for my war hammer. "Let me—"

KA-BOOM!

An ear-ringing blast echoed through the valley, sending birds squawking into the air. My heart nearly popped out of my chest and flew away with them.

A clump of snow fell to the ground next to me, barely missing my head. Doc yanked me backward and crowded me into the side of the building, shielding me with his body as large sheets of ice and snow slid from the roof and crashed to the ground at our feet.

"What the hell was that?" Doc asked when the snow stopped falling off the roof. He frowned in the direction of the old Plymouth.

"It appears the sky is falling," Cornelius said, brushing the snow from his one-horned Viking helmet. "Did your chicken warn you of impending doom recently, Violet?"

As a matter of fact, she had gotten her feathers ruffled down in the basement, distracting me from clock-watching with her squawking. It was hard to believe that had only been this morning. "Elvis the soothsayer chicken." I snorted. I dug my war hammer out from under the snow and ice. "That explosion was Harvey's distraction," I told Doc. "He was packing dynamite."

"No shit," he said, grinning.

I didn't mention that I was, too. Doc might not find that as amusing. I pointed my hammer at the loose board. "Are you leading now or am I?"

"I'm leading today, Killer." He knocked my war hammer aside and squeezed through the opening, his thick coat scraping over the wood and exposed nails.

"You go next," I told Cornelius, scanning the trees for trouble.

Doc held the board aside as Abe Jr. slid his thin frame through the narrow opening without a hitch. My curves got in the way when it was my turn, snagging my parka on a nail.

"Damn it." I scowled at the tear in my coat after I tugged free. "I'm going to run out of coats by January at this rate."

Doc let the board slide over the opening, shutting out the light. He clicked on his flashlight, shining it around a narrow, rectangular room with a ten-foot ceiling. Several broken boards lay scattered about the floor, covered with a thick layer of dust. Rodent droppings peppered the floor trailing in different directions, along with a set of boot prints that belonged to Cornelius heading through the doorway at the other end of the room. Where had he wandered off to?

In one of the corners, a nest of some kind was mounded about a foot high. A local critter appeared to be calling this place home sweet home. My guess was a packrat that liked to collect flotsam from the forest and had no problem pooping where it bedded down.

A broken chair sat crookedly next to a boarded-up window that leaked slivers of light around the edges. Crushed beer cans and broken liquor bottles told tales of drunken parties from long ago. The cold air smelled faintly musty with a mixture of dust, varnish, and urine. The walls muffled the outside world, giving a false sense of safety.

"We need to get moving," Doc said, grabbing my hand and towing me along behind him.

I trod carefully through the droppings and wooden boards. We stepped through a tall doorway into a much larger room, this one lined with broken-down shelves and an old store counter that ran the length of one wall. The packrats had been busy in here, too, building an even larger mound in an open cupboard door under a row of spiderweb-decorated glass jars.

"How soon until the chimeras figure out we're in here?" I asked.

"That depends on how long Coop and Harvey can keep them busy." He aimed the light at the top of the stairwell that ran up the side of the room. "We need to go upstairs."

"Why? What's up there?"

"The shadow I saw in the window yesterday."

"Where'd Cornelius go?"

The ceiling creaked overhead.

Doc pointed the light at more boot tracks in the dust, this time on the stairs. "He's leading the way now."

We climbed the narrow set of stairs, stepping more gingerly with each creak and groan underfoot. My hands were sweaty by the time we crested the upper floor.

"I hope those hold on the way back down," Doc said, aiming the beam down a long hallway running perpendicular to the stairs. A light flickered in one of the doorways partway down the hall.

We found Cornelius standing in a square room with no windows, Viking helmet still in place, his flashlight directed into one corner of the ceiling. The clock box lay on the floor at his feet.

What was this? A big closet? There were no shelves on the white plaster walls; no rodent droppings or broken boards either, oddly enough. The floor was dusty, but the room was clear of debris otherwise.

"We need to focus our energy in here," Cornelius said without looking at us. "It's the heart of the building."

I understood why Cornelius chose this room. Something about it felt right. The air was slightly warmer and the walls gave a feeling of security rather than confinement.

"Hold that thought," Doc said, disappearing into the hallway.

"What are you looking at?" I asked Cornelius, peering up at the corner, seeing nothing. Not even cobwebs. Once again, I had to wonder what this room had been used for, and why neither insects nor rodents desired to make it their home.

"The crown molding."

"What about it?"

"Whoever did the woodwork in this room was an expert finisher. The seams in the crown molding and the corners are perfect. I could use someone with similar skills at my hotel."

Doc returned, carrying a couple of pieces of wood. "I just heard Bessie's barrels sing out along with several shots from Coop's Colt." He closed the door behind him and jammed a broken board under the doorknob, wedging it at an angle on the floor. "Things must be getting exciting out there."

My pulse throbbed in my ears in the cottony silence of the room. I crossed my fingers and toes that Cooper and Harvey were holding their own and it was only exciting, not deadly.

"We need to hurry," Doc said, echoing my thoughts. "Are you ready, Killer?"

"I guess."

"What about you, Curion?"

Cornelius nodded. "What's the plan?"

"All three of us are going in, but you'll need to stay by her side while I figure out our way through. If Violet slips free of my mental tether, she may need help finding her way back."

"Back from where?" I asked.

"The dark," Cornelius answered. "Give me the candle, Violet."

I reached inside of my coat and plucked out the candle, handing it off and then adjusting the stick of dynamite so that it was now lodged in my inner coat pocket and not my cleavage. "You want the lighter?"

"No." He broke the candle into three pieces, and then pulled out a pocketknife and sliced the wick holding the pieces together. "We need to share. Here." He held out a piece of the candle toward me and gave another section to Doc. "I saw this used successfully once in Haiti. It should help us find our way back to one another in the dark."

I stared down at the piece of candle. "Can't I just use a flashlight?"

"It doesn't work that way," he said, lowering cross-legged onto the floor in the center of the room. When I frowned down at him, he patted the dust-covered wood next to him.

"Where will you be?" I asked Doc.

"With you but not."

"That's comforting," I said sarcastically.

He cupped my face. "I'll keep an eye out for trouble."

"What sort of trouble?"

"The kind that hunts Executioners." He kissed me softly. "Come back to me today, *cara mia*," he whispered before stepping back.

"*Oui, mon cher.*" I dropped onto the floor next to Cornelius.

Doc settled on the floor next to the door, leaning back against the wall. He set his flashlight on the floor, the beam lighting the opposite wall. He pointed at the box next to my knee. "Hold the clock in your lap. I have a feeling you're going to need it."

I did as told. "Like this?"

"Yes. Don't forget your war hammer."

I gripped it in my candle-free hand. "How do we know this is going to work?"

"We don't," Cornelius answered. "What's the code word?"

I glanced his way. "Why do we need a code word?"

"I need to make sure you are you on the other side and nothing is playing tricks on me in the dark."

Tricks in the dark? Yikes. I hadn't thought about that. "Monkeybutt?" I threw out.

"Monkeybutt?" Doc repeated, his tone edged with amusement.

"Sure."

"Monkeybutt it is," Cornelius said. "Take my hand." I clasped his palm. His fingers were cold. "Now close your eyes and meet me at the flame." He began to hum in a steady rhythmic tone, his usual soundtrack for sliding down the rabbit hole into our macabre version of Wonderland.

I stared at Doc. His dark gaze held mine in the dim light. "Don't go chasing shadows in there, Killer."

"I'll try not to. Get Cornelius out if shit starts heading downhill."

He saluted me and then closed his eyes, his chest rising and lowering visibly as he took several deep breaths.

Following his lead, I closed my eyelids and pictured a candle. Addy's and Layne's faces flashed through my thoughts. I squeezed my eyelids tighter, shoving all thoughts of my children away. I didn't want them anywhere near where I had to go today.

The candle flame in my mind flickered as I focused on it, sinking low until it was nothing more than a tiny flame of blue. One small sigh would blow it out. I hesitated, afraid to give life to the flame, my palms clammy about what was waiting in the darkness beyond. The cuckooing of the clock in my lap grew louder, making it hard to concentrate.

"Violet," Doc whispered in my ear. "Stay focused."

Pulling my attention back to the flame, I fed it energy, making it grow taller and brighter, watching it dance in the dark. The cuckooing faded until the only sound was my heartbeat, strong and steady.

I reached out to touch the flame. A pale hand grabbed my arm.

I sucked in a breath and looked up from the flame. Cornelius sat on the other side of the candle from me, his Viking helmet missing.

"What's the word?" he asked. His cornflower blue eyes seemed to glow in the darkness, reflecting the candle's flame.

"Monkeybutt."

He released my wrist. "What took you so long?"

"I was having trouble focusing. Hold this." I handed him the clock and pushed to my feet.

He stood as well, studying the clock. "The cuckooing must be hindering your channeling abilities."

"You can hear it?"

"How can I not? It's incessant."

Interesting. Was I using some sort of telepathy to relay the sound? Or was it … never mind. We had more important things to do than analyze the hows and whys at the moment.

"Now what do we do?" I asked.

A door opened behind Cornelius, answering my question. Was that a real door or only in my head? I shrugged. It didn't matter.

"Thanks, Doc," I whispered and scooped up my war hammer. After one last glance at the steady candle flame, I led the way toward the doorway. My fingers were crossed Doc was already there waiting for us.

* * *

Normally, I avoided going into the light. But today it beat freaking out in the dark while I waited for death to come courting.

It took a couple of blinks for my eyes to adjust to the brightness. When they did, I found myself standing in a room full of clocks. Only they weren't tick-tocking or hanging on the walls. Most were in pieces, spread out on a long workbench littered with clamps, pliers, and tweezers. On the walls, gears and chains of varying lengths and sizes dangled, as well as pendulums and hammers both big and tiny. A large magnifying glass hung from the ceiling on a hinged steel arm, hovering over the cluttered workbench. Several long-legged stools were scattered throughout the room. Three large windows let sunlight stream into the room, while pots full of dead plants lined the sill. The world on the other side of the glass was green and lush, not a flake of snow to be seen.

"What is this place?" I said quietly.

"I have a feeling we're not in Slagton anymore." Cornelius set the Wild Hunt clock down on the workbench and walked further into the room.

I chased after him, catching his sleeve. "Don't go too far," I said, glancing behind us. "Crud! Did you close the door?"

"I'm no doorman." He picked up a clock face that had upside-down numbers circling it. "What have we here?"

I returned to the door, twisting the knob. The door wouldn't budge. I turned the knob harder, tugging. "The sucker is sealed shut," I told Cornelius. "Like the closet door in Jane's office."

He set the clock down and joined me, trying the door as well. "Hmmm, it seems this is where we are meant to be."

"Or we're stuck."

He returned to the bench. "Everything will be okay in the end."

"What if it's not?" I followed him. "I'm here to face off with a hunter, remember?"

He shrugged. "If it's not okay, then it's not the end, is it?" He moved further down the bench. "Come look at this clock. The woodwork is more intricate than yours."

I studied the design, looking beyond the two-headed, gangly-armed version of Bigfoot carved in the wood with what appeared to be the body of an elk-like creature in one hand and the creature's head in the other. Cornelius was right. While there were similarities in the gruesome subject matter, the style was different. It reminded me of something Layne told me about the Maya civilization. How different stone carvers put their own flair into the glyphs they chiseled in the limestone—a distinct artistry visible in the design.

"Check this out." I pointed at a clock face sitting further along the bench. It had what looked like rune stone symbols in place of the numbers.

"That's peculiar. These symbols are from the Viking alphabet."

"You know the Viking alphabet?"

"That seems obvious, Violet, considering I wear a Viking helmet during séances."

Before I could make sense of that, a door at the other end of the room opened. I froze, my war hammer raised and ready to face off with whatever horror awaited.

A tall, willowy figure swept into the room, feminine in essence judging by appearance. The shafts of sunlight flooding through the window lit her, giving her long, white tresses an almost radiant glow. Her skin was the color of dark chocolate, visible through the transparent fabric of her cream-colored gossamer dress. Bright blue flowers were sewn into the fabric, concealing yet teasing with glimpses of what lay beneath. A pair of strappy flat sandals made of thin strips of leather wrapped around her feet, twining up her legs, disappearing under the sheer fabric.

"I think I'm in love," Cornelius said, his voice filled with awe.

The willowy female gasped, taking a step back at the sight of us. "What are you?" she asked, her tone dulcet, flooding me with warmth and happiness.

"You speak English," I said, not sure what I'd expected to come from the lips of such a mesmerizing figure. There was an accent in there, but I couldn't place it. Her words had soft edges, like her clothes and body. They flowed together, making me think of something Latin-based. A variation of French maybe?

"I followed your companion's lead," she said.

"Such an ethereal beauty," Cornelius said, his gaze still locked onto the willowy woman. "I want to compose a sonnet for her. To write tomes about her wavy white locks. To skim my lips over her luscious—"

I elbowed him in the gut. "Knock it off, Shakespeare."

While Cornelius coughed, catching his breath, I studied the woman. Was she the hunter waiting for me? If so, anonymity would work to my favor. "I'm here about a clock," I said by way of introduction.

She walked closer, her steps graceful and light, stopping before me. She was taller than Cornelius, midway between six and seven feet in height. The smooth and creamy texture of her skin made me want to reach out and touch her. Her eyelashes were a stark white against her dark eyelids, outlining irises the color of verdant grass in a spring meadow. The sweet smell of wildflowers in the sun filled the air.

My grip on my war hammer loosened, my internal warning system not reacting to her nearness. Something deep down assured me she was no enemy.

"You did not answer my question, stranger."

What question? I blinked out of her spell. "I'm a Timekeeper."

"Then why are you wielding a blade?"

"As a precaution."

She tipped her head to the side, studying me. "If you are a Timekeeper, why have I not seen you before?"

"I'm new on the job." I set my war hammer on the workbench next to the Viking alphabet clock. "I replaced Ms. Wolff."

One white eyebrow lifted. "Who?"

I thought of the name Prudence had used. "*Hoont.*"

Her eyes narrowed. "Why?"

"She was tired." That was no lie. Ms. Wolff had said as much before dying.

The willowy woman leaned forward, sniffing my throat, not unlike what Prudence had done in the past but without the creepy factor involved. "You have an odd scent. One that I know, yet I do not."

Most *others* could smell the *Scharfrichter* in my blood. How was it she could not? There was no way she was human, yet she did not react to my charm necklace, the one Aunt Zoe had made to trigger a response from the *others*.

At least I hadn't noticed a reaction yet. I needed to watch more closely, and not let myself be blinded by her beauty.

Her focus shifted to Cornelius, who stood almost nose-to-nose with her. "Your eyes are the color of my favorite flower." She sniffed him next, leaning even closer and taking another breath. His hand reached up to touch her hair, but I knocked it away, shaking my head at him.

"I know your kind," she told him. "You don't belong here." Her green gaze returned to me. "But you are an enigma. Familiar yet exotic."

If we were done with the smell-o-thon, we needed to move this train along before Harvey or Cooper ended up with tooth marks in their hides. "Can you help me with my clock?"

She looked down at the cuckooing clock, her lips pursed. "I did not make this clock."

She did not make ... Holy caca-moly! "You're a clockmaker!"

"Of course," she said. "Why else would you come to me?"

Never mind that I was there by dumb luck. Or was I? "I need your help," I told her. "I need to understand how the clocks work."

"How can you be a Timekeeper and not have this knowledge?"

"I'm still in training."

She searched my face for several seconds. "And what of your

friend?"

I looked at Cornelius, who was picking up random objects on her workbench, studying them. "What about him?"

He glanced our way. "What about me?"

"Not that one." She lifted her arms in the air, circling her hands. A glowing hole appeared in the ceiling. What the heck? Before I could make sense of it, a piece of tapered candle fell out of the hole, landing at my feet. "The Oracle who is hiding in plain sight."

My breath caught. She could see Doc? Or just sense him enough to take the candle from him? I'd always assumed he was safe when I was dabbling in the darkness and beyond. Then again, Mr. Black had warned of an Oracle's vulnerability around their mate.

I bent and picked up the piece of candle, stuffing it in my coat pocket, while I regained my composure. "The Oracle is none of your concern."

She smiled. "Do not be alarmed. Your entourage raises many questions, but I will keep your secrets. Now, what is it you seek to understand, Timekeeper?"

"What do the positions of the hands on a clock indicate?"

"Location. When the clock sounds, the position of the hands tells you the location of the gate through which the traveler is entering your world." She pointed at the hour hand. "This indicates what you would call longitude." Her long, thin finger hovered over the minute hand. "This indicates latitude. When you combine the two, you will know the location in which to seek the traveler."

"So how do I know which gate each number represents?"

"That is something you must learn, Timekeeper."

Crud. I'd sooner just kill the bad guys. "And if I move the hands, I change the location, right?"

"That is the risk. It is why the clocks must be watched over and protected. A clock in the wrong hands can end in disaster."

"But only Timekeepers can mess with the gates?"

She nodded. "Only Timekeepers can move the hands to make time work for them, which could be useful ... or detrimental."

"Why won't this clock stop cuckooing?" Cornelius asked.

"The traveler is waiting at the gate for some reason, unwilling to step through, forcing the gate to remain open." Her white eyebrows drew inward as she stared down at the timepiece. "It is curious. Why would a traveler not want a gate to close?"

"The squeaky wheel gets the grease," I said to Cornelius. Unfortunately, the only way to find out was to visit the gate myself.

I pointed at the hour hand. "I need to know where that gate is."

She made a weird, gurgling sound and stepped back. "Your ring!"

I looked down at the family heirloom Aunt Zoe had stuck on my finger earlier. "What about it?"

"I know that mark. You are a *Scharfrichter!*"

Damn. The gig was up. I stared at her in earnest. "Yes, but I'm also a Timekeeper. That was no lie."

She took several more steps back, her green eyes wide, her hands covering her cheeks. "I have never heard of such a combination. It's an abomination."

Abomination? Come on! Was my family line really that full of assholes? "I promise not to hurt you. I'm here because I need your help in keeping the balance in my world."

She lowered her hands. "Did you kill the Timekeeper before you?"

Crap. "Maybe just a little, but only because she insisted I kill her."

Cornelius snorted. "How can you kill a 'little,' Violet?"

"You're not helping," I sang to him between gritted teeth.

"Whose clock is this?" the willow woman asked.

"The leader of the Wild Hunt. At least that is what Mr. Black explained when he gave it to me."

"Mr. Black! He did not tell me a *Scharfrichter* had joined his cause."

Oops! Maybe that was supposed to be a secret. Oh, well. The executioner was out of the bag now. "Listen, Mr. Black told me I'm supposed to kill the hunter in charge of these creatures carved into the clock before they take over Slagton in a turf war."

"How did you arrive here?"

I pointed at the door behind me. "We came through that door."

"How did you know about that gate?" Her eyes widened. "Of course, the Oracle could see it." She took a step closer. "Where did you find an Oracle?" she asked in a lowered voice.

"I tripped over his books."

"Do you realize how rare they are? The trouble they elicit?"

I scoffed. "I'm a *Scharfrichter*. Trouble is my middle name."

"Why would a timekeeper sacrifice herself to a *Scharfrichter*. What would inspire such a daring decision?"

"Dangerous opponents. Listen, I don't have a lot of time here for explanations. If you help me find the traveler belonging to this clock at whatever gate it's waiting, I promise to return another time and explain everything to you in more detail. For now, you have to trust me."

She eased closer, sniffing in my direction again. "You do not smell like a *Scharfrichter.*"

"I usually do." Oh, hold on. I unzipped my coat a few inches and pulled the stick of dynamite from the inside pocket. "Maybe this is throwing you off."

"Is that what I think it is?" Cornelius asked, leaning away from me.

"If you're thinking old dynamite, then yes."

"Do you know how unstable that is?"

"Yep, you told me all about nitroglycerin, remember?"

She leaned close again, breathing in. "That is not the source. You smell like a wild animal, covered in mildewing plants and dead weeds."

I cringed. "That bad huh?" I had showered this morning and spritzed with some perfume afterward. Maybe I'd forgotten to rub on some pit-stick. "Wait." I dug in my bra and extracted the sachet Aunt Zoe had given me. "Is this what you smell?"

Cornelius hooked his finger in my neckline, peering down the front of my shirt. "What else do you have down there?"

I extracted his finger from my shirt, scowling up at him. "What I keep in my secret arsenal is none of your business."

The clockmaker sniffed the sachet. "Yes, this is the source." She leaned in close to my neck, her breath cool on my skin "Now I smell you, *Scharfrichter.*" She handed the sachet back. "This is an interesting disguise. You are quite clever."

I wished she'd tell Prudence that. I could use some testimonials on my Executioner résumé. The sachet, however, was Aunt Zoe's idea, not mine.

"What does a *Scharfrichter* smell like?" Cornelius asked, sniffing around my neck.

"Death. It is in their nature."

Nice. I reeked of death. Did they sell that scent in a shower gel and body lotion combo package?

I pushed Cornelius away, threatening to pop him in the nose, and stuffed the dynamite inside my coat and the sachet back in my bra. "We don't have time for this. I have to find the traveler on this clock immediately. How do I find the gate?"

"There is a shortcut for a Timekeeper."

"I'm all ears."

"Instead of going to the gate, you move the gate to you."

"How do I do that?"

She took my hands in her long fingers, helping me to nudge the hour hand halfway around the clock face and then bumping the minute hand up several notches. "Like this."

"So where is this gate now?"

She pointed at the door through which we'd entered. "It is in there, as is your traveler."

I grabbed my war hammer, looking up at Cornelius. "You ready?"

He picked up the clock. "No, however it doesn't appear that I have much choice."

"Thank you for your help," I told the clockmaker. "I'll return to explain more some other time."

She smiled. "At that time, I will teach you more about the clocks, *Scharfrichter*." She frowned toward the door. "If you live."

Right. Continuing to breathe oxygen after today would be just jolly.

"This is for you, human," she said, holding out her hand toward Cornelius. "You will both need it."

Both?

Cornelius opened his palm under hers. A blue flower like that on her dress fell into his palm. "I like your eyes," the clockmaker told him. "I would like to see them again as well."

Cornelius stuttered, his cheeks darkening as he stared at her.

"Okay, we're done here, Casanova." I dragged him toward the door by the elbow.

I paused at the door, telling myself I could do this. I was made to kill. This time, the handle turned with ease, and the door opened with little effort.

"Stay close to me," I told Cornelius and stepped inside. When the door closed, darkness blanketed us again.

"Doc?" I whispered. "I hope you're in here with us." The fact that I now had his portion of the candle made me wonder if we'd lost him.

Cornelius huffed behind me, his breath hot on my neck.

"Are you okay?"

"Are you talking to me?" Cornelius asked, his voice sounding far off, yet close. The darkness must be distorting sound as well.

"Yes, I'm talking to you. Who else would be panting in my ear?"

Silence filled the darkness, broken only by the sound of heavy breathing behind me.

"I don't know," Cornelius's voice sounded higher than usual. "Because I'm standing right in front of you."

Chapter Twenty-Four

This part-time executioner job was going to be the death of me. The workplace hazards were a nightmare, not to mention the on-the-job stress, which was going to send me into cardiac arrest one of these days, I just knew it.

Once again, here I was hanging out in some nameless dark place next to a mouth breather who was pining to rip me into tiny *Scharfrichter* pieces. I closed my eyes, digging deep into my core, searching for the strength to deal with whatever nastiness was waiting to spring its trap.

Turning to face my hunter, I pulled Doc's piece of candle from my coat pocket and held it out in front of me, picturing a flame in my mind. When I opened my eyes, the candle's wick flared to life.

I looked beyond the flame. A high-pitched whine rose from my chest at the sight of what had been lurking in the dark next to me. I stumbled back a step, putting some distance between me and the gray-skinned beast and its elongated, deformed face that I doubted even its mother could love.

The "hunter" stared at me through two sunken eyes nearly hidden beneath its bulging forehead. Black bubbles of saliva lined its lower lip, popping as it breathed through clenched sliver-like teeth framed by a large square mouth. Or was that black stuff its blood? The chimeras had bled black blood, too. While I cringed in horror, more of the dark, viscous drool leaked from one side of its mouth, sliding down its chin and dripping from its lower jaw. I noticed a faint scent of something musky and metallic, and gulped through the churning in my stomach.

Its teeth gnashed. The whine in my throat turned to a mewling cry. I tightened my grip on my war hammer, wishing I could trade in my Executioner Career card in this disturbing game for a profession with a lower "ick" factor.

The hunter's upper lip quivered as it lunged toward me from the shadows, but a leather strap held it in place against a large wooden door. I lifted the candle higher, taking a closer look at what must be the "gate" between realms. The huge door reminded me of something that would hang in the entryway of a castle, vulnerable only to battering rams and termite colonies. It stood alone in the darkness. How could a gate just be here in the middle of nothing? What if I walked around to the other side? Would I see the other side of the gate or nothing?

The hunter struggled to pull free again. Its muscular gray shoulders writhed against invisible chains while its nostrils flared and eyes bulged. More black blood oozed from its lower lip, trailing down its chin.

Someone touched my shoulder.

I squawked, whirling, war hammer raised.

Cornelius cringed, his hands held out to stop me.

I lowered my weapon. "Don't do that, damn it," I said, panting.

He frowned. "Are you feeling high levels of fear and anxiety?"

"Am I ... Hello! We're in the dark facing off with a monster. Aren't you feeling a tad nervous?"

"I've recently had my Third Eye chakra balanced to help me see everything more clearly. You, on the other hand, appear to need to open your solar plexus chakra so you can release some of that stuck energy and regain your strong sense of personal power."

I gaped at him over the candle flame. "Do you really think now is the time to discuss the current state of our chakras?" I pointed my thumb toward the hunter. "Do you not see that thing over there wanting to kill us?"

"See, this is what I'm talking about," Cornelius said. "Your voice is higher than normal due to the tension around your solar plexus chakra. Are you experiencing difficulties breathing due to a tightness in your chest? Have you been suffering from bouts of queasiness or diarrhea lately?"

I raised my war hammer in front of his face. "If you say the word *chakra* one more time before we get out of this place, I'm going to plant this in your Third Eye."

Behind me, the creature grunted and flailed. I turned to frown at it, my lungs tight with each breath. Stupid clogged-up solar plexus. "I don't understand what's going on here," I said to myself as much as Cornelius.

"You're looking at it incorrectly," Cornelius said. "Turn the candle upside down with your mind."

That didn't make any sense, but I did it anyway. When I flipped the candle around, I gasped at the thick, medieval-looking spike sticking out through the hunter's midsection. Black blood trickled down into the fur at its waist.

"Oh, Jesus," I whispered. "Why is it impaled on that thing?" It almost looked as if it'd been hung purposefully on the massive door, like some twisted version of a brass knocker.

Bait, said a voice in my head.

Wait a second. That wasn't one of my multiple personalities weighing in. The voice sounded like Doc's, only crackly, reminding me of a static-filled AM radio station in the middle of nowhere.

"Bait for what?" I asked aloud.

"Violet," Cornelius said. "If you're showing off your high cognitive functioning by having random conversations with yourself in the dark, I can assure you now is not the time, nor am I your ideal audience."

An Executioner. The voice was clearer this time, definitely Doc's.

He was listening to us in the darkness. Could he see what we were seeing? Were his hands trembling as much as mine?

"But this has to be the leader of the Wild Hunt," I told Doc. "It's here at the gate and its clock is still cuckooing."

"I'm not arguing that fact with you." Cornelius set the clock down and then grabbed the stick of dynamite that was poking out of the neckline of my coat, frowning at it. "Where did you get this?"

"That's not important right now." I grabbed back the stick, stuffing it in my pocket.

"You might want to take care with that stick, Violet, or you won't be important any more, either."

I turned my attention to the injured hunter, walking around the side of it with my candle held out to gain a clearer view of the spear jutting up through its chest. "If you are bait," I said. "Then who is …"

The candle flame went out.

A gush of cold air brushed past my skin, a hint of sulfur in its wake. Someone was coming.

I heard no footfalls, but my other senses alerted me to its presence by raising the hairs on the back of my neck, shooting tingling sparks through my limbs, and cramping my stomach.

I backed away from the creature, my war hammer raised and ready in the blackness that was so thick I couldn't see my hands. Where was Cornelius? I tried to hear the sound of him breathing amid the grunts and huffs coming from the impaled hunter.

"Cornelius?" I whispered. "Where are you?"

A whimpering sound came from the hunter.

I resisted the urge to whimper along with it, trying to focus inward and explore the darkness using my other senses.

A yowl of pain rang out.

The huffing stopped.

Then the cuckooing stopped.

My heart might have stopped, too.

Thump-thump. Thump-thump. Thump-thump.

No, it was still ticking even if the clock wasn't.

I held out the piece of candle again, picturing a flame bigger than the last. A flare ignited at the end of the candle, catching the wick on fire.

I glanced at the hunter. A shriek slipped out before I could cover my mouth. The creature had been gutted from neck to waist. Its body was still twitching on the spike, its innards slowly spilling from its torso. Bile rose in my throat. My stomach heaved.

Come back! Doc's voice crackled in my head.

I clutched the war hammer to my chest, not sure what to do, where to run, and how to find Cornelius in this shadowy in-between world. I needed Doc's sight, but our lifeline appeared to be experiencing technical difficulties.

My candle flame went out again, plunging me into darkness.

I fumbled with my candle, dropping it, losing it in the pitch black.

What do I do now, Doc? I thought as I patted my coat pockets for the other piece of candle and pulled it out.

I had to calm down. I could handle this. I just needed to …

I stilled.

Someone was in the dark with me. I couldn't hear any breathing or feel any air movement or see a single damned thing to confirm it, but I could definitely smell it. There was no mistaking the stench of sulfur.

"Who's there?" I whispered in the cottony silence.

I pictured the candle flame, bringing it to life, lighting the darkness again. The hunter was still dead, Cornelius was still missing, and I was still up shit creek in the dark world between realms.

Something smacked my hand, sending the candle flying. The flame was doused again.

Son of a motherfucker!

Now I was getting pissed. A steely reserve chased away my flutters of fear. Anger fueled my actions.

I searched my coat pockets again, this time for the lighter I'd grabbed at Aunt Zoe's. "Quit playing childish games and show yourself," I told whatever was messing with me, palming the tube filled with lighter fluid. "Or are you too chicken shit?"

Deep laughter rippled through the silence, twisting around me. "Your bravado is admirable, *Scharfrichter*, yet foolish."

I knew that voice! A wave of dizziness made me wobble in the dark. I staggered several steps back. *Not him. Please, not him.*

Bracing myself, I raised Aunt Zoe's lighter and flicked the flame to life with my thumb instead of my mind.

A superstar from my recurring nightmares leaned against the huge door next to the dead hunter.

"Wolfgang?" I croaked, but the voice didn't match the man.

Not real. Doc's voice was back, although not clear.

I stood taller knowing the Oracle was listening.

Wolfgang looked like the real deal to me, from his blond locks and deep blue eyes to his strong chin and broad shoulders.

A chameleon, Doc told me.

That explained the wrong voice for Wolfgang's face.

"Why are you here?" I asked, scanning the darkness for a sign of Cornelius. I hoped to hell he was hiding somewhere safe, because I had a feeling I was already up to my neck in quicksand here. Making it out of the dark alive was becoming less promising by the second.

"We have unfinished business."

My brain's voice recognition locked onto the chameleon's true identity: Kyrkozz. I stifled a groan. Damn, I'd rather have faced off with the hunter's spiky teeth.

"I'm pretty sure we took care of everything last time, Kyrkozz, before you peeled off your face and spit all over me." I purposely spoke his name so that Doc could hear it.

"You remember me."

That horrific scene had replayed in my dreams too many times to count. "You're hard to forget with your pretty orange eyes and twisty little horns, not to mention those lovely oozing pustules all over your skin. What's with the fleshy costume? Did you think I couldn't handle seeing your handsome mug again?"

He snickered. "So spirited."

It had been too much to hope I'd never run into this asshole again. "Why did you summon me, demon?"

"One cannot summon a *Scharfrichter*. I merely sent you an invitation to talk."

"So talk."

"I gave you an order before that you have disobeyed."

"What order? Remind me. My memory is short."

"I told you to leave this place, but you have returned to the dark time again."

"I've always struggled with following directions," I told him. "What did you do with my friend who was in here with me?"

"I did nothing. He opted to leave and I allowed it. The invitation was not meant for him."

Invitation my ass. Kyrkozz had baited me. Doc had been right all along. There'd be no living with him if I made it out of this mess alive.

"Well, you have me here, so now what?"

"You continue to interfere with my plans, *Scharfrichter*."

Which plans were those? Back in August, Lila Beaumont had wanted to use my womb as fertile ground for Kyrkozz's demon child seed. Was he still searching for a surrogate momma? Or did he have new plans for something even more sinister?

His chin lowered, his menacing smile sending chills up my arms. Why had I ever thought of Wolfgang as handsome?

"Since you did not heed my warning, you will die. After I remove your limbs one at a time," he said, "I am going to remove your head and mount it on a spike as a lesson for others. Disobedience will not be tolerated anymore."

Blind him, Violet! Doc spoke through the static, startling me.

Blind him with what? Aunt Zoe's lighter? My pathetic mental flame? My dim wit?

I lifted my chin in the face of his threat, donning a false bravado as I tried to figure a way out of the demon's trap. "Maybe I'll mount your head on a spike to teach the *others* like you what happens when you piss off an Executioner."

His laughter sounded hard and brittle. "You think that silly weapon in your hands can defeat me?"

"This?" I held up the war hammer. "Probably not." But I'd sure enjoy taking a few swings at him. The son of a bitch had haunted my nightmares for months. I was pretty certain that sinking the pointed end of my war hammer in Krykozz's forehead would be considered beneficial sleep therapy.

"You are weak, *Scharfrichter*. I can crush you. Your weapons are of no use to you in the darkness."

He was right. In the dark I was swinging blindly. I thought back to the day Cornelius and I sat up next to Wild Bill Hickok's grave in Mount Moriah cemetery and I first learned how to reach out in the darkness. That day I'd torn out something's tongue using my mind's eye alone.

My memory shifted to my last conversation with Prudence. What had she said about hiding my strengths? Something about distracting my enemy with my weaknesses instead.

Switching Aunt Zoe's lighter to my left hand, I swung my war hammer a couple of times in mid-air with my right, warming up my arm. "I don't know, Kyrkozz. My war hammer sure feels like it would pierce that fake outer shell you're wearing. How about we find out if I'm right?"

Violet, don't! Doc shouted.

"You cannot be serious, *Scharfrichter*."

"I don't joke with demons or clowns." I'd had my limit of both.

"I can rip you apart with my bare hands," he bragged.

"You talk the talk, but can you walk the walk?"

... *must blind him* ... Doc's voice wavered. ... *too strong for you* ...

Blind him how, dammit? It wasn't like I had a lighthouse beacon in my pocket. I should've taken one of the flashlights from ...

Oh, duh!

I held tight to Aunt Zoe's lighter. I'd get one chance at this.

"What say you?" I asked the demon. "Shall we dance in the dark?"

Before he could answer, I threw my war hammer at him. It spun through the air end over end.

He caught it in mid-air next to his head. He took it in both hands and broke it in half as if it were no more than a toothpick. "Surely you feel foolish now."

"Hand-to-hand combat it is," I said, bending to the side and reaching my right hand high in the air.

"What are you doing, *Scharfrichter*?"

"Stretching. Unlike you, I'm part human." I pulled my shoulders back, and then reached behind me. "I don't want to get a cramp while I'm kicking your ass." I bent down and touched my toes, the stick of dynamite that had been in my pocket now in my right hand.

"This is absurd," Kyrkozz said. "Your weapons are worthless against me. What makes you think you can defeat me with nothing more than your hands?"

"I'm optimistic that way."

Tired of talking, I stood up and threw the stick of dynamite at him, same as I had my war hammer, end-over-end.

He caught it with ease, holding it in front of his face. "What is this game you're playing?"

"It's called 'Hot Potato.' " I focused on the dynamite in his hand, picturing a blue flame, big and bright, in place of the fuse. "And I just stopped the music, so you lose."

I turned to run, but I'd made the flame too intense. An explosion flashed bright white, blinding. The shock wave sent me tumbling through the blackness. When I finally stopped, I was flat on my back in the dark abyss, the ringing in my ears deafening.

I lay there, disoriented, wondering if Kyrkozz would come for me. I doubted I'd killed him. Nasty sons of bitches like him didn't die that easily. Where was I, anyway? Being in the dark made it impossible to know how screwed I was. Would I ever find my way back? Would I die here in the dark alone? I felt my gut tightening and thought of my so-called solar plexus blockage, which led to wondering about Cornelius. Where had he gone? Had Kyrkozz done something to him? Had I doomed him to stay here in the dark, too?

A flutter of panic made me twitch, but I forced myself to lie still and let my body relax, focusing on my breathing. Now was as good a time as any to clear my clogged chakras. There was nowhere to run, nowhere to hide. All I could do was … Someone pinched my arm.

Ouch!

I sat up. Who did that?

Another pinch. This time harder.

I rubbed my arm. What the hell?

I realized I was still clutching Aunt Zoe's lighter. I held it up. The flame flickered, lighting the area around me. I was sitting in a small, empty square room. I looked at the ceiling, focusing on the crown molding, noticing the excellent craftsmanship in the corner joints. I knew this place.

Something nipped my earlobe.

I winced, touching it. The skin was hot. Pinches and ear nips—those were my revival techniques.

"Doc?" Where was he? I stood, looking around. The door was behind me, the board Doc had used to block it still in place. I kicked the piece of wood aside and turned the knob.

Out in the hall, the lighter's flame flickered, shrinking. I started toward the stairs, but the lighter died when I hit the first step. I stumbled in the darkness, my arms flailing as I fell forward.

A hand caught my arm, yanking me backward. I hit the floor hard, coughing in the dust.

"Violet." This time, Doc's voice sounded crystal clear. "Open your eyes."

I lifted one eyelid, fearing I was still stuck in the in-between place. That he was only a dream in the dark.

Doc stared down at me. "Both eyes, Killer."

I opened the other eyelid, blinking a couple of times. My hand shook when I reached up and touched his cheek. His beard stubble scraped under my fingertips. "Am I back?"

"Just barely." He captured my hand, brushing his lips over my knuckles. "Are you okay?"

"I am now. Did you bite my ear?"

His eyes crinkled. "A little. It's a wake-up trick I learned from a hot blonde with a wicked pinch."

"You sounded so far away. How did you find me?"

"The mushroom cloud was hard to miss." He scowled. "What in the hell were you thinking?"

"You told me to blind him."

"I meant with your candle flame, not a damned stick of dynamite. Christ, woman. You're going to turn my hair white if you keep charging hell with buckets of water."

I grinned. "Quit yer caterwaulin' and give me some sugar, Oracle."

He leaned over me, his gaze burning into mine. "When that explosion rang out, I thought I'd lost you in there for good, *cara mia*."

"Ah, *mon cher*. Don't torture yourself so." I framed his face, pulling him closer. "That's my job."

His focus dipped to my lips. "Damn, Tish," he whispered and kissed me, his mouth tender, his touch warming away the last of my chills. I wrapped my arms around his neck and clung to him. My heart overflowed, making a mess all over the place.

He groaned deep in his chest and then pulled away. "We're going to bookmark this and come back to it soon, Boots."

He helped me sit upright.

"We have to go back into the dark," I said. "I lost Cornelius."

"No, you didn't. I had to drag him out early. One of the chimeras had sniffed out our hiding spot. I needed Cornelius to keep it busy while I tried to find you and bring you home."

"You left Cornelius alone with one of those sharp-toothed predators?" I scrambled to my feet, swaying for a second.

Doc made sure I was steady before letting go of my shoulders. "He said he could handle the chimera, mentioned something about having recently flushed out his Third Eye. He took the crowbar with him." Doc looked down at my hands. "Where's your war hammer?"

"I sort of lost it."

"Not again."

"Yeah." I grimaced. "I don't think I'll get it back this time."

"What about the clock?" he asked.

"I forgot it in the dark." I doubted there was much of it left after that blast.

A war cry resonated up the stairwell.

Doc beat me down the stairs.

We found Cornelius in a room in the corner of the building—an old kitchen with a cast iron stove in the corner. On the floor at his feet lay a chimera larger than any of those I'd battled by the old Plymouth, the crowbar buried in its neck. Black blood pooled around its head, reminding me of the impaled hunter at the gate that Kyrkozz had used as bait. I shivered, looking up at Cornelius who was wiping off his jacket with a handkerchief. His Viking helmet lay on the floor next to the dead creature.

"How did you …" I trailed off. Apparently, there was a lot more to Cornelius than hairy knees and a crooked smile.

"Why didn't you use the Glock?" Doc asked.

Cornelius bent down and grabbed his helmet. "Gunfire hurts my ears." His cornflower blue eyes landed on me. "You're back. How was the return trip?"

"A bit mind blowing."

Doc guffawed.

The floorboards creaked behind us.

All three of us turned.

Cooper stood in the doorframe, his Colt .45 in hand. His face was splattered and streaked with black blood. A red cut sliced across his cheekbone. At the sight of the dead chimera, his shoulders sagged. "Is it over?" he asked, blinking slowly, his eyes red rimmed.

"For now," Doc answered.

"Where's Harvey?" I asked, my breath held as I waited for his answer.

He holstered his gun. "Waiting outside in the pickup."

"Is he all right?"

"All right? It was a fucking shootout at the OK Corral out there." Cooper said. "Uncle Willis was hooting and hollering the whole damned time, blasting the shit out of anything that moved. Not to mention that he blew the woodshed to hell and back with that stick of dynamite. The old coot had the time of his life." He rubbed the back of his neck. "Jesus, my ears aren't going to stop ringing for a week."

"Was there anything hiding in the woodshed?" I asked, thinking of that yellow eye staring at me through the knothole. "Before Harvey blew it up?"

"Yeah. My informant."

I cringed. "Was he in pieces?"

"Nope. He's still very much alive and talking. You're going to want to hear what he has to say about this screwed-up town." Cooper's bloodshot eyes locked onto me. "Masterson gave you false information."

Dominick lied. That slick bastard. What was his game? Had he been in cahoots with Kyrkozz?

"You owe Dominick a chimera," Doc reminded me.

Cooper leaned against the doorjamb. "That might be a problem. We didn't leave any breathing."

"That's okay," I said, walking over to the dead one on the floor at Cornelius's feet. "I have an idea."

* * *

I didn't talk much on the trip back down to Deadwood. My brain was too busy processing the shitload of images and information dumped on it to be able to form coherent sentences.

We'd dropped Cooper's yellow-eyed informant off at Harvey's ranch since he had nowhere else to go for now and needed to hole up for a few days until this mess blew over. I hadn't asked his name. Cooper knew it and that was enough for me at this point. The guy looked normal enough, maybe a little long in the tooth when it came to his scraggly gray ponytail and hairy knuckles, but otherwise easily mistaken for a human hermit.

He'd filled my head with tales, opening my eyes and then some. It turned out that most of Slagton's oddball remaining residents weren't human. They'd stayed put after the mine pulled out because they had a job to do: guard the gates—as in more than one.

"How many gates are we talking?" I'd asked the informant.

"Enough to require sentinels on guard at all times, *Scharfrichter*," he'd said. "But now that you're here, we have another purpose."

"What's that?"

His answer had made me cringe.

I wasn't ready for this wave. All I wanted to do was go home and hide in the corner of my closet amid Elvis's feathers and plug my ears until it all passed.

Harvey dropped Cooper, Doc, and me off at Doc's place, heading out to take Cornelius back to his apartment above Calamity Jane Realty and then swing by Aunt Zoe's while we cleaned up. He had big tales to tell and was happy to hold off on a shower and catch Aunt Zoe up instead.

Once inside Doc's house, Cooper headed straight for the shower.

He had to be at work in an hour. Finding his informant alive seemed to have made him much less crotchety. Or maybe it was playing shooting gallery for real. He did share blood with Harvey, after all.

Cooper had even helped me collect what I needed for Dominick without snarling at me. When he'd chuckled about what crazy mess I was going to land him in next, I'd begun to suspect Harvey's dynamite had knocked something loose in Cooper's brain. Witnessing this side of the law dog was almost as scary as facing off with Kyrkozz.

While Cooper showered, I sat at Doc's kitchen bar and drank a beer, staring at the bubbles in the bottle. Doc gave me breathing room, seeming to understand I needed space to sort out what had happened in this world and the other.

"You're next," Doc said to me when Cooper came down the stairs in jeans, a button-up shirt, and tie.

"You go first," I said, still nursing my beer.

Before climbing the stairs, he invited Cooper to stop by Aunt Zoe's later for supper if he had time to take a break.

Cooper poured himself a glass of water. "What are you going to do about the Slagton situation?"

I finished off my beer. "I don't know."

He gulped down the water and stuck the glass in the dishwasher. "You were right about splitting up," he said.

I blinked. Twice. "What did you just say?"

"You heard me, Parker. I'm not going to say it again."

"Did you hit your head fighting those things today?"

A grin flitted over his features. "I did take a hit to the face when the shed blew up." He pointed at the cut on his cheek. "Maybe that piece of wood knocked something loose."

"Be careful, Cooper. If you say something else nice to me, I might suspect you're starting to like me in spite of my big nose and curls."

He pursed his lips, staring at my nose and then my hair. "Nah. I'm just tired as hell and don't feel like fighting right now." He grabbed his Deadwood police coat from the back of the other bar stool. "Once I'm caught up on sleep, I'm sure I'll find you irritating as ever."

"Then I guess I'd better make hay while the sun is shining." I hopped off the stool and walked over to him.

His eyes narrowed as I neared. "What are you doing, Parker?"

I held out my hand. "Breathe easy, law dog. I only want to thank you for being there today and keeping those things away while I dealt with what I had to on the inside."

"Why was the clock stuck cuckooing?"

We didn't have time to go into detail now, so I kept it short and sweet. "A demon had impaled the clock's owner on the gate between realms in order to lure me there so he could tear me limb from limb and mount my head on a spike."

"Are you fucking with me?"

I shook my head.

"How did you escape?"

I smiled. "Harvey wasn't the only one sporting dynamite today."

He scowled. "Jesus, Parker. That dynamite was a ticking time bomb. You could have blown yourself to pieces."

"That thought had crossed my mind once or twice." I stared up at him. "Thank you, Cooper. For everything." I wrapped my arms around his rigid torso and gave him a quick hug. It bordered on awkward, but at least I didn't get bit while standing that close to him.

When I stepped back, he gave me a lopsided smile. "You keep life interesting, Parker."

"That's what Doc says."

"I don't envy him. You're hard on a guy without even trying." He grabbed his keys off the counter, pausing at my side. "I might stop by your aunt's place later for some grub, if that's okay with you."

I nodded. "I think Nat will be there with us. If you play your cards right, maybe she'll chastise you with another kiss."

He smiled. "Or she'll just chew me a new asshole again."

"Or that."

He patted my shoulder. "Try to stay out of trouble for one night. I could use a break." Without another word he left.

I deadbolted the door after him and then turned to look up the stairs. "And then there was one."

I peeled off my shirt on the way up the stairs and plucked the sachet from my bra, dropping both on the floor. After locking Doc's bedroom door behind me, I stepped out of my jeans and socks. The bathroom door was open a crack. I closed it after me, breathing in the steam of the shower. I could see Doc's form through the curtain. He was letting the water beat down on his head, his chin tipped up.

You're hard on a guy without even trying.

Today had been hard on all of us. There was so much to break down and analyze, so many words and actions that didn't make sense. But now was not the time. Now, I just needed to *feel*. To show Doc how much I appreciated him. How much I loved him.

I left my bra and underwear on, knowing he really liked it when I got wet. His eyes widened when I joined him on the other side of the curtain, then his attention drifted downward and his surprise turned into a hungry smolder.

He hooked his finger in the center of my bra, towing me closer. His hands framed my face, tipping it up. His thumbs brushed over my cheekbones. His gaze lingered on my mouth for several seconds, then lifted to my eyes. The love shining back at me melted my heart.

"Kiss me," I whispered.

"Once I start, I'm not going to stop."

I wrapped my arms around his neck. Warm water bounced off his shoulders, misting my face. I moved my hips against him. "You're getting me all wet."

He shifted, pressing me back against the shower wall. The tiles were cool on my skin. "You're overdressed for the party, Boots." He caught my wrists, holding them against the wall over my head with one hand. Then he leaned back and let the warm shower spray pelt my chest, watching the water run down my skin.

His barefaced admiration made my body hum. "I hate being overdressed. Maybe you should take off my bra."

"Not yet." He raised his other hand, brushing his knuckles over the wet satin fabric, first one side and then the other, giving equal attention. His dark eyes lifted, watching me as he repeated his stroking, this time with his thumb.

I writhed under his touch, biting my lower lip.

"God, that's hot," he said and let go of my wrists. He leaned down, using his mouth this time, still teasing me through the fabric. I grabbed his head, holding him against me. I tipped my head back, closed my eyes, and moaned as his talented tongue stoked the flames burning inside of me.

His fingers made quick work of the bra clasp, stripping the wet material off and draping it over the top of the shower curtain rod.

He grabbed the soap, starting with my arms, lathering along the way. I watched his hands move over my curves, my need for him burning hotter and hotter. He lost the soap somewhere along the way. I lost my patience a short time later, taking his hand and sliding it inside of my soaked panties. "Feel what you're doing to me."

He groaned and lowered his mouth to mine, his fingers working their magic.

"Yessss." I scratched my nails down his shoulders.

His fingers delved deeper, his thumb strumming, while his tongue stroked along mine. He spun me higher and higher, making me dizzy with need, until I cried out with release, quivering under his touch.

"I love it when you do that," he said, sliding his lips along my cheek. He pulled his hand from my underwear.

"I love it when you make me do that." I reached down and took him in my palm, my body still tingling. "I want to do it again."

His mouth returned to mine, growing bolder. His body tensed under my touch.

I sucked his tongue into my mouth, kissing him how I wanted him to love me, hot and hard, making me even wetter.

"Keep that up," he said against my lips, "and I'm not going to last long enough to get you to my bed."

"I want you here. Now. In the shower." I kissed him again, tightening my grip, mimicking my tongue stroke for stroke.

"Damn, Boots," he said, bracing against the shower wall on each side of my head. He pressed into my hand, his jaw taut.

I trailed my lips down his stubble-covered jaw, nibbling on his collarbone. Then I dragged my mouth to his earlobe, sucking on it.

"Violet." His voice sounded deep and raspy, sensual.

I let go of his ear, looking up. "What?"

He stared at me, his eyes nearly black with need. "Let me inside."

"Take off my panties."

He pushed them down over my hips, helping me step out of them. "Turn around." I did as told, facing the wall, hands flat on the tiles. He skimmed his palms down my ribs and then spanned my hips.

I arched my lower back, looking over my shoulder. "Now, Doc."

He pressed into me, his breath hot on my neck. I moaned, adjusting to take all of him.

"Oh, God," he gasped, his teeth sliding along my shoulder. His body moved against mine, taking ownership, lighting me on fire. "I can't get enough of you, *cara mia*." His hands moved north to cup and fondle while he made love to me with his mouth and body. One of his hands slid down and rubbed over me, making my knees grow wobbly, winding me up again. I reached down and helped him, my fingers covering his, moving with him as one.

My legs almost buckled when I reached the apex. I arched in pleasure as my body convulsed around him. He growled in my ear when I finished, ravaging me against the shower wall, all control gone. His body strained against mine, his face buried in my neck as he groaned my name. I felt his muscles quiver with release, and then he stilled, panting.

We both stood there under the warm water, neither moving, letting it cascade down our skin.

"You can shower with me anytime, Boots." His lips were warm on my shoulder blade after he pulled away.

"Doc?" I said, turning in his arms.

"What?"

"I don't know what to get you for Christmas."

He burst out laughing, taking a step back.

I frowned up at him. "This isn't funny. I don't want to get you something that freaks you out."

"Like what?" He moved under the spray, letting it cascade over his head. "A demon's tongue?"

"No, smartass. I mean something sentimental that makes you think I'm too clingy."

"You're never too clingy."

I continued while watching him rub soap over his chest. "I don't want to get you some expensive but boring electronic gadget that doesn't really show you how important you are to me, but that's what all of the catalogs suggest for the man in my life."

"Sweetheart, you just gave me an amazing gift."

I rolled my eyes. "You get my body all of the time. It's not a gift."

"I beg to differ. You give yourself to me without hesitation, letting me live out my fantasies with you. That's the best gift ever."

"But don't you want something more?"

"I think you underestimate how much I fantasize about being inside of you, especially when you're wet and willing."

"I'm almost always wet and willing around you."

He grinned. "I know. It's sexy as hell, too." He rinsed, switching places with me under the shower.

I tipped my head back under the water, soaking my hair. He had shampoo in his palm when I finished. I turned around and let him lather it in my hair. "You must have a big hot water heater."

"I installed it after I moved in. I bought the largest tank I could with you and this in mind."

"Really? You actually planned on taking long showers with me?"

"Oh, yeah." He massaged the shampoo into my hair.

After I rinsed the shampoo out, I asked, "Will you stay the night with me again?"

He was quiet for a few beats. "You don't get it, do you?"

"Get what?"

"I'm nuts about you, Violet. I want to spend every night with you." He poured conditioner in his hand. "Turn around again."

Every night, huh? I smiled and turned, warming my front side in the spray. "But you have a nice new bed."

"It's boring under the covers without you beside me." He massaged the conditioner into my curls. "Just as my shower will be now when you don't share it with me." A short time later, he slapped my backside playfully. "Time to rinse again."

I faced him while I washed out the conditioner. He leaned his shoulder against the shower wall, ogling me like I was naked and wet. Figuring some suds might up the heat in his gaze a notch or two, I reached for the soap.

He sucked air through his teeth when I circled my way south.

"I fear you getting tired of me," I told him, rubbing the bar over the tops of my breasts.

"I fear you not coming back from the dark and having to live without you." He grabbed the soap from me, making me extra sudsy in my more sensitive places.

I watched him wash my skin, wanting him inside of me again, making me his. "Doc?"

"Yeah?" He let go of the soap, using his hands now instead.

"How much longer do you think the hot water will last?"

"Another ten minutes, maybe."

"What about you?"

His eyes met mine, his pupils dilated. "What about me?"

I stepped closer, getting soap on his chest. "Can you go another ten minutes, too?"

"That depends." He ran his hands down my sides. "You're pretty slippery."

"Is that a problem?"

"Yeah. The best kind of problem." He met my mouth halfway, his kisses rougher, giving it to me just right.

He was wrong about the hot water, though. To make it up to me, he kept going long after the spray had turned cold, warming me up inside and out while getting his sheets all wet.

Chapter Twenty-Five

Y ou gave Dominick *what?*" Aunt Zoe asked me later that evening. We were holding court in the kitchen after filling our bellies with Harvey's homemade chili and corn bread. The supper dishes were washed and the kids were hanging in the living room while yet another holiday classic played on the television.

"Shhhh," I said, stuffing a bag of leftover grated cheese into the fridge. "Addy and Layne don't need to hear this."

"Addy and Layne don't need to hear what?" Natalie asked, returning from the living room where she'd been helping Addy string colored popcorn into garlands. Her pink fuzzy sweater had pieces of popcorn stuck in it.

"Ya got a bad cat on the line there, Sparky," Harvey said from his seat at the table next to the cookie jar. "Yer gonna need to circle the wagons the next time that devil comes callin'."

"What did I miss?" Natalie asked Doc, who was leaning against the counter. His black thermal shirtsleeves were still pushed up from helping me dry dishes.

"Violet told Zoe about her special delivery this afternoon."

Natalie wrinkled her nose. "Oh, that." She took a seat next to Harvey, stealing a cookie from his hand. "You get more twisted by the day, girlfriend."

"It comes with the job." I offered Doc a beer from the fridge.

He nodded. When I brought it over, he caught my arm, pulling me back against him. I settled in between his long legs and let his body warm mine through my cardigan and yoga pants.

"I don't understand," Aunt Zoe said. "Why give Dominick a chimera's head?"

"To teach the slick bastard a lesson. We had a deal."

"What lesson does a head in a burlap bag teach?" Natalie asked.

I'd called and told her my plans for Dominick earlier before leaving Doc's house. In addition to filling Natalie in on my mad, mad life, I'd wanted to make sure she planned to come for supper for two reasons—the first having to do with the recap of our adventures in Slagton; the second revolving around a certain Deadwood detective who might stop by for some grub.

"Dominick lied to me," I answered Natalie. Although he denied that when I delivered my present, claiming he'd been misinformed as well. Hoodwinked or not, if he was going to make deals with me, he needed to make sure his information was accurate prior to delivery. "I wanted him to understand that I'm not someone with whom to fuck."

Aunt Zoe crossed her arms over her worn, flannel work shirt, her gaze narrowing. "And you condone this, Doc?"

He took a hit off his beer. "Condone? Not really." He wrapped his arm around my waist, fitting me even closer against him. "But I understand Violet's objective after today's adventures in Slagton."

Natalie stole another cookie from Harvey. "What's her objective?"

"To show the manipulative jerk that I'm not his bitch." I looked at my aunt. "I'll finish the *lidérc* job because of what's at risk, but after that, I'm no longer an Executioner for hire."

"What was his reaction to the chimera head?" Aunt Zoe asked.

Doc spoke first. "Initially, he looked wide-eyed and winded, like Violet had landed a surprise right hook in his breadbasket."

"Then he tried to act insulted," I joined in. "But I called him on it, so he switched into charming mode."

"But Violet would have none of that either." Doc took another drink before adding, "She reminded him that Executioners were killers, first and foremost."

"Are you nuts?" Natalie sputtered. "That guy can control people with his mind."

"But his tricks don't work on me. Dominick can die by my hand as easily as others, even if he is as old as dirt."

"In other words," Harvey said, brushing cookie crumbs from his beard. "Ya spit in the wildcat's eye."

Natalie scoffed. "I'll say she did. He can kill you, too, you know."

Of course I knew that. "He won't, though, because he needs me right now."

Aunt Zoe was still studying me. "How do you know that?"

"If Dominick is being honest about being misinformed about the Slagton informant, then he has trouble with his subordinates." I borrowed Doc's bottle of beer, taking a sip. "Make that *more* trouble. Remember, Caly was one of his pets and she went rogue. My guess is that she isn't the only one."

"So now what?" Aunt Zoe asked.

"Now I find his *lidérc* and finish my dealings with him as an Executioner." I was still willing to work with him on the real estate front, though, since it not only lined my pocketbook, but kept me in the know on some of his activities. However, now was not the time to disclose my monetary inclination when it came to Dominick.

Harvey hooked his thumbs in his yellow suspenders. "Did ya find out why that snake was sharin' some tongue varnish with yer ex?"

"Dominick says he met Rex by chance during a Lead Chamber of Commerce meeting at the lab that afternoon."

Doc took his beer back. "Masterson claimed it was a simple small-town coincidence that Rex is Violet's ex."

One of Aunt Zoe's eyebrows lifted. "But you don't believe him."

"Of course not," I said. "But I played along for now."

"So this game of cat and mouse continues," Natalie said.

"Exactly."

The doorbell rang. Doc set me aside to go answer the door.

"Violet," Aunt Zoe said. "I don't want you to take any unnecessary risks when it comes to me."

"What's that supposed to mean?"

"Dominick may try to trick you and succeed."

I crossed my arms. "I won't let him have you."

"I appreciate you saying that, baby girl, but I'm telling you if it comes down to life or death, let me go."

Harvey scowled. "Sparky ain't gonna take off her spurs and call it a day that easy. She has too much gumption flowin' through her veins."

Aunt Zoe sighed. "Yes, but—"

"I ain't gonna let her toss ya to the curly wolf, neither. You can beat yer gums to death about this, but all that hot air is fallin' on deaf ears."

Doc rejoined us with Cooper on his heels. The detective must have left his coat in the other room. His tie had been tugged on, his hair was a mess of blond spikes. In between those north–south borders, his face looked like ten miles of rough road.

"Hey, Coop." Aunt Zoe smiled up at him. "You have some room for supper? Your uncle made a big pot of chili." She pointed toward the stove, where the chili sat cooling.

"I'd love some, thanks." His gaze flitted around the room, landing on Natalie last, who was busy breaking her cookie into small pieces while not meeting his gaze.

"No Reid tonight?" I asked Aunt Zoe.

"I need to keep that heartbreaker at arm's length." The worried frown on her face spoke volumes about her rekindled feelings for her old flame.

I opened the cupboard behind me and grabbed a bowl. "Any trouble with a corpse-eating ghoul tonight, Cooper?"

"Not so far." He took the bowl and walked to the stove. "But the night is young."

"And Mr. Haskell's body?" I set a glass on the table for him.

"Eddie says the old guy hasn't risen from the dead so far."

Doc grabbed the pitcher of lemonade from the fridge, filling Cooper's glass. When he finished, he returned to the counter, standing next to me.

I waited for Cooper to fill his bowl. "Your uncle figures you two killed about twelve chimeras today. Do we need to go back tomorrow and take care of the bodies?" If I were to stab them after they were dead, would they still turn to ash? Probably not.

He took Doc's usual chair, sitting next to his uncle. "No. Brown says the bodies will be gone by morning."

"Who's Brown?" I asked.

"My informant."

Mr. Brown and Mr. Black. I was beginning to see a pattern here.

"Who's going to remove the dead?" Aunt Zoe asked him, pushing her chair back. She walked over to the fridge, grabbing a couple of beers.

"I didn't ask, but I assumed the other residents that Brown told us about."

"You mean the sentinels?" Natalie asked, taking the bottle Aunt

Zoe handed her. "Thanks."

Cooper shot a look her way over a spoonful of chili. "It appears someone already filled you in on today's events."

"Your uncle may have mentioned something about old dynamite and a shitload of bullets." She met his gaze for a second or two.

Harvey had told his side of the story before supper while the kids were upstairs finishing homework. He explained how Cooper found fresh footprints leading into the woodshed next to the old Plymouth. Inside, several clues led to a trap door in the shed's floor. Under that door was a small root cellar in which the informant was hiding with his Ruger rifle and a half-empty box of shells. He'd been hiding there for days due to the chimeras. They had come to Slagton in a surprising wave, isolating and killing several sentinels. Those remaining had to flee or hide. If I hadn't come along and killed that first one at Brown's place, accidentally entering the battle, he might not have seen the light of day again.

By the time Cooper had helped Brown out of the cellar, the building was nearly surrounded by the predators. Cooper and the sentinel had run out the main door with guns blazing away while Harvey lit the dynamite and snuck out another door. The explosion had scattered the predators, giving the three of them time to return to the pickup where they held their ground against the toothy bastards, taking them out one by one. Only the largest chimera—the alpha male in the pack according to Brown—had escaped, which Cooper had tracked to the store. In the end, Cornelius had finished the job for them.

"Willis," Doc said. "Did you tell Zoe what Brown said about Violet's standing in Slagton when we dropped him off at your place?"

"Nah. I wanted to wait 'til Sparky was here fer that part."

Aunt Zoe turned to me. "What did he say?"

"I won the turf war."

"For now," Doc added.

"What does that mean?" Natalie asked.

"According to Cooper's informant," I explained to her, "Slagton is like a frontier town on the border between worlds. The sentinels are there to keep order and monitor what comes and goes."

According to Brown, this explained the decapitated predator we'd found hanging from his porch. It turned out the message painted on the store about trespassers being hung and gutted had been a warning from the sentinels meant for troublemakers passing through town. The big-horned creature was a bounty hunter notorious for torturing its prey for pleasure. Brown and another had killed it and put it on display to warn others like it.

When Doc had asked if by *others* Brown meant the chimera, the informant told us that normally these troublemakers were few and far between. They would make an appearance once every decade or so, such as the bone cruncher digging up graves and the faceless sentinel from Slagton that we'd found in Harvey's safe who'd been naïve enough to try to take it out on his own. But lately, the amount of traffic coming through Slagton had increased tenfold.

For whatever reason, the tide had turned and predators were now coming in numbers larger than any time in the last century. While Brown had been happy to see me, he wasn't sure that one Executioner would be enough to balance the tide. His words echoed Ms. Wolff's before her death, as well as Prudence's warning several months prior. In short, I was up shit creek and paddling wasn't going to do me much good.

Tonight, I didn't feel like talking about this dismal situation to Aunt Zoe and Natalie. Instead, I explained how our defeat of the chimera made me the current head honcho in Slagton, which meant Brown and the other sentinels would be reporting to me the comings and goings of Slagton's more notorious visitors. Cooper had agreed to act as our middleman so the detective stayed in the know.

When I finished my tale about the battle for Slagton, Aunt Zoe sat back in her chair, her face lined deeply around her mouth. "What were you doing while Harvey, Cooper, and this Brown character were shooting up the town?"

I glanced at Doc. He nodded at the question in my eyes.

Taking a deep breath, I spilled it all. I started with Cornelius and my visit to the clockmaker, giving a brief lesson about what the hour and minute hands represented on the clocks, and ending with lighting the dynamite in Kyrkozz's face. When I finished, wrinkled brows and wide eyes stared back at me, except for Doc, who'd already heard it all before while I lay sprawled on his chest after we'd finished warming up from our cold shower.

"Why did Kyrkozz look like Wolfgang?" Natalie was the first to break the silence.

"Doc has a theory about that. The first time Kyrkozz and I met was when I fell asleep during a séance. Wolfgang was my most recurring nightmare back then, so Kyrkozz latched onto that image, knowing Wolfgang filled me with terror." I smirked. "The asshole needs to catch up with the times, though. Wolfgang doesn't hold the crown in my dreams anymore."

"Doc," Aunt Zoe said, "how were you able to find the clockmaker in the dark?"

Good question. "It was you who opened that door, right?"

He nodded once. "When I'm in there, things look different for me than they do for you."

"Different how?" Cooper asked, lifting a spoonful of chili to his mouth.

"You see only darkness, but I sense light and sounds, sort of like white noise, in the space between here and there."

I tried to picture that. "Was it this 'white noise' that kept disrupting our communication?" His voice had been laced with static until after the dynamite blast.

"Yes. It also makes it hard to know where you are."

"You were able to find Cornelius in the dark—I mean light."

"Cornelius is very focused, while you emit continual waves of energy. Sometimes the waves are thin, and I can penetrate them to locate you, such as after the explosion when you were lying still, listening. Other times, when you're in the thick of action, you blast energy like a solar flare, knocking out my radio towers, if you will. It takes me time to regroup and find you in the brightness after one of your flares."

Harvey stroked his beard. "It seems like if Sparky is shootin' out energy, it'd be easier to locate her. Like watchin' lightning strikes."

"Imagine walking blindfolded into a large room with a stereo turned up to full volume," Doc said. "And you have to figure out where the speaker is." He caught my hand. "With Violet, I have to try to use a combination of my other senses to find her through the brightness. It's not easy, but I'm getting better." He raised my hand to his lips. "I'm determined to figure out a way to keep track of her in the light."

I blew him a kiss.

"You didn't finish answering the question about how you knew what door the clockmaker was behind," Aunt Zoe said.

"That's the tricky part." Doc lowered my hand, but didn't let go. "What I've learned over time with Violet is that each time she goes into the darkness, the setting shifts. Don't think of it as me finding places for her to go in a made-in-stone maze. Think of it more as, depending on her situation during the point of entry, the characters, doors, and trails inside the maze will vary from the last time she visited the dark. But the maze itself is still based on Violet's point of view because she is the channeler who is leading the way. In other words, if I were able to go into Cornelius's darkness with him at the helm, the setting would be different, the characters unique to his abilities and state of mind."

I tried to wrap my head around that. "You mean not all darkness is the same?" I hadn't ever considered that it would shift depending on who was leading the way into the dark, but that made sense.

"Exactly. You have an exceptionally dangerous dark side, Killer. I doubt anyone else in here would have near the horrors waiting for them that you do." He looked at Aunt Zoe. "The clockmaker's workshop wasn't the first door I checked in there, but when I saw all of those clocks, something told me our new resident Timekeeper needed to stop there first."

"If I want to go back there, would you be able to find it again?"

He rubbed over his beard stubble. "Possibly, but you'll have to go through the dark again."

That meant there was always the risk of my not making it back out. As Mr. Black had said, I'd have to trust in the Oracle's abilities to see where I could not.

"But you're getting better at finding Vi when she's in the dark," Natalie said.

"Yeah, but she keeps getting better at scaring the hell out of me while in there."

"What about Cornelius's broken candle?" I asked. "Did that help you keep track of me?" Maybe we could try that trick again next time.

He nodded. "I could sense the tether between us until the clockmaker pulled it from my hands."

"How did she do that?" Aunt Zoe asked.

Doc shrugged. "Your guess is as good as mine."

"How did you know Violet needed to blind Kyrkozz to escape?" Cooper asked, pushing his empty bowl away.

"In that book she 'borrowed' from Lila Beaumont about the demon, there is a drawing showing Kyrkozz recoiling from light reflecting from what I believe is a mirror." Doc looked at me. "I think Kyrkozz is stuck in that dark realm. It's his prison."

"So when I go into the dark, it's like I'm visiting his cellblock in Alcatraz?"

"Yes, but he's not the only one stuck in there. There are others."

Were the others like me? Had they ended up stuck in there with him? I shivered. Talk about hair-raising nightmares. I was beginning to rethink that return visit to the clockmaker.

"Until Kyrkozz can find his way free," Doc continued, turning back to Aunt Zoe. "The darkness is where he must reign. According to the book, he's developed the ability to see in the dark. I'd intended for Violet to blind him with her candlelight somehow, not blow up a stick of dynamite in his face."

"Do you think Violet managed to get rid of him for good?"

"No," I answered for Doc. "He's still in there, I could feel it afterward. But the blast threw him off."

"If the clockmaker could sense an Oracle was near and take your candle," I asked him, "do you think Kyrkozz could sense you, too?"

If he could, Doc was even more at risk than I was.

"I don't think so. When you were at the clockmaker's, I had a lock on you and was able to easily listen in to what was being said. She somehow picked up on my eavesdropping, whether via my scent or my energy imprint. After you went into the darkness, I lost you in the light. I would guess that our disconnect saved me from being discovered."

"But you could see Cornelius clearly enough to pull him out?"

"Yes. As I said, he's focused and pulls in energy, receiving rather than blocking me." He frowned at Cooper. "It was a similar situation with you at Ms. Wolff's the night Violet killed the Timekeeper. I was able to sense you clearly except for that brief moment after you made contact with Violet."

"You mean when she plowed into me and gave me a black eye."

I gave the detective a pouty lower lip. "Poor baby."

"Again, Violet's energy waves were blasting that night. I need to keep working with her to develop the ability to keep a leash on her in other realms without being knocked out of the ballpark when her emotions peak."

Maybe I needed to work on not reacting so strongly, but feeling my way through the dark was not like skipping through tulip fields. It was hard not to scream when things jumped out at me ... or breathed down my neck.

Speaking of breathing down my neck, I looked at Cooper. "Did you ever find out who called you that day and pretended to have news on your informant? The one who lured us back into the trap the chimera had set up?"

"No. Brown said he didn't know anything about it. He'd been hiding in the shed by then. He heard us pull up outside the woodshed, which was why he was watching through the knothole when Violet passed." Cooper took his bowl and glass to the sink.

"I'll wash your dishes later, Coop," Natalie said. "You probably need to get back to work."

He stared at her for several seconds, possibly trying to figure out if that was a dig or not, just like I was.

I dragged my focus from Natalie. "How did your informant know I was a *Scharfrichter*?"

"He said he could smell you. That sentinels have developed an acute sense of smell for creatures as part of their watchdog ability."

"Does he know what happened to the hunter's corpse that had been hanging on his porch?" I asked.

"He figured the chimeras ate it."

I thought of those blue guts and grimaced.

"Thanks for supper," he said to nobody in particular. "Duty calls." He said his good-byes, sliding Natalie one last look before Doc walked him out.

I hit Natalie with raised brows after he left. She bit her lower lip and turned away. Apparently, she was going to keep fighting her attraction. While I felt bad for Cooper, I applauded her willpower.

After Cooper left, Aunt Zoe headed back out to her workshop while the rest of us joined the kids in the living room until bedtime. Addy asked Doc to go up with her and listen to more of the old radio program starring Cinnamon Bear, which he did without hesitation. My eyes were heavy by the time he came back downstairs. Natalie and Harvey said their farewells shortly thereafter and headed home.

I went upstairs not long after and brushed my teeth. It had been only five days since I'd taken that not-so-joyous ride with Cooper out to check on his informant and accidentally killed a chimera. Five short days that felt like a year. I was losing myself to the Executioner part of my life, no longer questioning the idea of realms and creatures beyond my wildest dreams and nightmares. Or was I accepting it as part of who I was? To think that a short time ago, I thought Doc was a little odd because he said he could sense ghosts.

Damn, how quickly life had changed.

When I got to my bedroom, Doc was already in bed waiting for me. I crawled under the covers, seeking his warmth.

"Christ, woman. Your feet are icicles. Did you walk through the snow before coming to bed?"

"Maybe," I said and snuggled closer.

"I'm going to get you heated socks for Christmas."

I smiled at him. The moonlight coming through the window added a silvery glow to his skin. "Thanks for listening to that radio program with Addy."

He toyed with my curls on the pillow. "You want to know what I want for Christmas, Boots?"

"What?"

"Your family."

I stilled. Was that a marriage proposal? "My family?" I croaked.

"I can't remember Christmas with my parents," he explained. "I was too young when they died. My granddad did his best, but he was a loner, so holidays were never big events for us."

My heart squeezed in my chest, making my eyes water.

"I want to see what Christmas is like surrounded by your family." He pulled my hips closer. "From putting presents under the tree on Christmas Eve to waking up early Christmas morning and watching Addy and Layne tear into their gifts. I want to experience the holiday with you."

I pushed him onto his back, rolling on top of him and smiling down at him. "You know the kids might get into a fight and ruin our happy little family moment."

"I don't care."

"Addy is going to expect you to make us cinnamon-swirled French toast for breakfast."

"I'm happy to deliver."

"Layne will want you to practice sword fighting with him."

"Swords are cool."

"And their mother is going to want a lot of kisses under the mistletoe when they're not looking."

"Kissing their mom is one of my favorite things to do, day and night." He pulled my mouth down to his, showing me.

When I came up for air, I whispered, "You're crazy to want us for Christmas."

"You and your kids are the best thing that ever happened to me."

My tears threatened to return. "Even with my cold feet," I jested, sliding one ice cube up the inside of his calf.

"Seriously, woman. You have circulation problems, I swear."

I laughed, nuzzling his neck. "Maybe, but my hands are warm." I slid my palm south over his abdomen. "See?"

His body responded to my heated touch. "Two times wasn't enough for you today, Boots? I'm an old man, you know."

I sobered. "After the dynamite blew up, when I was there in the dark all alone, I thought I might never see you again." I kissed his chin. "How do you feel about just lying here and letting me love you this time, *mon cher?*"

He cupped my face, his eyes dark pools in the moonlight. "That's French, Tish."

* * *

Wednesday, December 19th

Something was making scuffling sounds next to my head.

I opened my eyes. Doc's profile filled my vision. He lay sleeping quietly next to me in the early morning light. He'd turned his alarm off after I'd finished having my way with him, deciding to sleep in rather than hit the gym today. I lay still, listening to the house creak. The furnace whirred to life.

I must have dreamt the scuffling sound. Yawning, I closed my eyes and rolled over to give my left shoulder a break.

I heard it again.

It was almost like a fluttering noise, reminding me of a moth flapping around in a light fixture.

I opened my eyes. Bogart the cat watched me from his perch on my nightstand. What was that damned cat doing in here again?

Scuffle-flutter.

The cat shifted. Movement under its front paws drew my eyes downward.

A small bat with one freed wing struggled to buck off its furry captor. Its little black eyes stared at me as it struggled to flap its wing. Meanwhile, Bogart leaned down and licked the top of the bat's head, purring loud enough for me to hear.

Holy flying terror! I blinked and pushed off my pillow several inches.

My movement sent the bat into a fluttering panic. It opened its mouth wide and let out a piercing squeak.

I jerked backward with a gasp.

Bogart hissed at me and hopped off the nightstand, leaving the bat behind. It stretched its other wing and tried to take off, only to crash onto my pillow next to me.

I screeched, backpedaling across the bed, slamming into Doc.

The bat tried to take flight again and flew right into my shoulder, landing on the quilt at my chest.

I screeched even louder this time and scrambled over Doc, remembering to be careful of his bruised ribs at the last minute, and fell out of the bed on the other side. My knee thunked on the floor, shooting pain up to my hip.

"What the hell, Violet?" Doc frowned down over the edge of the bed at me.

"Bat!" I yelled.

As if on cue, the little flying beast took to the air again and slammed into the window, dropping to the floor.

The door opened. "What's wrong, Mom?" Layne asked, rushing into the room. Addy raced in after him.

"Addy's stupid cat caught a bat." I pointed toward the window.

"Oh!" Addy kneeled next to where the bat lay, not moving. "The poor little thing. What did you do to him, Mom?"

"Me?! I didn't do anything," I pulled myself topside again, grabbing my robe from the end of the bed. "The thing panicked. It must have knocked itself out."

"It wasn't the only thing panicking," Doc said, chuckling from where he lounged in bed still.

"That's real nice, coming from a big strong man who lay there while his poor woman got attacked by a flying vampire."

Doc laughed even harder. "Layne, we're going to need something to wrap the bat in to get it out of your mom's bedroom."

"I'll get a pillowcase," Layne said.

"Not a pillowcase," I yelled after him. "Get an old towel."

"Addy." Doc sat up. "We need to put the bat somewhere safe until it wakes up. Don't you have a cat carrier in the basement?"

"I'm on it!" She raced off to get it.

Doc climbed out of bed after they left, grabbing his lounge pants from the chair. "You sure keep life titillating, Killer, both in and out of our bed."

Our bed. I liked the sound of that. "It's not my fault. Addy's cat likes to mess with me, I swear."

He grinned, pulling me into his arms. "I can't blame Bogart. I like to mess around with you, too. Especially in bed, but the shower is a close second."

Layne returned with a towel. I left Doc and the kids to remove the bat from my boudoir and escaped to the shower. Life was back to normal today, which meant I had real estate to sell.

An hour later, I kissed Doc and the kids good-bye as he shepherded them out the door and into the Picklemobile to take them to school. He left after I promised to stop by his office later at lunch.

Aunt Zoe had headed out to her workshop after breakfast, a frown of determination on her face. I didn't ask what was on her mind, figuring she'd tell me soon enough.

I grabbed my bag and drove down to work. I was halfway across the parking lot, checking my messages, when I looked up and noticed Ray walking toward me. He must have come from Calamity Jane's. Picking up his last check, maybe?

I slowed, narrowing my eyes. Crud. Here we went again.

His overly tan face scrunched up, ugly as ever. "This is your fault, Blondie." He wrinkled his upper lip at me. "Trust me, this shit between us is far from over."

Bummer, and here I'd hoped it was just a fall fling. "What did I do? You're the one who got busted screwing over your coworker."

"You and Tiffany are in this together, I know it."

"Ray, why would I be working with Tiffany to get you fired?"

"Because you two know that I can outsell the both of you."

"Wow! That ego of yours must weigh a ton some days."

"You two thought you could knock me out of the race, but I'm not going anywhere. Three can play at this game."

"What game is that?"

"You had Tiffany string me along and make me think she could get you shit-canned if I helped her steal a client or two."

"Dang! Who knew I had such power?" I sure hadn't.

"Then she ran to Jerry and tattled on me, turning him against me with her lies."

I sighed. It was too cold outside even for this steaming load of crap. "Ray, you screwed up. Quit trying to drag me down with you. This is all on you, not me." I started to walk away.

"We're not done here, Blondie. You wait and see."

I flipped him off over my shoulder.

"She's coming for you next!" he yelled. "She told me so."

I snorted. Like that was news to me.

I thought of Slagton and the shit parade heading my way.

Tiffany was going to come for me, was she?

"Bring it, bitch," I said under my breath and stepped inside Calamity Jane Realty.

The End ... for now

About the Author

Ann Charles is a USA Today bestselling author who writes award-winning mysteries that are splashed with humor, romance, paranormal elements, and whatever else she feels like throwing into the mix. When she is not dabbling in fiction, arm-wrestling with her children, attempting to seduce her husband, or arguing with her sassy cats, she is daydreaming of lounging poolside at a fancy resort with a blended margarita in one hand and a great book in the other.

Facebook (Personal Page):
http://www.facebook.com/ann.charles.author

Facebook (Author Page):
http://www.facebook.com/pages/Ann-
Charles/37302789804?ref=share

Twitter (as Ann W. Charles):
http://twitter.com/AnnWCharles

Ann Charles Website:
http://www.anncharles.com

More Books by Ann

Books in the Deadwood Mystery Series

WINNER of the 2010 Daphne du Maurier Award for Excellence in Mystery/Suspense

WINNER of the 2011 Romance Writers of America® Golden Heart Award for Best Novel with Strong Romantic Elements

Welcome to Deadwood—the Ann Charles version. The world I have created is a blend of present day and past, of fiction and non-fiction. What's real and what isn't is for you to determine as the series develops, the characters evolve, and I write the stories line by line. I will tell you one thing about the series—it's going to run on for quite a while, and Violet Parker will have to hang on and persevere through the crazy adventures I have planned for her. Poor, poor Violet. It's a good thing she has a lot of gumption to keep her going!

Short Stories from Ann's Deadwood Mystery Series

The Deadwood Shorts collection includes short stories featuring the characters of the Deadwood Mystery series. Each tale not only explains more of Violet's history, but also gives a little history of the other characters you know and love from the series. Rather than filling the main novels in the series with these short side stories, I've put them into a growing Deadwood Shorts collection for more reading fun.

The Jackrabbit Junction Mystery Series

ANN CHARLES — DANCE OF THE WINNEBAGOS | **ANN CHARLES** — THE GREAT JACKALOPE STAMPEDE | **ANN CHARLES** — JACKRABBIT JUNCTION JITTERS | **ANN CHARLES** — THE ROWDY COYOTE RUMBLE | **ANN CHARLES** — THE WILD TURKEY TANGO

Bestseller in Women Sleuth Mystery and Romantic Suspense

Welcome to the Dancing Winnebagos RV Park. Down here in Jackrabbit Junction, Arizona, Claire Morgan and her rabble-rousing sisters are really good at getting into trouble—BIG trouble (the land-your-butt in jail kind of trouble). This rowdy, laugh-aloud mystery series is packed with action, suspense, adventure, and relationship snafus. Full of colorful characters and twisted up plots, the stories of the Morgan sisters will keep you wondering what kind of a screwball mess they are going to land in next.

The Dig Site Mystery Series

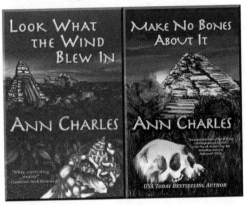

Welcome to the jungle—the steamy Maya jungle that is, filled with ancient ruins, deadly secrets, and quirky characters. Quint Parker, the renowned photojournalist (and lousy amateur detective), is in for a whirlwind of adventure and suspense as he and archaeologist Dr. Angélica García get tangled up in mysteries from the past and present in exotic dig sites. Loaded with action and laughs, along with all sorts of steamy heat, these two will keep you sweating along with them as they do their best to make it out of the jungle alive in every book.

From the Future Goldwash Mystery Series

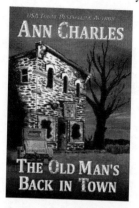

This short story is a bit of a puzzle. Each scene is a different variation of the same story for a reason, which you'll learn at the end. See if you can pick up on the clues along the way and figure out the puzzle before you finish the story. Thank you for giving it a try!

~ **Ann**

Overview...

In the lonely mining ghost town of Goldwash, Nevada, Christmas has come early. Unfortunately, the local bar owner must be on this year's naughty list, because Santa brought her something even worse than a piece of coal on this dark, cold winter night—her old man.

Made in the USA
Lexington, KY
21 May 2018